Lightborn

"Engaging mix of chaos, angst, and manners [that yields] some answers, including genuine surprises" —*Locus*

"This story world is highly complex and certainly unique.... Readers should find the plot and players fascinating. . . . What will the imaginative Alison Sinclair come up with next?" —Romance Reviews Today

Darkborn

"Alison Sinclair's unique world of two societies, mortally divided by sunrise and sunset, provides a fascinating backdrop for a fast-paced thriller of politics and intrigue. Delightful!"
  —Carol Berg, national bestselling author
  of *The Soul Mirror*

"Alison Sinclair's *Darkborn* plays like a sweeping historical novel in a teeming preindustrial city whose residents are divided into those who can only tolerate light and those who can only exist in darkness. A sprawling cast of characters argue and scheme and practice magic in secret— until a calamitous chain of events reveals the whole city to be under siege from a mysterious and ruthless enemy. Despite swift action, broad conspiracies, and monumental life-and-death stakes, the heart of the book is a delicately rendered love triangle that tracks the human cost of any grand adventure. I can't wait to read the next book about these complex and engaging characters."
  —Sharon Shinn, national bestselling author
  of *Troubled Waters*

continued . . .

Also by Alison Sinclair

Darkborn
Shadowborn

Lightborn

Alison Sinclair

A ROC BOOK

ROC
Published by New American Library, a division of
Penguin Group (USA) Inc., 375 Hudson Street,
New York, New York 10014, USA
Penguin Group (Canada), 90 Eglinton Avenue East, Suite 700, Toronto,
Ontario M4P 2Y3, Canada (a division of Pearson Penguin Canada Inc.)
Penguin Books Ltd., 80 Strand, London WC2R 0RL, England
Penguin Ireland, 25 St. Stephen's Green, Dublin 2,
Ireland (a division of Penguin Books Ltd.)
Penguin Group (Australia), 250 Camberwell Road, Camberwell, Victoria 3124,
Australia (a division of Pearson Australia Group Pty. Ltd.)
Penguin Books India Pvt. Ltd., 11 Community Centre, Panchsheel Park,
New Delhi - 110 017, India
Penguin Group (NZ), 67 Apollo Drive, Rosedale, Auckland 0632,
New Zealand (a division of Pearson New Zealand Ltd.)
Penguin Books (South Africa) (Pty.) Ltd., 24 Sturdee Avenue,
Rosebank, Johannesburg 2196, South Africa

Penguin Books Ltd., Registered Offices:
80 Strand, London WC2R 0RL, England

Published by Roc, an imprint of New American Library, a division of Penguin
Group (USA) Inc. Previously published in a Roc trade paperback edition.

First Roc Mass Market Printing, June 2011
10 9 8 7 6 5 4 3 2 1

Copyright © Alison Sinclair, 2010
All rights reserved

RoC REGISTERED TRADEMARK — MARCA REGISTRADA

Printed in the United States of America

Acknowledgments

With thanks to my editor, Anne Sowards, and my agent, Caitlin Blasdell, for their encouragement, insightful comments, and, above all, patience.

One

Telmaine

She had *never*, thought Telmaine Hearne, been so glad to have a train journey *over*.

Not because the bells were tolling sunset, and the end of the killing sunlight. Not because they had come to the end of their journey without any sign of threat. Not even because, a scant twelve hours before, she and her dear husband had run for the coast-bound train with no certainty that both or either of them would return.

No, it was the company she kept, and the explanations that would be awaiting her at the end of this journey.

Small consolation if her fellow passenger shared her feeling. Lord Vladimer Plantageter, her noble cousin and half brother to the archduke, had all the prejudices of his sex and class, enhanced by a temperament both reclusive and distrustful. Only the urging of a man he respected and who had just saved his life would have made him accept the company of a woman on this journey, much less a woman who was also a mage. And as for Vladimer accepting her protection . . .

Nor would she have done it, except at the behest of the two men who had asked her. She sighed, but silently. Who was it who wrote, "I can mind my enemies, but the Sole God protect me from my friends"? Had her husband been with her, she would have asked him, but even at this moment Balthasar might be boarding a train bound south to the Borders and a threatened invasion.

That, too, she could set against Lord Vladimer's account.

She heard the door to the stateroom open. Her sonn resolved a man in the blazer and cap of the railway who leaned into Lord Vladimer's private cubicle to apologize that they could not draw up to their regular platform as two specials were preparing to depart—the hour after sunset being the busiest hour of the night—and would have to use one of the public platforms.

"Have it cleared," Vladimer said without hesitation. "And have a coach waiting."

"And for the lady . . . ?" the conductor said.

"The lady comes with me."

He might at least *try* to avoid giving the impression that he was taking her in for interrogation, if only for the sake of her reputation.

Which he could ruin with a very few words, should he choose. Amongst Darkborn, mages belonged on the fringes of society, not in its finer families and upper social circles. She had stepped out of her class to marry Balthasar Hearne, whose fine old blood was attenuated through generations of daughters and younger sons, but was still acceptable. To be revealed as a mage would be not a stepping out but an irredeemable plunge.

To her husband, a physician and one insatiably curious about mind and society, the Darkborn aversion to magic and mages was less because of history than because of present society. Eight hundred years ago, magic had divided Darkborn from Lightborn, condemning the Darkborn to perpetual darkness, the Lightborn to perpetual light. In daylight, the Darkborn burned to ash; in darkness, the Lightborn melted excruciatingly away. But eight hundred years ago was a time long past, particularly for the forward-facing Darkborn; Balthasar thought the aversion was less due to what mages had done than what they could do, even though the knowledge that had underlain the Curse was lost. Even the weakest mage could read thoughts with a touch, and most had strength enough to heal. A stronger mage, such as she seemed to be, could cast her thoughts into another's mind, influence others with her will, force sleep upon the unwilling, walk—she swallowed at the memory—

unharmed through a burning building. Such powers were an affront to propriety, disruptive to the order of society, and a threat to earthly and divine authorities.

She understood that; she believed and agreed with that; yet these were the powers she had, and had been forced to use.

She could hear the sudden change in the reverberation of the engine as the train entered the enclosed space of the station. It shuffled and jolted, switching points, and she swayed gently in place, hand on the writing case tucked beneath her skirts. The case contained the letters Balthasar had written in case he did not come back, bidding farewell to their daughters, his sister, and the Lightborn woman Floria White Hand, Telmaine's rival on the other side of sunrise, Balthasar's first, impossible love, and lifelong friend. That last letter, she wished she dared burn. Polite Darkborn did not speak of Lightborn any more than they must, given that they shared the city and the land with them. Lightborn mores were shocking, their politics violent, and rumor held that the Lightborn court was ruled by mages.

But the journey was over. She would deliver Vladimer safely to his brother's palace, and let him initiate the schemes that he had surely been planning all these silent hours. He was the spymaster who, while still a teenager, had put organized crime in the city docks in such disarray that it might not recover in his lifetime, and had gone on to guard his brother's back against the schemes of his own dukes and lords. Ruthless and brilliant—even in the opinion of his enemies—but also profoundly vulnerable, alas, to magic.

All she need do, she told herself yet again, was sense and warn, and thwart any use of magic against him. She lacked training, yes, but Ishmael di Studier was convinced she had power in abundance. And as she, and Balthasar, and Ishmael, had just demonstrated, even a mage was not immune to bullets.

Ishmael, she thought. After a week's acquaintance, she should hardly be so free with her thoughts of a man neither husband nor brother, never mind one with his reputation. But propriety hardly allowed for Ishmael. The man who had saved her husband's life, her daughter's life, and not least her own. The man who had recognized her as a mage, because he was one himself, and shaken her magic loose from its lifelong restraint. The man whom she had begun to love, though she loved her husband not a single portion less. She and Balthasar could have no better ally in these strange and dangerous times, and Lord Vladimer and the archduke could have no better servant. Ishmael was born to inherit one of the great Borders baronies, where the civilized lands abutted the regions around the ancient mages' last stronghold. He had spent his adult life hunting marauding beasts from the Shadowlands, though it had been Vladimer, not Ishmael, who had imagined the prospect of men and women emerging from those poisoned lands to raise chaos with their intelligent schemes. Which made Vladimer the Shadowborn's enemy, too, and unlike Ishmael, he could not sense their magic. She, Balthasar, and Ishmael had saved Vladimer's life as he lay unconscious and fading under ensorcellment.

The train stopped with a final, settling lurch. Gladly, she picked up the writing case and tucked it under her arm as she stood, shaking out skirts creased with travel. A bath would be the utmost luxury, even with the slightly antiquated plumbing in the archducal palace. A bath and breakfast with her daughters; what better reward and fortification?

The steward returned to tell them that the platform had been cleared. In the doorway to his cubicle, Lord Vladimer steadied himself on his cane and gestured her impatiently to precede him. She paused in the doorway, taking a careful sweep of the platform with her mage sense, and finding only Darkborn. Their enemies' magic carried with it a distinctive, repulsive taint. The air was familiar, acrid with smoke from the pulsing trains all around her. Bolingbroke Station, the main interchange of Minhorne, its vast sealed canopy and night-and-day bustle making it a hub of Darkborn business and middle-class society.

Telmaine extended a hand to the steward to allow him to steady her on the long step down, and alighted with poise. As the steward turned to assist Lord Vladimer, she cast sonn around herself with the gentility expected of a lady, a muted cast that visualized no more than a dozen yards around her. She could not but recollect that the first words she had spoken to Ishmael were a rebuke for his too-forceful sonn, cultivated in dangerous places but quite inappropriate for polite society. Thinking of that, and what he would expect of her, she cast again, defying her inhibitions. Thus she caught the two men filing toward them along the side of the engine, guiding themselves with their outstretched fingers along its flank.

They were Darkborn, with no taint of magic or Shadowborn on them. To her mage sense, they belonged. They wore the uniform of railway engineers. But she knew them. Though she and they had come face-to-face for but a moment, and the burns on their faces were quite healed, she would *never* forget the men who had burst from her husband's house, leaving him dying behind them, and snatched up her elder daughter as a token of blackmail.

Their forward creep halted at the touch of her sonn. They had been as prepared for discovery as she was unprepared. She had no word of warning readied. *No*, and *Lord Vladimer*, and *You* tried to come together; all she achieved was a choked cry. She sonned the unmistakable gesture of a man swinging up a gun; sonn surged from fore and aft; she could not have said who fired first. She shrieked at the re-evoked horror of their fight with Lord Vladimer's first Shadowborn assailant, and threw herself down in a huddle as the guns fired again. Something clattered down the side of the train behind her. She smelled a man's sweat, sonned, and found him only steps from her. He disregarded her in her shrinking helplessness, speaking past her. "Move aside, you fool. It's him I want." She had heard that voice before. It had said, "Tell Hearne that when we get Tercelle Amberley's bastards, he gets his daughter back."

She had got their daughter back. She had walked through an inferno to do so. *Push the fire back*, Ishmael di Studier had said, and she had *pushed the fire back*. And now, as she had then, she *pushed* with all her magical strength at the assassin's outstretched arm. The gun swung wide; his head turned after it, shock in his face. From behind her there came a snap, and she felt something hiss past her head. The man grunted and her next cast showed a stubby dart jutting out beneath his ribs. His hand groped, gripped, pulled, pulled it free. Then his mouth opened; his face twisted in disbelief and rage that *he* had come to this. With shocking finality he pitched backward. His legs thrashed briefly, like a neck-snapped rabbit's, and he collapsed into a mortal laxness. She smelled blood and ordure, as his bowels and bladder released. Ear and sonn found the other man, sprawled where she had first sonned them, choking on the blood from his shattered lung, and no threat to anyone.

She *should* have been distressed. She should have felt some little pity for them. But she remembered her first touch of Balthasar's shock-chilled skin, her first sense, through her magic, of his terrible injuries, inflicted by these men. She remembered Florilinde's screams as those men carried her away, and again when the warehouse blazed around her. And she understood the impulse that compelled decent men to spit on fallen enemies.

Then she heard the steward shout again for help, and twisted where she knelt, too swiftly to dread what she might find. But Lord Vladimer was sitting—yes, sitting—in the door of the carriage, his head turning, alert to sound and sonn. Her first, absurdly relieved thought was that he looked like a marionette abandoned in a nursery corner, with that length of leg so carelessly deployed. His right arm hung by his side. His left hand gripped the hilt of his cane, which rested across his lap, pointing in her direction.

Two against one, Telmaine thought, *and that one taken in ambush.* Ishmael would not have been particularly surprised at the result. She scrambled to her feet, uncertain of what to say: a lady's training in etiquette, comprehensive as it was, did not address this particular situation. Vladimer's sonn pinged her, hard, and he shifted the cane slightly. He still did not move, and Telmaine, tentatively extending her magic to sense his vitality, abruptly understood that though he had survived, he was not unhurt. His stillness was that of a man who knew the next movement would be excruciating. She took an uncertain step toward him.

Then men came scurrying across the platform, encircling Vladimer and the dying assassin, shouting orders to one another but heeding none. A woman's voice beside her shocked her into a pulse of sonn sharp enough to make the speaker flinch. The attendant was one of the ladies' stewards—a controversial innovation that acknowledged the increasing number of venturesome ladies traveling together or even alone. The woman had to repeat her questions before Telmaine—whose hearing was still baffled by close gunfire—both heard and understood. Would the lady like to rest in the ladies' waiting room? Did the lady need a doctor? Was the lady being met?

She moved a gloved hand vaguely toward Vladimer's voice by way of explaining why she could not leave. He was saying snappishly, ". . . just my arm, so stop measuring me for a bier and secure the area. Send a runner to the nearest station of public agents; get someone down here." He would have been more convincing if his voice had not had the irregular pulse of a shudder running through it. She could quite understand; she was ready to shudder herself with the deathly cold of—

Oh, sweet Imogene. They're here.

With a puff of warm air that was as gentle as the opening of a door into a hearth-warmed room, fire bloomed from the undercarriage of the engine and stowage car. The first screams were as tentative and muted as the fire. Then the doors on the engine and stowage cars slammed open and men hurled themselves and one another onto the platform, the rearmost shoving the others ahead of them, to land running or sprawling, the first man to rise dragging the others clear, injured or otherwise.

Briefly, as though a wind had shifted, the sense of Shadowborn magic ebbed. But it was no more than a gathering of breath for effort—and she *heard* the breath drawn. She turned toward it, her sonn catching at its limit an indistinct figure. She thought it might be young, and it was dressed as a male, standing apart, exuding chill, pollution, and triumph. His arm swept toward them in a grand gesture worthy of an actor or orator. A man screamed, "Get away from the train!" in the raw Rivermarch accents of the apothecary who had been assisting Ishmael. Who had, like Ishmael,

survived the inferno that had destroyed nine blocks of the
Rivermarch, a fire that was surely Shadowborn-set.

No, Telmaine thought, *you shall* not. In the blazing warehouse she had pushed the flame aside; now she reached
out with the full force of her magic and tore the fire from
its root in the burning engine and whipped it around the
Shadowborn. She risked no exchange of words or thoughts;
she had tried that with his kin back at Vladimer's bedside and had all but lost her mind to him. As the vortex
of flame enfolded him, the Shadowborn screamed in the
half-broken voice of an adolescent boy. Sonn caught his
frantic flurry in the midst of the shimmy of flame, and the
fire rippled and bellied around him as he paddled it away,
stronger than she would have imagined. She felt a blast
of heat and oily vapor, and terror of immolation lent her
strength to tighten the vortex; she knew no other response.
Then chill and foulness slapped at her, and the fires were
instantly snuffed by his magic. The Shadowborn reeled in
place for several heartbeats, and then, as people started to
gather warily around him, he screeched a vulgarity in her
direction and stumbled away.

The train and coach burned on with a sullen natural flame, its smoke thickening the enclosed station. Telmaine's legs abruptly surrendered beneath her. With the
ladies' steward pulling uselessly on her arm, she sank down
amongst her pillowed skirts, gasping for breath. Two men
caught her up, emergency overriding propriety, and bore
her past the onrushing fire crews with their buckets and
hoses.

Telmaine

"What," said Vladimer, "exactly happened back *there*?"
The last word came hoarsely as the carriage jolted over
rough pavings. Vladimer had directed it on a tortuous approach to the archducal palace, a precaution he might be
regretting as it wound through side streets.

"Those two men were the ones who beat Balthasar and
kidnapped Florilinde," she said, almost whispering. She
would rather not have been answering these questions

now, and certainly not in a coach with guards riding over-head. "They were also with the group who shot Guillaume di Maurier and left him for dead. When I—when he was telling me where Florilinde was, he was remembering."

And she had been holding di Maurier's hand, easing his agony with her magic. To be a mage, to be any level of mage, even a first-ranker like Ishmael di Studier, was to be a touch-reader.

Which was why her timid offer to heal Vladimer's wound, once they were alone, had been harshly rebuffed. He had allowed the apothecary to apply a bandage, ignoring the man's warning that it needed proper attention, and hurried them to the coach.

"They had nothing to do with the fire," he said curtly. "They were dead before it started."

"There was a Shadowborn," she said, and swallowed against threatened nausea from the jolting of the coach and the recollection of the magic. "I said there were two."

"*Two?*"

"The one Ishmael killed, and this one."

"Ah, so that is your accounting." His humorless smile needed the barest twist to become a grimace of pain. "Curse it, I'll have words with someone about these roads," he muttered. "So the fire was Shadowborn-set. You sensed it."

"I sensed it."

He withheld any reproach as to why she had not sensed the Shadowborn's presence sooner. "Why start with the engine and stowage if they wanted me dead?" Then he answered his own question. "The corpse of the one di Studier shot at my bedside." His lips tightened in irony. "The strongest evidence I could offer my brother and his counselors to support this wild story of ours. The fire will have done for it."

"He was about to burn our coach," Telmaine said.

"And you turned his fire back on him. You seem," he said coolly, "to be making great gains with this neglected power of yours."

She knew exactly what he was implying, his doubt that she was as unpracticed with her magic as she claimed to be, as she *was*. "All I did was distract him," she lied desperately. "It was his own magic turned on him."

There was a silence, which did not tell her whether he had believed her. "A great shame it did not burn him worse."

Another bend in the road brought them onto the smoother roads of a quality neighborhood. She had quite lost her bearings, but knew they could not be far from the archducal palace. "Lord Vladimer," she ventured, trying to keep her voice from going soft and high in appeal—which he would revile as feminine wiles. "Lord Vladimer, *must* you tell the archduke about me? It will—it will *ruin* me in society."

She knew little of the archduke's attitude toward magic, but the little she did know suggested that he was no more sympathetic than any other aristocrat, and possibly even less.

"I do not have the impression that your husband would repudiate you," Vladimer noted.

He could have had no sense of the new complexities of her marriage, now that Balthasar knew the secret she had kept from him all those years. If ever a man was set for lifelong bachelorhood, Vladimer was the man. But he was right that Balthasar would not repudiate her for being a mage, would not add to her stigma that of divorce. And she would not plead being thrown back on Balthasar's inferior social status after all these years of cultivating loving indifference to it. "I know," she said, humbly. "My husband honors his vows, and he loves me—more than I realized. But we have daughters, Lord Vladimer." Children she and Balthasar had left behind in their dash to save Vladimer's life, she thought resentfully. "Their happiness, their marriage prospects, their place in society—all would be ruined if it were known that I am a mage." Her voice wavered with desperation and fatigue.

There was a silence. While he weighed her plea, and she tried not to amplify it.

"You are—however irregularly—in my service, it seems," he said, slowly. "It is to my advantage as much as to yours, I think, not to have your capabilities known. As

long as you remain—" He seemed about to say more, but
the coach went through a sharp turn, jolting them both, and
forcing a gasp from him. She started to put out a gloved
hand to steady him, but snatched it back before he perceived the gesture. Then they were rattling along the side
of the archducal palace, toward the private entrance that
Vladimer used.

She slithered down from the coach, gloved hands futilely
trying to set right rumpled skirts, ruffled lace, disordered
veil, disordered *self*. Two—or was it three?—nights ago,
she had arrived at this entrance as a refugee from multiple
disasters, with Balthasar battered and too weak to stand,
and one daughter missing through abduction. She had been
appalled then at the thought of coming here, with her life
and social armor in such disarray. But at least then she had
not had to face the entire ducal household, as it seemed
she must now: Sejanus Plantageter himself had descended
to greet them. She recognized his broad, reverberant sonn,
like no other. In the converging echoes of the entire household's sonn she perceived the archduke closing on his
brother, by his manner equally poised to embrace him and
to shake him. *"Vladimer,"* he said, in the ominous tone of
someone who had waited and worried and was ready to
lose his temper with the object of the waiting and worrying.

Vladimer, his head low, muttered, "Janus, I don't *need*
this circus."

"Then don't go frightening us like that," the archduke
rebuked him. "First they had you at death's door, and then
I heard there was trouble at the station." At the same time,
with sharp sweeps of his hand he was waving dismissal all
around. Then he sonned Vladimer sharply and said in a low
voice, "You're ill. Or hurt."

Vladimer shook his head minimally. "Not till we're in
private. It will take some explaining."

"When does it not with you, Dimi?" the archduke said.
He started to turn, and his sonn caught Telmaine, in her be-
draggled state. "Lady Telmaine," he said, in surprise. "Mrs.
Hearne."

She dropped a deep curtsy. Now in his late forties, the
archduke was a man of arresting appearance who shared

with his illegitimate brother their mother's distinctive bony features, high cheekbones, and broad brow—augmented in Sejanus's case by the equally distinctive Plantageter nose. Telmaine's acerbic-tongued sister had once opined that the dynastic prowess of the Plantageters was surely due to that nose; where it appeared, paternity was never in question. Sejanus had been archduke for nearly forty years, and was as respected as his brother was feared.

"Lady Telmaine was good enough to accompany me from the coast, a decision I fear she came to regret," Vladimer said.

The archduke's brows arched. He had surely last heard of Telmaine as sheltering within his walls, and his brother was not known for dashing around the countryside with other men's wives. But if the expression was meant teasingly, its target missed it. His brows drew down again, less in displeasure than worry.

Telmaine dipped a shallower curtsy. "If I may be excused, Your Grace, my mother and children will be wondering where I am."

The archduke eased the frown from his face, turning to say considerately, "Ah, yes, before you become concerned, I should let you know that your mother and sister have taken your daughters back to your sister's household. They thought the children would be more comfortable in familiar surroundings."

None of her immediate impulses—to bolt out the door, to scream in panic, to rage at her imperious, managing, *clueless* sister—would have made the least sense to pragmatic Sejanus Plantageter—at least not until he had heard Vladimer's report. The archduke's brief, sympathetic smile said he was well aware of the personalities in his circle, even those of dukes' daughters. Not to mention the challenges of dealing with a difficult sibling.

Perhaps fortunately for what she might have confided, his attention was diverted by the arrival of Casamir Blondell, hurrying in with a jubilant *"My lord Vladimer."*

Vladimer raised a baleful face. "Blondell, what is this about having charges laid against Baron Strumheller for murder and sorcery?"

She could almost pity Blondell for having his joy at his lord's return so harshly quenched. The spymaster's city lieutenant drew himself up, saying in a firm voice that verged on pomposity, "It was a necessary temporizing measure, my lord, to reduce suspicions of the Lightborn and interracial tensions, and there was sufficient evidence of di Studier's presence at the scene of the murder to make it plausible."

"It makes a mockery of justice and came near to being a fatally stupid measure," Vladimer rasped. "Janus, I need to speak to you now. Blondell, you should hear this, too."

"Just tell me why I shouldn't have you put to bed first," Sejanus Plantageter grumbled. "Come on, upstairs." He nodded toward Telmaine. "Lady Telmaine. My house is yours, as ever."

Vladimer, who had set his cane preparatory to taking a first step, hesitated and said through half-gritted teeth, "Lady Telmaine should come as well, if she would."

If this was as unexpected or unwelcome to the archduke as it was to her, he did not show it, only set a firm grip on Vladimer's sound arm, a grip that Vladimer did not resist. Casamir Blondell's curiosity was almost palpable, but he had the courtesy not to probe her with his sonn.

The archduke steered them into the first room at the top of the stairs. "Claudius is here; shall I bring him in on this?"

"Yes." A footman peeled off to carry the orders. Vladimer faltered before the challenge of lowering himself into a chair with only one working arm. The archduke said, "Come," set his hands under his brother's armpits with a readiness that suggested he had done this before, and eased him down. Vladimer leaned carefully against the cushions, letting his head fall back.

"Right arm, is it?" Sejanus said.

"Yes."

"Happened at the station?"

Vladimer's lips twitched. "And you accuse me of never waiting for a story to unfold. Yes, we were ambushed as we came off the train."

"The person responsible is dead or in custody, I presume."

"Two of three."

"Only two of three. You must be losing your touch."

Telmaine was still trying to decide whether this was meant as brotherly humor or archducal rebuke when Duke Rohan arrived. Claudius Rohan had been the youngest member of the regency council during the archduke's long-ago minority, and, though fifteen years Sejanus's elder, was still his closest adviser and friend. His relationship with Vladimer, however, had the meticulous formality of two men who subsumed their incompatibility in a strong mutual loyalty. "Vladimer," he greeted the archduke's brother. "Welcome back. What's this about bullets and fires at Bolingbroke Station?"

The archduke said, in a tone of distinct irritation, "You already know more about this than I, Claudius. Sit down. Vladimer has a report for us."

"I think . . . I will ask Lady Telmaine to explain, since much of what I know I heard from her, her husband, and Baron Strumheller. It is largely thanks to those three I am sitting here now."

Telmaine froze, first with simple social dismay at being thrust from her observer's role, then with concern—was he having her tell it because he did not have the strength?—and finally with horror as she understood his strategy. He was inviting—or challenging—her to perjure herself before the archduke. Her tongue suddenly seemed too large for her mouth.

"Strumheller?" said the archduke, sharply. "I had a report he'd died in prison."

"A necessary ruse, Janus. Telmaine, if you would be so good. Tell my brother the story."

She heard a double meaning in that, no doubt intended. But it stiffened her resolve. She *would* tell the archduke the story. On her, as much as on Vladimer, lay the responsibility to convince him of the threat.

She sought just the right tone of reliable willingness. "Your Graces, when I was down at the summerhouse, at the last grand ball, Baron Strumheller asked me if I would permit him to escort me back to the city. Lord Vladimer had asked him to consult with my husband—" She faltered, aware that the men around her had stiffened at the mention of Ishmael's name, and remembering that Blondell at least was hostile enough to have Ishmael charged conveniently with capital crimes. Did these men know that those years going in and out of the Shadowlands themselves had left Ishmael with a dangerous compulsion to return? The people who lived along the Borders, Ishmael's people, knew it as the Call to the Shadowlands, and dreaded it. But if the archduke did not know, she would not expose Ishmael's vulnerability. "Regarding a personal matter," she amended. No one challenged or contradicted her. She continued her account, keeping her tone steady with some effort: arriving at her door to have her daughter snatched from her arms as a token of blackmail. Finding her husband severely beaten—abruptly, she decided to omit all mention of the magic used to save Bal's life, hers, *and* Ishmael's. Learning what the kidnappers wanted: the bastard twin sons of Lady Tercelle Amberley, recently delivered by Balthasar and his sister, Olivede. Children whom Balthasar believed to have been born sighted, as no Darkborn had been since the Curse that had created their races.

"Tercelle Amberley," Rohan said sharply. "Ferdenzil Mycene's betrothed." His tone was skeptical, though no more than she would have expected. Tercelle Amberley had been betrothed to the only son of the second most powerful duke in the land, after the archduke himself.

"There have been rumors, Your Grace," put in Blondell.

Vladimer stirred slightly; Telmaine's sonn caught a quelling hand gesture toward his deputy.

"There are always rumors," the archduke said. "Where is Hearne now?"

"On a train to the Borders," Vladimer said. "Continue, please, Lady Telmaine."

Charging Ishmael to find her daughter. Waking to the smell of smoke from the blazing Rivermarch, hearing the rainstorm summoned by the Lightborn to drown the fire— making no mention of the magical tempest that had almost sucked her into itself. The return of Ishmael di Studier, burned and suffering from smoke poisoning, to sweep them away to what he believed was a place of safety here in the archducal palace. Ishmael's arrest for the murder of Tercelle Amberley and the suspected ensorcellment of Lord Vladimer, found unconscious at the ducal summerhouse. Learning where her daughter was, from one of Vladimer's other agents, and setting out to rescue her.

"Very foolish of you, Telmaine," Vladimer said, in a tone that was dry, but otherwise not interpretable.

"I am a mother, sir," she said, realizing only then that he might be referring not to the act itself—of which he knew the true story—but of her daring to lie about it here. But *he* had set her up to do so.

"This ensorcellment," prompted the archduke, toward his brother.

Vladimer's lips tightened. "I don't remember, Janus. I was in my private study, I heard a sound behind me, and the next thing I knew, I was waking up in my own bed, four days gone."

He had said the same to Ishmael, Balthasar, and herself. Balthasar believed that he lied, that the sorcerous coma had followed a sorcerous seduction, cruel and damaging to a man as aloof and distrustful as Vladimer. Did Sejanus Plantageter, with his lifelong knowledge of his brother, hear the lie?

If so, he did not pursue it, "Go on," he said, equally to Telmaine and Vladimer.

Telmaine did. Though she thought with some despair it seemed a wildly coincidental tale, a fire breaking out in the warehouse at just the right moment to distract her daughter's guard. No mention of her own walk through the inferno. She prayed that it did not differ too greatly from anything else the archduke might have heard.

It seemed so wrong that she could not tell them what Ishmael di Studier had sacrificed to save her and Florilinde from the flames.

Vladimer said, "You'll notice a pattern in this. The Rivermarch. Now warehouse thirty-one. Our enemies like fire, as a weapon."

The other men made noncommittal noises. The archduke said, "I heard about that fire. Malachi is keeping me apprised of the investigation." He considered a moment, and then leaned toward her. "A word of advice, Lady Telmaine: you might be best to admit to your accomplices. Given the circumstances, it will likely not go too ill with them, or with you."

What he meant to imply, she realized after a moment's bewilderment, was that he thought *she* had had others set the fire for her, as a diversion. While she gulped, he said, in that same quietly warning tone, "I am given to understand that some of your personal effects were recovered from the hands of people from the area."

The reticule and jewelry she had lost during the rescue, including a distinctive silver love knot that Bal had given her during their courtship. Were the archduke and his agents assuming that those had been her bribes? Her mouth was very, very dry at the thought the public agents had been speaking to people who were on the Lower Docks. She'd thought she could not possibly have been sonned walking out of the flames, because of the chaos and turbulence, but suppose—

In undermining her listeners' disbelief in the potent and strange, she was undermining her own best protection.

"I would be p-pleased to talk to the superintendent, should—should his inquiries not satisfactorily conclude. But I know—no more than I have told you." Should she appeal for their protection, in the name of her sex and class? She had no idea.

Shaken, she stumbled on with her account, which grew yet wilder toward its conclusion. Receiving word of Ishmael di Studier's supposed death in prison. Being persuaded by her husband that they should take the day train down to the summerhouse because—because Balthasar strongly believed in Ishmael's innocence and Vladimer's importance, because Balthasar had past experience in a small way of being an agent. It all made her Bal seem desperately reckless, whereas while the decision *had* been his, driven by his profound sense of civic duty, it had been made with knowledge from both herself and Ishmael that there were Shadowborn mages at work in the city.

"But why did Balthasar take you with him, Telmaine?" Claudius said, worried. He had been a friend of her father's; she knew he felt protective of her.

She pressed gloved hands together. "Lord Claudius, you have no doubt heard that my dear husband is a terrible marksman. *Someone* had to go with him, for his protection."

He frowned, gently disapproving. "And what did you find, when you reached the summerhouse?"

With no guidance, not even a twitch of a lip, from Vladimer, Telmaine forged ahead, once more eliding the contribution made by her magic. She and Balthasar had found a man who resembled Balthasar's estranged brother at Vladimer's bedside, while Vladimer's entire household lay unconscious around them. The intruder had threatened both Balthasar and Vladimer. She had wounded him with a borrowed pistol and Balthasar had fought him bodily, and while he was thus distracted, Ishmael di Studier had stepped in the door and delivered the death shot. Dead, the assassin had appeared quite different than he had when living.

"In what way, Lady Telmaine?"

She swallowed nausea, remembering. "It was a—a hideous sight, Your Grace. Baron Strumheller's last shot had—split his skull—it was mostly gone, above the brow. But his face was still whole and no longer resembled Lysander Hearne in the least."

"Lady Telmaine," the archduke said, slowly, "if I were to ask you to take an oath that that is what you witnessed, as if in a court of law, would you still say so?"

To *that* she could. "Without the least hesitation, Your Grace."

Did she imagine the archduke's sigh? "Go on."

"And then Lord Vladimer woke up," she said, omitting mention of Vladimer's initial reflex, which was to hold a revolver to Ishmael's head. "We explained to him what had happened, and why we were there, and he ordered my husband and Baron Strumheller to the Borders to prepare for an invasion, and I asked to accompany him back to Minhorne, because of my children."

"How did Strumheller escape from prison?"

"With the assistance of the prison apothecary," Vladimer said, "who declared him dead."

The archduke grimaced slightly. She could not tell him how near Ishmael had then been to death from overspending his magic to save her from the fire. "There were *two* attempts on his life while he was in prison," she said.

It did not, she realized, help. "You are quite certain he was Strumheller?" the archduke said to Vladimer.

Vladimer smiled briefly. "He had all Strumheller's nerve." He didn't elaborate.

"What happened at the railway station?" the archduke said, his head twitching toward his brother.

She told it, as she had observed, once more omitting that part that was hers and magical. The archduke would surely believe that Vladimer had dispatched both assassins—he knew his brother's accomplishments—and he might be persuaded that the Shadowborn had overreached himself in his alarm.

"You concur with this, Vladimer?" the archduke said.

There was a silence long enough for Telmaine to wonder, if Vladimer betrayed her, what she would do, take flight, or face the archduke and the ruin of her life square.

"Vladimer?" said the archduke, casting toward his brother.

"Yes," said Vladimer, rousing himself. "There is a threat, I am certain of that. Janus, I will pursue these Shadowborn with all my skills and resources, but the Borders need the ability to defend themselves properly. I told Strumheller I would get a ducal order to allow him to raise forces. I'm asking you to suspend the order of six twenty-nine."

Even the most indifferently tutored lady knew of the Borders uprising and civil war that followed, and the ducal order that had come with the peace. The order of six twenty-nine restricted the standing forces that could be maintained by the nobility, especially the Borders baronies, lest they be held in insurrection.

"You told Strumheller that you would get a suspension of six twenty-nine," the archduke said, in a tone so uninflected as to be ominous. To Telmaine's surprise and perturbation, Vladimer seemed unaware of his misstep. A soft brush of sonn showed him braced in the chair, head lowered. Overcome with faintness, she feared. If the archduke realized, he did not—whether out of consideration for Vladimer's pride or out of annoyance—acknowledge it. "I'll take your word that Strumheller is who he claims to be," he said, narrowly. "I'll grant he's done well by you and the Strumheller barony, but you know I've never shared your trust in him. The man's a mage. You can't convince me that he didn't influence the man who helped him escape. Giving him a ducal order to raise forces in the Borders would be—"

Telmaine bit the fingertip of her glove, stifling her urge to give the archduke a piece of her mind. Which would be disastrous, since most of the things she knew about Ishmael di Studier, including the greatness of his heart and the depths of his loyalties, she knew only because she had touched him as a mage touches another, mind and heart.

Vladimer interrupted before the archduke found the word he sought. "Janus, Strumheller has not influenced *me*, if that is what you are so carefully not implying. He has neither the power nor the malevolence." A shudder ran through the last word—he had but lately encountered one who had both. "He's as loyal to you as I am. And there's no one knows the Borders, knows the Shadowlands, knows the danger, better."

"I've already signed the order of succession recognizing Reynard di Studier as Baron Strumheller."

Vladimer jolted upright. "*What?* When did that arrive? They'd barely have had word of his death."

"A courier came by day train," the archduke said, his tone making Telmaine wince; powerful men did not like being placed on the defensive. "The haste was a touch indecent, yes, but there seemed no reason to delay. The report of di Studier's death came from Malachi himself."

"Reynard di Studier's not the man for this. Please, Janus, I'm begging you: rescind that order of succession. Quash those charges. Give Strumheller a chance to—a chance to—a chance—" The archduke moved even as he sonned, catching Vladimer as he slid forward, and propping him carefully away from his right shoulder. Vladimer muttered something. The archduke's reply was tart, for all the words themselves were inaudible. Telmaine thought she deciphered *utterly pigheaded*.

"I will give it the most careful consideration," the archduke said, straightening, his steadying hand on Vladimer's sound shoulder. "Once I call the physician."

He circumvented further argument by going himself to the door to speak to the footmen outside, and staying there until the doctor arrived. The physician obviously had prior experience of Vladimer, effectively deflecting objections while he organized footmen to carry him. Telmaine heard the archduke quietly ordering the halls to be cleared. "I'll be along," he promised his brother and the physician as they left.

Returning, the archduke brushed his hand down the chairback, and sat down, frowning and wiping his fingers on a handkerchief. "Have that cleaned, once we're done here," he said to the remaining footman, and dismissed him, turning his attention decisively back to his adviser. "Well, Claudius, *now* what do I do? You know Dimi: he's highly strung and this has to be quite the wildest story he's ever laid before me, but he's never once cried fire without *something* burning. And he's barely escaped an assassination attempt—two, if that uncanny illness of his were indeed sorcery. But he's asking for a ducal order suspending six twenty-nine in the Borders—and that will not make my dukes at all happy," he finished, in tones of wry understatement.

"Your Grace," said Casamir Blondell, "surely you do not have to decide immediately. I can investigate further—"

"No," the archduke told him, heavily, "I've never doubted Vladimer's judgment in these matters, and I will not start now. And I've no reason to doubt any of the barons. But curse it, why'd Vladimer tell di Studier that he'd get this done before he said anything to me? If I don't do it and there's trouble, there'll be yet more bad blood between the Borders and the north."

Telmaine chewed the finger of her glove until her teeth bruised skin.

"Vladimer's right that di Studier's done journeyman's work strengthening the Borders defense, *and* kept it within the limits of six twenty-nine, or as near as is not worth mentioning. You can be sure I'd have heard otherwise if not. Vladimer trusts the man—as much as Vladimer trusts anyone—and in all honesty I don't think there's undue influence working. But di Studier's still a mage, and"—this to Casamir Blondell—"accused of sorcery."

Blondell said nothing. If he felt any chagrin at his false accusation, it did not show on his face. Nor did he retract it.

"What if you were to address the ducal order for Strumheller to Reynard di Studier?" Claudius said. "You've already signed the order of succession in good faith, and there's every reason not to rescind it until Ishmael di Studier's legal status is resolved. Even if Vladimer denies the sorcery, there's still the murder of Tercelle Amberley in question. Her betrothed won't be satisfied with quashed charges, and if there's going to be trouble, as Vladimer seems to think, you can't risk any conflict with the Mycenes."

"Reynard di Studier," the archduke said slowly. "I don't know the man well; he keeps to the Borders. He's, what, three or four years the younger—it's the sister who's much younger, isn't it? Is he solid?"

"He's no Shadowhunter," Claudius admitted. "In all truth, Janus, I'd be less happy about it if it weren't for Strumheller's—Ishmael di Studier's—having organized the defenses for the last decade. But I recommend you send the ducal order to Reynard. Even if nothing comes of it, you'd find out what he's made of."

"Except Dimi promised it to Ishmael di Studier," the archduke said, with a sigh. "Well, he's overstepped himself there, and I'll have to have that out with him when he's fit for it. I'll write the ducal order for Strumheller to Reynard di Studier, and I'd best send an agent after Ishmael di Studier. Get him back here to sort out the legalities, and keep him out of trouble in the Borders."

Telmaine, forgotten, waited in suppressed fury until they had left the room. "That rat bastard," she breathed. "How dare he! Ishmael's spent years, blood, and pain in his service." Just in time she stopped herself for reaching out for Ishmael with her magic; he'd have no protection from her rage.

I might change his mind, came the thought, half bidden. Horrified, she rejected it, but it crept back into her mind like a foul smell. She might indeed change the archduke's mind, but would he know it? Would anyone else guess it? Claudius? Balthasar? *Ishmael?* A shiver passed through her, with the sense of how corrupt she had already become, how much magic had already degraded her, if only the thought that they might catch her stayed her from forcing the mind of her ruler. No matter that it was for the sake of those she loved.

All that she had to her credit was that she would *not*, even for the sake of those she loved.

But she must warn Ishmael that agents would be waiting for him in Strumheller. She paused a moment to pass her mage sense carefully over the palace. She had been taken by surprise at the train station; she must not be so again. Nothing seemed out of order. Then she made her way along the corridors to the rooms that had been her and her family's refuge.

It had been most thoroughly cleaned out, even to her own dresses and toiletries. The purge was the mark of Merivan, at her most officiously efficient. Telmaine would cordially detest her eldest sister if not condemned to understand her. Had Merivan been a man, she would have been a superb barrister and no doubt, in time, a judge. As a woman, cleaving to propriety as a principle, she seethed with boredom unrelieved by childbearing and the endless social round.

Merivan ought to have a secret, Telmaine thought. It would make her life ever so much more interesting.

She rustled over to the armchair and sank into it. Sitting, she realized how weary she was. She could not sit long, or she would fall asleep. She swept her mage sense out again, finding Lord Vladimer, and the archduke, close by each other now. Both their vitalities were distinctive, yet more alike than their very different temperaments would suggest. Was blood relationship evident in the texture of vitality? She had never thought to wonder. She turned her head slightly in the direction of Merivan's home, a mile distant, and extended her senses, seeking, and finding, the two living presences more familiar than any other, her little daughters. Those seemed quite distinct, Florilinde in her boldness, Amerdale in her curiosity. Both marred now with unhappiness and anxiety in a way that hurt her to sense. She caressed them gently, unfelt, making them a soft, unheard promise: soon. *Soon I will be there. Soon we will go home. Soon this will all end. Soon.*

Ishmael di Studier on the Borders Express seemed but a little farther away, so distinct was his presence to her. His spirit still had that banked-ember heat she had warmed herself against, though her sense of his magic was dim, crumbled charcoal. There was no justice that he should lose, and she should keep, what was so precious to him and so burdensome to her. She had said, when first they discussed magic, that she would gladly give him all of hers—and she would have. But that was not the way magic worked: his was merely first-rank, hers possibly as much as sixth, when the strongest living Lightborn mage was said to be eighth-rank. Generous as ever, he had guided her magic, gifted her with his learning and best understanding of its structure, and finally overreached his own meager powers to save her.

She would carry all those gifts, and her sense of him, next to her heart for as long as she lived, and if it was improper in a married woman, so be it.

<Ishmael,> she whispered in his mind.

She sensed his sudden wakening, and then his movement as he sat up and reached across to shake the man dozing beneath a quilt on the couch next to his chair—her husband, Balthasar Hearne.

"Telmaine," Ishmael said, speaking aloud in his distinctive Borders accent. "How good it is t'hear from you. Are you in th'city?"

<Yes. I'm fine. But Vladimer couldn't—*we* couldn't—persuade the archduke to issue the ducal order to you, or to quash the charges against you. Ishmael, the archduke has signed the order of succession already. He is sending the ducal order to your *brother*.>

He sighed; she felt him settle his frame deeper into his own armchair, shaken gently with the pulse of the train. "Well," he said, "th'order's gone out, and that's the important part of it. I'd a worry that th'archduke would not be sure of Vladimer, with th'ensorcellment, but it's only me he doesn't trust."

She had been trying, so hard, not to let him know that. Foolish to think she could, when he'd lived with society's judgment against his magic all his adult life. <The archduke said he was going to send an agent to Strumheller to bring you back, so you couldn't interfere.>

She sensed his amusement. "Telmaine, if I cannot outfox a city agent in my own lands, a drafty cell's no less than I deserve." She nearly protested—the last drafty cell had nearly been the death of him. "But please be so good as t'let my lawyers know that th'charges still need answered." She felt his attention shift. "Your husband asks, how are th'little ones?"

<Tell him—tell him my sister has been her usual officious self, and carried them off to her house. I will go over there now.> She would not tell him about the attack at the station when neither he nor Balthasar could do anything about it other than fret—but even as she had the thought, the thought she meant not to have, he said, <*What was that?*> and for the first time reached toward her with his magic. His pain was immediate and shocking, mounting with cruel intensity. She could feel his heart falter as the effort drained away his vitality.

<Best we stop now,> he managed. She released the contact instantly, and leaned forward with her head in her hands, trembling. She wanted to reach out to him again, to know if he *was* all right. She dared not. He had told her his magic was damaged, but not so damaged that he risked his life with its use. She knew it now.

The knock on the door brought her upright with a violent start, mage sense skittering out to confirm all was well with the archduke and Vladimer. She brushed Vladimer's vitality closely enough to judge he was asleep, though uncomfortably so. The knock had to come again before she remembered that she had no maid to answer the door.

It was the apothecary who had helped Ishmael escape, a narrow-faced, stooped young man in a second- or third-hand physician's frock coat, accompanied by two footmen. "M'lady," he said, preempting her greeting, or their introduction. "I need you to put in the word for me."

"Yes?" she said, coolly.

"There's a question, as t'why Lord Vladimer wanted me with him."

Work or a prison cell, she recalled Vladimer saying, with his mordant humor. Unfortunately, those hearing it would have no means of disambiguation in Vladimer's absence. Her mage sense registered him as Darkborn, exuding common anxiety. He had smuggled the comatose Ishmael out of the prison, and come with him to the summer palace to guard his back. Now he was jobless, homeless, and likely penniless, having aided the escape of a fugitive from the law—and no doubt expecting that the aristocratic Lady Telmaine would neither appreciate nor empathize. He would be quite right were she any other aristocrat.

But she was not; she knew exactly what it was to stand in peril of losing everything by her own rightful action. And he had saved Ishmael's life.

"I will take responsibility for him until Lord Vladimer decides what he wants to do with him," she said, calmly. "Please arrange servants' quarters. Kingsley, a word."

"M'name's Kip," the young man said.

The corner of her mouth tucked in. She had been there when he'd explained the lack of patronymic—in terms most unflattering to his mother—to Lord Vladimer. "Not in my service, it's not," she said, firmly, and stood back to let him in.

He certainly had none of the instincts of a servant in a noble household, for he seemed oblivious to the lack of a maid or chaperone. He did, however, have the basic breeding not to throw himself into a chair unbidden. "My thanks, m'lady. I thought it was to be the prison cell for sure."

She settled back into her chair with a loud murmur of fabric, not quite sure whether to bid him to sit. He decided the matter for her by dropping abruptly down on the carpet to sit cross-legged. From there, he sonned her, with a lighter touch than she expected. "Magister di Studier said I was to put myself at *your* service."

Her lips parted in surprise, both at the instructions and at the reference to Ishmael by his seldom-used mage's title.

"It was while you and your husband were saying goodbye. He hunted me up, gave me orders." He grinned like a street urchin, as at a private joke. "Promised to pay me the going rate this time; I'll believe that when it happens."

The grin, and the insult to Ishmael's generosity, offended her. "You will be paid, I assure you."

The grin fell away; his expression was pure feral River-rat. "I'm not doing this for pay, your ladyship. I lost a child when the Rivermarch burned, a little child who'd done no one harm in all her brief days. Whoever were that set the fire, I want to pi—trample on their ashes."

Telmaine caught her breath, thinking how easily her own child could have died in fire. "I understand."

"How's Lord V.?" he said, abruptly. "That wound of his needed properly dealt with."

"It has been. The archduke made sure of it."

"Ensorcellment, a bullet, and then fire." He could not control his shudder at the last, and Telmaine remembered the raw terror in his scream of warning. She wondered how close his escape from the Rivermarch blaze had been. "They want him dead about as badly as they want Magister di Studier. You heard about the poison, and the knife, in the prison?"

"I heard," she said, certain that he was in some way testing her. Did he know the reason for Ishmael's final collapse?

"M'lady, let me be straight with you," he said, setting a hand flat on the carpet. "I think we should contact the Broomes. They're the leaders of the Darkborn city mages, and they do a fine job with the magic and the politics, for all the father's daft and the brother's a slavering republican. It was Magistra Phoebe Broome brought di Studier round, her and Magistra Hearne—" She could not but start, hearing her married name coupled to *that* title, but he was referring to Balthasar's sister, Olivede. "They're two women as staunch as any you could have on your side. They'll be able to sense those Shadowborn, and if there's any trace of what they did to Lord V. That's not something you or I can do."

Telmaine gulped, as impressed as she was appalled by the man's audacity at making such a suggestion to *her*, Telmaine Hearne, Lady Telmaine, and suddenly, dizzily, terrified at the thought that he might suspect. "That—that decision is for Lord Vladimer to make."

"It's a decision he's got to live to make," the apothecary

said grimly. "We're well out of our league here, your lady-ship. If I'd any doubt of it before they set light to th'train, I've none now. It's a blessed miracle we all survived."

She swallowed. "I will—think about that," she said, lying. The last thing she wanted to think about was the Darkborn mages. When they had healed Ishmael, how much had they learned about the *reason* for his overreach? Had Ishmael himself already inadvertently betrayed her?

The apothecary did not, it seemed, wish to challenge her further. She said, "I want you—I want you to get close to Lord Vladimer. I know you aren't a mage—you can't sense the Shadowborn—but you do know and believe in what we're fighting."

"Thought you'd say that," the apothecary said, and pushed himself to his feet. "He'll have doctors, y'know."

"You seem to me an inventive young man," she said, not rising.

"I'm a right hungry one," he amended. "Soon as I can get fed, I'm yours."

Two

Floria

*F*loria White Hand leaned against the curved glass of
the high balcony, gazing over the palace ballroom
below. In stately, rippling rounds the dancers paced out
their steps, the Lightborn court uniting to carouse at the
coming of age of their prince's heir. The bold colors of the
north intermingled with the muted earth hues of the south,
and gems sparkled in the lights mounted at every joint of
the coffered ceiling, every bracket in the walls and around
the balcony columns. No shadows were allowed in this hall.

Though how they could dance after that hours-long feast,
Floria could not imagine. All she herself wanted was a quiet
place to negotiate with her outraged stomach.

Beside her, Prince Isidore's voice said softly, "He's come
on well, hasn't he?"

The ruler of the Lightborn leaned against the balcony at
her side as casually as if he were merely one of the Prince's
Vigilance and not their earthly master, robed and cauled
in the royal blue and star sapphires that only the prince
and his lineage were allowed to wear. The captain of the
Vigilance guarded his back, and two senior lieutenants his
right and left, protecting his person and, for the moment,
his peace.

She followed Isidore's gaze to the center of the dance, to
find the tall, gangly figure of Fejelis, his heir. Fejelis danced
as he did almost everything else, with attention, precision,
and a perceptible hesitation before committing himself. He

was invariably a half beat behind the music. She found it illuminating to observe the effect on his partners.

"I like to see this one from above," the prince remarked. "For the effect of the waves. I've been told it goes back centuries, before the Sundering, and was an invocation of the sea."

She made a sound more dutiful than interested.

"You look a little wan, Mistress Floria."

"Indigestion, my prince," Floria said.

"Ah," he said, with a trace of chagrin. The heir's mixed heritage had been celebrated in food as well as decoration, music, and dance. As a palace vigilant, daughter of generations of vigilants and assassins, Floria's duty was to guard the life of her prince and those he designated. Several generations ago, an ambitious head of the White Hand lineage had contracted with the Mages' Temple to supply and maintain an asset of immunity to poisons for a member of the White Hand lineage. The cost had beggared and the controversy divided the lineage, but the asset had descended first to Floria's father, and then to herself. With it had come the duty of being the prince's food taster, and as such, she had to follow where his tastes led.

Unfortunately, where the prince had been able to develop first a tolerance and then a fondness for the highly spiced fare of the south, Floria had been unable to do likewise. The asset that protected her, and by extension the prince, seemed unable to distinguish between certain spices and poison.

"Oh, I'll live," she said, rubbing her stomach.

"White fish in milk tomorrow," the prince promised. She made a face, as he no doubt expected.

The heir was dancing with one of his southern cousins, a voluptuous young woman whose lush brown hair had been woven into a stiff cornice with beads and gems. The girl was asserting the rhythm, her bare stiff back expressing her resentment at being shown up by her partner. His eyes were fixed politely on her face. Beside Floria, the prince chuckled. "I shouldn't be surprised if he were figuring out which bit of that hair to tug on to bring the whole lot tumbling down. I could tell him, I suppose, but I think I'll leave him to find out for himself."

She glanced sideways at him, knowing that there was nothing idle in the remark. His eyes had strayed to where his consort was sitting amongst her entourage, on the dais at the far end of the hall. Helenja's hairstyle was even more ornate than her young cousin's, its faded roan length woven into an ornate sculpture evocative of a shell.

The marriage between north and south had been a political and economic necessity. It had been intensely unpopular with the northerners, and the consort's relatives had intrigued against Isidore from the start, appalling the court. There was a code and style to deposition of leaders. Two of Helenja's brothers and several of their supporters had died at the hands of the Prince's Vigilance before the southerners had learned. Yet by the glint in his eye, the prince was thinking of the mischief he might make with that sculpted hair. South and north might conspire against each other, but the man and woman themselves had found an accommodation, even mutual affection.

Floria wished him well, tonight of all nights. Helenja's mood was bound to be difficult. Of their children, Fejelis was far from Helenja's favorite—that was his brother, Orlanjis, prancing through the elements of the dance at the far end of the room from brother and mother. He was a handsome boy, much more so than his brother, growing evenly from a compact, appealing child into a well-shaped, winning youth. His auburn hair was intricately braided and wound close to his head, like a princely caul. Not by chance, Floria was sure. Fejelis's sandy hair was no more than shoulder-length, blunt cut in the northern style—as short, as his mother complained, as a servant's—and swung free as he spun lightly on his feet. A single star sapphire bounced on its chain at his throat.

"Do you remember when Fejelis cut his hair?" the prince said. There were times she had to wonder whether he didn't have a trace of magic himself, but Isidore was nothing if not observant. "Looked like a new-hatched chick, he did, all the yellow down standing up in tufts. That

was the day I was sure he was going to be his own man. . . .
You will watch out for him, Floria, won't you?"

He would be thinking, as she was, of the consequences
of that haircut. Three days later, Fejelis was poisoned by
members of his mother's retinue. He would not have lived
but for luck, and a mage's willingness to flout the law. The
outrage around the poisoning of a child had one good consequence—it divided the southerners and resulted in exile
or execution for the worst of them. Helenja might countenance the assassination of her consort, but she would not
countenance the murder of her son.

Floria studied the broad sullen face of the woman on
the dais, and wondered if she still would not. She feared
otherwise. Fejelis had survived with his health and spirit
intact, but with a new wariness. As far as she knew, he was
close to no faction at court, neither south nor north, which
might protect him from becoming ensnared in the enmities
of his allies, but gave him no allies against his own enemies.
But until Orlanjis came of age, Fejelis should be safe—or
at least as safe as his father—or at least from that quarter.

She shifted her eyes back to watch Fejelis weave
through a line of other dancers, the swift turns and partner
exchanges evoking the disorder of foam spilling onto the
shore. Yes, he would be his own man, and not a puppet of
the southern factions. But was he his father's as much as
Isidore seemed to think? The Prince's Vigilance monitored
his activities, of course, but he could be disconcertingly
adept at dodging their observation, when he so chose.

Again the prince's unsettling perceptiveness. "I'm well
aware that he has affiliations he prefers I not know about
and far more radical ideas than I. But I've never believed
that policy should outlive the prince. The world changes,
year by year, for all we deny it. If nothing else, our friends
on the other side of sunset would see to that."

The intrepid, inventive Darkborn, who filled the night
with the sounds of their industry and, with their light-
sealed factories and day trains, were encroaching upon the
day. Their inventions crept across sunset, no longer merely
affecting the lower classes. Several of the costumes down
on the dance floor were dyed with by-products of Dark-

born chemistry. The Vigilance carried guns made according to Darkborn designs; alas, so did their enemies. Even the precariously static world of the Lightborn would not remain unchanged, with them near.

"Did your Darkborn friend recover his daughter?" Isidore said, unexpectedly.

She glanced at him; she had forgotten that she had told him about Balthasar's troubles. "I haven't been home since shortly after Ishmael di Studier took him and his family to the palace, thinking they'd be safe there." She would have been more worried about Balthasar had not the influx of visitors—southerners—for the ceremony kept her preoccupied with the well-being of the prince. Except for intervals of snatched sleep, she had been standing guard and tasting food for days.

Tomorrow she should be able to stand down, if only for a few hours. Then she could return home, send a message by day courier to the archducal palace. Find out what had happened to Bal, to Florilinde, even to Balthasar's prickly wife.

Isidore said, "Fejelis thinks the Darkborn are most important for our future."

She swung her head to look at him. He half turned toward her, his patrician face in three-quarter profile. The molding of the caul picked up the lines of his cheekbones and followed his brows. They exchanged glances, hers dubious, his calm, a gray so light as to be silver, like mirrors. About some things, even a prince could not speak openly.

Seven hundred years ago, the last remnant of Lightborn mages had thrown themselves on the mercy of the strongest chieftain of the sundered lands. From their bargain had arisen the compact that governed the use of magic in the affairs of those without magic, the earthborn, to this day. It prohibited mages from using their magic in their own interest where earthborn were involved. It prohibited mages from using their magic either for or against earthborn, except at the behest of another earthborn. It established a complex and rigid set of laws as to when and how an earthborn might righteously contract the services of a mage. Any acts under contract were then the responsibility of the earthborn; the mage was made immune by law.

Thus the mages had survived, and the chieftain had ended his days as master of the daylight lands. Would he have made the compact, Floria wondered, if he had envisioned that the few dozen desperate petitioners would become thousands, with some amongst them with the power to become essentially immortal, or conjure up a storm, or—it was rumored—reverse time itself? If that chieftain had envisioned that one day the earthborn palace, large as it was, would be . . . shadowed . . . by a Temple tower four times its height? Or that the transfer of wealth from hundreds of years of contracts would leave his state a hollow shell?

Had he known that, he should have had his petitioners' hearts pierced then and there, or been deserving of righteous deposition.

The Darkborn had resisted making such a bargain, had thrust magic to the periphery of society, and had nonetheless prospered. Idealistic and radical factions within Lightborn society wished to follow their example, and escape their dependence on magic, a dependence that extended—she glanced upward—to the very lights they lived by, through the night.

The dance ended. Fejelis had no sooner bowed to his partner than another southern cousin pushed through the throng to claim him. She was as fair as the first had been dark, but no less shapely and supple. Floria sensed a campaign, Helenja's, or someone else's. From his not-so-casual remark about his son, Isidore seemed at ease with the idea that Fejelis might ally with a southerner.

Floria was not, but then she was the one who, for eighteen years, had tasted every dish the prince ate and cup he drank. Fejelis would be safer if the southern faction thought he could yet be brought to heel—unless the northerners turned against him, determined that there would be no more southern alliances.

Even the Prince's Vigilance could fail in its task.

"I do worry about him," Isidore said. "His strongest alliances are not within court, but outside—though there are some that are potentially formidable—" She glanced aside at him, and caught the suggestive glint of a silver gray eye. None of the prince's associations known to the Vigilance could be described that way. Disruptive, yes, formidable, no. Isidore continued. "It is time he built stronger support of his own within court; he will need it when this job falls to him."

Useless to protest that statement; it was the reality and they were realists. There would come a time when age or cumulated mistakes made Isidore's deposition more acceptable than not. There would come a time when even the Prince's Vigilance would stand aside, for the good of the state.

But it should be years yet. Years.

"He's in danger of being too careful," Isidore stressed. "Of not taking the risk of letting people close. Of not trusting people he should."

This was, she thought, a disturbing conversation to be having on the evening of the heir's coming of age. Fejelis was now considered able to rule without a regent. There were those who would risk an unrighteous deposition to have a prince on a string.

Did anyone have Fejelis on a string? What was the formidable association Isidore had alluded to? Isidore himself did not seem perturbed by it—but why alert her?

"He has reason, of course. So I've been having a quiet word with a few people *I* trust," the prince said.

He said little after that, and presently left, his guards following. Floria knew she had received—along with those other few—a commission, though a commission to do what, she was not sure. She let the prince go down the stairs, and then padded along the corridor to a locked cabinet where the Prince's Vigilance kept some of its provisions. Find water and a glass, mix in one of her own preparations to settle her stomach. In a while, she would be summoned to taste the food and drink the prince was taking into his chambers with him, and then, perhaps, if her indigestion, or this last conversation, allowed, she might sleep.

Telmaine

Had she been but a little quicker, she would have escaped.

It was not to be. As she closed her door, on her way to

visit her daughters, she heard footsteps on the stairs at the end of the hall. Superintendent Malachi Plantageter, with Ishmael's lawyer trotting at his heel.

An impulse to dive into the bedroom, squirm childlike under the bed, and pretend not to *be here* died stillborn. "Lady Telmaine Hearne?" said the superintendent, though he well knew who she was. They had exchanged words when he arrested Ishmael. "Is this an inconvenient time?"

"I was just going to my sister's to visit my children," Telmaine said, coolly. "But I suppose this will not take particularly long." She stepped back and let the two men in, the long-boned man with the distinctive Plantageter nose—which he came by quite legitimately, if through the distaff line—and the small rotund lawyer.

"I understand your husband is out of the city," the superintendent said. "Would you prefer that one of your brothers or your brother-in-law were present?"

She couldn't imagine which would be worse, to have her rigid eldest brother, Duke Stott, either of her two smart and mocking younger brothers, or her sister's husband, Lord Judiciar Erskane. Merivan's husband would be her best ally against the law, but if anyone found the missed stitches in her lace of lies, it would be he. She shook her head.

"The archduke said he thought you would prefer to have your own legal representation," Malachi Plantageter continued. She sonned the lawyer, noting his shrewd face with mixed relief and apprehension. Di Brennan was not her family's usual lawyer, but he represented the same firm, and he and Balthasar had spoken about Ishmael's arrest; he knew at least part of the story—one of the stories.

"Thank you," she said meekly. "What would you like to speak to me about?"

Without a word, without a theatrical flourish, the superintendent held out both hands. In one was a lady's reticule; from the other dangled a silver love knot.

She knew her hands would tremble, but she had no choice but to accept both. She laid her hands down atop the reticule, the love knot held in her closed fist.

"Is there anything you would like to tell me, Lady Telmaine?" he said quietly.

"I thought I had lost them," she said.

"How much money was in the reticule?"

"Sixty, sixty-five." She ventured a small shrug of the shoulder, the insouciance of a lady to whom money comes easily.

"Perhaps," di Brennan said to the superintendent, "you might explain."

Plantageter leaned back with a sigh that she felt in her own weary bones. "Yesterday evening young Guillaume di Maurier was found seriously wounded—he had been shot in the abdomen." The lawyer's brow drew briefly in sympathy. "I sent one of my agents to take a statement. Di Maurier said he had been searching for a lost child—you may know he acts in an irregular capacity for Lord Vladimer—and had traced her to a warehouse in the Lower Docks. It was while he was there he was shot. He had given this information to the child's mother with the expectation that she and"—a slight emphasis on the contested title—"Baron Strumheller would act to free the child. As the young man seemed in extremis, the agent did not tell him of Strumheller's arrest. A kindness, you understand, if he were to die." Telmaine made a small sound in her throat; Plantageter paused, awaiting her question, but both sonned di Brennan's warning headshake. Breathing shallowly, gripping Bal's love knot, she held her peace.

"That was around one fifteen of the clock. A little after half past, a coachman delivered a lady matching Lady Telmaine's description to the Upper Docks. Further reports had the lady walking in the direction of the Lower Docks. At around two of the clock, fire broke out in a warehouse in the Lower Docks. An extremely fierce, hot fire. One or two witnesses claim they sonned a woman carrying something from the direction of the fire, but in such conditions such testimony could be challenged. Somewhat later, the lady returned to the waiting coach, smelling strongly of smoke and with a sick child in her arms. She asked to be driven to the archducal palace, claiming to have lost her money but to be acting in Casamir Blondell's interest. Out of sympathy for the child, the coachman agreed. He was paid on arrival, and the cloak he had lent to keep the child

warm returned. I received the information from Casamir
Blondell that the child Florilinde Hearne had been restored to her parents. He knew of no female agent assigned
to work the docks."

Telmaine controlled her breathing and her expression
with an effort. He waited; she had a sudden impression of a
cat waiting by a mousehole, and felt a flare of unwise temper at the idea he should toy with her.

"I also received a message from the prison that Baron
Strumheller had collapsed and expired at about the same
time the warehouse burned. However, I now know that is
not so."

"In what way?" said di Brennan, frowning.

"He is not dead."

"The order of succession has been dispatched, and we
are making the arrangements required to execute the late
Baron Strumheller's will."

It was, Telmaine thought, a cat-to-cat contest now, and
she was very glad to crouch quietly in her mousehole.

"I would hold on that will," Plantageter said, with a
trace of humor. "Lord Vladimer Plantageter arrived by
the train from the coast just after sunset tonight. By his
account Lady Telmaine, her husband, and Baron Strumheller interrupted an attempt on his life and killed the
sorcerer responsible. Strumheller had escaped prison with
the collusion of the prison apothecary, whom I believe he
had known in the past."

"I am truly gratified," di Brennan said after a pause. Telmaine heard genuine emotion in his voice, and her heart
warmed to him. "I have known Ishmael di Studier, boy,
man, and baron, since I was a student, and despite all his irregularities, I have never felt that by serving my client I was
not serving justice." Then the unguarded moment passed;
the lawyer returned, keen-edged. "Then the charges are
dropped?"

"We must discuss that at a later time, Master di Brennan," Plantageter said.

Smoothly, the lawyer accepted that with a murmured "Of
course."

"The charges must be dropped!" Telmaine said, unable

to restrain herself. "We know who tried to kill Vladimer and we know who killed—who must have killed—Tercelle Amberley."

"Unfortunately, my lady, knowing and proving before law are two different matters," Plantageter said, with some emphasis. "The remains of four men were found in the ruins of the warehouse." A flush of heat washed over Telmaine as she remembered brushing by the foot of one of the corpses. That realization, that distraction, would have been the death of her and Florilinde, but for Ishmael's sacrifice.

"Lady Telmaine, did you arrange for that fire to be set, to enable you—or someone else"—as di Brennan shifted in his chair—"to free your daughter?"

"Of course not!" Telmaine said, in what she hoped was the tone of someone hearing that outrageous accusation for the first time.

"Did you bribe anyone to set the fire, with the money in that reticule and your jewelry?"

"My husband gave me this when we were *courting*," she said in a thin voice. "It would be the last thing I would *ever*—"

"Did Baron Strumheller start the fire?"

Now she was genuinely appalled. "No! Baron Strumheller—" She caught herself; di Brennan's hand signal was redundant warning. "Baron Strumheller was in *prison*, half the city away." And, brazenly, "I know he has the reputation of being a mage, but I—I simply don't believe it."

"Baron Strumheller's supposedly fatal collapse occurred at the time the fire began," he noted, but without any real conviction. "Lady Telmaine, what did you plan to *do* when you confronted those men in the warehouse?"

She would *not* think of Ishmael's agonized scream in her mind as he had reached across the distance between them to hold back the flames—an impossible effort for a first-rank mage. "I planned to bribe them to free my daughter," she said, as steadily as she could. "I would have promised them no one would know. They could not know that Master di Maurier had been able to give testimony. Is he—" Her voice wavered. "Is he still alive?"

"I believe so, but if he does live, it will be a miracle. It does make me ask what you thought you were doing, going to the same place."

She bit her lip. "In truth, Superintendent, I fear I was a little mad. My husband had been beaten, my daughter stolen away from me, and the man who had been helping me find her accused of the vilest crimes."

"You should have come to us, Lady Telmaine."

She clutched her gloved hands together. "It was—I was afraid of the publicity, Master Plantageter. Afraid that it would hurt my daughter. Baron Strumheller promised us he could use Lord Vladimer's networks. And Master di Maurier found her. I do hope he lives. When he told me— Florilinde was all I thought about."

He leaned back in his chair and his sonn washed deliberately over her. "I cannot decide whether you are a blessed innocent who has used up a lifetime's luck in a night, or a woman so cunning she has been able to conceal all the traces of her crimes." He paused, and sonned her again, catching her with her mouth a little open as she sought— truly sought—to find an answer for him. "When did the fire in the warehouse start?"

"As I set foot inside the building."

"The description was that it was explosive."

"It may have seemed so from outside," Telmaine said, steadily, her heart beating hard. She must hold her nerve, hold it with all her strength. If she did not waver, they must take her testimony for what it was, or think the unthinkable. "The downstairs was passable."

"But the guards did not escape," he said. "And if there was time for you to reach and free your daughter, there was time for them to flee. Did you have them drugged, Lady Telmaine? Was that what your bribe money was for?"

"No," she said, cleared the croak out of her voice and said again, clearly, "I did not drug them. I do not know why they did not escape. I paid them no heed. All I could hear"—a shallow gasp, quite unfeigned—"were my child's cries."

There was a silence. Plantageter said, in a confiding voice, "I suspect, Lady Telmaine, that not a court in the land would convict you."

"Do not respond to that, Lady Telmaine," cautioned di Brennan.

She sonned di Brennan, her brow furrowed in temper. "No court should even *charge* me, sir. I have done nothing wrong."

There was a silence. She did not dare sonn the man's expression until his sudden movement startled her into a nervous cast that visualized him rising from his chair. "Thank you for your time, Lady Telmaine."

Di Brennan rose also. Telmaine remained where she was, resisting the desire to melt into the chair. Di Brennan followed the superintendent to the door but, instead of following him through it, closed the door softly and firmly behind him.

Turning, he sonned her lightly, his face thoughtful. "When I met your husband, I thought him a clever young man. Now I appreciate he has an equally clever wife."

"I don't understand you, sir," Telmaine said, struggling to summon up offense. "I have done nothing wrong. If the Sole God were not watching over me, then his *mother* was." She regretted the statement immediately: the Mother of All Things Born was the goddess of Lightborn and mages, not of respectable Darkborn. She brought her hand to her lips. "Forgive me," she said, from behind it.

He said, "Please mind what you say, Lady Telmaine. Even to me."

Floria

Floria woke, unrested, eyes squeezed against the dazzle of the lights overhead. She had slept naked for want of her usual night attire, a thigh-length lace vest, Darkborn-made, that Balthasar had given her as a birthday gift years ago. Tangled sheets bound her legs; the sheet against her back felt clammy. She threw an arm across her face, ignoring the prickling of her shadowed skin, and tried not to taste the inside of her mouth. The thought might be unworthy of the prince's loyal servant, but she could not help hoping that Isidore had paid just a little for yesterday's overindulgence.

But the festivities had passed without major incident.

Yes, several duels, three with pistols—a deplorable habit adopted from the Darkborn—and two deaths. Many alliances and schemes, some of which would no doubt lead to trouble. Numerous dalliances, some of which would produce inconvenient children. The Lightborn did not have the Darkborn's sensitivities about legitimacy, since magic could answer questions of paternity, but alliances amongst their brightnesses were of necessity political, and even the brightest were susceptible to base jealousy. But today the guests would begin to disperse, taking with them the most uncouth from the south and the least forgiving from the north, and she could stand down.

At least there was no occasion around breakfast. The business of the princedom must go on, whether or not a son comes of age, and the prince habitually woke early, worked before breakfast, and then ate breakfast privately with one or more intimates. Today, it was his flighty daughter Liliyen. Floria angled her arm to view the clock; it was as early as she feared, given the way she felt, but not, alas, as early as she hoped, also given the way she felt. She kicked free of the sheets, rolled to her feet, and began her morning stretches.

Stepping wide for a side lunge, she bruised her bare foot on one of her own shoes. She caught it up and pitched it beneath the form carrying her court costume before she thought—*she* had not left it there.

She had not left it there, and none of the palace servants could possibly have come into this room without her knowing. Which left—she began a methodical search of the room, looking for the evidence that would surely be there if one of her own colleagues was counting coup on her. It had to be a game, for if someone had found a way into her room with malevolence in mind, she would not have lived to awaken.

She found nothing, no mocking note or hidden counter. Perhaps, she thought, that was the object, to unsettle her. Sooner or later someone would make a point of letting her know.

She rounded off her exercises in irritable haste and went to bathe. One of the compensations of an overnight stay

at the palace was the sybaritic facilities. The huge bathtub
and sink were milky porcelain, chipped and marked with
the fine frieze of age. They had originally been enspelled to
absorb the daylight from the wide window, but subsequent
economies replaced that by the usual magical lights in mirrored brackets. By habit, she noted their healthy color and
brightness. A light whose store of sunlight was dwindling
passed through all the colors of sunset before it went out.

It was too early to open the shutters, still before dawn.
She turned away from the light and found herself facing
a mirror. She assessed herself with detachment. A woman
of more than average height, lean, muscles like straps and
cords, bulkier on the right arm and leg. Fine lines of age
around eyes and mouth, but only to those who came close.
A little softening by time of the contours of breast and but-
tocks, but only to one who remembered. Shoulder-length
hair, not much darkened from the white gold of youth, a
fortunate color amongst Lightborn. She should consider
it so; it was what made her father notice her mother, all
those years ago. Several old scars, white on fair skin. The
tattooed mandala of faded yellow and brown that spread
across most of her upper abdomen.

She rubbed the mandala lightly. She had not been awake
when the asset was cast upon her, the tattoo cut into her
skin. Her father's doing; he knew she would not have con-
sented, otherwise, to assume the asset that had preserved
his life and profession until then. Only one member of the
White Hand lineage could carry it at any one time.

For the remaining four years of his life, she had tasted his
food, too. Then he had set aside his caution, and died. Another had brought the poison to the table, she understood
that—and had had her vengeance—but he had brought his
indifference to living longer, now that the weakness of age
was fully upon him.

On her, the marks of age were slight, the marks of weakness none.

It was, she thought, unfair on a woman: her father was
a decade older than herself when he sired her, yet if she
were to pass the asset on to a child of her own, that child
would have to be conceived soon. The alternative would be

to pass it on to a cousin. She could not but find fault with all her young cousins, in some way or other.

She would think about this later, she decided, not for the first time.

Frowning at her vagrant shoes, now resting one across the other, she pulled on underclothes and trousers, blouse, and tunic. The front and rear of the blouse and tunic were opaque, the narrow side panels transparent. The fabric of the sleeves and trousers alternated stripes of translucent white with opaque silver, to muddle an enemy's eye. Light-born could not endure too dense a shadow. Black tarpaulin was even a weapon of assassination, though a victim had to be extraordinarily negligent, drugged, or sodden drunk to be taken that way.

As she buttoned the tunic up its side, memory niggled: sometime during the night, she had fastened these very buttons as part of a peculiarly prosaic dream of walking through the brightly lit halls to the prince's quarters with—something in her hand. All she could think of was a little wood and ivory box that Balthasar had given her for a birthday years ago, filled with a sandalwood perfume cake. She had never told Bal that her asset reacted to the perfume, and the delicately carved wood and ivory were stained and mismatched, ugly to her court-refined eye. Though she still kept the box, because she treasured the friendship. Why she should dream of carrying that to her prince, she did not know, except if it had to do with his comment that the future lay in people like the Darkborn.

She shook her head in self-reproach. Of all the ills that could beset her after long duty and spice-laden banquets, why she should choose to fret over this one, she did not know. Or for that matter, why consider it a nightmare?

She combed out her hair, spun it into a coil at the back of her head, and contained it with a white mesh. Shoes, soft-soled with closed toes and mesh uppers. Glove on right hand, soft suede palm, mesh upper. Sword on left hip, pistol on right. Her great-grandfather had schemed to acquire an asset that would deflect bullets, but he had never been able to persuade the family to support the purchase of another asset, when their fortunes had still to recover from the first.

The prince carried such an asset, cast on a talisman for his father. The price had been a province, one of the last pieces of land outside the city owned by the princedom.

Her father had always told her that politics was no concern of a vigilant. But when the impoverishing of the princedom led directly to the southern alliance, it had closed his lips on that argument.

As she opened her door, she heard the screaming. Faintly, from the direction of the prince's chambers. She sprinted, hand gripping the sword hilt to steady it, through galleries, past where servants were gathering to open the many shutters, once certain of dawn. As she reached the last corner, the screams dwindled to a harsh mewing, more ghastly than the shrieks.

Prince's consort Helenja and one of the consort's Vigilance stood before the door to the prince's rooms. At their feet was the prince's daughter Liliyen, tumbled onto her side, her head lolling on her arm, her bare hand outstretched to the threshold. Floria noted the faint motion of her breathing, though that meant only that she was not, at the moment, dead. The vigilant was staring into the doorway with a face flayed with horror, fatally oblivious to everything about her. It was from her throat that the mewling came. Helenja turned her head. Her face was whey-hued and moist, her eyes wide to bulging, her broad jaw sagging. Her mouth silently opened and closed like that of a fish dragged into a boat to smother in air.

Slowly, Floria turned toward the door. It stood ajar, pushed wide open. The light from the corridor fanned across the floor and reflected dimly from the near furniture, on the periphery of a room in utter darkness.

Three

Telmaine

*A*lone in her rooms, Telmaine picked wearily at a late supper, grilled fish in an herbed butter sauce. She had scant appetite, having eaten a nursery supper with her daughters in an attempt to reconcile them to staying with their cousins. The effort had met with little success: though the nursery itself was familiar, the children sensed her ambivalence at leaving them there. But she could not—she would not—bring them back to a household under such threat as this one.

To her relief, Merivan had been indisposed with her latest pregnancy, delivering her ultimatum that she and Telmaine must speak *later* from beneath a mint-scented facecloth. She had not even asked what had become of Balthasar. Telmaine had had to speak to Merivan's husband about her daughters' protection, a small ordeal, that. Despite careful forethought and despite invoking Lord Vladimer's name to account for both her fears and her constraint, there had been several precarious moments. The lord judge understood better than most Vladimer's capabilities, ruthlessness, and limitations. She maneuvered carefully between convincing him and alarming him, lest he feel it his duty to order her under his own protection. In the end he let her go, making her promise that she would ask for help if she needed it, while he promised in turn to shelter her daughters. He was, she thought, more than Merivan deserved.

She had wept all the way back in the carriage, barely

caring about threats from sunrise or Shadowborn, or the presence of her maid.

So she dipped her fork in sauce, and wondered whether she should summon the maid from her own late supper to pour her a bath, or defer the bath for tomorrow, or simply fall asleep where she sat. The archduke's vitality pulsed in her awareness; even three hours after sunrise, he showed no indication of retiring. And Vladimer had, in the last hour, awakened and grown restive.

Nevertheless, the note was an unwelcome surprise. Kip carried it in one hand, hurrying her unhappy maid along with the other. The note was brief, untidily punched, but quite legible. "Join us, immediately. Oak receiving room. V."

Of course, she thought, a man who could fire a fatal bolt from a cane, left-handed, would surely be able to write passably with that same left hand.

With the help of her maid she scrambled into a fresh dress, still damp from the pressing it had received in Merivan's laundry, and pulled her hair into approximate order. Veils covered a multitude of sins. Kip was chafing in the sitting room when she came out; she thought for an unsettled moment that he was going to take *her* by the arm to hasten her along. But he contented himself with keeping her pattering after his long stride. He had, she noted, acquired a footman's uniform that fitted tolerably well, though not the graces to go with it.

Since she couldn't protest to Vladimer, she did so to Kingsley. "A lady needs time for her toilette."

He halted and turned so abruptly she almost collided with him. Snapped sonn before and behind them, confirming the corridor was empty. Bent his head to hers to say in a low voice, "The archduke's about to go into session with the dukes over the ducal order and this and that that's happened—the Rivermarch fire, and Lord V.'s ensorcellment. But Lord V.'s just had a message—something's happened with the Lightborn, something serious."

"Will Lord Vladimer be there?"

"Yes, more fool he," said the apothecary. Shook his head. "Don't suppose he's much choice. Here we are. Over to you, m'lady."

Over to her, indeed. Quick pat of hands to veil, hair beneath it, collar, bodice, gloves, skirts. Draw spine very straight and sail forward into the sonn of the two footmen. "Lord Vladimer is expecting me," she proclaimed, with emphasis on the name.

She could hear voices raised in argument behind the closed door, muffled by its thickness, unnervingly loud as the doors swung open before her. She almost shied on the threshold, but forceful interlaced sonn pinned her there like a naturalist's beetle, and the voices went suddenly silent at her unexpected appearance.

"Lady Telmaine!" said Claudius's voice. There was a general rustle of movement as the men rose to their feet. The movement struck her then as peculiarly sinister, a closing of ranks. She walked steadily forward, striving to project composure. "Lord Vladimer asked me to attend, Your Grace."

"Thank you, Lady Telmaine," Vladimer's voice said. "Indeed I did."

There was a brief, low exchange; though she could not make out the words, she could well guess the content. Then Sejanus Plantageter's voice said, "Bring a chair for the lady. *There* will do."

There was in the empty space at Vladimer's side, Sejanus dealing a little discomfiture Vladimer's way. She risked a light stroke of sonn over the figure in the armchair, the one who had not risen. Vladimer was fully dressed, even overdressed, his formal coat more suited to winter than summer. Social armor, or warmth? His left hand rested atop his cane in a familiar pose—and she would think very respectfully of that cane hereafter—and his right arm was propped carefully on the chair arm. His face was drawn, his lips dry, but his expression was alert, his sonn crisp. Too alert, and too crisp, for a man with his wound. She tallied signs she had learned from Balthasar, with his interest in treatment of addictions, and realized that the apothecary's "more fool he" was not merely a comment on Vladimer's being on his feet. Stimulants could negate the effect of injury and blood loss, for a time.

"I trust," the archduke said dryly, "that we can now proceed."

"Yes, Sejanus. I apologize." Trying for bland, Vladimer sounded merely sardonic.

"Then, my lords, I was explaining why, on Vladimer's request, I signed and sent ducal orders to the Borders, authorizing the raising of troops by the five baronies beyond the allotment stipulated in the order of six twenty-nine."

"And I was saying," Sachevar Mycene growled, "that it is the most ridiculous farrago I have ever heard—" and once again, everyone was talking at once.

Telmaine started as a hand gripped her sleeve; it was Vladimer, leaning over to hiss beneath the hubbub, "They're all themselves, I take it."

"Yes," she breathed.

"A shame," said Vladimer, and eased himself upright, leaving her to ponder his twisted humor. Which of them would he prefer were a Shadowborn, or Shadowborn touched? Sachevar Mycene, the archduke's political rival? Xerxes Kalamay, devout follower of the Sole God, opposed to the least accommodation with the Lightborn?

"What's happened?" she risked whispering.

"Wait."

Though she had met these men at social events, here, in their power, they seemed to use up all the air. Of the four major dukes, the next tier of rank down from the archduke, three were present.

Xerxes, Duke of Kalamay, did not turn his head at her sonn, though its pitch and quality would have marked it as feminine. As with the archduke, experience and character had engraved itself on his face. It might have been a benign face, had he achieved his youthful aspirations to the service of the Sole God and the hand of the merry daughter of a fellow cleric. But one short summer's night his elder brother wandered staggering drunk from his fellows and was not missed until past sunrise, and within two years Xerxes was his father's deputy and wed to a melancholy heiress. Time had scored his disappointments deep.

Beside him sat Sachever, Duke of Mycene. He was small and wiry, like his son, with a finely shaped, hairless head that, in its poise and swift turning, evoked a hunting hawk. Time rode him lightly. Even in his sixties he was pugnacious, driven, and a master of sports and weapons. He delighted in outwitting or outlasting men a third his age, and still made his plans as though he expected to pluck their fruit himself, even fruit thirty years in the ripening.

The Duke of Imbré sat to her left hand, the nearest of them all to Vladimer. He was more than eighty, as eroded and immutable as a sandstone outcropping; no predator but time would pull him down. Age had brought him wisdom and the respect even of his enemies.

The five Borders barons stood approximately level with the next tier of dukes in social rank, though their vast, sparsely populated lands encircled the Shadowlands and extended almost to the south coast. Two of the five were here, with the heir to the third, Stranhorne. And Ishmael's city representative, a cousin, surely, with that broad figure and blocky profile.

The archduke's raised hand elicited silence. "Perhaps we might like to hear each other's questions."

Sachevar Mycene had half sprung from his chair. "Di Studier murdered my son's betrothed and he and his—associates are using this—farrago of lies and insinuations—to distract us from his guilt."

"For all we know," the heir to Kalamay said, "*he* seduced the lady."

"There was no seduction and there are no children," Mycene snarled. "The physician who claims so—"

"Lady Telmaine's husband," Vladimer murmured.

"—was in Ishmael di Studier's pay."

"My *husband* was in nobody's pay."

Vladimer tapped Telmaine's arm, in caution. "I have two independent examiners' reports that Lady Tercelle Amberley had borne a child within a few days of her death."

There was a shocked silence. Imbré winced and shook his head. "This is an outrage!" Kalamay said. "To violate a lady's modesty so in death—Sejanus, your brother has gone too far!"

The archduke, Telmaine suspected, might have agreed; even she herself, with no love whatsoever for Tercelle Amberley, was dismayed. Vladimer continued, unruffled as a pond in summer. "While I have no wish to slander the lady's memory"—a lie, given his indifference to slander against his own reputation—"or offend your lordships' sensibilities"—another lie—"we do know at least one other man might have an interest in Tercelle Amberley's life or death."

"The child was Strumheller's," Randalf Kalamay said.

"An extraordinary feat of magic, that, given that he was in the Borders at the pertinent time."

Vladimer, Telmaine decided, was *enjoying* this exercise of wits too much.

"There was no child," Mycene said, "and my son will have anyone who repeats this slander outside this room on the dueling ground."

Which was a threat to give anyone in this room pause. Ferdenzil Mycene's aim had publicly been proved deadly on several such occasions.

Old Duke Imbré said slowly, "You must know how implausible this sounds, Vladimer. Ferdenzil's bride is dead. The child or children have disappeared, so their origin or even their existence cannot be proven."

"Never mind these children," Duke Kalamay himself said. "Sejanus, is it my understanding that you have given a ducal order into *Ishmael di Studier's* hands?"

"As a matter of fact, no," the archduke said, calmly. "I received an order of succession for Strumheller prior to the issuing of the ducal order. I had no reason then not to sign and seal it. Reynard di Studier is now Baron Strumheller." A small, pointed pause. "As for *Ishmael* di Studier, last evening I commissioned Lord Ferdenzil Mycene to travel down to the Borders and apprehend him."

Telmaine heard herself gasp. She swept Vladimer's face with sonn, demanding explanation. His face was still and his grip on his cane, knotted. The announcement had surprised him, too, unpleasantly. She felt ill, remembering Ferdenzil Mycene, when he had paid court to her, or rather to her bloodline and properties. Herself, he had perceived as no more than a pleasing female shape and a vessel for his dynastic ambitions. She had seldom touched a man so potent and so cold.

"I thought it more than likely Ferdenzil would take matters into his own hands," the archduke said. "And Ishmael di Studier loose in the Borders is too much fox for any city agent. I was quite explicit that di Studier is to be returned alive, and frank in my displeasure if any harm comes to him. If he is innocent, then I wish his name cleared; if guilty, then he shall be punished by law."

The Duke of Mycene seemed to be examining his son's commission like a gift of dubious providence, uncertain as to its hidden purpose or price. The Strumheller representative raised his jaw from his fist. "It might seem t'me that you do not trust Bordersmen t'respect th'law."

"Lord di Gruner," the archduke said, gravely, "I trust the majority of Bordersmen to respect the law, but there are precedents when fugitive Bordersmen have been sheltered within the Borders."

"Aye, and northmen have hidden in the north from retribution from their crimes," di Gruner said, in a Borders accent achingly like Ishmael's. "Th'baron near died three times in th'cells. It needn't be guilt that makes him shy t'return."

"Then set your mind at ease; he will be well protected until the truth of the charges is known."

"Yes," said Vladimer, one spare word, heavy with the weight of his reputation.

"Now, I had thought to have Superintendent Plantageter report to you on progress with the investigation of the Rivermarch fire, but decided to defer that report. In brief, the fire started simultaneously a dozen places and burned extremely fiercely. Since it started in daylight, we asked for reports from the Lightborn. There was suspicious activity near two of the locations, but it proved to be ordinary criminal activity. There is no evidence of coordinated arson."

"They would say that," said Kalamay.

"A second such incident involved a fire in a warehouse in the Lower Docks, this time at night. The warehouse had been largely unused for some time, except for illegal purposes. Again it appears that the fire started in several places at once and burned extremely fiercely.

"A *third* such incident occurred this evening, on a train newly arrived at Bolingbroke Station." He clearly did not want to mention whose train. "Fortunately, the fires were contained before great damage was done or injury sustained."

Claudius said slowly, "Janus, are they saying the fires were unnatural?"

There was an uneasy, shifting silence. "I know," the archduke said, "you find mention of magic distasteful. You do not believe it exists; it offends your piety and your sense of the order of things; it seems too much like wish fulfillment, bringing a man too easily things he should achieve only with effort or not at all. It is an invitation to corruption and a childish gratification of whim."

Telmaine realized she was hearing Sejanus's own convictions. That might be said of her, whose power came so easily, but Ishmael di Studier's magic had taken everything he had. "But there is another aspect of magic, a part that we prefer not to acknowledge: it is potentially very dangerous. An attempt—two attempts have been made on my brother's life. And a little while ago, Vladimer received word that an attempt was made on the Lightborn prince's life, and was successful. Isidore is dead."

Not a man spoke. Lightborn or no, the prince was a ruler, and the rulers had their own fraternity. What struck at one struck at all. Sejanus seemed the calmest man in the room, including Vladimer, whose knuckles sonned like bone on the head of his cane and whose expression, turned toward his brother, was stark.

"How?" said Kalamay.

"The light in his chambers failed during the night. Dissolution was, as burning is for us, near instantaneous. As these lights are enspelled to create light, their failure is unlikely to be either by chance or nature."

"Then that puts the southern bitch's son in his place," said Baron Rutgegard grimly, and not a man rebuked him for language in the presence of a lady. The new prince's great-grandfather, named Odon the Breaker in Darkborn histories, had set out to rid his lands of Darkborn. The Borders in particular had never forgotten, or forgiven, that year and a half of genocidal slaughter. "They've won at last."

"Barbarians," said Kalamay. Thwarted in his religious

calling by his elder brother's death, Xerxes Kalamay had quarreled even with members of his own church over interpretations of doctrine that suffered mages and Lightborn in their midst.

"Perhaps," the archduke said mildly. "Young Fejelis may surprise more than the southern factions, I suspect. But that is outwith our powers to decide. My lords," he said, formally, "aside from my brother's concerns, on the other side of sunrise there are powers we do not understand, powers that may exceed anything that we can match, and whose motives are unclear. Furthermore, whatever the logic of their protocols of succession, Isidore's assassination will result in turmoil, during which the southern factions are certain to make a renewed bid for power. If Fejelis does not survive that turmoil, the succession is liable to pass over to his younger brother, who *is* a creature of the southern factions.

"Whether the greater threat proves to be Lightborn or Shadowborn, as Vladimer believes, we must prepare. I have sent a ducal order to the Borders to permit the raising of forces to resist a Shadowborn invasion. I was weighing a ducal order to yourselves, to permit the raising of forces within the city to meet any associated crisis—"

Vladimer's cane rattled against the chair, startling sonn from her. He was leaning forward, the tendons of his neck sharp, his hand clenched on his cane. "*No*, Janus," he whispered.

The warning went unheard, or was ignored. "The documents will be in your hands within the hour."

She felt a surge of triumph from the Duke of Mycene, though not a muscle moved in that raptor's face. The Duke of Kalamay bowed coldly. Imbré leaned over and briefly laid a time-gnarled hand on Sejanus's knee. Vladimer lowered his head.

"This will not be used as an excuse for persecution of those—Lightborn or mageborn—who have committed no crime." This, Telmaine knew, was directed at Kalamay. "We have lived in peace if not in amity with the Lightborn for nearly three hundred years, and I can revoke these orders as readily as I grant them. Now I will ask you to leave me;

it is late, and we are all tired, and we will no doubt make an early start tomorrow evening. Please consider my household your own." He stood, and set his hand on the back of his chair while the other men rose and filed out, Mycene and Kalamay shoulder to shoulder, already conferring. Telmaine remained as she was, half in determination, half in paralysis.

"Well, Dimi," the archduke breathed. "Say it."

"What is there to say?" Vladimer said huskily. "As you have but lately reminded me, you are archduke. I hope you can as successfully persuade Mycene and Kalamay of that."

The archduke's expression was a warning. "I could not issue a ducal order to the barons without issuing one to the dukes, not after this. Do I have your backing?"

"Always," Vladimer said. "And at least you have them mewed up for the day."

A sketch of a grin of appreciation. "Do what you have to, and get some rest, or you're going to pay for this. Lady Telmaine," he acknowledged her, belatedly, not lingering as she rustled to her feet to bob a curtsy. The footmen carefully closed the door behind themselves and the archduke, leaving her alone with Vladimer.

"Ferdenzil Mycene should *not* be hunting Ishmael," Telmaine said, in a suffused voice.

Her sonn caught the movement of Vladimer's left hand toward his right arm. He let the hand fall. "Lady Telmaine," he said, bitingly, "some things are under my control and others are not, as you have heard. And we have worse problems, which you should also have heard." He lifted his head and snapped a burst of sonn at her. "Have you been able to warn him?"

Telmaine hesitated, caught between anger and inhibition.

"Talk to me, woman," Vladimer said. "We won't be interrupted."

"I can reach him, yes," Telmaine said, equally sharply. "But it's no use. The damage to his—to his magic is worse than he told us. If I try again, it might kill him."

Vladimer's jaw clenched. His fisted hand thumped the chair arm once, and braced itself there. Less harshly, for he was genuinely affected, she said, "He did seem to think he could stay ahead of pursuit."

Vladimer nodded, stiff necked. "It seems so. I've had word your husband arrived at Strumheller Station alone. The archduke's agent thinks Ishmael is making his way cross-country for Stranhorne. I think it's likely: next to Strumheller, Stranhorne would bear the brunt of any invasion. And Stranhorne and his family are no friends to Mycene."

"And what about Balthasar?"

Vladimer rubbed his temple. "Ah, finally some wifely concern."

"Stop needling me," she snapped. "I promised Ishmael and Balthasar I would protect you, *despite* you, if need be."

Vladimer smiled thinly. "I cannot tell you how much it reassures me not to have you cozen me."

"You mean if I were bent on harm, I'd speak sweetly to you?"

"*She* did," he said, his voice going hollow.

Hearing that change, she wished intensely that Bal were there. All those years she had spent striving *not* to know the inner thoughts of others, he had spent in avid study of the mind.

She thought what Bal might say. "Lord Vladimer, *that* wasn't a woman. That was an enemy out to destroy you and taking pleasure in causing you all the pain and humiliation it could."

His sonn raked her. "How did you know that?" he said, harshly.

"Balthasar," she said, her heart jumping. "Bal guessed."

He swallowed, and for a moment she thought he would be sick. "Can these—creatures—touch-read?" he said, thickly.

"It and I—communicated—as mages do," she said. "But—whether they could touch-read an—a normal person—I don't know."

"You and it *communicated*?"

"Vladimer, stop—*lashing* at me. It was a horrible experience. It told me—called me Magistra; and then said I wasn't a mage, but an ill-taught apprentice, and it—it—"

The sense came back to her, of the foul, chill aura of the Shadowborn, of its power welling up around her and its voice insinuating itself into her thoughts. *Let me show you*, it had said, and then it had begun to press into her mind the structure of its own magic, like a seed meant to grow monstrous and consuming.

"It, *what*?" snapped Vladimer. "Please restrain your hysteria, Lady Telmaine. It merely tries my patience."

She drew a shuddering breath, stinging at the rebuke. She would be light-struck to confide in him. "When Ishmael shot it, I *felt* it die. I felt as though I were dying, too."

"That is an experience," he said, "I do not envy you."

Sweet Imogene, but she missed Bal. She missed Ishmael. She missed men who did not treat a woman's feelings as weapons slung at them. "Have you ever *loved* a woman, Vladimer?" she demanded, intemperately.

There was a long silence. She resisted sonning him, to reveal the expression on his face. Indeed, she was rather appalled at her own temerity.

She was about to apologize for the question when Vladimer said, "Do you think, Lady Telmaine, you can learn how to quench these fires?" He paused, and, receiving no answer, said, "Because so far they have deployed two weapons against us, and the latter is by far the more devastating."

"I don't know," she said. "I know—I can turn back the fire against one, but I took him by surprise."

"Yes," Vladimer said. "I have set my agents to follow up on the descriptions that you and others have given. I wish I'd been able to do so sooner. At what range can you sense Shadowborn? Ishmael's sense was so limited that he found it more distraction than advantage, but yours seems broader."

"I'm not—certain. But I do not have to be in the same room. The Shadowborn in the summerhouse, I sensed as soon as we entered. But, Lord Vladimer, it may be only the workings of their magic I sense. I only felt the one at the train station as he started the fire."

"You were distracted," he granted. "But despite my inconvenient weakness when we arrived, I have not been idle. I doubt anyone will be able to circumvent my precautions for the safety of my brother's household *without* using magic."

She had only a vague sense of what those precautions might entail, yet Ishmael had been convinced of Vladimer's effectiveness. She must take comfort in that. "Lord Vladimer, would you extend your precautions to Lord Erskane's household, and my children?"

His lips compressed briefly, and then he said, "Inasmuch as I can do so without provoking inconvenient questions, consider it done."

"Thank you," she said softly.

Mere chance allowed her to catch his brief, bitter smile. She wondered at the thought that had provoked it, but dared not ask.

"I know you cannot stay on guard night and day," he allowed, "though there are drugs that enable a man to stay alert for stretches of several nights." He did not, as Balthasar would, qualify that statement with the full risks to constitution and reason—did he even consider them, even for himself? She rejected his veiled suggestion with a firm headshake, a contradiction that could go safely unobserved. He caught the whisper of her veils against her shoulders and tilted his head inquiringly, awaiting her voiced objection.

"I would prefer you to remain alert until sunset," he said when she offered none. "It may be pure atavism for me to think the threat is greater during the day, but our vulnerability certainly is."

She could not plead desperate tiredness to a man who had dragged himself from his sickbed. "Yes," she said, in a low voice. "I can do that."

"You may sit in the botanical library. I will ensure you are not disturbed. My rooms are behind it, and Sejanus will be using the legal library next door; he will probably allow himself four hours of sleep, if that." He cast light sonn over her. "I will advise my staff that you have the right to wake me in an emergency. If there is no time, go straight to Sejanus. Those are my orders."

Floria

Floria paused before the prince's antechamber, bracing herself for what she would find inside. By the sound of it, the antechamber was full, humming like a hive of crimson bees, an impression confirmed as soon as she opened the door. Their brightnesses, who had gathered to celebrate the heir's coming of age, now crowded the antechamber to petition for a private audience with the new prince.

There were no chairs, because no one would use them. To show infirmity was to invite righteous deposition; to invite another to show it, an act of contempt. Floria set her back against a wall, and exchanged nods with the other vigilants present, standing as she stood, observing the gathering of their brightnesses.

Wondering, as she wondered, which one had slain their prince.

The subtle unease of the minority who wore less than full mourning pleased her, but did not signify. Every brilliant claimed the right to depose a head of lineage who was so senile, corrupt, or incompetent as to risk collective interests. Equally, they defended that right against any who abused it. Only in melodramas did unrighteous usurpers and assassins betray themselves by penitence or trickery and declaim guilt in iambic pentameter.

Prince Isidore's father, whom her father had served so long, had been a man of great charisma and recklessness. Any other prince would have been righteously deposed over the decision to bind his ten-year-old son to the sixteen-year-old daughter of a southern barbarian. Prince Benedict had wooed their brightnesses with promises of profit and stability through expansion, and though that program was extremely successful, he had sacrificed his son's domestic peace, and the later tolerance of his first signs of mental frailty.

He had also sacrificed the regard of the Darkborn, who had no such expedient reason to forget the genocidal reign of the consort's grandfather. Since the Darkborn nobility measured blood as carefully as the mages did in their lineages, they would not mark the new prince's lineage in his favor.

And fully a quarter of the people in this chamber showed some signs of southern origin or aesthetic. For all their barbarity, southerners were austere in their attire. Their decorations depended more on texture than color, almost as the Darkborn's did. Floria approved the simplicity and functionality; had the choice been neutral, she might have favored the style herself.

The consort's surviving brother and two sisters had deployed themselves on either side of the door of greater privilege, though four impassive vigilants stood between themselves and full possession. Orlanjis stood with them, despite being underage for this gathering. He wore a red vest and sash, and his hair was coiled into a red mesh net at the nape of his neck, a judicious choice. The skin beneath his eyes looked bruised with sleeplessness, and he could not keep his gaze from the lights. Isidore considered Orlanjis the most imaginative of his children, and Fejelis the least, for all the heir's other virtues—but imagination too easily became a liability.

To Floria's surprise, her wait was over almost before it had begun. The new prince's secretary emerged from the door of lesser privilege and crossed with hushed step to invite her to be received. He was another southerner, but one who had found his natural home and loyalties here; he wore full mourning, and his face was haggard with grief.

As they approached the lesser door, the door of greater privilege suddenly burst wide, to expel Helenja herself, a heavy woman dressed in the textured earth color of southern habit, and four of her vigilants. That the dowager consort made the barest concession to mourning, in the form of the crimson ribbons decorating arms and waist, did not surprise Floria in the least. Helenja would not offend her supporters by mourning her husband openly, whatever her private feelings.

Though her slab of a face was crimson enough. "You're making a mistake!" she hurled back over her shoulder—the gesture was rendered faintly absurd by being thrown into the face of the vigilant trailing her. Seeing Floria, she glared. "If anything happens to my son—"

Floria dipped a bow, inferring what had happened: Fejelis had turned the dowager consort out of his private councils. "Your son, Highness? I rather think that is a prince in there."

Whether true, or wisely said, it was satisfying to see the woman vexed. If Helenja had had any part in Isidore's death, Floria would claim the right to see to her righteous—and to Floria's mind overdue—deposition.

She slipped through the door of lesser privilege as Helenja demanded of Orlanjis, "What are *you* doing here?" Oh, she was ruffled, to publicly rebuke her favorite so.

Then Floria halted, guard up. Fejelis was alone in the room. That, she had not expected. She stepped aside from the door, setting a wall that she knew to be solid at her back. Was that it—the dowager consort's words, his being here, alone—part of a plan? She was to make a move, and then to be brought down, by a dagger or a dart, attempting revenge. She need not even make the move. His word would stand against her silent corpse.

"It will work but once," Floria said, calmly. "You might not want to waste it on me."

The young prince regarded her steadily, showing neither comprehension nor confusion. His face was composed but pale, made even more so by its contrast with his full crimson mourning. He had a northern complexion, which she had always thought fortunate, and his eyes were his father's, silvery and as unrevealing of his thought as mirrors. His head was bare of the princely caul, his light hair slightly disarrayed. He had a southerner's height, though had yet to fill out his spidery frame, and his habitual hesitation of speech and manner left one constantly expecting a stumble, and not noticing when it did not happen. How many people knew how he had worked at training hesitation out of himself in the *salle*?

Time, she thought, might yet lend him distinction, if he lived. He was already a sound blade, with a deadly advantage in reach, and around his neck he wore the talisman that turned aside bullets. What remained to be seen was whether he could command loyalty where it mattered. What remained to be seen was who his real allies were.

He said, mindful of the ears outside, ". . . The first thing I want to say to you is my father's death was not my doing."

More direct than she expected. An experienced courtier, she responded in kind. "Was it your mother's?"

". . . I do not know. She says not. You are," he reminded her, "my servant." The statement was not entirely free of question.

"I am a member of the Prince's Vigilance," she said. "With all that implies."

". . . How long do I have to prove myself?" To whom, he did not specify.

"As the inheritor of an unrighteous deposition," she said quietly, "you have very little time."

His eyes closed briefly, although she could have told him no more than he knew. ". . . I did not kill Isidore. I did not conspire for his death. I'm not ready, and I know that." He did not protest that he would *never* have conspired to kill his father, or wished him dead, though Orlanjis, in such a position, would have protested—and believed it of himself. Fejelis said, ". . . Will you give me a chance to convince you that I am not stupid enough to do this?"

". . . I am your brilliance's servant," she said. *For now* remained implied.

"Of all vigilants, he kept you closest."

"That," Floria pointed out, "was because of your mother's exercises in poison."

To give him credit, he did not flinch or evade the implication. ". . . If this is Helenja's or the southerners' doing, why should they not wait until Orlanjis came of age?"

She fed it to him, hard. "Because you will take all the blame and anger for Isidore's death to your own darkening, clearing the way for your brother."

His self-control was not quite equal to hearing so stark an assessment. But, impressively, the wavering was only momentary. ". . . Until and unless I am deemed deserving of righteous deposition, will you continue to serve me as you did my father?"

"On one condition," she said. "Please, go sparingly on the spices."

He smiled. "That will be a pleasure. I've lost count of the number of times I left my parents' table with my stomach burning. Now"—the smile fell away—"tell me what you know about my father's death." ·

"The prince—" He did not react to that petty impropriety. "Your father," she allowed, "retired to his rooms last night as usual. The magical checks were carried out on the wards, and the usual inspections. We left him wine, water, and food that I had tested myself.

"And we all missed something," she said, though she doubted he would have insisted on the admission. "As far as we can tell, sometime shortly after your father retired, the light in his chambers failed."

He glanced at the blazing lights arrayed across the white and silver ceiling. "... How could that happen?" he said, his voice hushed.

"Here are my thoughts so far," she said. "The lights are enspelled to absorb daylight during the day and release it through the night. The light normally lasts two, three days without being recharged. A light that is nearly discharged changes color, conspicuously. Anyone in the room would have noticed.

"Next, the magic. Magic dispels when the mage dies. For that reason, quality lights are enspelled by at least two mages. The prince's were enspelled by no less than four. In the rare event that the enspelling itself is flawed, the light fails within minutes of its first use.

"So the magic did not naturally dispel, and did not fail; therefore, it was annulled. The manner of the prince's death prompted immediate inquiry into any unusual magic exercised in or around the palace. The mages have admitted no such activity.

"There are assets against certain kinds of magic, although the pricing is prohibitive. For an individual with an asset to use that asset, he or she would have to be in the room, and would die with his victims. Not necessarily a deterrent to some, but there was no evidence that anyone else was in the room, except for your father, the captain of vigilants, and two of the staff. And the Temple has a record of all living assets.

"A talisman, though, could have been created years or

decades ago. Lights are talismans themselves. One need only be given to an individual—mage or nonmage—with access to the prince's quarters. And its action could be delayed.

"The weakness in all those theories is that the members of the Temple Vigilance contracted to the palace should have sensed that magic."

". . . And what about the Darkborn?" he said.

"Darkborn law and policy does not countenance assassination," she said. "Or they'd have dealt with your great-grandfather, or with your mother before she even bore you." Privately she doubted that chance alone had led Odon the Breaker to his end in the claws of a Shadowborn that normally hunted at night, while he was chasing refugees into the Borders. The baronies made their own laws. "And the only way for a Darkborn to have reached your father's rooms would have been from the outside, at night."

She weighed telling Fejelis the strange tale of Tercelle Amberley. She still thought it more likely the children had been born of an ordinary dalliance of the kind that so offended Darkborn morality, yet on its account, Balthasar Hearne had been nearly battered to death and his daughter kidnapped from his doorstep.

". . . And the mages amongst the Darkborn?"

"Perhaps fifty able to dispel midrank magic, but again, the Temple Vigilance would know."

". . . So, once again, it comes back to the Temple Vigilance. Whom can we trust?"

She smiled, very thinly. "Your father once said that trust was irrelevant now."

She watched him for his reaction. Isidore had been careful to maintain equal distance from all his children, marking none out for favor—a care that had become even more scrupulous after Fejelis had nearly died. But it was obvious that he and his father had grown closer, and last night's conversation—*last night's only*—suggested that Isidore considered Fejelis a political player with his own mature agenda, and an ally.

"Why should they cause trouble?" Floria concluded. "They have everything they want."

"... Is there any one of them we can trust?"

For the first time she paused, to weigh her reply. "I believe we could trust Magister Tammorn."

"... I've heard that name," said the prince, after a longer pause than usual. "He is not contracted to the palace."

Could he remember? She had taken a risk—for all three of them—in putting that name before Fejelis. But surely after ten years ...

"Your father may have mentioned him, or you heard some gossip," she spoke lightly of that. "He hasn't been around the palace much. Tammorn is not of the lineages; he was born up in the northwest. His magic came in late and unrecognized, and brought him all kinds of trouble. He was a petty criminal when he crossed paths with my father, who used to advise for the city watch. My father recognized him for what he was, had a word with the prince, and brought Tam to the Temple's attention."

Without Isidore's patronage, the high masters might have elected then to burn out Tam's magic, for all his past offenses—including his great impertinence of being born with power outside their carefully tended lineages. "Tam will be one mage who'll be wearing full mourning, and meaning it."

Fejelis blinked, but otherwise betrayed nothing. "... His rank?"

Might Fejelis actually *remember*? A nine-year-old child, fatally poisoned, muscles spasming uncontrollably, face mottled slate gray with asphyxia. Chance—in the form of a desultory flirtation—had put Floria in the orchard with Tam at her side when they heard the sounds of what they thought at first was a small animal in distress. Tam had acted before either of them thought of the compact and the law, and the contracted mages who should, rightfully, be summoned. Even the saving of a child's life was a grave violation of the compact.

"Fifth, by Temple reckoning. Were he not a sport, it might be higher." Even after five years with his magic bound, the Temple had not forgiven Tam.

"Ask him," the prince said, without hesitation—the effect almost one of blurted words. "... Have him come to the *salle*, at the end of my regular practice time."

"And may I tell him why?"

Fejelis nodded slowly, light sliding on his hair. ". . . Yes," he said, at last. "Tell him why."

Floria

Unlike most high-ranked mages, who lived in the Temple or in its immediate vicinity, Tammorn lived in Minhorne New Town, across the river from palace, Temple, and indeed any destination of any account. Which meant that the brisk mage wind that cleared the lingering smell of the burned Rivermarch bore it toward the New Town. All the way across the bridge, the smell of ash followed her.

Yet almost as soon as she reached the far bank, the breeze abruptly changed direction, and leaves, litter, and scorched scraps whirled suddenly skyward. The wind tugged her tunic, lifted her hair. Ten yards on, the air was sweet, still, and flowing lightly from the north, as the clouds indicated. Somebody with power enough to deflect winds cared about the place. She thought she knew who.

The New Town was home to artisans, merchants, and craftsmen who had failed, through lack of luck, industry, or skill, to establish themselves in the city proper. It was also the gathering place of an unruly collection of self-styled revolutionaries and idealists who preached liberation from dependence on magic, and enthusiastically adopted Dark-born inventions. An unlikely place to find a high-ranked mage—but then, Tam was an unusual mage.

He was sitting on a bench in his front garden, gently jiggling the infant draped over his thigh and gumming on a double fistful of his scarlet trousers. That particular red was one of the new chemical dyes, a by-product, ironically, of the blind Darkborn's experiments with tar. Its touch made Floria's asset-imbued skin itch. She had been meaning to take the matter up with Balthasar when his next term on the Intercalatory Council came around: there were poisons enough in the world without creating more.

"Tam, you can wear that color; just don't let her chew on it." Tam's expression took on a momentary expression of focus as he used his magical senses, and then he nodded and righted the baby, setting her so that she straddled his knee. Thwarted, she promptly turned puce—she had her father's complexion—glared at Floria with tearing eyes, and began to screech.

Tam glanced toward the door of the house behind them. A tall, fair-haired woman in a potter's smock emerged and came to retrieve her daughter with a wary glance at Floria and a reproachful frown at Tam. She was Beatrice, Tam's lover of some six years. She was not mageborn, but an artisan, and to the Temple she would never be other than a concubine, for all the Temple had also shown little interest in Tam as a contributor to their own precious bloodlines. Tam's eyes followed her warmly as she carried the child into the house, arriving at the door just in time to thwart the escape of their venturesome three-year-old son.

Tam looked weary. Mourning red drained his pink and freckled complexion and clashed with his ginger hair and brows. He looked to be in his mid-twenties, although she knew him to be at least a decade older than herself. To a high-rank mage, accomplished in healing, arrest of aging was almost trivial. The archmage was more than three hundred years old.

"Can you ensure we're not overheard?" she said.

He sketched a tiny circle in the air. "Done."

"Magister Tammorn," she said formally, "the prince wishes to discuss a contract with you."

Tam blinked. "Fejelis?" he said, surprising her by his ready use of the first name. "Did he say what?"

Could there be any question? "To find those responsible for his father's death."

His eyes narrowed. "Why?"

"I recommended you as one likely to do a thorough job of it."

"Floria—" He stopped, and gestured. "Sit down." She did, tilting her rapier, and observing him closely. It was obvious he was disconcerted. The question was, why?

"There are mages contracted to the palace, mages whose contract Fejelis now holds."

"Yes," she said, "there are. But the way the prince died—I cannot see how magic could not have been involved. The prince—Prince Fejelis—asks that you visit him in the *salle*, at his usual practice time, which is four of the clock."

"Has he anyone else?" he said.

"No. I suggested you; he accepted it."

Tam stared away into the distance. She did not even think he saw the Mages' Tower, which even from here loomed immense on the skyline. "What do *you* know about the prince's death, Floria?"

There was a stress on the pronoun that he surely did not intend to betray. Despite her certainty of her own blamelessness, despite the sunlight, she felt uneasy. Mages—unsettled—even a mage she had known since her father brought home the ginger-haired vagrant who spoke in monosyllables and refused to meet anyone's eyes. What did he know that she did not?

She recited the same analysis she had given the prince.

"You are so certain," he said, "that it could not have been done other than by magic."

"The lights were discharged, dark, not removed, not covered, not smashed—even then the fragments would have continued to glow. Besides the prince, there were three people in the room, one a captain of the Prince's Vigilance. Their—residues—were all exactly as I would expect them to be: prince and secretary by the desk, Captain Parhelion by the door, and the prince's manservant readying the bedchamber. All the lights, in all the rooms—and there were seventeen of them—were affected at once, with no warning, no signs of a struggle or an attempt to flee."

He was watching her with a disturbing intensity. "Are you certain that the three other men in the room with the prince were who you thought they were? Quenching leaves very little—just fragments of clothing and personal ornaments. You assume that the clothing was being worn by the people you expected to wear it."

"If there had been anything anomalous, Captain Parhelion would have raised the alarm. If he had not been in his appointed place, the prince or the prince's secretary would have questioned it. Tam, it was our routine."

The corner of his mouth twitched. "You think Helenja was involved?"

"Had it happened the morning of Orlanjis's coming of age, there'd be no doubt. But to depose the prince now and elevate Fejelis—"

"You think Fejelis is unacceptable?" Tam said, in a neutral voice.

Less so than she had thought, she privately admitted, but it did not change the realities. "I give him six months, less if there's a crisis. That's for your ears only, Tam."

The mage's expression was in-turned. "What has been done with the prince's rooms?"

"The residues have been removed, and the rooms were searched by members of the Prince's Vigilance and the Palace Vigilance."

"And yet you want me?"

"We missed this, vigilants and mages both."

"Yes," he said slowly. "You did." He stood. "I want to see his rooms."

"The contract has not been signed."

"Members of the Temple might be involved; I want to see the rooms."

"Magister—"

"Mistress Floria, even *you* could be involved, being in the palace on the night."

She let out her breath. "The prince wanted your involvement kept covert until the contract was declared."

"It will be. But before I declare any contract, before I agree to do this, I want to see the rooms and speak to the prince."

Tammorn

High in the Mages' Tower, Tam leaned against the wall to catch his breath, feeling magic pushing at him like a blustering wind before a squall. <It's me,> he sent, needlessly, for the mage he had come to see already knew it. The courtesy was just another example—like his climbing the stairs rather than using power to glide up them—of the earthborn habits that caused the Temple to regard him with suspicion.

On the other hand, Magister Lukfer was entirely capable of dropping an importunate visitor down the shaft, intentionally or unintentionally. He had done that to Tam at the beginning of their relationship. Although that, Tam had concluded, was meant as the old bear meant when it greeted the cub with a cuff to test its spirit before taking it in its jaws to confirm its proper bearish taste. It was an initiation.

Even so, he braced himself before nudging open the broad, bronze door with a magical touch. Lukfer kept his rooms nearly as dim as a bear's lair, disquieting to all, and painful to many, including Tam. His eyes fixed at once on the windows on the far side of the room, curtained though they were with a half-opaque fabric. Sweating, he crossed the length of the room to clutch and push back the curtains, drinking in sunlight. Only then could he acknowledge the man sitting in shadows.

Like Tam, Lukfer was a sport, born in a small desert village amongst people even more desperately poor and ignorant than Tam's own mountain clan. Unlike Tam, whose powers had been bewilderingly slow to emerge, Lukfer had had touch-sense almost from birth. The unrelenting intrusion of the anger, fears, and suspicions of those around him had driven him mad before his fourth birthday. The Temple's care had restored his sanity, but neither their efforts nor his had enabled him to control his power. By now, he should have been one of the high masters, occupying these rooms by right. Instead, he was the high masters' ward, kept close so they could contain him, if need be. His living in shadows, disturbing as it was, bled off his power in constant healing effort.

Meeting Lukfer, knowing how much worse his own fortunes might have been, had been a salutary experience for the surly lout whom Darien White Hand had brought before the high masters. In the bright-lit amphitheater at the apex of the tower, Tam had stood scowling in disapproval at the opulence around him, studiously ignoring the discussion of his fate. He remembered the check in the deliberations, and the shocking sense of his bitterness and resentment, washing back against him as though from an emotional mirror. He whirled round to stare at the man who had floated above the stairs' wide shaft: a hulk of a man, bald and dressed horrifyingly in black.

"So this is the new sport," the man had said. His voice had startled Tam with its quality, a velvety rasp like a wolf skin taken in winter. "Sixth rank, maybe seventh, by the feel of him. Take good care of him, or you'll have another like me." To Tam, he said, "I'm Lukfer. You'll hear about me; what's not tripe is true. When you've some control, come and see me."

And he had, despite what he had heard, and found a perilous teacher and a true friend.

"I need your help," he said now.

Lukfer had been staring at him from the moment he entered. Eye and pointing finger converged unerringly on Tam's pocket. *"What is that?"*

He should not have been in the least surprised, though he had tried to shield the thing before carrying it into the tower. He drew out a small pouch and, handling it with his fingertips, set it down unopened on the wide arm of Lukfer's chair.

"*This*—inside—was in the prince's chambers." He faltered, wanting to warn the other man, who suffered so from his sensitivity.

Lukfer's eyes narrowed; magic pulsed; the pouch twitched and spit out its contents. The item skidded across the arm, stopped just before the edge.

It was a tiny, octagonal box, less than a palm span in diameter, such as the Darkborn used for blocks of scent. It was exquisitely carved in scrolls and sprigs of tiny flowers, but from unevenly hued wood and stained ivory. The craftsman capable of such carving should have rejected such unsightly variations. Had he been able to see them. It still smelled of sandalwood, but the magical aura of it was like a charnel stench. Lukfer's massive body shuddered, his nausea threatening to overset Tam's control. Reciprocity would have them vomiting their hearts out. "Sorry—" Tam snatched the pouch and brought it down over the box, as he would net a poison beetle. Lukfer's black-gloved hand closed on his wrist. "Leave it."

Tam gulped and, as Lukfer released him, backed away. From the door—as though that made any real difference—he watched Lukfer carefully remove his gloves to touch it with his bare hands. Tam swallowed harder.

Lukfer laid it down. "Now you can cover it."

Bare hands gripping the arms of his chair, Lukfer watched Tam net the vile little thing with the bag and jerk the laces violently closed.

"Have a seat," Lukfer said.

Tam toppled into a chair, sapped of strength by renewed exposure to the sense of *darkness*.

"I have been offered a c-contract, by the prince, to investigate his father's death," he said. "M-Mistress White Hand brought me the message. The contract hasn't been negotiated or formalized yet—I haven't spoken to Fejelis—the prince; I don't think anyone knows. I went by Isidore's rooms first, wanting—wanting to see them as soon as possible. And I found *that*. There were other mages there, but—but they didn't even seem to sense it. I didn't know whether they were pretending or—but when I palmed it"—a skill he had mastered in his first months in the city—"nobody acted as though they noticed."

Lukfer let out a breath. "Keep it that way. Now, open the curtains, would you."

The curtain was stiff with disuse; it took a magical push to send it lurching back. A broad stroke of golden sunlight fell across the bloated figure in his chair. Beneath his olive complexion, Lukfer was ashen. Tam half rose. "Master, what is it? Are you all right?"

Lukfer waved his concern away.

Tam sat down, watching him worriedly. "That's a talisman of some kind, isn't it? Is it possible that that—is what nullified the magic in the lights?"

"You tell me." That sounded more like his teacher.

In sudden horror, he snatched up the pouch and started out of his chair. Lukfer's magic snagged him, making him stumble. "Boy," Lukfer said, brusquely, "I thought of that; that's why I had you open the curtains. There's no magic so powerful as can quench the sun. Put it down."

He did, hands shaking. "Master Lukfer, do you know *whose* magic this is?"

Lukfer watched him with an unreadable expression, eyes honey yellow in the sunlight. "If you mean to do more than pay lip service to that title, then decline that contract, and forget this ever happened. Will you do that, for both our sakes?"

"I—can't," he said.

"I tell you, as your master, that this concerns mysteries of the Temple that have nothing to do with a mage like yourself."

"I've sensed this before. I don't know what it is, but I've sensed this before."

"Tam, as you love your life, let the matter be."

"The f-first time I sensed it," Tam pressed on, "was when the Rivermarch—that Darkborn district—burned. I was one of those called to put out the blaze, lest it spread. I felt it then. I didn't realize that no one else had, not then. The second time was—a day or so ago, just after sunset, from the Darkborn district, the covered railway station. The third was with this box, here."

"That, that was not the third," Lukfer said.

"Not?" Tam faltered.

"There was at least one other."

He had thought, when he finally heard the gossip about Lukfer, that Lukfer had said, "When you have control—" for Lukfer's comfort. Only later did he realize Lukfer meant it for Tam's safety, too. Though after the first few meetings, after he had met and passed Lukfer's tests, and Lukfer had begun to relax with him, he had lost his fear of the older mage, and then he began to love him. But fearing or loving, he had never been able to lie to Lukfer.

"It was on Floria White Hand, too," he sighed.

"Ah," Lukfer said quietly, unsurprised. There was a long, long pause. "Have you ever visited the Borders?"

"The *Borders*?" he said, bewildered at the irrelevance. The Borders had been left to the Darkborn so long ago that hardly a trace of Lightborn remained, all their works swallowed by the land or dismantled by the Darkborn for the building of byres and field walls that had in their own turn gone to ruin. The only Lightborn who lived in the Borders were those who had gone to work for the Dark-born railroads and agreed to tend the track through the Borders—antisocial, miscreant, eccentric, fugitive, or simply desperate for work.

"Some years ago, I had reason to," Lukfer said.

Tam remembered Lukfer's absence, unique for him, but at the time Tam himself had been under punishment, exiled from the Temple, with his magic bound. Lukfer never had said why he went to the Borders; he did not say now. "Do you have any notion as to why Lightborn by and large do not live there?"

"I—when I thought about it at all, I assumed it had to do with safety from the Shadowborn. But what has that to do with—?" He gestured toward the talisman.

"Yet the Darkborn stayed, handicapped as they are by their blindness and lack of magic, to hunt these creatures and drive them back across the Borders. . . . I've exchanged a few letters with one of their Shadowhunters, a weak mage himself. You have heard of glazen, creatures that ensorcell men and then slowly devour them alive."

Tam had heard the stories told by children to their credulous peers. Wise in the ways of bullies, he had accepted none of them. He said so.

"Monsters out of fantasies, maybe," Lukfer said. "But that"—a gesture toward the pouch—"is no fantasy. The mage I corresponded with recognized my description of what I sensed."

It took Tam a moment to understand. "You think that is *Shadowborn* magic."

"I know it is; I have sensed it before."

"Then *that* is why we left. That sense." *That* Tam could believe.

Lukfer interlaced his fingers, staring steadily over them at something Tam could not see. "You said none of the mages in the palace behaved as though they sensed the box. It is my belief that *no* mage bred in the Temple lineages could have sensed this box."

Tam stared at him in disbelief.

"Have you seen anything around you to suggest they might have?"

"Wouldn't the masters of lineage realize that? Surely they would breed it back in?"

The golden eyes shifted to him. "I do not doubt they tried. They may have failed. Or they may have succeeded, but not cared for the results. Perhaps with the ability to sense comes a diminution of power—sports as strong as ourselves are rare. Even for the masters of lineage, breeding strength is not that precise an art." He shifted his shoulders beneath black-trimmed carmine. "Whatever the reason, lineage mages cannot sense—or manipulate—a form of magic that is potentially deadly."

"Mother of All Things," Tam breathed. It seemed completely implausible, and yet it explained why this small, deathly object should have passed unnoticed. "Master, the archmage and the others—do they know that this magic is in the city itself?"

"No," said Lukfer, mouth setting hard. "And you will not tell them."

"But—"

"The Temple looks after its own interests, boy," Lukfer rasped. "We've made vast fortunes from our magic, and the magic as much as the compact protects us against retribution from our greed. But what would happen if the earthborn knew that there was a form of magic that Temple mages could not sense and counter, and was powerful enough to quench enspelled lights and kill a prince? They are already restless beneath the inequity; *you* know that better than any. This could mean the magic and mind of any mage who knows it, and the life of any earthborn—*do you understand*?"

Lukfer's magic suddenly surged against him from all directions, a fierce pressure mounting to pain. Tam held it off, gasping with the effort, and sagging as it withdrew as abruptly as it had come.

"Sorry, lad," Lukfer said. "But if anyone should tell them, it will be myself, alone."

Tam started to remonstrate; Lukfer slammed his hand down on the arm of his chair. Around the room, ornaments burst into fine shards of glass and then spun themselves together again. Lukfer's voice rasped, "You have no sense of *history*. Amongst high-ranked mages, you are still a child in years, and you have no lineage and therefore none of the—received awareness that mages pass amongst themselves, parent and teacher to child and student."

"Indoctrination, you mean," Tam said, unfairly—he well knew what Lukfer meant, the magical transfer of knowledge from mage to mage, master to student. No one was likely to give *him* such a gift, and Lukfer's magic was too uncontrolled for him to bestow it. "They did their best with me."

Lukfer shook his heavy head in rebuke. "The archmage is three hundred and forty years old. He was raised within the Temple by members of the first generation to emerge with real power, who were bred and trained in utter secrecy, in fear of what the earthborn would do when they learned the Temple was trying to rebuild magic. His attitude, and that of many of the high masters, is at its root shaped by the Temple's situation *five and six hundred years ago*, when the earthborn still had the ability to eradicate us. The high masters may have grown powerful enough to disdain earthborn, and would never admit to fearing them, but that first fear lives on in them, in that place that fears acquired in childhood do."

"This *magic* killed the prince."

"Not magic," Lukfer said, "the mind behind the magic."

It was a distinction frequently underscored by Temple mages, and Tam detested the hypocrisy of it. No high-ranked mage took a contract he did not agree with, not anymore. "We cannot let this go on—magic or mind—killing unchecked. If we cannot take it to the high masters, *we* have to find that magic and its users, and, if need be, destroy them. In other words, if we cannot go to the Temple Vigilance, *we* must be the Temple Vigilance."

Slowly, Lukfer nodded.

Fejelis

I have one friend at least, Fejelis thought as he returned his practice épée to the rack and crossed the *salle* to greet

Magister Tammorn. A servant approached with towel in hand and he waved her away, preferring to spare only just enough attention to track her whereabouts rather than weigh the possibility of subtler threats.

He studied the demeanor of the mage, instead. Disregard the wan cast that that scarlet shade lent him, and it was still a burdened man who stood there. Stricken with grief for the prince, or for another reason? "Magister Tammorn," he said formally. "Welcome."

"Your brightness," said the mage, with a small dip of the head. "What may I do for you?"

"...Come with me while I wash," Fejelis said. He turned and led the mage between the pistes, conscious of the tapping of the other's hard soles on the tiles. His own feet, in their soft soles, squeaked intermittently. Their mirrored images tracked them along all four walls of the room; at this time of day, only the skylight was clear to the sky. Two of the four walls were also windows, and reflected only when in shadow, as now, with the sun on the far side of the palace. Fejelis preferred his practice at this time of day: exertion in direct sunlight was tiring, and shade did keep down the audience.

Locked doors played their part, too, at least for ordinary courtiers, though no locked door could keep out a mage.

He waved the servants out of the dressing room, too. He wanted no witnesses to this conversation, and the servants seemed—they were—more nervous than usual. He was not greatly concerned: he could attribute that to his sudden elevation, the rumors around his guilt, or the company he kept.

He turned to Tam, emotion closing his throat at the sight of the mage's face. He had urged his trainers to drive him hard, so as to force everything else out of his mind but the moment. Now, however—unable to trust his voice, he put out his arm to be clasped in greeting. The mage used the grip to draw Fejelis against him in an importunate but welcome hug. "Jay," he said against the prince's ear. "Oh, *curse* it, Fejelis. I am so sorry."

Fejelis allowed himself to rest against Tam's peasant-bred strength, a strength that had nearly fifty years of living behind it, and not always easy living, either. Then he eased himself away. Above all, he must remain clearheaded and clear-eyed. Grief was for men secure in their position.

". . . I know, Tam," he said, huskily. "It's far too soon to lose him, and in such a terrible way. But we both knew the risks." His watchful eye caught Tam's distress, and he made note. What risks did Tam know about that he did not?

"What are you going to do?"

". . . Survive," Fejelis said, simply. "Father would be thoroughly disappointed in me if I did not." Then with irony, "I'm rather offended that anyone might think me fool enough as to have my father assassinated on the very night I came of age."

"Others have, or at least attempted it," Tam pointed out.

"Well, I'm not one of them. And if you yourself have any doubts, let us lay them to rest now." He offered his bare hand. If it trembled slightly, it was with muscle fatigue. He intended to sleep well tonight. Whether he might safeguard himself by taking up with one of his erstwhile dancing partners, or merely add to his danger, he had yet to decide.

Tam sketched a gesture deflecting the touch. "I trust you."

". . . Then you're probably unique," Fejelis said. ". . . Mistress White Hand told you I want you to investigate his death. Are you willing?"

To a man who had schooled himself to pay attention, Tam's open face could be as readable as a child's. ". . . You already know something, don't you?"

For a moment he thought the mage would object that there was no contract between them, no payment negotiated, no public declaration made. That would have been a lawful objection, and the puddle of muck that remained of his father attested well to the consequences of a broken law.

But this was Tam, the mage who had acted outside contract and compact to save a dying child. "I—can't tell you, yet. It's a Temple matter."

". . . Does that mean you are declining the contract through conflict of interest?"

"I am not declining the contract," Tam said, flushing,

though the question was entirely proper at such a juncture. "This is something that . . ." He caught himself. "Who exactly killed your father, and who else was involved, is not something I can tell you at present, because I do not know."

Fejelis weighed the answer. ". . . If you cannot tell me who was responsible, perhaps you might be able to tell me who is not? It would help if I know whom I might trust."

". . . Yes," the mage said.

". . . Shall we discuss terms of payment, then?"

With an air of challenge, Tam named a sum that matched a skilled artisan's wages.

Fejelis laughed, the first laugh he had enjoyed since he had learned of his father's death. "You mean that, don't you? How do you ever plan to become obscenely rich, as befits your rank?"

The mage's revealing face showed not irritation but frank anger. "You know why," he said, grimly.

Fejelis already regretted his reaction. Indeed he knew why. Tam had lived the consequences of the beggaring of the provinces, the poverty that broke spirits and bodies, the desperate ignorance. ". . . I do," he said, soberly, "and I respect you for it. I am sorry to deny you the chance to express your principles, but I cannot have this contract seen as a mockery of my father's death."

"Then offer what you think fit. I do not care," the mage said. He ran a hand over his face. "I would do this unpaid if I could, for your father, and you."

". . . And wouldn't that be a scandal." Fejelis turned to ply the lock of his cabinet. From within the cabinet, he took two bottles, examined the seals of both with care—intact— and offered one to the mage. Then he pressed the lever to reset the lock, and closed the door. Leaning against the cabinet, he took a long swig of water.

". . . There's an estate on the outskirts," he said. "Nine acres and a manor house. I've been trying to think how to get it to you for some time. With some work it would be suitable for the hostel you've spoken about." The mage had been contributing to the city's charities for destitute immigrants since he had a coin to spare. ". . . Or you could turn it into a workshop for our friends the artisans. You'll have to figure out the Temple tithe yourself. . . . Be warned; Mother had some notions as to what I might do with it. Did she have a part in Father's death?" he asked, launching the question without a beat's hesitation.

"I . . . can't say," the mage said, the momentary pleasure at Fejelis's offer leaving his face.

". . . You do have the information? Or hesitate to say? Please tell me that, at least."

The mage met his eyes directly. "I do not have the information."

That would have to do. ". . . Are you starting to regret taking the contract?" he asked.

"I do regret it," Tam said, low voiced. "I will regret it. But I would regret it far more if I did not—I know and sense and feel that."

Fejelis gave little weight to some mages' claims of prescience, but that statement lifted the hairs on the back of his neck.

He sighed. ". . . My mother took great pleasure in telling me that she had learned that Mistress White Hand had visited my father's rooms in the early hours of this morning." Watching, he saw the mage's perturbation. ". . . Can I trust her, Tam?"

Tam started to say something, and then stopped. "Jay," he said, "this is for friendship, not for contract. I—cannot exclude the possibility that Floria *was* involved. Knowing how she loved the prince, I can hardly believe it, but I cannot exclude it. The basis of my suspicions I—cannot tell you yet. I need to investigate further."

He looked more than tired now; he looked white, sickly almost. Fejelis set down his bottle—on the top of the cabinet, where he would not lose sight of it—stooped, and hefted the bench some six feet from its original position. The skylight was mirrored outside, the roof well patrolled during sunlight, but he did not, and would not, create opportunities. The servants would be able to describe the layout only as it had been. "Sit down," he said.

Tam sat; Fejelis sat beside him, stretching to ease a twinge in his back. He'd have to get lighter benches in here if he was to have these conversations often.

Neither of them spoke. He settled back on his hands, studying the deep blue sky. He remembered the sweetness of the poisoned peach as he lapped its juices from his hands, standing in the orchard beneath a late summer's sky, just like this one. He had been alone, and the solitude, like the peach, seemed a gift to nourish him. He felt himself expand to his full height in it, relieved of the constantly watching eyes, the constant waiting for him to declare himself one way or the other. He could feel the breeze cooling his scalp through his close-cropped hair, the haircut that had so appalled his mother and her entourage.

He had cut his hair for the most childish of reasons: he had been jealous of his brother, little flame-haired Orlanjis, the pampered darling of the southern faction. He had wanted attention. He had wanted to announce he was different.

In that, he thought, he had certainly succeeded. The delicious peach, the delicious solitude, had, of course, been engineered. The Vigilance drawn away, himself lured—by a girl three years older than he whom he worshipped—into the far orchard, to the peach trees, to the low-hanging peaches. She, three years older, six inches taller, could reach past those, quite naturally. They had plucked and devoured the fruit with muffled glee. Then she had blurted that her mother would be looking for her, and dashed away, leaving him licking the juice from his fingers, until the dizziness began, and the painful muscle spasms.

In a sense he had died that day. Whoever had been carried from the orchard, it had not been the child who wandered so blithely in.

". . . Does the Temple want me dead?" he said quietly to the mage beside him.

"No," said Tam. "Not to my knowledge."

Fejelis twisted to study the mage, weighing those words. ". . . I could almost wish they did," he said, half whimsically, half bitterly. ". . . Then I would know they thought we had a serious chance."

"I wish," the mage said, "I had half your courage."

The prince prodded him. "I'll hold you to artisans' wages on future contracts. We will shake the foundations of the Temple yet."

My courage, he thought, *is of your making, though you may not know it*. He remembered the moment when he had been able to breathe and hear again, the quietly spoken, "He'll be fine now." By the time he had opened his gummy eyes to stare at laden peach trees, and Floria White Hand's frightened face, the two of them were alone. But the voice had lingered, the voice of a god speaking benediction on him. *He'll be fine now*. The words carried the accent of the west foothills, but gods lived in places remote in place and time; the western mountains seemed as likely a place as any.

He held that promise close throughout the slow convalescence that followed—for Tam had not erased all the ill effects of the poison, merely the death in it—and the investigations that, largely unknown to him, led to arrests, executions, and banishments. He was made aware of those only once, when he woke to the sound of the girl's voice crying his name from the outer rooms—she had briefly escaped her captivity, come to beg him for her life. Her voice had filled his throat with sweet, poisoned juice. He rocked miserably on his pillows, hands over his ears, straining to hear the remembered voice of the god. *He'll be fine now*.

In time he had realized that his savior had to be a mage, not a god. But by then the promise had counteracted the last effect of the poison, the one on his spirit. He might be changed, but he was not broken.

He had been fifteen when he finally met the man. By then, he was a boy of guarded actions and many masks, who regularly shed the Vigilance—or so he thought—to wander the city in disguise, studying people unnoticed. In the persona of a rebellious young palace servant, he had fallen in with students from the artisan colleges. Observation guided him to the group at the periphery who spoke quietly amongst themselves of the arts of the people on the other side of sunrise, of firearms that could shoot hundreds of yards with precision, of trains that rode their tracks more swiftly than a horse could run, night and day. And of a magic that was not magic, called electricity, that could—it was in the equations—move impossible loads and heat wires until they glowed with brilliant light.

Much of what he learned, he took back to his father, at their private breakfasts. Isidore listened closely to Fejelis's accounts of Darkborn wonders and the concerns and complaints of people outside court. Isidore in turn spoke of his discussions with the Darkborn archduke, whom he found both shrewd and sympathetic, though Sejanus Plantageter's distaste for magic was profound and he was hampered by the prejudices of his dukes. Lightborn-Darkborn affairs were mediated by a low-level, relatively powerless shared council. And as Fejelis grew older, Isidore spoke often of the consequences of the compact and the stranglehold that the mages had on the princedom's wealth.

But as Fejelis listened to the young artisans argue about whether heated wires could glow as brightly as the sun, he knew his father would not find this interesting, but alarming. Light was the one form of magic that every Lightborn had no choice but to depend upon. And by their suddenly lowered voices, the artisans knew it, too.

Even as he tried to steady himself, he became aware that he himself was being watched. At a nearby table, a man caught his eye, and crooked a finger. Fejelis took in the red hair, the broad, freckled peasant face, the sharp gray green eyes, the dress of a journeyman artisan. Quite ordinary, but very much a stranger. And he might have been sitting on the other side of a mirrored window, for all the others seemed aware of him.

He knew then what the man was. He pushed his chair back and walked quietly around the table, his fellows' glances sliding off him. He sat down opposite the man; yes, even from here, he could hear every excited whisper.

There was nothing to indicate who held the mage's contracts, and therefore nothing to indicate whether Fejelis could lawfully order him away. Nevertheless, ". . . You ought to leave," he said. "You don't belong here."

The mage's eyes narrowed. "I would say the same of you," he said. "You're no servant's boy. Not watched as you are."

He twitched, but managed to resist looking around to find the guard he had missed. Even so, the man smiled. "Not today, I'm afraid I've made sure of that. . . . What do you think"—he tilted his head toward the artisans—"of their notions?"

He did not trust the lightness of that word, for one. ". . . I think," he said, measuring out his words, ". . . they are very clever, but innocent. They do not understand the implications."

"Not as well as you do, perhaps, but well enough to be dangerous."

". . . Magic is not involved here. Law says this has nothing to do with the Temple. . . . Let's walk out together. I can make it worth your while." He slid his hand across the table, opening his palm to show a single star sapphire on a fine chain. Only those of the reigning prince's blood were entitled to the stone.

There was no surprise recognition in the mage's face at the sight, only relief. With a gentle touch, he pressed Fejelis's hand closed. "I do believe you are right." His fingers flickered, and suddenly the students clustered around them. *"Tam."* One of the girls, landing a flirtatious kiss on his wavy hair. "We didn't see you. I see you've met our latest recruit—" She caught Fejelis's expression and looked uncertainly back at the mage.

Who said comfortingly, "Yes, we've met. He'll be fine now. But you do need to be more circumspect, my children, when you're plotting to turn the world upside down."

Fejelis's world turned upside down. *He'll be fine now.*

"You're smiling," Tam said now, at his side.

"I'm thinking about the day we met," Fejelis said, "when I tried to bribe you, and you rather more successfully turned me into a coconspirator. . . . If any good is going to come of this terrible thing, it will be that I can do what we've only just talked about until now. Having a workshop in the manor would let our friends build more and larger prototypes and generators. Now I can push to elevate the standing of the Intercalatory Council, get some higher-ranked earthborn on both sides involved. I also want the palace judiciary to explore the wording of the concord and all subsequent rulings to determine what is and is not allowed within the concord—we have to be protected against interference from the Temple."

"Jay, you have to take care," Tam breathed.

Isidore had said the very same to him, on occasion. But along with grief, he had a heady sense of possibility: he was prince, with all that entailed. He might die tomorrow, from southern ambition or northern schemes. What purpose holding back, then?

". . . The best help you can give me is to find out how my father died." He would push no further, at this moment. Even friends could turn.

He thought about Floria White Hand. Tam had said that she loved the prince, and he trusted Tam's judgment, though no doubt the vigilant daughter of vigilants would scorn such sentimental terms. Isidore had trusted her with his life against repeated poisoning attempts—nine that Fejelis knew of, and more in the years of his infancy. In the palace, Fejelis himself had obeyed Isidore's wish that he eat only dishes that Floria had tasted first. He said, slowly, ". . . I think I must have the Vigilance hold Mistress White Hand."

The mage flinched. Fejelis continued. ". . . What Mother said, I might discount as malice." Though his mother's survival instincts, he knew, were superb. "But along with what you said . . . if *I* cannot rely on Floria's loyalty, I cannot rely on her asset. And she is herself an expert with poisons."

The sudden taste of ripe peach in the back of his mouth made him want to gag. Hearing the stifled sound, and perhaps mistaking it for a sob, Tam reached over to squeeze his arm briefly. "It's a good decision," he said. "If she's been somehow ensorcelled, you dare not trust her."

Fejelis did not acknowledge either the moment of weakness or the gesture of consolation. ". . . It'll make for a hungry few days, until she's cleared or I have a replacement. But I'll live. If I share Mother's and Orlanjis's table, aside from being vulnerable to our common enemies, I'll burn my stomach out." He stood up. "I need to get washed and dressed and back upstairs. Fortunately"—his smile twisted—"I doubt anyone will want to risk my company, come sunset."

Tam lifted his head. "You're wrong. I'm staying with you now. I intend to find the person or persons responsible for this attack. There's more riding on it than I can tell you, but your life is by far the least."

Floria

Balthasar's letter came into her hands in the late afternoon, delivered by the secretary of the Lightborn half of the Intercalatory Council with profuse apologies for its tardiness. Her lips thin, Floria silently cursed the woman for an incompetent—a letter meant for a recipient other than the one it was addressed to was hardly a rarity in her work—and, back against the lintel of the window of the west-facing gallery, turned the letter toward the sunlight. The script was thinner and more untidy than usual, and there were mistakes in the ciphering. It was dated two nights past.

> *Floria, Baron Strumheller has been arrested for Tercelle Amberley's murder and for sorcerous harm to Lord Vladimer. . . .*

Oh, my friend, Floria thought, reading his plea for information on the whereabouts of his kidnapped daughter. *I am desperate. . . .* And Strumheller, their capable ally, charged with sorcery. She turned the letter over in her hands, feeling the stippling of the Darkborn script, and paused to decipher the covering letter to the head of the Intercalatory Council, Bal's careful strategy for disguising the message to her from his own people. She shook her head: maybe she had taught him too well.

With the prince in no immediate need of her special services, she surely had time enough to go home and check for any further word, and time enough to send an inquiry directly to the archducal palace if there was none. Tam was with the prince; she would speak to him as soon as possible thereafter. A word to the new captain, Lapaxo, and a promise to return promptly before dinner gained her leave to go.

Smoke-tinted sunlight painted the west walls of the palace. Already the first of the palace administrative staff—those not involved in executing the elaborate funeral arrangements—were beginning to return to their own homes in the periphery of the palace round. All wore red jackets over their work clothes. Whether a deposition was rightful or unrightful did not matter to the civil service; tradition ruled.

She lifted her eyes, looking across the garden toward the wall that enclosed the palace. Four or five centuries ago, before the crops and fields had been torn up for gardens, piazzas, and buildings, and while the palace and its staff were still small, this inner city would have been nearly self-sufficient. That was a time when princes still might expect to die in bed.

Mother of All, but she was wearier than she could ever show, here in the Lightborn court. Perhaps she could understand her father's mortal resignation, in the aftermath of the death of his own prince. But she did not think Benedict had ever charged Darien to look after Isidore, as Isidore had charged Floria on Fejelis's behalf.

She set a hat of broad-brimmed mesh on her head and glanced through its filter at the sun. Lightborn she might be, but the sun scalded her. Pale as a Darkborn, whispered the more fanciful of her enemies. But neither she nor they had ever seen a Darkborn, to know whether a Darkborn's skin was as pale as milk, as some speculated, or dark as onyx, as others did. The Darkborn themselves could not know.

She avoided the servants' common ways, disliking crowds, taking a series of open paths across open lawns and alongside still pools that reflected the stippled clouds overhead. *He will never see them again*, she thought, and the loss pierced her, daggerlike. *Mother of All, whoever is responsible will not escape their own deserved and rightful deposition, and I will make it painful.*

The red-clad guards on the side gate passed her through without a word. The next breath she took seemed freer, and she did not look back until she had reached the corner. Turning then, she did, at the wall, at the wide- but blind-windowed upper stories of the palace behind it, and at the monolith of the Temple tower at its back, the white walls, balconies, and crenellations blazing in the sunlight. Every generation the tower grew in grandeur, until even the Darkborn, enthusiastic builders though they were, protested that it could not stand safely. The sight never failed to disquiet her, but she shook her head at the futility of dispute with the order of things and continued toward her own modest home, on a border between Lightborn and Darkborn districts.

She took careful note of her surroundings as she approached. Her home lacked shrubbery or statuary, or ornamentation. The stone was polished smooth and fitted close, and the woodwork and shutters were a glossy gray that would show any crack. When she was a girl, she had pointed to the Mages' Tower and whined about the drabness. A little later, her father had taken her with him to the death scene of a member of the Prince's Vigilance. The assassins had entered via a shutter left unlocked by the artist hired to decorate it.

Years later, Floria had learned that her father had arranged the assassination himself, and why. Corruption within the Vigilance could not be tolerated.

She wondered why that memory made her feel so cold. Perhaps because she could envision one type of person who might be so trusted, and so skilled, and so ruthless, as to kill a prince in such a manner.

She unlocked her front door with care. Just inside was a decorative curtain, a silvery mesh that was another Darkborn invention. Push it aside in the usual way, and the links would fall into a new and recognizable pattern. But the pattern was undisturbed; the mesh had not been touched.

Nevertheless, something was wrong.

She slid past the curtain and moved silently to the archway of the large front room. The mesh on the windows was undisturbed. The open back and mesh of furnishings offered no cover. Carefully placed mirrors exposed hidden corners. Another gliding step took her to the archway to the smaller side room. Again, nothing anomalous.

Upstairs, then, pausing to slip her key from within her belt and disarm the traps on the stairs. She knew, as soon as she reached the first landing, what was wrong. The familiar smell was subtly altered by the scents of Darkborn furnishings and Darkborn furniture treatments. Habit made her pause on the landing to check all rooms before she turned toward the half-open door of her *salle*, the room that, via a paper wall, abutted the home of Darkborn Balthasar Hearne. Discipline kept her eyes from fixing first on the huge rent in the paper wall and the mesh that reinforced it; she glanced over the room entire, seeing nothing else anomalous, and then back at the wall. A flap, like a doorway, had been cut away, and now hung curled under its own weight.

"Balthasar," she whispered. On three sides of the room, the mirrors returned her reflection, color drained to the verdigris pallor of a corpse.

Her reflection had its rapier in hand as it crossed the floor. There was enough light cast through the rent for her to live by, and more than enough light to burn any Darkborn to ash. She drew a deep breath, and stepped through, entering Balthasar's home for the first and likely the last time. She noticed the mismatch of hues in the wood of the bookcase, the patched leather of the armchair, and the blank spines of the books. His utter sightlessness was borne in on her again. She took a deep breath and made herself look down at the carpet for the mound of fine gray ash amongst fragments of fabric and metal that marked a Darkborn caught by light. She saw nothing, except for dark stains of dried blood at the base of the wall. Here was where he had lain dying, the night two men came in search of Tercelle Amberley's twins. More blood spatters helped her reconstruct the choreography of the attack, to which she'd been condemned to *listen*, until she had had the desperate idea of attacking with a blade of light, a torch shone through a tiny slit in the wall. . . . There was the patch where she had driven the needle in.

In the doorway to the hall, pain and weakness warned her that she could go no farther. Slowly, staring through the half-lit hall, remembering the prince's dark room, she backed into the light. Balthasar *must* still be at the archducal palace, where she had suggested Ishmael di Studier take him, and his family, two—yes, two days ago. He must be.

She wiped her damp face with a sleeve, and turned to examine the damage. She would not have expected anyone to be able to cut through the wall, since on Telmaine's insistence Balthasar had installed Darkborn-made mesh, as strong as metal came without magic. A heavy knife with a serrated edge had been used, with a powerful shoulder behind it.

The edges curled toward her. The cut had been made from the other side.

She whipped round, at no sound, only a sudden conviction that now must be the moment that someone would step out behind her. There was no one there.

Then the intruder's object must have been to find, or to leave ... something. Her eye went at once to the lights, blazing in their brackets. Of all the rooms in her house, this was the only one that had no window, was entirely dependent upon the enspelled lights, day and night.

She resisted the impulse to run from the room. She moved her eyes over the mirrors, the racked weapons and equipment. All was as she had left it four days before; all was as she had always left it. Disorder did not become a vigilant, who should be able to notice the least anomaly. She thought once more of the misplaced shoe, and the dream.

The thought guided her across the landing, into her bedroom, past the undisturbed bed, and to a tall cabinet with mesh sides and fretwork doors. In it, she kept family ornaments and memorabilia, and her own collection of inconsequential treasures. With the hilt of her dagger, she hooked the handle and drew open the doors.

The box was gone, the ugly but well-crafted little wood and ivory box that Balthasar had given her for her fourteenth birthday. The box that she had dreamed she was taking to the prince. Everything else was there. Bed, bedding, night vest, side table—all were unchanged from the state she had left them in.

From downstairs came the soft shivering sound of the links of the mesh cascading into a new configuration.

Whisper-footed on the tiled floor, she crossed the bedroom to look out and down the stairs. A flicker on the floor, a shadow briefly cast by sunlight against the lesser lamplight. A pair of feet, shod in mourning red, moved toward the stairs.

She sprang for the *salle*, but too late. "Mistress White Hand!" The voice was that of Tempe Silver Branch, of the vigilants' judiciary. Like the White Hands, the Silver Branches possessed a family asset, theirs the ability to detect lies in the spoken word. It was by no means as sure an asset as the ability to detect poison, Floria's father had said. Nevertheless, Tempe held considerable influence. "Floria, we need to talk to you."

There were three vigilants besides Mistress Tempe: Mortimer Beaudry, a captain she disliked, and two lieutenants. One she knew from the *salle*; his skill with a rapier equaled hers, although he was more temperamental and erratic than she. The other was unusually short statured for a vigilant, but had a reputation for mechanical artistry that some said approached magic. Talk? This was an arresting party, if ever she had seen one.

She locked the door to the *salle* as Tempe set her foot on the stairs. It would gain her only a little time, but that time should be enough. Two of the lights went into a mesh equipment bag, with a semiopaque sack over the outside. The first knock on the door interrupted her brief consideration of a third light, but the weight would hamper her. She slung the bag through the rent and dropped it on the floor.

"Floria?" said Tempe, from the other side of the door. "Why are you reacting like this?"

Everything she said would be weighed and judged through Tempe's asset. She lifted down two of the four remaining lamps and pushed them into one of the closets. "Have you a warrant?"

"Do you expect one? Have you something to fear?"

Had she? Aside from a dead prince, an inexplicable dream, and a missing box.

"Floria, there are rumors around the palace that you visited the prince's rooms last night."

"You're coming to arrest me on rumors?"

Within the door, she heard a click. A gap appeared between door and lintel. Fingers probed, blanching as they took the strain. The gap widened, opening on Tempe standing with the lieutenants flanking her and the captain at her back.

"Prince Fejelis ordered your arrest." She held out a long, narrow, cream-hued fold of paper. "Read it, if you would."

Her eye, drawn to the paper, caught in passing a glint of metal in the shadow of their bodies, as Captain Beaudry cleared a revolver.

She lunged through the rent into Balthasar's study. Snatched up the bag and let her momentum take her through the door, across the landing, into the curtains across an alcove on the far side. She knew terror then, floundering against fabric that, in the half-light, was black as death itself. She rolled out of the alcove, curled around the sack containing the lights.

"Beaudry, what are you *doing*?"

A shot punched into the fabric above her.

"It's not a death warrant! *Floria!*"

Floria scrambled out of the view of the doorway, holding the bag against her ribs, panting with the shadows. She swung her feet onto the stairs and, with a hand that slipped on the smooth uprights of the banister, heaved herself up.

She heard footsteps in flight down her own stairs next door, all stealth abandoned, and a step in the study behind her. They had divided their numbers, thinking to cut her off. She fell, more than ran, down the stairs. At its foot she took the briefest moment to choose between front door and side door to the tiny garden—and heard someone stumble on the shadowed landing above and begin to scream for light. She herself was close to the limit of her endurance of shadow and pain, hardened though she was by vigilant's training, and her own explorations of her limits. Those explorations told her she had no more *time*—she grabbed the front door handle, tore open the door, let in the streaming sunlight that made the gray unfinished wallpaper beautiful, and the well-varnished parquet radiant.

She staggered down the steps into the deserted street. At the curb stood one of the products of the Darkborn's obsession with machinery, Baron Strumheller's chemical coach, abandoned in his flight days ago. She passed it at a run, angling across the road to a shadowed lane that Darkborn traveled freely and Lightborn, seldom. She prayed that there had been no new construction since the last time she had explored these lanes. The next street, too, was Darkborn, with only a few passersby. She plunged across the road, down another lane, onto a street that bordered a park. At this time in a late summer's day, the shadows of the bordering trees had spread halfway across the grass, and the parkgoers had followed the sun. She dodged into the shadow, across the grass, and down the steps into the moist, thick shadow of one of the creeks that laced the city. Stopped, gasping, to drag the translucent covering off the mesh, and release the full strength of her lights. She could not hear any pursuit. Few Lightborn came down here, even in daylight, while the trees were in leaf. But the board-walk—a fashionable stroll for the Darkborn at night—led upstream to the gardens of the archducal palace itself.

Four

Telmaine

*T*elmaine caught herself drowsing, not for the first time. The coffeepot on the table at her side was cold, the thin sandwiches dry and unappetizing. Balthasar's lower-class tastes had affected her, she thought wryly; she liked her sandwiches cut thick, with abundant moist filling, each a meal in itself.

She stood up in penance for her lapse, and began to circle the library again. Unlike the ducal summerhouse, the city palace had never been a place for childish exploration and games of hide-and-seek, even for the children of dukes. So she had not previously been in the botanical library. It smelled of resin and dried flowers. Three walls were shelved from floor to ceiling, to house old monographs and journals from natural-history societies. The fourth wall was given over to a bank of small drawers, each containing desiccated samples of leaves, flowers, or seeds. When this was all over, she *must* arrange permission for Bal to visit, even if she would not see him again for days. When this was all over . . .

The archduke had retired hours ago, and was deep in an untroubled sleep. She supposed a man with his cares had to learn to set them aside, or let care wear him out. Vladimer had been sleeping and waking throughout the day, his vitality marred by his wound. Around her, the palace was sunk in its daytime lull, only the day staff awake.

Throughout the day she had been thinking about magic. Ishmael had been deeply concerned about the hazard her untrained power posed to others and to herself. Should she do harm, she would come to the attention of the Lightborn mages, who, being far more numerous and powerful, determined the use and abuse of magic on both sides of sunrise. Then she risked having her magic, and perhaps her mind, destroyed.

But if they were so *cursed* all-knowing, Telmaine thought, where were *they* when the *Shadowborn* ensorcelled Lord Vladimer? Where were *they* when the Shadowborn set the firetraps that killed those men in the warehouse and nearly killed herself and Vladimer at the station? Or since the victims were Darkborn, were their fates a matter of indifference to the Lightborn?

Ishmael would have helped her, had intended to help her work with her strength, even at a remove. He had not realized how dangerous the use of *any* magic would be to him. Perhaps—as Bal would say—he had not *wished* to realize it.

But when Malachi Plantageter's agents had seized upon him for the murder of Tercelle Amberley, he had given her a gift, overextending himself to convey to her his understanding of his own magic. She had not yet fully unwrapped that gift; it lay, warm with that dimming-ember sense of him, quietly in her mind and magic.

As did the far more malevolent bequest of the Shadowborn mage she had fought at Lord Vladimer's bedside. Not even Ishmael knew all the details of that encounter; not even he knew that the Shadowborn had begun to impress upon her his structure of his *own* magic at the moment at which Ishmael killed him. She could feel *that* also in her, like some obscene seed.

But surely, it, too, could be used. Unlike Ishmael, the Shadowborn had been a mage at least as powerful as she. He had been able to set traps—like the firetraps in the warehouse—that did not need him to be present to trigger. She *liked* the idea, indeed she did, of the Shadowborn ensnared in traps of their own design.

She returned to the least comfortable of the chairs in the room, a straight-backed wooden chair that her deportment mistress would have approved. Settling into it, she leaned her head back, muted her sonn, and brushed the sleeping archduke and the restless Vladimer. She reached farther, sweeping her mage sense over the palace and finding all as she hoped it would be. A little longer stretch, a little greater effort, let her touch her daughters. Reassured, she returned her attention to Ishmael's gift.

He had given her, indeed, a sense of how he had learned to extend and manipulate his own vitality to achieve insights and effects beyond the physical. It was an unsettlingly masculine vitality and there was a pleasurable indecency in contemplating it. As she had once told Ishmael, had she met him at the age of seventeen, she would have fled. Innocent virgin that she was then, she would not have been able to name the feelings that so disconcerted her—though she would have been well aware of their impropriety. As a married woman, and one with a thoughtful and—sometimes embarrassingly—curious husband, she was well able to name them—and was still well aware of their impropriety.

What she had not expected was the memories. She had forgotten the strange dreams she had experienced the first day after his arrest. She was not sure whether the sharing was intended, or accidental, but she tiptoed delicately amongst them: that rock-hewn old man must be his father, though surely Ishmael in forty years would be of warmer humor. That lovely woman must be his mother. Younger brother and much younger sister—both inheriting from their mother. Sister . . . Ishmael's first unwitting working of magic, emptying himself into the fluttering chest of the tiny, premature baby. If this was how he had been born as a mage, little wonder he would not let it go. Memories of other healings, many desperate and some less so. The odd magical mischief. The curmudgeonly mage who had taken him on as a student. Phoebe Broome, mageborn daughter of the only seventh-rank Darkborn mage living. She wouldn't—she *hadn't*—mages had *no* morals.

She sat a moment with her hands pressed to her heated face. Sweet Imogene, now she had further reason to hope never to encounter Magistra Broome.

Composing herself, she checked upon her charges once more, and turned her attention back to examining Ishmael's magic. While they plotted Florilinde's rescue together, she in a carriage on the streets and Ishmael in a prison cell, she had sensed him thinking how well they worked together. And indeed, his use of his magic, the way he used it to shift vitality throughout his body and into the body of another, seemed natural to her. He was primarily a healer, limited to the manipulation of living flesh, which had a pliability far exceeding inanimate matter. Even then he was able to help only a few at a time. But by that power he had defined himself, and she could weep for its loss, as she would never have wept for the loss of her own. Oh, Ishmael.

Sounds in the corridor recalled her to self and place, the first sounds of stirring of the great household. Reluctantly, she turned her attention to the other mage's gift. There were memories there, too, but fragmentary and repellent and inexplicable. Bal had tried to explain to her how the eye could see much, much farther than sonn could be cast and return, by the *light* of a sun immensely more powerful than anyone's sonn. He had tried to describe *horizon*, *clouds*, *stars*. She had listened resentfully, knowing he had these descriptions from Floria White Hand. But that line there was *horizon*, where the earth curved away from the sky—or ended, as some said. And those, those were houses, windowed houses like the houses of the Lightborn. And faces—the face of a boy with features—features very like Lysander Hearne's. The faces seemed to rearrange themselves as they moved—were they all shape-shifters? But no, Bal had talked about *shadows*. A woman's face, as proud and remote as that of any dowager duchess—evoking in the mage a sense of worship, fear, and hatred. Who was she?

She shivered. She had no idea why the Shadowborn had forced this on her, save to triumph somehow over Ishmael. She had been unwillingly privy to more than one man's fantasies about the daughter or wife of an enemy. But why such hatred? Because Ishmael was a Shadowhunter, scourge of Shadowborn? Because he was a mage? Some other, as yet unknown reason?

Had their enemy intended to enslave her to his will? He—or another of his kind—had certainly demonstrated himself capable of it; Tercelle had yielded to the lover who had ruined her. And Vladimer . . .

She sensed—she knew—that she should take this information to *someone* who might be able to infer from it what she could not. But Balthasar and Ishmael were beyond her reach, and Vladimer—Vladimer was the last person to whom she could confess. And surely his agents or Vladimer himself would read any letter she tried to send.

No, she was alone with her magic and the knowledge it brought her, as she had been alone with them all her life. Brief, illicit intimacy did not alter that.

Tentatively, she examined the Shadowborn's magic. Were those bizarre manipulations of vitality to reshape tissue the basis of their shape-shifting? It was repugnant to imagine such corruption of the healer's magic that Ishmael practiced so diligently. . . . She remembered the moment, after she had secretly granted Guillaume di Maurier a chance of life, when she had finally understood *why* Ishmael had thought his home and inheritance fair exchange for his meager powers.

Could she, with this knowledge, with *her* power, reshape *herself*? She raised a hand, and sonned its familiar shape, remembering the claws that had raked Balthasar's face as he and the Shadowborn struggled together in Vladimer's bedroom. Almost, almost, she knew how to do it. Revulsion at the very thought stopped her from full realization. How could anyone, any*thing*, reshape his flesh into something *monstrous*? Even the speculation tainted her with corruption, as had the speculation that she could change the archduke's mind. She shuddered.

No, she merely wished to learn how the Shadowborn set their traps, so that she might neutralize them if she met them again. Vladimer's idea that she learn to quench their fires was a sound one. She carefully did not consider what Ishmael might have thought, or said.

But to quench a fire, she might light a fire. In one of the drawers she found several sheets of loose writing paper, and walked over to the unlit fireplace, folding the paper into a small, neat fan. Holding it over the hearth, she concentrated on the sense and essence of fire. With that sense came the memory of the warehouse. Searing heat washed up her face; she barely stifled a shriek and dropped the blazing paper, and staggered back from the hearth clutching her hand, her nostrils full of scorched lace. On the hearth, fire utterly consumed the paper, leaving a smudge of ash.

Several minutes passed before she could compose herself enough to heal her hand and tuck her burned glove up her sleeve. With a trembling hand and a hearth brush, she swept the ash into the fireplace. She wondered what the housemaids would think. Secret messages. Or more likely, love letters. She should disturb the stylus and frame before she left.

She folded another sheet and this time set it down on the hearth, touching it only with a finger. She carefully held in her mind the sense of an unlit fire, then a flame no larger than an orange blossom, and snatched back her hand as the entire paper burst into a bounding blaze. This was more difficult, more unnatural, than she had thought. She would have to lay hand on a supply of paper, one other than expensive palace stationery. Frugal Bal would be appalled. Carefully, she extended her magic, and muffled the blaze into a small flame, the flame into embers, the embers into smoke.

Three sheets of paper later, each of which had flared up like the one before, she heard the sunset bell with a sense of relief she remembered from the schoolroom. She cleared the last of the ash into the fireplace, and replaced the cleaning equipment. She had done what Vladimer asked, tested her ability to quench flame, but she was vexed and dissatisfied at her tenuous control in the lighting; she would need more practice. At the desk, she took care to shift the position of the stylus and writing frame. If only she dared write to Bal, and to Ishmael . . . but no. A few hours' sleep, and then her vigil would resume.

Telmaine

Vladimer's summons roused Telmaine two hours into her craved-for sleep. Sweet Imogene, but the only other time she could remember being this tired was the last weeks be-

fore Amerdale was born. With her maid's help, she put on
a moderately formal evening dress and set her hair in good
order. By the time she arrived at the botanical library, she
was walking more or less straight and wishing that Vladimer were not himself ailing; archduke's brother or no, he
was due a piece of her mind for treating her like some clerk
to be ordered to his whim.

"Your husband's letter case was delivered to me," he
said, by way of greeting. "One of them was ciphered." He
had read them, read her husband's heart openings to the
people he loved. "Can you interpret that cipher?"

It was too much to hope that Vladimer be ashamed of
himself. "No."

"What is your husband's relationship to this Lightborn
woman?"

"They are friends from childhood," she said. Only her
mother and her closest friend, Sylvide, knew what she felt
about Floria White Hand. Vladimer certainly did not need to.

"She was highly placed in the Lightborn Prince's Vigilance, was one of Isidore's special agents. What," Vladimer
said, "would he tell her?"

She caught herself, realizing that there was more staked
on this than her womanly pride. "He would tell her," she
said, carefully, "everything he thought she needed to know
as a servant of the Lightborn prince."

"Did he not trust the official channels of information?"

Vladimer might distrust her, but he must *not* distrust
Balthasar. "My husband has served several terms as an Intercalatory Councilman. He *is* part of the official channels
of information."

Vladimer braced his cane and pushed himself to his feet.
"We have an unexpected visitor. I trust you will tell me if
she is who she claims to be."

He led her through a labyrinth of stairs, halls, and corridors, all the time providing steady commentary on the history of the palace. Merivan's two eldest sons, reluctant students and with the gruesome tastes of young boys, would
have been enthralled. For herself, she found Vladimer in
the role of history tutor disconcerting, even without his re-
cital of treachery, villainy, and horrific death.

They turned into a corridor as wide as some dancing halls she had seen, whose finish did not disguise its rough construction. Two massive doors separated it from the rest of the palace; at the moment, both stood open, but the aspect was not inviting. This was no wing for guests, even unwelcome ones. Vladimer jerked his head toward a plain door. "Execution room," he said, and she thought—with relief—he would not elaborate, but he said, "The skylight can be opened from outside. Been more than a few traitors who've ended there, quietly. And a number of criminals."

And for those he had sent there himself—for he surely had—he showed neither pride nor regret. Something she would not have understood before these last days.

"It's not always a boon in law to be wellborn," Vladimer added. "The common-born have protections that may be denied us."

Any explanation he might have offered was preempted as they turned a corner and arrived at another narrow door. "This needs two hands," Vladimer said. Telmaine pressed where he indicated, and pulled as she was bidden, until the door opened. She followed him into a tight vestibule, and waited as he struggled one-handed with the mechanism of the inner door. Grudgingly, he yielded up that secret, too, and let her open it.

The room they emerged in was small, and, like the study in Bal's family home, the far wall was no more than paper reinforced with mesh. She caught her breath in visceral alarm.

"Lord Vladimer," she hissed. He gestured her to silence and pointed to the wall. She sensed a familiar vitality on the other side. And an equally familiar taint, faint, but detectable.

"Mistress White Hand?" said Vladimer. His sonn, and his frown, prompted Telmaine to nod in confirmation, of that identity at least.

On the far side of the wall, a body stirred. "Balthasar?" Floria's voice said.

"No. But I have with me his wife."

"Telmaine?" Telmaine had no desire to respond; she had never accepted that she and Floria should be on first-name terms. And with that taint about her . . . "Telmaine," Floria persisted, "is Balthasar all right? Where is he?"

"Balthasar is quite well," she said, politely. "Thank you for inquiring."

The woman on the other side of the wall gave a choked laugh. "This is hardly a social call, not at this hour, Telmaine."

"Mistress White Hand invoked the law of succor," Vladimer said, neutrally. "Arriving at the palace as the sun-bell was tolling. She is in one of the rooms we keep for the purpose. It goes without saying that she brought a light source with her."

"Who are you, sir?"

"I am acting in the interest of Lord Vladimer Plantageter," Vladimer said. "You may regard everything you say to me as being said to Lord Vladimer himself." There was a small table with recording materials against one wall. He set his cane across the table, and eased himself down into the chair. Telmaine stood beside him, her mage sense extended through the wall.

"Very well, sir," Floria said. "I will take you at your word. I need asylum. I'm suspected of being involved in the unrighteous deposition of the prince. I had hoped Balthasar Hearne would be here to speak for me."

Vladimer's left hand slid into his pocket and his balance shifted forward. "You did not mention that before."

"No," she said. "I wanted to speak to someone with the authority to grant my request for asylum."

Vladimer weighed the request, while Telmaine stood without breathing. It was a long moment before he settled his spine back against the chair, guarding his arm, and waved Telmaine to sit down in one of the other chairs. "Please tell us what you know of the prince's death. Consider me Lord Vladimer's ears."

He might, Telmaine thought, curb that undertone if he thought to protect himself by denying his identity. Floria White Hand was astute enough to hear it.

After a brief pause, the woman on the far side of the wall said, "The prince retired to his rooms last night, later than his usual hour: the court had been celebrating Fejelis's coming of age. The usual checks were done on the wards in his rooms by the mages contracted to palace service. The vigilants carried out their usual inspection. With the prince were a secretary, a servant, and the captain of vigilants. Sometime late in the night, the lights in his room failed completely. We know that it happened with little warning because of the position of the residues: none of them had made an attempt to escape."

Telmaine was a moment understanding what she meant: while daylight burned the Darkborn to ash, darkness dissolved the Lightborn away to— To their daughters, Balthasar had said water, and to herself, who had not invited it, not much at all. The Lightborn were too familiar with magic for her to want to know more of them. She preferred—or *had* preferred—to regret ignorance rather than knowledge.

"Go on," said Vladimer, unmoving. "The lights failed, you said; how?"

"How much do you know about how we make sunlight last through the night, Master—Ears?"

Telmaine stiffened, wondering how the woman dared provoke from her position, but Vladimer's chancy humor was teased. "By magic, I presume."

"The lights capture sunlight during the day and reradiate it through the night. Since magic dies with the mage, even the cheapest lights are enspelled by at least two mages. The lights in the prince's chambers were enspelled by four."

"So the failure of the lights implies the involvement of a mage." Vladimer had his chin propped on his sound hand, listening intently.

"Yes," Floria said, sounding stifled. "We began inquiries— the usual inquiries amongst the earthborn staff—"

"Earthborn being nonmageborn," Vladimer supplied, in an aside that made Telmaine twitch, exquisitely sensitive as she was to the mention of magic.

"—as to people entering or leaving or seen around the prince's rooms. What do you know of the—arrangements— between Lightborn mageborn and earthborn?"

Vladimer said, in his didactic tone, "Mageborn cannot use their magic to influence the affairs of nonmages, but they can engage in publicly declared contracts to act in their interests, and in doing so are indemnified under law. The nonmageborn who engages a mage becomes liable for all their acts in his or her interest."

"That's—right," Floria said.

"It seemed an advantageous solution, particularly to the early warlords and potentates able to hire such mages—who, after all, would hold them accountable to the law but their fellows? I do not believe its developers anticipated a time like the present, when mages would number in the—what, thousands?—and command powers that are, frankly, barely to be imagined by the nonmageborn."

But someone like you would have, Telmaine thought.

"The economic consequences have also been significant," Vladimer observed, "given what amounts to a one-way transfer of wealth from nonmageborn to mageborn—there being few services that the nonmageborn can render that would offset the service of magic. Your system is not sustainable, Mistress White Hand."

There was a silence. "Might I have the pleasure of addressing Lord Vladimer Plantageter himself?" Floria said.

"The very same."

Telmaine tensed, extending her senses, but Floria only breathed out, audibly. "My lord, I have heard a great deal about you."

"Not too unctuously flattering, I trust. What were your initial hypotheses?"

Her tone was distinctly crisper, as though reporting to a superior. "A light that is nearly discharged changes color, conspicuously. The prince, or anyone else in the room, would have noticed. There was no evidence that they did."

"Mm," Vladimer prompted her to continue.

"Next, the possibility that the lights were faulty. In the rare event that the enspelling itself is flawed, the light fails within minutes of first use."

"Without—fail? As it were?"

"Always. However, any magic can be annulled by a stronger mage. But the activities of higher-rank mages are of great interest to other mages, and the mages have admitted no such activity."

Vladimer collected Telmaine's attention with a curl of his hand and pointed a finger at the wall. Calling her attention to the statement.

"So we come to talismanic magic, magic cast on inanimate objects and maintained by the vitality of the mage—lights are talismans themselves. Talismans can be created that annul magic. One need only be given to an individual—mage or nonmage—with access to the prince's quarters."

Vladimer tapped his fingertips lightly on the desk. "And is that what you are accused of?"

Floria's indrawn breath was audible.

"It is a not-unwarranted deduction, is it not?" Vladimer said. "Did you?"

"Lord Vladimer, I would have said—not. But I have—I remember—or I dreamed—going to my prince's rooms during the night. I would never willingly have harmed the prince." Her voice had thickened with tears, extraordinary to hear in this woman.

"Ensorcellment," Vladimer said, in a voice utterly without inflection.

"The palace mages would have sensed it on me. That was another reason why I wanted to speak to Balthasar: I know there are nonmagical means of subverting the will."

Telmaine drew her breath to make Balthasar's argument that such means could not make people do things that were completely against their will, and let it out unused.

"What had your palace mages to say?"

"The mages contracted to the palace sensed, or say they sensed, *nothing* untoward. I was not satisfied; I decided to contract a mage I knew personally, a sport—a mage who—" She hesitated.

"I know what a sport is," Vladimer said. "Continue."

But I do not, Telmaine thought, perversely piqued. She cleared her throat softly, drawing Vladimer's attention. Vladimer said, not without malice, "The Lightborn masters of lineage breed mages, Lady Telmaine, as horse breeders do prize stock, to strengthen certain traits. A sport is a mage whose powers have arisen without benefit of such pedigree; all Darkborn mages might thus be considered sports."

Her face heated with embarrassment at the reminder

of Lightborn immorality, and the even more pointed reminder of her magic.

"I thought—though Tam would not say—he seemed to sense something in the room the prince had died in. He seemed troubled. He said he must make inquiries of the Temple. Almost the next I knew was the vigilants coming for me with a warrant from the prince."

"Ah," said Vladimer. He thought, briefly. "Mistress Floria, it is not unknown, is it, that a sufficiently powerful mage may take the form of another?"

"Such magic around the prince would have been sensed. *Any* ensorcellment—they should have sensed."

"And so we come back, once again, to what may or may not have been sensed," Vladimer said, half to himself. "What part might the prince's son, or the mother, have had in Isidore's death?"

Telmaine shivered at the casual allusion to assassination and patricide.

"The timing is simply wrong. Fejelis said he would not be so stupid as to arrange his father's deposition the very day he came of age, and, Mother of All help me, I believe him. And if Helenja meant to elevate one of her sons, it would be Orlanjis, but he is only fourteen—and Helenja would *not* be chosen regent."

Vladimer considered that in silence, his skepticism palpable.

Floria said, a little desperately, "I'm asking not only for succor from the night but also for asylum. This is the one place that the mages cannot lawfully harm me, or the Vigilance reach me."

"Your safety is conditional," Vladimer noted, "assuming you are right about the existence of a talisman that can annul light, and mages lawless enough to use it."

"That did occur to me, yes," she said, quite steadily.

"That said, I will grant you asylum, and we will—see—as you would say, what manner of petitions arrive for your surrender." He pushed himself to his feet, bracing himself with his cane.

"Thank you, Lord Vladimer."

Telmaine trailed after Vladimer through the small anteroom, into the hall, and waited while he rang a bell and delivered instructions to the servant who answered for Floria's continued care.

"You're not going to—tell her about the Shadowborn?" she said as they started back toward his rooms.

"Not now. It will be revealing if she lives to tomorrow's dawn."

Little as she cared for the woman, she was dismayed by such calculation. "Do you—what do you think of the Lightborn mages sensing nothing? Because I had wondered— Ishmael said that they punished abuse of magic. Yet your ensorcellment, the firetraps set in the warehouse . . ."

"Those things had occurred to me, Lady Telmaine," he said.

On their return, there were no macabre diversions; he was noticeably flagging. Despite her skirts and his longer legs, she easily kept pace with him through the corridors, all the way back to the botanical library. He let himself down into one of the comfortable armchairs, Telmaine into the straight-backed wooden chair.

"What did you sense?" he said.

"It was Floria White Hand. But there was Shadowborn magic about her. Faint, but there."

"Was she telling the truth, as far as she knew it?"

"I—I think she was."

"Think?" he said stingingly. "You cannot let your emotions interfere with your purpose, Lady Telmaine."

She would, she decided, find some opportune moment to quote his own words back at him.

"I have not asked you this before, but do you sense any aura or influence around me?" His voice was very controlled, and she had seldom been so relieved as to be able to say, "No."

"Which may mean, simply, that the one that ensorcelled me"—he said this with only the faintest hesitation—"is indeed dead. If Mistress Floria were ensorcelled . . . But the timing, the timing is wrong. The mage died before the prince. And the ensorcellment about Mistress Floria lingers." He drummed his fingers restlessly on the arm of the chair.

"Floria said—lights were enspelled by more than one mage," she said tentatively. "Perhaps this also involved more than one Shadowborn. We know there are at least two."

"So does this taint she bears come from ensorcellment, or contact with this putative talisman?" Vladimer said. "Tell me, when you interviewed Tercelle Amberley, did you or di Studier sense such a taint around her? You did not mention it."

"No," she said. "But—Tercelle may not have seen her"— she threw herself at the word—"lover—since—they were last together." He received the opinion as mere fact, to her relief; another man might have leered or reacted with distaste at such indelicacy. Emboldened, she said, "And if she *had* been ensorcelled, she might not have fled to Balthasar, since everything that has happened suggests the Shadowborn did not *want* Balthasar involved."

"Then we have several possibilities. The Temple colluded in the assassination of the prince. Or there is a form of ensorcellment that no mage can sense. The alternative that comes to mind is an impersonation by Shadowborn. And the other concern I have is whether a talisman created to annul light might also be created to *cast* light."

Telmaine shivered with horror. Vladimer, catching the shiver with his sonn, smiled narrowly. "Had I been sufficiently prescient, I should not have sent Ishmael into the Borders. As it is, I must rely upon you. It is entirely likely I shall need you again tonight, so please hold yourself in readiness."

Telmaine

Vladimer summoned her again shortly after the midnight meal, another savory but solitary repast picked at without appetite. She was trying to compose a letter to her daughters, well aware how poor a substitute it would be for her presence, for either sender or recipients. So Vladimer's note was almost welcome.

This time, the footman escorted her to Vladimer's own chambers, tucked well in the depths of the older part of the palace and doubtless connected via hidden passageways to a dozen other halls and rooms. The footman announced her at the door and left her. She wondered what Vladimer had done with Kip—Kingsley.

Vladimer was sitting in an armchair, cane to hand. By the evidence of the plates on the table to his right, he had made an indifferent essay at his own lunch. A bottle and a small medicine glass sat beside the plates, the glass drained of its contents. His sling was nowhere in evidence.

"I am about to have a visitor," he said without preamble. "I would have preferred to meet her elsewhere, but my physicians—and my brother—insist I should not be going about. They are concerned about fever."

They should be concerned about more than that, Telmaine thought, if they were paying attention. His vitality shimmered with unnatural intensity.

"I want you within reach but not within sonn. My visitor will be quite aware of you, but I fully expect you will discourage any unseemly interest: she is merely of fourth rank."

"A *mage*?" she breathed.

"By the name of Magistra Phoebe Broome."

She caught her breath in mingled social shock and fear. Vladimer continued. "Ishmael speaks well of Farquhar Broome's and his daughter's loyalty, though the elder Broome reportedly is quite deranged. Phineas Broome is a vocal republican and no friend to the nobility. Ishmael commended Magistra Broome to me as the most reliable of the three." Telmaine, her face warming, wondered if Vladimer knew that Phoebe Broome had been Ishmael's occasional lover.

"You asked her to come *here*!"

"Believe me, I would much rather not. You can imagine the uproar were Kalamay and his ilk to find me consulting with mageborn. Even Sejanus would not be best pleased. But she will be able to give me answers you cannot. I, however, need you to tell me if *she* has any Shadowborn influence about her."

"Lord Vladimer—," she began. One did not refuse the archduke's brother. But surely a lady might—*must*—say no to a proposition that threatened her virtue, as this did. And might expose her secrets, as this might.

"I might remind you," he said, "that you depend upon my silence. But I think I am a sufficiently good judge of your nature to think I might better remind you who it was gave me into your keeping. I will show you where you are to sit."

Teeth clenched, he levered himself out of the chair. She did not move, gathering herself to object. "Lord Vladimer, I—" Mage sense, extended throughout the palace, rippled and flinched back from a sudden intrusion. "They're here," she said, in a half whisper.

"They?"

"Two of them."

"So she brought an escort," Vladimer said, sounding almost amused. "Or the escort brought himself. Not what I would expect of the lady." He *did* know about her from Ishmael, Telmaine thought.

"I sense no Shadowborn," she said, in faint hope that he would be satisfied and release her.

"Here," said Vladimer, swinging open a panel in the wall, opening up a cubby with a single seat and a tiny table with a writing frame, stylus, and sheets of paper.

"They'll know I'm here," she protested.

"I count on it," he said, leaning against the panel. "But your husband's sister is a mage, is she not? And all the years she has known you, she has never discovered you."

Clutching that as a desperate hope, she yielded to his will, drew her skirts around her, and slipped into the alcove. He closed the panel on her.

She heard him summon a footman to tidy away the residue of his neglected meal and set out a chair for his unexpected guest. Her heart was beating so hard from combined fright and the expectation of discovery that she was surprised the mesh was not jingling. Through the rush of her own blood she barely heard Lord Vladimer's guests announced and the woman's breathless, "Lord—V-Vladimer."

Phoebe Broome, she knew, had social ambitions and an unqualified admiration for the nobility. That stammer might have been excitement or fright or a sudden attack of social uncertainty. Whatever it was, Vladimer responded with a smoothly ironic "Magistra Broome . . . and this is Magister Phineas Broome, I presume."

The man with her was something else: masculine energy and revolutionary ardor looking for an outlet, and finding it in that tone. The upsurge of hostility alarmed her; its sudden shift toward her, even more. "What's that?" and followed with a bruising <*Who are you?*> She repulsed him, hard.

"There's another mage here," Phineas said, in a tone so shaken that she felt contrite.

"Yes, Phineas Broome," Vladimer said, calmly. "And as you have obviously just discovered, one quite capable of making you mind your manners."

"What do you want?" Phineas Broome demanded; he was obviously the kind who would fight if surprised or set back. "Why did you bring us here?"

"As I recall, it was your sister I invited, not you," Vladimer said. "No matter. There is a force at work in the city using magic for assassination and mayhem in an effort to—I believe—destabilize both the Darkborn and Lightborn states, set Darkborn and Lightborn against each other, and possibly ready us for invasion."

"Your kind fancies conspiracies everywhere," Phineas sneered. "You know your days are numbered."

"On account of a rabble of posturing intellectuals who cannot even agree on the wording of their own manifestos?" Vladimer retorted. "I get full reports of your meetings, though frequently I mistake them for reviews of theatrical farces."

Telmaine winced, wishing Vladimer could get out of the *habit*.

"Phineas," Phoebe Broome said—in a tone that suggested kindred feeling, "*please*. You've often enough said the same." There was a brief silence. "Lord Vladimer, I should say that Baron Strumheller told us you had been ensorcelled when he left us the last time. I am very glad to know you have recovered."

"Am I?" Vladimer said, narrowly.

"Yes," she said, steadily. "I sense no trace of ensorcellment about *you*. Though I do not think you are entirely well."

"Ensorcellment leaves a trace, then?" Vladimer said, in that same sharp-edged manner.

"Unless the mage releases his or her victim, or dies."

"Dies, then. Courtesy of Ishmael di Studier."

"I am so relieved. I was very worried about Ishmael. His household sent us an urgent summons, and we found him more dead than alive. He had overspent himself badly, doing what, he would not say. I feared he would be permanently impaired."

"He never could accept," Phineas said snidely, "that the noble Baron Strumheller himself could be only first-rank."

She had not, Telmaine decided, slapped him *nearly* hard enough. She sensed a ripple of magic passing between sister and brother; she trusted it was a sharp rebuke.

"How much did di Studier tell you?"

"Neither my sister nor I," Phineas said, "will be answering any more of your questions until you tell us why you wanted us here. You're no friend to the mageborn, whatever your lackey believes."

Phoebe said, with the air of a woman trying to salvage a hopelessly blighted conversation, "My lord, he set out to catch the day train as soon as we could get him back on his feet. He had time to give us no more than an outline. But he had told us about the sighted babies, earlier, if there is a connection."

"Had he indeed?" Vladimer said, sounding not at all pleased.

"He thought then that these children might be the products of sorcerous interference. We—our community—deal with sorcery wherever we can, rather than rely upon the Lightborn. We had but barely begun to investigate when the Rivermarch fire . . . but just before he left, he told us it was Shadowborn magic."

"To which I say he's finally cracked," Phineas said.

"Do you?" Vladimer said. "Then I submit certain items for your consideration. Item one: the Shadowborn raiding patterns have changed; in fact, there have been no raids into the Borders this summer. Why? For what purpose might they be withholding their forces?

"Two: the children you spoke of were born and were put into foster care, and two days later the physician who had attended their birth was severely beaten in an attempt to make him divulge their whereabouts. Which, to his credit, he did not. To my knowledge they have not been found.

"Three: their mother was murdered, and an attempt was made to entrap and kill Ishmael di Studier at the scene. He is still being hunted in connection with the murder.

"Four: my own ensorcellment, which occurred around the same time, at the ducal summerhouse while it was full of guests.

"Five: the Rivermarch fire, a fire that defies natural explanation.

"Six: di Studier and others broke into the ducal summerhouse in time to prevent my assassin from completing his task. I have reliable testimony that, upon death, the assassin's face and aspect changed; I have Ishmael's testimony that the assassin's aura was that of a Shadowborn; and I have his speculation that the assassin was capable of changing his appearance. My prompt awakening established that this was the same mage as had ensorcelled me.

"Seven: on my return to the city, I had a second unpleasantly close encounter with a Shadowborn and his agents. Fortunately my—lackey, as you term him, sent the other off with his tail between his legs." Telmaine, her breath held, waited for a challenge from either of the mages to that "he." It did not come.

"Eight: the Lightborn prince was assassinated last night by what has been suggested was talismanic magic used to annul the lights in his room."

Phoebe Broome drew in her breath sharply. Even Phineas was silenced.

"In short, a series of events that cannot be explained without considering magic." He paused. Waiting, Telmaine thought, for protest that he would summarily dispatch.

There was none. He continued. "The archduke sent a ducal order to the Borders yesterday, permitting the raising of troops from reserves beyond those allowed by the order of six twenty-nine. With the death of the Lightborn prince, the archduke has extended his ducal order to the north, giving Mycene and Kalamay, among others, leave to activate reserves and move armaments into the city."

"That's—not good," Phoebe said, faintly.

"No, Magistra, it is not."

Phineas broke in. "It would be like you to try and entrap us into something you could call sorcery before the courts."

"I sincerely hope," Vladimer returned, "you have had nothing to do with any of this, or I would have to kill you, here and now."

"You could try," Broome growled.

"I would succeed," Vladimer said, "in the same manner that Ishmael di Studier and his ally killed my would-be assassin. Ishmael's strength as a mage was, in this case, irrelevant, and I assure you I am every bit as good a shot."

Telmaine pressed her hand to her mouth, tasting bile. He had given her no intimation that this was in his mind. He had summoned them to accuse them, to provoke an attack, knowing she must protect him. And then, as Ishmael had the Shadowborn, he would have executed them.

She hardly heard his next words for the blood surging in her ears. He would entirely deserve it if she fainted and made herself useless to him, but fainting would leave her vulnerable to Phineas Broome's intrusions. She braced her elbow on the small table and propped her head on her hand. She heard Vladimer say, "The individual—we are presuming a Shadowborn—who attempted to assassinate me was powerful enough to take the shape of either man or woman. What does that tell you, about its power *and* that of my ally?"

"Shape changing is—not a form of magic we know, Lord Vladimer," Phoebe said, sounding dazed at his frank ruthlessness. "I—expect it is an extension of healing, the reshaping of tissues, but it does not seem to have any beneficent purpose. After Ishmael told us about the infants, we started to investigate the possibility that there was a mage working in—tissue shaping."

"And have you found those infants, or any other evidence of that mage?"

"I thought you had a dead Shadowborn," Phineas said. "You've not left it out in the sun, have you?"

"The body was destroyed in the attack at the train station."

"How vexing," Phineas said, with heavy sarcasm.

"Exceedingly," said Vladimer, in an identical tone. "But entirely in keeping with the general turn of events."

"Lord Vladimer," Phoebe said, forcefully, "we—our community—had *nothing* to do with any of the events you described. Our activities are entirely within the law, if not within custom."

"I am pleased to hear that."

"What do you *want*?" Phineas demanded.

"Information, first of all. The city is under threat, I am sure of that. If the Darkborn mages are not the source of that threat, then the source is either the Lightborn or some other party. Magistra Broome, by just how much do the Lightborn exceed yourselves in numbers and magical capacity?"

"Considerably," said Phoebe Broome. "But the Lightborn hardly concern themselves with our doings, as long as we avoid what they—and we—would consider sorcery."

"We'll return to that point in a moment. Please quantify 'considerably.' Take, for instance, the sixth rank—how many Lightborn and how many Darkborn?"

"Nine to one," Phineas said. "We're not telling you numbers."

"I have a fair sense of yours already. What is the overall ratio of all Lightborn to all Darkborn mages?"

"Three or four to one," Phineas said, through set teeth.

"So they are succeeding in concentrating power at the higher levels."

"Lord Vladimer," Phoebe said, "the Lightborn mages have no interest in doing us harm."

"Magistra Broome, please do not come the naive schoolgirl with me. It is common knowledge in the Lightborn court that the Lightborn mages aim to rediscover or recreate forms of magic lost since Imogene's time. The Temple's exploitation has beggared the Lightborn state, no matter how pretty the facade that remains. The Darkborn state has been protected largely by the distrust of its leadership, because sunset is no barrier to magic. But as mages you are outnumbered and, to borrow Ishmael's phrase, outgunned."

"And what are we supposed to do about that?" Phineas Broome demanded. By the sound of movement and the shift in his voice he had come vehemently to his feet. "It's persecution by people like you that have cost us our numbers and our learning, so don't come weeping to the door at sunrise. Phoebe, let's go; we've heard enough. And you—*mage*—I hope you've been listening."

Phoebe Broome said, slowly, "Lord Vladimer, our faith and philosophy is that magic is a gift, from the Mother of All Things Born, a largesse that has been sorely abused, but not rescinded. Magic should not be used as the Lightborn use it, or as Imogene and her fellows used it, to twist nature and control the lives of others."

"In any contest concerning power, the one willing to use it to dominate always wins."

"There are many kinds of power."

"But few that matter," Vladimer said. "Do not weary me by preaching 'moral power.'"

There was a silence. "There are certain types of power one has to experience to know," she said, with quiet conviction.

Vladimer said sourly, "Sit down, Magister Broome, if you are staying. Leave if you are going." He sounded stung. Perhaps even he was susceptible to virtue, Telmaine thought. Which was an odd opinion for a respectable lady to form about a woman who was both a mage and a loose woman, but there was an undeniable uprightness about Phoebe Broome.

"As you pointed out, unless something has substantively changed, for the Lightborn mages to mount such an elaborate and oblique attack on us makes no sense—and the Lightborn head of state appears also to have fallen victim. Which, finally, leaves the Shadowborn. Ishmael di Studier describes their magic as having a particular quality—repugnant and chilling. That description has been confirmed by a second mage, who has never visited the Shadowlands. So I return to my original question as to whether you might have sensed something similar recently."

"Yes," she said, slowly. "Maybe."

"Around the Rivermarch?"

She swallowed. "Lord Vladimer, you must understand what else we sensed—sense—around the Rivermarch. A hundred and sixty people died there, their vitality riven from their flesh in the most excruciating manner. Eight Lightborn mages summoned a storm; the sense of that lingers. So yes, perhaps there was a—taint—there, but—I cannot say for certain."

"Anywhere else?"

She faltered. "Not—for certain. No, not for certain."

He waited, but she offered no more.

"Well, then, I bid you good evening and thank you for coming. I hope you will be prepared to inform me should you learn more, and I may ask for your help again. And I trust that events simply do not overtake us both."

She heard him ring the bell for the footman, and give instructions as to how his guests were to be shown out. She lifted her head from her hand and slumped backward in the chair, the many unbreakable rules of a lady's deportment remote now.

The club of Phineas's magic through the wall took her by surprise, like a crude hand thrust into her face to tear away her veils. She lashed at him, hard, with her magic, <Get away from me!> and through the contact between them heard him cry out. She thrust him away, forcefully, but without the revulsion that she had felt for the Shadowborn; indeed, the sense of his magic was not unpleasant, almost reminiscent of Ishmael's. But his hostility was palpable. How *dared* he? <Stop,> he cried.

Then she smelled smoke, sonned before her, and found the blurred roil of flame that was several sheets of paper. Frantically, she snuffed it out.

"Telmaine," Vladimer said from outside, "if you would be so good as to join me."

He must not smell the smoke, he *must* not. She crumbled the charred, chilled paper into her reticule. A sweep of her hand found the latch; she released it, half fell into the room, and slammed it closed behind her. Vladimer's sonn caught her as she stumbled against an armchair and braced herself upright on shaking arms.

"You didn't tell me that you didn't trust the Broomes," she accused before he got out his first word. "You didn't tell me that you would have had me hold them while you shot them. How *dare* you!" A lady's carefully groomed vocabulary had no words to express his offense and her outrage. Had she been near enough, she would have slapped him. Had any object been in reach, she would have thrown it. The impulse quivered in her muscles, tingled in her gloved palm, but she was deeply grateful it was afforded no outlet. Vladimer's response might not be tempered by gentlemanly courtesy, but she was even more afraid of something inchoate and inadmissible, something embodied in the heat and turbulence of flame. If she let herself be as angry with him as he deserved, she did not know what might happen.

Vladimer sighed. His energy was once again palpably on the ebb, his voice hollow. "I had to be certain that they had no part in it. The woman may protest their unworldly intent, but I do not disregard their power."

"You baited them," she rasped. "You used me as a stalking gun."

"Should they consider aligning themselves with the enemy, I intend them to know that their treachery will be known and rewarded—the brother is my concern, there. You did put him in his place, I trust." He sounded satisfied and she again wanted to slap him. Men could struggle for mastery with impunity; for a woman it was dangerous.

"If those two have any wisdom, they will apply their powers to the information I—and Ishmael, it seems—have given them, and confirm and extend it. I will be interested to hear my informants' reports." He paused. "Thank you, once more, Telmaine."

Five

Telmaine

Vladimer's third summons of the night interrupted Telmaine's bath, though at least his timing had allowed her a little time to savor it. She sent his messenger back with a firm promise that she would be along when she was ready, and settled to let her maid dress her hair. That maid was a source of perplexity to Telmaine's sisters, since she lacked the refinements they expected in a lady's maid, and Telmaine had driven their mother's housekeeper to distraction with her fussiness—for reasons she could never explain. But this maid had a gift for mathematics, and it occupied her to the exclusion of all merely human interests or intrigues. Her touch, with its flow of mental shapes and symbols, its warm absorption in the abstract, was as unobtrusive as any Telmaine had experienced.

With her maid's help, she donned a new and lushly fashionable visiting dress that she had ordered before going to the coast. Every season, she outfitted herself to remind society that, whomever she had married, she was still the daughter of a duke. Tonight, she needed to remind *herself* of that, that Lady Telmaine in full feather had *nothing* to do with the woman whom Vladimer had co-opted to his intrigues. She tucked her embroidered gloves into the cuffs of the inner sleeves with relief; autumn meant covered arms, no more conspicuous long gloves.

Vladimer was waiting in his private rooms. His lips compressed with irritation, though whether at her tardiness or her plumage, he did not indicate. Spreading her abundant skirts carefully, she sat where he directed.

"I've had a telegraph from Baronette Strumheller to say that Ferdenzil Mycene came through Strumheller and insisted on taking your husband on with him. They left on horseback, bound for Stranhorne."

Telmaine caught her breath. She had traveled in the Borders only twice in her life—while visiting her best friend Sylvide's family—and her recollection was of exhausting carriage rides on bone-jarring roads. "What are you going to do about that? Balthasar is not strong enough—"

"It is but five or six hours' ride, by roads that are reasonable in the main." He paused, sonning her face, which was unimpressed, since she very much doubted Vladimer had entrusted his precious bones to Border roads at *any* time in his life. "He will simply have to find the strength. I shall ask Maxim Stranhorne to advise his father that no formal charges have been laid against your husband."

"I would be most pleased," Telmaine said, stiffly, "if you would remind *everyone* of that."

She resolved that she would *not* ask after Ishmael and allow Vladimer to torment her. Though he did not seem to be in the mood for torment. He sat gripping the head of his cane, hunched around his sling, his expression grim. Her sense of his vitality betrayed what his pride would not: he was feverish and in pain. She would *not* feel sorry for him. She eased back slightly so that her back was just touching the back of the chair, and waited.

"There is something I need you to do," he said, at last.

Courtesy would demand she acknowledge his statement. She decided that she did not feel in the least polite toward him, either.

He twisted the tip of the cane into the carpet, head lowered. "If I had thought that Sejanus would broaden the ducal order, I would never have urged him to issue it to the Borders. But I was so fixated on the new threat that I overlooked the old." He lifted his head. "Mycene would take back the archducal seat if he could. Kalamay would be another Odon if he could. I have to know what they mean to do with the forces released to them under the order."

She could understand that, she thought, but what had it to do with her?

"They have requested an interview with my brother. I will arrange that they wait together. Though I doubt they will talk about their plans here, they will surely think on them."

Now she understood. "No, Lord Vladimer," she said, in a stifled voice. "No, I will *not*."

"Will not," he noted. "Not cannot."

"I agreed to protect you against Shadowborn. I did not agree to spy for you! You would not ask this of Ishmael!"

"Ishmael had not the power," Vladimer said, matter-of-factly. "They would never have allowed him near enough to touch. But you do have the power. Our enemies have agents here, in Minhorne, as you well know, and who knows what kind of allies."

"There was no taint of Shadowborn on Duke Mycene or Duke Kalamay," she said. "I told you that. But beyond that—" She was trembling. "Beyond that, I will not go."

He leaned on the chair arm, casting that probing sonn over her. "Very well," he said wearily. "But I shall still ask you to confirm that there is no taint to them before they speak with my brother."

She hesitated, distrustful. She had expected a longer, more taxing argument. Was he feeling so ill that he would simply accept her refusal?

His smile was thin, with an edge of malice. "Kingsley will show you to where you should wait."

She knew the room, having waited here herself with her family before an interview with the archduke, the last time to discuss her father's death and her marriage. She drew in a sharp, disconcerted breath as he released the catch on the heavy decorative fretwork on one wall and swung it aside on its hinges to reveal the alcove it hid. He gestured her forward and in. She carefully gathered in the rustling billow of her dress. It would be in need of ironing after this. She noted the position of the catch as Kingsley closed it on her.

The alcove was open on both sides. Benches spanned the alcove at each end, barely wide enough for the shoul-

ders of a slight man, or a woman. She settled into the one
nearest the hatch she had entered by. But no sooner had
the dukes entered the waiting room than she realized she
could never leave the alcove unheard, not in this dress.
She could hear every rasp and creak of clothing, and they
would hear hers. Now she understood Vladimer's smile.
The two men were quite free of Shadowborn ensorcellment, but her own ill judgment and Vladimer's craft left
her condemned to listen to their every word.

"Kalamay," Sachever Mycene said, and the other,
"Mycene."

She heard a creak of leather and a crack of knee joints
as the Duke of Mycene sat. Even his formal attire followed
the style for riding or some other vigorous pursuit. Yet for
all she knew Mycene was ambitious, she could not believe
him treasonous. Vladimer's envy—for surely a man crip-
pled at nineteen must envy a man so vigorous at sixty—
must be distorting his judgment.

Would that the archduke summoned them soon.

A footman arrived to reassure the visitors that the archduke would see them presently. They accepted the offer of
tea, but she heard cup light on saucer maybe twice, the barest gesture. Kalamay coughed, dryly. His cologne filtered
through to her, a faint scent of lemon and lavender that
she associated more with dowagers than dukes. She had
just decided that they were going to wait in silence when
Kalamay's husk of a voice said, "Have you heard from
Ferdenzil?"

"He telegraphed from Strumheller Station," Mycene
said. "He'd had word that the train arrived, but di Studier
had jumped it, likely going overland to Stranhorne Manor.
Ferdenzil planned to mount and pursue."

"Ferdenzil should be here now, not playing public agent."

"Oh, he's not playing," Mycene said, distinctly. "Trust
my son not to miss his chance, if it comes to him." There
was no doubt about what he implied. Telmaine's hands
fisted in the lace of her sleeves.

"Di Studier has been an affront to the Sole God and
society for decades." Telmaine set her teeth, though the
impulse thus contained was less one to speak out than to

snarl. Kalamay continued, quite deliberately. "Signing the order of succession nine years ago was a mistake; I counseled Sejanus so then."

"I suspect he knows that now," Mycene observed.

There was a brief silence, as actors pause after the opening of a play to note the temper of the house.

"Though di Studier's dangerous," Kalamay said. "Twenty-five years Shadowhunting."

"Twenty-five years vermin hunting," Mycene said, dismissively.

"Do you think he killed the woman?"

"No," Mycene said, without hesitation. "I'd lay my money it was the father of her bastard." The other man shifted, with a rustle of his austere vestments. Mycene continued. "I had my physician examine the body. She bore a child. Regardless of who goes to the shackling post for her death, I'll settle with the man responsible, for the insult he's dealt my son and my name."

"And what of that fancy of Vladimer's?"

"I think a commonplace explanation far more likely, don't you?"

"I presume you've not been able to get at her servants, yet."

"Not yet. But I might have something better. Di Studier has so far eluded arrest, but Ferdenzil has his traveling companion. He's Balthasar Hearne, the same one as attended Tercelle in childbed. I'm told that a woman often cries out the name of the father of her child at such a time. I have telegraphed ahead to Stranhorne to suggest that Ferdenzil send the man to me, if he cannot bring himself to question him himself."

Telmaine, trembling, gripped her hands in each other. If either tried to force a name out of Balthasar . . . Her magic had healed him physically, but his helplessness, suffering, and near death had left raw wounds in his spirit.

"Ah, yes, the husband of Telmaine Stott. Can you press him, given the family's interest?"

"The family don't much care for him," Mycene said. "It was a misalliance. Anaxamander Stott was a dying man when he gave consent."

"Ferdenzil had an interest there, didn't he?" Kalamay bestirred himself to say, not without malice. "Though all she's thrown are daughters, and only two of those, so there's little to regret there."

Telmaine's face burned. Matrons and dowagers discussed breeding prowess in terms every bit as frank, but to hear those two *men* . . .

"Are you going to wait out the mourning year?" Kalamay continued. "Your son's past thirty, already."

"For my own name's sake, I'll show the proper respect to the faithless . . ." Whatever epithet he would have applied, he withheld; Kalamay was renowned for not only his piety but his propriety. "It's as well it was Vladimer who brought the charge; enough men hate him to make loud with their disbelief."

"If Ferdenzil were to wed one of the other Amberley daughters, you might shorten the waiting. I doubt they'd plead finer sensibilities, and you'd keep the marriage portion."

"The sisters!" That provocation cracked the other man's mask of indifference. "The younger is as near to a whore as makes no difference, and the older is a plain-faced shrew with intellectual pretensions. The Amberleys will deliver the marriage portion anyway—or I *shall* ruin her name and theirs."

"As long as you can keep the details out of the broadsheets," Kalamay observed.

"Men come cheap who claim first allegiance to the truth. I can keep her name out of the broadsheets." He shifted in his chair with a creak of chair and breech leather. "Sejanus must have pressing business."

There was a brief, knowing silence. "The youngest Stott girl is due to be presented next year," Kalamay observed. "She seems healthy and biddable enough, though no great beauty, and a late bloomer. She's still growing."

Telmaine stiffened in dismay. They were talking of her youngest sister, Anarysinde, sixteen and aching to be presented to society and become eligible for courtship and marriage. A girl had only a little grace period before being relegated to hopeless spinsterhood, whereas Ferdenzil Mycene could still be a prime bachelor at thirty. Telmaine's brother the duke, Anarys's official guardian, would be as flattered at the thought of Anarys marrying the heir to one of the four major dukedoms as he had been appalled at Telmaine's refusal. To think of blithe, romantic Anarys . . .

Mycene said, irritably, "Height's not something to be let matter." He was, like his son, sensitive about his own height, Telmaine thought. "I hardly know the girl. Biddable, you say. I'd insist on assurance of her virtue. I'll have no repetition of this."

You arrogant—hypocritical—, Telmaine thought furiously, the thought broken off when Mycene said suddenly, "Do you smell smoke?" She stifled a gasp, and reached out with magic and fingers to quench a smoldering edge of wallpaper.

Kalamay said, "It's from the Rivermarch."

Telmaine pressed her fists to her temples, deeply shaken. She could not—she *would not*—let her temper be her undoing, no matter how provoked. But they *would not* barter her sister in this way.

At that moment, the door opened; a footman's voice advised the men that the archduke would see them. With a rustle of heavy fabrics and a scratching of leather, the two men rose. She thought, *They cannot go now; I need to know.* . . . Vladimer forgotten, her refusal forgotten, compelled by anger and fear for Balthasar and her sister, she reached out and swept her magic across Mycene's mind.

Telmaine

Several minutes after the men had gone, Kingsley came to free her and escort her back to Lord Vladimer. Her first impulse, and still her prevailing impulse, had been to *run* to her sister's house, snatch up her daughters, and carry them far away from this cursed city.

"Lady Telmaine?" said the apothecary, more than a simple question in his voice.

She pulled her wits together before Kingsley could start reaching his own conclusions as to why, for instance, Lord Vladimer should have set *her* to this task.

"They were talking about my *sister*," she said, her voice unsteady. "About a marriage between her and Ferdenzil Mycene." Even as she said that, she wondered if he could possibly understand her not wanting her sister married to a major ducal heir.

He surprised her. "That's no family for your sister to marry into, from what I hear. But," hesitantly warning, "but Lord V. won't care about that, likely."

"I will *make* him care."

He drew a shallow breath, but did not argue further. He preceded her toward the door, carefully opened it, and listened for the sound of passing footsteps. Impatient, she swept her mage sense before her, and pressed closer to his back. "Let's *go*."

They returned to Vladimer's private rooms, finding him sitting in the same chair, in almost the same posture. The cane had slipped down and now lay beside his foot. The untrained Kingsley missed Vladimer's prompting gesture toward it. Vladimer sighed and said, "Please hand me up my cane, and consider yourself dismissed." Kip lifted the cane, set it in Vladimer's hand, frowning. Vladimer sonned the frown and shook his head, sharply. "Later."

Kingsley nodded to Telmaine—another solecism—and left.

"Did you know," she said, before he could ask her, "did you even *suspect*—what they would talk about?"

"I admit," he said, "I had assumed it would be innocuous." He paused. "I assume from your manner that it was not so."

"Mycene thinks Balthasar might know the name of Tercelle's lover. He does not believe in the Shadowborn. We have to get Balthasar released from Ferdenzil Mycene's hands *before* Mycene tries to force a name out of him!"

"As I have said before," Vladimer said, "my options are limited."

They would see about that. "My sister's name was mooted, in the most degrading terms, as a possible bride to Ferdenzil Mycene."

"And you are not delighted at your sister's potential elevation," he said. "Tush, Lady Telmaine, such jealousy does not become you."

She fought down the heat of temper. "I *refused* Ferdenzil Mycene's suit myself, Lord Vladimer, of my own free will, and for good reason."

"Lady Telmaine, frankly I would be delighted if Ferdenzil Mycene were to marry your sister. Your family, illustrious as it is, possesses no assets—not blood, or land, or resources, or talents—that Sachevar Mycene does not already possess a surfeit of. The marriage to Tercelle Amberley, on the other hand—"

"The Amberleys are supplying him with munitions."

There was a beat. "And what," Vladimer said, pulling himself forward, "does he plan to do with those munitions?"

This was the moment—this was the moment to insist that he should do as she wanted, ensure Balthasar's immunity, her sister's freedom. "Lord Vladimer, I want—"

"No," he interrupted her, like a guillotine blade dropping. Her voice stalled, against her volition and determination. "Do not attempt to dictate to me. Either tell me or do not tell me, but should you withhold what you know, and harm comes to my brother, the state, or even myself, you will have me for an enemy, woman or no."

She recognized that she was finally meeting the Vladimer his enemies knew, devoid of the defensive shell of suspicion and mockery. This Vladimer had no need for either.

"They're going to destroy the Lightborn Mages' Tower," she whispered, with no more volition than had been involved in her falling silent a moment before.

"They're going to do *what*?"

She had finally shocked him, and his reaction left her as terrified as she had been when he had caught her as a child trespassing in his private study. She sat as mute as that child, expecting at any moment to be struck or shaken. But mastery seemed to lend him patience. "Tell me," he said quietly. "Tell me everything."

She said, "I—I—" and blurted sonn at him as she heard him struggle to his feet and retrieve a decanter and glass from the side cabinet. He uncorked the decanter with a clumsy one-handed motion, sluiced the drink into a glass, and, abandoning the cane on the cabinet top, limped to thrust the glass in front of her. "If I must get you drunk to loosen your tongue, I will, whatever the cost to your precious reputation."

The smell of brandy rasped her nose. She drank as he demanded, coughing at the strength of it. He gave the lie to his threat when he snatched the glass away unfinished, spilling brandy on her bodice. "Enough. I need you coherent." He limped back to his chair and, standing, drained the last of the brandy himself. Then he simply let the glass fall. To her befogged wonder, it bounced gently on the thick carpet, unbroken. *"Now,"* he rasped, lowering himself into the chair again, "something about what they said overset you sufficiently to forget your most vehement refusal."

"They were so vile," she whispered, "speaking of Balthasar and Anarysinde as though they were no more than—pawns—in their games."

"Ah," Vladimer said, tautly ironic. "They would have thought that when their conversation was reported to me, I would think it of no account. But you, it fatally provoked."

"The footman called them away. I *had* to know what Mycene meant to do about Balthasar, about Anarysinde. But he had already stopped thinking of them—he didn't care—he was thinking what he meant to say to the archduke, how to get certain streets evacuated that run close to the tower. He was wondering if it was worth the risk of arousing your suspicions, when those areas contained no one of real importance."

Vladimer made a soft sound in his throat, almost a growl. He had the reputation of holding the city in his mind as clearly as a game board. For herself, there was only one street and only one house adjacent to Lightborn territory that she cared about: Balthasar's narrow town house that stood back-to-back with Floria White Hand's. He had been born in that house, he had inherited it with his parents' deaths, and while she wished he would part with it, it was not in this way.

She gulped. "That was his clearest thought, that and satisfaction at ridding the state of such a threat. He—hates the notion that there should be a greater power than the state—than himself—that is not his. He—he *envies* mages their power." She shuddered at the memory of the envy, a voracious envy that would destroy what it could not have.

"How is it to be done?"

"I'm not—I don't know. It came to me mostly as impressions. Ishmael—" But she could not speak of Ishmael, having so utterly violated the principles he had tried to share with her. He had violated them himself once, in venturing to touch-read Tercelle Amberley, but that was for Florilinde.

"If you cannot give me sufficient information to work with," Vladimer said, dispassionately, "I will give you further opportunity to find out."

She gulped in air, but refusal would merely have been bluster.

He resumed, patiently, "Will they attempt it during the daytime or the nighttime?"

"I think—just before sunset. So that the Darkborn are not yet out in the streets."

"Ah, some vestige of social responsibility," Vladimer said, with his old mordant humor. "Or tactical polish, since the Lightborn will be at their most helpless if their walls are breached after dark. Though how, if they plan to do it by day, shall they accomplish it?"

"It has—something to do with Duke Kalamay's estate on the other side of the river."

"The munitions are stored there?"

"No, I think—I think the guns are there." That was not derived from any explicit thought, but from a cluster of impressions and sensations: a stone crypt, smelling of gunpowder and metal. And an anticipation of the first salvo that was almost sexual in quality, a stone-shattering challenge to the power of the mages.

"I did wonder," Vladimer said slowly, "how they proposed to approach the tower through Lightborn areas, and with mages inside."

"They think the Lightborn mages do not pay attention to—nonmageborn Darkborn. They look upon our machinery and munitions as children's toys."

"The mageborn in the tower, perhaps, but the Prince's Vigilance concerns itself with more secular threats. . . ."

She swallowed. "Mycene also has a contact amongst the Darkborn mages, who has been helping him."

"Ah," said Vladimer, slowly. His sonn swept over her, but what he was probing for, she did not know. "And the name?"

"He does not know it, though he has tried hard to find out."

"Darkborn," Vladimer said thoughtfully, "or Shadow-born; would he know the difference? Is there any Light-born collusion in this?"

"I don't know," she said, again in trepidation.

"But the munitions are in emplacements in Kalamay's grounds on the far side of the river, within reach by shell of the tower. They have the range, and angle and inclination of fire, and the precision machinery to control. They will have tested them elsewhere. . . . They will have to hit with the first salvos; with mages, they will have no second chance." He stopped suddenly, and shuddered. With fear or fever, she did not know.

"Lord Vladimer," she said, half rising.

"Let it be," he said harshly, gripping his right elbow.

"I wish I had not done it," she whispered. "I feel—foul."

"Such an attitude reeks of self-indulgence," he rasped. "Would you have us not learn of this conspiracy until the first salvo was fired?"

"But where—does one stop, Lord Vladimer?" she said, in anguish, knowing the futility of asking for consolation of this man, especially.

There was a silence, several heartbeats long. "One does not *stop*, Lady Telmaine," he said, in a much quieter voice. "I suppose being a bastard in a noble family is not unlike being a woman," he mused, ignoring her indrawn breath of affront. "Every aspiration beyond silence and obscurity is a threat. If I'd had sufficient cunning or good counsel, I should have played the half-wit—as a lady is obliged to play the light-wit—and saved myself much trial. Fortunately for me, Sejanus ignored his counselors and treated me as a brother and an ally instead of a shame and would-be usurper. In an-swer to your question, I will not *stop* while there is a threat to his standing and state remaining."

"I—can't do that," she whispered.

"Can't you? You already have abandoned conventional morals on behalf of your husband, your daughters, and Ishmael di Studier. The state and I are merely incidental beneficiaries. Love, Lady Telmaine, is not the tender emotion portrayed by the sentimental literature. Whether they speak its name or not, it brings people to dare, and do, what they would consider unthinkable. I suggest, my lady, that you visit your daughters, and remind yourself."

Telmaine

As the carriage made its sharp turn into the long side driveway to the ducal palace, Telmaine's unhappy mood deepened. In bitter rebellion at the use Vladimer had made of her, she had taken him at his word—let him manage his own safety—and had asked a carriage to be brought to drive her to her sister's house.

It had not been a relaxing visit, between Merivan's questions and her brother-in-law's inability to promise her that Balthasar's safety could be assured. "It's a dangerous game your husband's been drawn into," he said. "Even without the more—fantastic elements. He's traveling with a known fugitive, and you say it was willingly."

"*Lord Vladimer* asked him," she stressed.

"In the absence of a warrant," he said, "the arrest can be challenged. I warn you of two things: a warrant could be easily obtained, and it will not protect Balthasar from coming to immediate harm." He sat, tapping his lip lightly. "I will arrange for one of my representatives and two of my agents to proceed to the Borders first thing tomorrow." He smiled. "It may also prevent Balthasar's idealism from leading him into further jeopardy."

If the price of Bal's safety was that Theophile judged him naive and incapable of fending for himself, she would gladly pay that price. Outside the courtroom, Theophile judged with tolerance.

And the children ... she had thought a brief visit to their own home would cheer them up—it had certainly cheered her to review the earthshakingly ordinary matters of meals

and domestic supplies in preparation for their eventual return. She had thought the children could collect any little
treasures they wanted for their stay at Merivan's. But she
had not considered how the children would react to *leaving* again and how the crying and shrieking—Amerdale
had evidently adopted this new tactic from Merivan's next
youngest—would affect her shattered nerves. Bal would
be upset she had shouted at them. *She* was upset she had
shouted at them.

. . . *Curse* Vladimer, she thought, huddling in abject misery in the corner of the coach.

If she were a different woman, she would retire to her
room indisposed. Though if she were a different woman, she
would not have let them put her in this *impossible* position.
And she was not, she realized, going to have even a moment's
reprieve. Kingsley was skulking in the hall outside her room.
Oh, Sole God, what now? She unclenched her mage sense to
sweep it over the household, relieved to find Vladimer's and
the archduke's distinctive vitalities unchanged.

"Can't stay long," Kingsley said as soon as she closed the
door behind them. "Wanted to let you know there's maybe
trouble simmering. Lord V.'s none too well, and he and
Blondell had a knock-down-drag-out of an argument, there
in Lord V.'s bedroom. Staff said they've never had anything
like it before. Someone said they'd heard Blondell shouting
about 'treason,' and you can imagine how the whispers're
spreading. And there's gossip about what happened in the
summerhouse, come back with some of the summerhouse
staff; they're talking about ensorcellment. People are starting to repeat old gossip about Lord V., and about his influence on the archduke."

"Lord Vladimer," Telmaine said tartly, "is not overly concerned with gossip or reputation." His own or other people's.

"They've never had ensorcellment to cast against him,
m'lady," Kip said somberly. "Last time I crossed paths with
Blondell, he was wearing an ugly great amulet against
magic. Maybe that was the quarrel, over the rumors of
ensorcellment." He shook his head slightly, qualifying the
speculation. "When I come by more, I'll let you know."

Alone, she sat and nibbled the finger of her glove. An

amulet against magic—could there be such a thing? Was it a talisman itself, or a fake? She must avoid Casamir Blondell, either way. As for the argument, Vladimer could provoke even a follower of one of the contemplative disciplines. But gossip was a poison she understood. Even though Vladimer's seemed a reputation apart, the archduke must eventually take heed. Was this merely a whispering campaign, taking advantage of Vladimer's indisposition? Or could Mycene and Kalamay suspect that Vladimer knew about their guns? Was that the treason Blondell alluded to?

The memory of how she had learned of those gun emplacements brought her to her feet to shake off uncomfortable recollection. She wished she had been better able to use the information to force Vladimer to protect Balthasar and Anarys. Or even—should she have gone directly to Mycene? But how, then, might she plausibly have come by the knowledge? Vladimer was the only one she *could* tell, because he already knew. She could only wish to be better at blackmail, and that—she did not desire.

But if she *could not* depend upon Vladimer to protect Balthasar, her children, or even herself, if he did not judge it in his own interests, she must thank him for the lesson in realities, and make her own arrangements.

Resolute now, she called her maid to her, satisfied herself that her dress provided the best possible compromise between appropriateness and unobtrusiveness, and set out to follow the route Lord Vladimer had taken her to Floria White Hand's prison. Blessedly, she met no one on the way, and blessedly, too, the little interview room was empty. For a heartbeat she thought, from the silence, that Floria was gone—liberated, surrendered, or melted away as her lights failed. Then she brushed the familiar vitality and the familiar taint.

"Mistress Floria?" she hissed.

"Lady Telmaine," said the other, with distinct relief. "Is anyone with you?"

"No," she said. "I came—Balthasar would—he would expect me to ensure your well-being." Having more or less decided why she was here, she still did not know how she should explain it. "Are you well?"

She expected the woman to deride her social airs, but all Floria did was sigh. "Has the prince asked for my surrender?"

Telmaine's hands closed to fists in her lacy sleeves. She would have said she had no desire to know what the other woman was thinking, ever. Now she was appalled at the temptation to fling a defining question at her and sweep from her mind the true answer.

"Not yet," Telmaine said, instead. "But the sun has yet to rise."

Floria said, "Maybe you can help me. The skylight is closed, and the door to the outside courtyard locked behind me when I came in. The lights I have with me will need to be recharged, sometime in the next twenty-four hours."

She did not want to admit that she was here without Vladimer's knowledge or leave. "You would be best to speak to one of Lord Vladimer's servants."

There was a silence, in which Telmaine realized that Floria preferred not to reveal her vulnerability to anyone else.

"When do you expect Balthasar back?" Floria said.

She subdued the reflex to tell the woman that was none of her business; why else had she come here except to hope for an ally?

"Oh, spare me, Telmaine," Floria uncharacteristically snapped, misreading her silence. "You Darkborn think marriage means that you possess each other body and soul, and Bal's friendship with me is tantamount to infidelity. Balthasar has been my friend from the time he was barely old enough to lisp his first questions through the paper wall, long before he even met you."

"Balthasar's questions got him into this," Telmaine said bitterly, wifely loyalty or no.

"You mean Tercelle Amberley's children," Floria said, her voice moving toward the screen. "I had forgotten—did Strumheller find Florilinde? Is she safe? Bal sent me a letter, but I had only just received it before all this."

Letter, she thought—but it could not be the letter now in Vladimer's custody. That "I had forgotten" outraged her. "Florilinde is safe. A young colleague of Baron Strumheller's located her, and *I* got her back." Foolish, reckless, to claim so, she knew immediately, but she knew that the Lightborn woman regarded Darkborn women as willfully enfeebled and passive. She waited for Floria to say, in disbelief, "How?" but the Lightborn woman only said, "Good."

A silence, and then she heard Floria begin pacing. She bit her lip. She was aware how much Vladimer had withheld the first time they spoke, and had he dealt fairly with Telmaine, she would have continued to observe his wishes. But he had used her unconscionably, as bait and tether on the Broomes, and as spy upon the dukes. He might argue it was necessary, but she suspected he also believed that it was his *right* to use her so. He would use her, and Balthasar, and Ishmael, to shame and destruction if he chose.

Telmaine was as much a novice at spymasters' games as she was at magic, but she must find a way to protect herself and her own, even from Vladimer. And even if Floria was a prisoner now, and possibly even ensorcelled, she was also a veteran of the intrigues of the Lightborn court.

She said, slowly, "Mistress White Hand, the reason Balthasar is not here now is because two nights ago, Balthasar and Baron Strumheller saved Lord Vladimer from dying from an ensorcellment set"—what *was* the correct verb?—"by a Shadowborn mage."

"A *Shadowborn mage*?" Floria said, disbelieving.

"I was *there* when Baron Strumheller killed him." And had nearly vomited at the shattered skull and spilled brain matter, but she let that pass unsaid. "When we first faced him, he was wearing the form of Lysander Hearne."

"Balthasar's *brother*?"

How much had Balthasar confided to Floria about Lysander's cruelties? "I never knew Lysander Hearne, but the man I met resembled Balthasar, in appearance, at least." She had taken his voice for Balthasar's—or *one* of their voices for Balthasar's—when first she heard it. "But the dead *body* did not resemble Lysander in the least. Baron Strumheller said that he must be some kind of shape changer."

She could hear agitated breathing from beyond the paper wall. "What are you *saying*?"

"Maybe it was one of *them* who took your guise, and carried the talisman to the prince."

"That's impossible. The prince holds—*held* the contracts of a dozen mages of fifth rank and higher, to guard his person and secure his work. They sensed *nothing*. Telmaine, I swear, by your gods or mine, I would never have done anything to harm my prince. My family has been in the services of the princes for ten generations."

Two weeks ago, she would have accepted—even welcomed—Floria's guilt, assuming the worst of a functionary of the corrupt Lightborn court. But then, two weeks ago, she would not have imagined that a mage could be *falsely* charged, and that the gossip and headlines, however outrageous, might not contain some truth.

"Baron Strumheller was arrested on charges of murder and sorcery, our enemy's doing."

"Strumheller is just a first-rank mage, Telmaine. He kept Balthasar alive, yes, but as for sensing what the Temple Vigilance could not—"

"While he was in prison, a guard tried to poison him, and a prisoner tried to knife him. He barely escaped alive"—though his narrowest escape had nothing to do with Shadowborn. "Surely that suggests *something* to you. *That* is where Balthasar has gone, south to help him prepare the Borders for an invasion that Vladimer thinks is coming."

There was a brief silence, in which, no doubt, the Lightborn woman weighed up her own prejudices. "Telmaine," she said, with audible reluctance. "I think I know what the talisman was. A trinket box Balthasar gave me, years ago."

"Balthasar! How dare you—"

"Telmaine, for the Mother's sake—he was seven years old! It was taken from my house—I think by someone who came in through Balthasar's and cut through the paper wall. But I'm—it's possible *I myself* took it to the prince, though my memory—and I do not know why . . . ," she finished, forlornly.

Though she did not want to, she could not help but soften toward that tone. "This is what I know. . . ." Once again she recounted the events that had brought her here and Balthasar to an uncertain fate in the Borders, ascribing anything that she could not attribute to coincidence to Ishmael's magic. To her relief Floria was too preoccupied with the intent and powers of the Shadowborn to question her in detail about how she had survived the burning warehouse; unlike the superintendent and dukes, Floria would not defer to feminine delicacy of feeling.

"I've heard no rumor that there was magic behind the Rivermarch fire," Floria said. "And no mage should take it on—such an atrocity, even against Darkborn, would attract Temple retribution."

"Is it possible," Telmaine said slowly, ignoring that "even," "that only certain mages *can* sense Shadowborn magic?" Vladimer had essentially asked the same of the Broomes.

"A low-ranked mage like Strumheller able to sense what Temple mages cannot?" Floria said skeptically. "Though from what you say, he sounds underranked."

If nothing else, she should keep Floria from speculating about Ishmael's capabilities. "Maybe," Telmaine said, "maybe because Lightborn left the Borders so long ago, the—familiarity was lost. Your mages no longer know what Shadowborn magic *feels* like." Though she had needed no prior familiarity and no training to sense and be revolted by it.

"Telmaine," Floria said, "you do not understand very much about magic."

That, Telmaine thought, was too much. She rose, in a rustle of silks and lace. "No," she said, coolly. "I don't suppose I do."

"At the same time," Floria said, apparently unhearing, "it could explain the Temple's inaction. It could explain why—why nobody sensed the delivery of a talisman to the prince's quarters." Her voice quickening. "It could explain why no one sensed a shape-shifter, if it were a shape-shifter, or an ensorcellment if it were—Mother of All," Floria breathed. "It *fits*. It fits better than any other explanation I've been able to think of. Telmaine, is there notepaper on your side? If I write a letter, will you see it reaches its destination?"

The unfamiliar verb, "see," distracted her briefly. "It can't be an hour to sunrise," she protested.

"Couriers come and go between the houses of state at all hours of day and night. You have only to find the daylight postbag and get the letter slipped in. It will only be readable to my—to Lightborn."

She thought rebelliously that she had not come here to make herself Floria's tool instead of Vladimer's, but for her own purposes and for Balthasar's sake. "He loves you," she blurted, a challenge she had been longing to fling at the other woman for years. "Balthasar loves you."

Floria did not deny it, saying impatiently, "And I love him, Telmaine, but that does not *change* anything in your and his relationship. I wish you understood that."

She wished she understood it as Floria did, because for her it mattered, painfully so. "I came to ask you to help me to protect him. Duke Mycene—" But she could *not* tell Floria what she feared from that quarter, because she could *not* tell Floria how she had learned it. "Ferdenzil Mycene—Tercelle Amberley's betrothed—has Balthasar prisoner, because Balthasar was traveling in Ishmael's—Baron Strumheller's—company. I'm frightened for Bal. We have to find out who the Shadowborn are, what they intend, before Balthasar—or our children"—or, sweet Imogene, Ishmael himself—"get further hurt."

"I do understand," Floria said, sounding beleaguered. "My *own* life hangs on this, too. Let me write the letter."

"Who is it to?" Telmaine said, in a tone she used to children and servants, one that implied no yielding in the question.

"To a friend of mine—the mage I spoke of."

Telmaine trapped the question, *Is he your lover?* between her teeth. Aside from the impropriety—at least asked of another Darkborn—the answer was truly none of her business. She collected some paper—trying not to think of singed edges and smoke—and slipped it into the *passe-muraille* that served as a conduit for more than words between the two rooms. She sat tensely listening to the faint scratching of nib on page. Occasionally, Floria asked for confirmation or clarification of a detail; she had Balthasar's gift for listening well. Eventually the scratching ceased, and Telmaine could hear her blowing softly to dry the last of

the ink. Balthasar's exercise of writing with ink had fascinated their children, and his closing ritual of blowing on the
apparently unmarked sheet of paper had always set them
giggling.

She heard Floria open and close the small door. "I've
addressed it," she said. "Thank you, Telmaine."

There seemed not much more to be said, Telmaine
thought with relief, going forward to retrieve the letter, a
smooth folded sheet quite blank to her fingers. She bade
the woman good night, realizing the infelicity even as she
said it.

"Telmaine, I know you'll think this presumptuous of me,
but I'm surprised—at the courage and initiative you are
showing through this. Bal always said there was more to
you than the society lady."

"You're right," Telmaine said, "it is presumptuous,
but—a lady learns to take compliments as intended.
Good—day, Mistress Floria." She slipped into the vestibule, feeling oddly satisfied. Admiration from a rival was
always gratifying. She tucked Floria's letter carefully up
her sleeve before stepping out into the corridor. Kingsley
would surely be able to find out where the daylight post
was collected, and she would simply tell him—ah!—that
Lord Vladimer had finally released her husband's letters,
and she had chosen to send this one on.

She had taken the first measured strides toward the corner—*a lady, taking a walk*—when around the corner and
straight into her came Casamir Blondell. Her skirts and his
quilted jacket cushioned the impact, but they sprang apart
with guilty vigor. Her sonn caught his dismay; she was
certain his did hers. Their apologies washed against each
other, *all my fault*, *needed a walk*, *not paying attention*. She
checked herself first; of course it was proper that he should
apologize to her. But what was *he* doing here? Surrepti-
tiously, she probed for the letter in her sleeve, confirming
it hidden.

"Dear me," she said, "I thought this part of the palace
was less used. I might as well take my constitutional in
Bolingbroke concourse."

He bowed to her, submitting to her rebuke. "Perhaps,"

he said, a little brusquely, "I might escort m'lady back to her rooms."

"Of course," she said, graciously; what else could she do, aside from wonder how to prevent him from reporting this encounter to Vladimer? Working in Lord Vladimer's service, Blondell had surely met bribes far beyond her purse, and refused those of any significance; Vladimer would not have tolerated him otherwise. Should she appeal to his sympathies? But how, without stirring his suspicions? She would simply have to hope that her air of innocence, and his reported quarrel with Lord Vladimer, would be enough for this to pass unremarked.

Unless *he* knew about Floria White Hand, and was appalled to find Telmaine so close? Then he would be thinking as hard as she, wondering how he might find out what she knew and why she was here, without arousing *her* suspicions. If so, he had the sympathy of a fellow sufferer.

At least she now knew that Blondell's amulet was nothing to fear, since she had been as close to it as a decent woman could come. It was a medallion at least four inches across, solid metal with an ornate knotted border and with several large symbols cast in relief upon the flat face. Whatever they were, neither they nor the metal itself had any potency that she could sense, either to detect or to repel her.

So all she need do now was divest herself of Floria White Hand's letter in the direction of the postbag, and polish a plausible account of their conversation for Vladimer, in case. She could, she thought, tell mostly the truth. She would omit only the letter.

Six

Fejelis

"...What?" Fejelis greeted his reflection in the mirror. "Not dead yet?"

"Not funny yet, either," Tam said sourly, propping himself in the open doorway to Fejelis's dressing room.

Fejelis lifted the prince's caul from its stand, his smile falling away. Its stiff supporting mesh still contained the shape of his father's skull. A few hairs, the color of winter grass, quivered in the gem-encrusted rim. "I'll need to get this fitted," he said quietly, turning it in his hands to study the arcs and swirls of gold filigree and cobalt blue and indigo stones. The largest gems had been sold first, the gold wire last, in his great-grandfather's time; the caul was, in short, a fake.

Its fit was close, closer than he had expected, just a little pressure on the temples, a little looseness on the forehead, his skull slightly broader than his father's. The face that stared back at him, framed in gilt wire and blue glass, had a likeness disconcerting even in his own eyes.

Tam, by his huffed-out breath, also saw it.

"...Have you anything to report?" Fejelis said.

"There were no attempts on the lights overnight," Tam said.

"And Mistress White Hand?"

"At the archducal palace." A fleeting hesitation. "Quite safe."

"...They'll say her flight implies her guilt," Fejelis noted.

". . . But I didn't like the report I had of Captain Beaudry's actions." He lifted off the caul and set it aside, binding his hair back into a tight knot at the nape of his neck.

"Will you ask for her surrender?"

". . . I have no choice," Fejelis said. ". . . The manner of my father's death is too evocative. I think I shall leave it a few hours yet, see what transpires."

Over a red vest, he drew on a red jacket with stiff breast panels and sheer sides and sleeves, embroidered with swirls in deep blue stitches and blue semiprecious stones. It was merely the latest of a succession of princely mourning jackets passed down the generations. He returned the caul to his head, checked its fit with a glance, and turned quickly away from the mirror.

". . . Why is it, do you suppose, that the Darkborn do not practice deposition, yet are not burdened by senile and incompetent rulers?"

Without answering, the mage handed him the sash. He tied it around his waist, set the knot, and bloused the fabric. Stretched and twisted to ensure he could move freely, and turned to face Tam. ". . . Shall I pass?"

He watched the mage consider, and reject, a cautionary word. "Yes."

". . . Then I propose we venture forth. If we wait for them to summon the courage to knock, we shall get no breakfast."

"I am glad your terms of employ include breakfast."

Fejelis gave him a scimitar smile. ". . . You've never eaten breakfast with my family."

His father's intimate dining room was a solarium on the southeast corner of the palace. Two long galleries subtended on two sides a rooftop garden. A shallow pool was its centerpiece, and the base of the pool formed a skylight to the prince's private study on the floor below. Even on a dull winter's morning the light was restorative.

This morning a wall of cloud, silver-limned, stood off the horizon on the east, sparing them too much glory. The faces of his seated family—families—turned, as one, toward him, giving him a reflex twinge of expected retribution. But whatever the other penalties of his position, being prince meant he would never be late again. *Don't let it go to your head*, his father's voice chided.

As one, they stood to acknowledge him, red-clad northerners on one side facing drab-hued, red-ribboned southerners on the other. Mother, brother, sister; mother's sister, brother, and cousins. Father's cousins. The fifteen people most likely to have killed his father and most likely to kill him.

Not a job for the fainthearted, as his father had once said.

He heard a sound like a suppressed sob from Liliyen's direction. While Orlanjis had cultivated charm and a reputation for blithe-spiritedness, and Fejelis had cultivated caution and a reputation for dullness, she had cultivated high sensitivity and a reputation for flightiness and fragility. Making her probably the smartest and toughest of them all, as Orlanjis was the most melancholy and he, the least cautious.

Of his other sister, Perrin, no one spoke at all.

Orlanjis looked harrowed and sleepless. Which would make Fejelis's opening sally a simple one. He would offer him the vacant suite on the southwest corner on the prince's floor, a suite he knew Orlanjis coveted for the sunlight and the space to cultivate his desert gardens. It had stood empty too long. Moving would ease Orlanjis's nerves and remove him from the immediate vicinity of Helenja's coterie. Give him space to know his own mind, away from the southerners who had influenced him for so long. Their satisfaction over Isidore's death would surely grate on Orlanjis, given the obscene nature of that death.

Helenja was staring at him, flat-eyed, certainly seeing the resemblance to her dead consort. She, too, looked as though she had not enjoyed an easy night's sleep, though she still wore no more than red ribbons to sketch mourning. What she truly felt for Isidore's passing he doubted she would ever allow him to know.

Which, he thought, had a certain justice in it, because he had no intention of letting her know what *he* felt. He and his father had hidden the closeness of their relationship as carefully as any pair of unfaithful partners.

Though Helenja, too, he would court, if he could. She

was no longer the willful young woman who had seen her
marriage as a conquest and her consort as a temporary
inconvenience, or the mother who had tried to press her
silver-eyed son into the mold of a southern prince. She, and
her entourage, had learned subtlety as well as survival over
the years.

And how is this good? he all but heard Tam comment.

On the northerner side of his table, facing Helenja, sat
his cousin, son of Benedict's younger brother. Of Isidore's
four brothers, none had survived him, which left Prasav
and his daughter as Fejelis's principal rivals, after Orlanjis. Prasav's eyes, a pale hazel gray like a tarnished mirror,
were unreadable as he took in Tam by Fejelis's side. Fejelis remembered then that Prasav was lord of much of the
northern and western provinces, including the poor mountain region that had bred Tam. Prasav's shrewd economies
had stemmed the loss of wealth, but he had done little to
ameliorate conditions in the struggling provinces. Fejelis
regretted that he had not thought to acknowledge Tam's
feelings in this; he would later.

Prasav bowed slightly toward Fejelis. His slight build
had come from Fejelis's grandmother and he lacked Fejelis's height, but he also had her handsomeness, and his
profile would grace a new-minted coin more finely than
Fejelis's. He wore full mourning crimson and a caul set
with emerald and jade—the caul of the northern lords who
had once styled themselves princes—with his silvering hair
finely braided and pulled back beneath it. *Those* stones
were likely genuine.

By his side, facing Orlanjis, sat his eldest daughter and
heir, Ember, a decade Fejelis's senior. She swept the gathering with depthless brown eyes, and met Fejelis's nod of
greeting with one that managed to be both sympathetic
with his hopes for this breakfast and amused at his folly.
She was an immensely accomplished woman, possibly the
most capable of their generation. Fejelis would not have
given an artisan's day wage for Prasav's long survival past
his first serious lapse in trade or politics.

As Isidore had more than once remarked, he could receive no better education in politics or strategy than surviv-

ing his family, and Fejelis supposed—he was sure—it was a fatal ambition to wish for more than survival. But how he wanted to harness Helenja's contacts and determination, Orlanjis's imagination, Prasav's mastery of economics, Ember's elegant strategy, in restoring earthborn independence, wealth, and pride.

And if they were not constantly having to guard against one another, a plethora of expensive mage's contracts—like the very one he had signed with Tam—could be dispensed with.

Fejelis took his place at the head of the table, Helenja to his right. Tam, prompted by a subtle gesture, moved to his left. The mage regarded the cutlery dubiously. *Peasant*, Fejelis thought, amused, though *he* was hardly in a position to judge. True southerners ate with their fingers. It was difficult to poison fingers.

He considered the dishes set before him, each one with its glass cover. He selected one, and pointed it out; the servant, after a moment's hesitation, spooned a little onto Tam's empty plate. With a flicker of his fingers, Fejelis indicated the correct fork. The mage took a small, dubious bite. Though Fejelis had selected one of the moderately spiced dishes, he could still see the perspiration moistening Tam's upper lip.

"Let's—try this another way," Tam said, a breach of the etiquette that dictated silence for the first courses. He touched the lid of first one dish, then another, almost as a priestess of the Mother of All Things would bless the four sacred chalices at the midsummer ceremonials. He stood up to reach those dishes that were farther away. The ones that were beyond reach he floated toward him, held lightly, and set back in place. Fejelis could tell that he was expending effort, moving inert matter, though he doubted anyone else could except for the four mages of the Temple Vigilance, standing guard along the walls. He did not look in their direction, but simply settled back and watched the show. Using magic to move objects was not a low-rank skill. Which was probably Tam's point.

Tam set the last dish into place, and sat collectedly down. "You need to check the plates and the cutlery as well,"

Fejelis murmured. Tam passed his hands lightly over Fejelis's setting and his own and nodded.

Fejelis would dearly like to open his hands and bid them all eat without regard for precedence, but Tam had already done custom enough mischief. Fejelis indicated his selection, waited as the servant spooned out the brightly hued grains and vegetables. His mother tapped lightly on her plate with a spoon, recalling the attention of her own mage, who had been watching Tam's performance with an ambiguous expression. Prasav gestured to his own food taster, a gaunt individual who looked like no food had agreed with him for five decades. No mage, but possessor of an asset like Floria's. Orlanjis obediently waited for his mother to be done, while Liliyen, with a giggle, gestured imperiously with a ringed finger to her own server, her veiled glance bent on Tam. Fejelis sincerely hoped this was not the blazing up of one of Lili's infamous infatuations. Ember commented with a raised brow, her hands still on her lap. Each member of the breakfast table had him- or herself served in turn, as protocol decreed. Tam requested plain rice and vegetables. Fejelis warned him off an innocuous-looking white sauce and watched Ember suppress a smile.

The sun broke above the bank of cloud, gloriously. It cost Fejelis his only moment of discomposure, remembering how his father's head would turn at such moments. *He loved the sun—there could be no death more cruel.* His eyes, he knew, were glistening. Liliyen chose that moment to glance up, to see, and to break into muffled sobs, drawing the attention of the entire table to her. *Thank you, little sister.*

The savory was cleared away, the sweet pastries brought out, each carried within reach of Tam before being set down. Custom allowed conversation now, though no one could speak before the reigning prince.

Strange how a pastry could dry between one mouthful and the next. Rather than sip, he carefully chewed and swallowed. ". . . I don't think you know Magister Tammorn," he said, choosing informality. "The final contract will be available by this afternoon." Their brightnesses received immediate notice of any published contracts from the Mages' Temple, proving, as his father had observed, how magic could be a boon to bureaucracy.

"Where is Mistress White Hand?" said one of his more distant northern cousins, who Fejelis noted had eaten only what Tam and Fejelis had.

". . . Mistress White Hand is currently absent from the palace. Magister Tammorn kindly agreed to substitute."

"What is his rank?" said his consort. She was a notorious miser who would surely be reckoning the costs.

". . . Magister Tammorn is considered fifth-rank."

"I am told," Prasav said, "that he is underranked, because of problems with discipline."

That flush on Tam's face was surely more than spice. He should know the custom of treating contracted mages, vigilants, and servants as though they were not present. Children, too, until the age of four. Orlanjis had reacted with screaming tantrums. Fejelis had tested the bounds of invisibility with mischief, as had Perrin.

". . . I am satisfied," Fejelis said, "that Magister Tammorn is fully qualified for his contracted tasks."

"And these are?" Ember said, with a cool glance at Tam. "There was no report of a contract in the digest."

". . . I expect that the draft will be waiting for me on my desk. . . . To determine who, and what, killed the prince, and to stand in, for the moment, for Mistress White Hand."

"Yes, and what *has* become of Mistress Floria?" Helenja said, her voice cutting across his.

". . . I requested that she be detained."

He let them wait until he had taken a bite of a small almond square, laid it down, and continued. ". . . There was a question about her behavior on the night the prince died."

"I heard she has run to the Darkborn," Ember said.

". . . There appear to have been some irregularities in the behavior of the arresting party—shots were fired—and she appears to have decided she was safer in the hands of the Darkborn than her colleagues." His eyes briefly held his mother's. He had no proof, and doubted he ever would, that the guard captain had been paid or otherwise given incentive to shoot rather than arrest Floria.

Helenja's hatred of Floria had a foundation that her son found both ironic and hypocritical. Southern custom emphasized the sharing of meals between intimates. But for their entire life together, the prince had shared his dishes first with another woman, rather than his consort, as a precaution against her, and her relatives', attempt to murder him.

Oh, Mother's Milk, Fejelis thought, half despairing. After this morning, there'd be those in the southern contingent who would style himself and Tam lovers, for the purpose of slander if not out of conviction.

"And will you request her surrender?" Helenja said.

Fejelis simply nodded. He had, as he had said to Tam, no choice. But he would have to do so in a way that did not offend the Darkborn.

"You would be wise to," his mother advised him. "You do not wish to be seen to be obstructing the search for those responsible for your father's unrighteous deposition."

Fejelis tilted his head toward his mother, acknowledging both point and hit.

"Has he anything to report?" Prasav asked, with a bare twitch of the head toward Tam.

". . . Nothing that I am prepared to share."

"Ah, then I shall withhold my congratulations"—this straight across the table to Helenja—"until another time."

The dowager consort's broad face set. "Believe me, Prasav, you will get no congratulations from me. I know you have coveted the princedom for years."

On the far side of Helenja, Orlanjis abruptly pushed his chair away from the table. "Fejelis—Prince Fejelis—may I be excused? I don't . . . feel very well." He stood bent over, hands kneading his stomach. Fejelis forced his clenched hands to relax on the arms of his chair as the entire southern contingent came to their feet as one and carried their distressed favorite out.

All eyes, except Prasav's and Ember's, turned to the half-eaten iced tart on Orlanjis's plate, and then to Tam. Who placidly reached for another tart himself. Fejelis swallowed the taste of ripe peach and tilted his chin down to conceal his pulse from Prasav's keen eye. Much as he wished to follow Tam's example, he could not, but he gave a short nod, as though drawing his own meaning from the mage's calm, and pulled a deep draft from his glass of lemon water.

Ember's raised eyebrow said, as surely as if she had spoken aloud, *Surely you don't believe that display.*

Prasav turned to the lesser family members on his right, and Fejelis realized he was about to dismiss them. He rapped his plate sharply with his knife, reminding them all whose table this was. He had a question for Prasav about a boundary dispute between himself and a Darkborn duke, which neither was willing to pass through the low-status Intercalatory Council. He and Isidore had discussed using such disputes as leverage to elevate the status of the Darkborn-Lightborn interface.

Admittedly it made for breakfast conversation as dry as the pastry, but he kept herding the conversation in the direction he wanted it to go. When he allowed the family to excuse themselves, Prasav made no attempt to stay behind. Fejelis had no doubt he would receive full measure of his cousin's advice and opinions later. But at least the tales carried to Helenja would not include confidences over breakfast.

". . . So do I fire my food taster, or curse the brat for a flawless performance?" he muttered to Tam, once his guests were gone. He was fairly sure which one, but he knew his voice was too brittle; he could still taste peach.

Tam put a hand on his shoulder and leaned close. "It wasn't poison. Not in anything *he* ate."

The slight emphasis on the pronoun made Fejelis look sharply at him. ". . . I may be maligning Orlanjis," he admitted. "Ever since he was little, he's had stomach pains when he's upset. But Mother of All, Tam, his *timing*."

Tam's fingertip traced a small circle in the air, signing that he had closed off their conversation. "There was something in the white sauce."

". . . The white sauce? Orlanjis didn't touch it. Only Mother and . . ." He stopped. The implications were unavoidable. "Do you know what it was?"

Tam gave him a dry look. "Fejelis, I've studied the underlying structures beneath assets like Mistress Floria's, but I haven't got eighteen years of experience." He tugged his red cuff. "Floria was scolding me for letting Juli chew on this, only yesterday. But there was something there inimical to life. I neutralized it, but I'd thought by tasting it I could have learned more."

Fejelis snorted. ". . . Trust me, with that sauce, you wouldn't have. When your vision starts to blur, it's not your eyes watering but your eyeballs cooking. . . . Are you sure it's not just the spice you sensed? Mistress Floria can have difficulty telling the difference."

"I'm pretty sure."

". . . Curse it," Fejelis said. There'd been little chance of such a poisoning succeeding, at this table, but . . . "And so it begins."

Fejelis

"And lastly," said the master of protocol, "there is the question of the prince's name."

Fejelis rubbed his forehead, wondering how, over the course of a morning, the caul could have shrunk so.

He had known this one was coming, of course. As prince, he was now entitled to choose whether to follow the naming conventions of his father's people or his mother's people, or select his own. It was a choice every bit as fraught as that long-ago haircut.

". . . I think," he said, "that since this has come on me suddenly, I must take time to consider." There was no harm, he thought, in making that point, though he was already decided to keep his father's family name, Grey Rapids. As his father had once dryly remarked, one of the side benefits of having the southerners as enemies was that the northerners sought to differentiate themselves by being exceptionally well behaved.

The white sauce at breakfast, alas, had given the lie to that.

"Of course, Prince Fejelis," the master of protocol murmured, gathering together his documents.

Fejelis let him dismiss himself. As his father had also observed, the prince might rule the land, but the staff ruled the palace, and woe betide the brightness who disrupted their routine. He opened his notebook, and checked off half a dozen items dispensed with over the last fifteen minutes, and contemplated the thirty added.

He glanced up at the skylight, where fish shadows slowly turned against the sky, and out toward the waiting room. The glazed wall was covered by a translucent drape, but he could still see the shifting mass of red outside.

The red, interestingly, seemed to be parting. To his side he could hear the small chink of the vigilants' chain armor as they came to point. The door opened, and the secretary came in, looking harassed and slightly pale against his red. "Prince Fejelis, some representatives of the Temple are here to see you."

". . . Show them in," Fejelis said, by which time the mages were in the doorway of greater privilege. None of them he knew, a man and two women, all wearing the formal robes and chains of their rank. The two most senior mages under palace contract followed. Servants carrying chairs were already filing through. Fejelis closed his mouth, rather than give any further redundant directions. The three Temple mages deployed themselves, facing him. The two vigilant mages moved off, carefully indicating allegiance to their contract, or at least neutrality.

Fejelis waited. With mages, ordinary protocol did not apply. Furthermore, he had no idea of their names. He wished Tam were here.

Or perhaps not, because the woman in the center gestured, and the second woman stood up to lay a sheet on Fejelis's desk: the contract that he and Tam had negotiated the previous night.

". . . Is it not in order?" Fejelis said.

The woman in the center gazed steadily back at him with a northerner's pale eyes. Unlike the other two, who were handsome to an unsettling degree, she was broad-faced, broad-nosed, and broad-lipped, and around his mother's age. Which in a higher-ranked mage meant she could be anywhere from eighteen years old and fed up of looking so cursed *young*—with which he could empathize—to more than a hundred and making no apologies. Her chains suggested fifth-rank, though her authoritative air suggested otherwise.

"Surely you are aware that the Temple is conducting its own investigation."

". . . I have no doubt," Fejelis said.

"And that the findings would be made available to you."

". . . Thank you."

"Is that not satisfactory?"

". . . It is quite satisfactory," Fejelis said. ". . . It is not sufficient."

By the ripple in her lips, she had very nearly snapped, *Explain.*

". . . My father's death represents a—singular, as far as I can tell—failure in the Vigilance."

"All men die," the mage said—not entirely comfortably.

". . . But not by magic. We contract with mages to protect ourselves. The last prince to have died by magic was, what, nearly two hundred years ago, and that was only after due warning by the Temple that his contracts had been canceled. My father had no such warning."

He held his breath. He was convinced that nothing *he* had done even approached that long-dead prince's outrages against the Temple, but it was quite possible that he had offended them all unwittingly.

"Our objection," she said, "is to the individual contracted. You are surely aware, Prince, that he was born outside the lineages." Fejelis simply nodded. "He came late to training. And in the past his standing has been in question."

". . . In what way?"

"He was disciplined for practicing outside the compact."

He did not blink. Did not look at the mages vigilant. Did not, he believed, reveal in any way that he knew exactly what she meant. They could probably feel the strain in his vitality, but he had no choice but to trust that the mages vigilant would fulfill their contract and guard him against magical intrusion.

". . . He is in good standing now, is he not?" he said, after a suitable pause. "Magistra—" She tendered no name in response to his suggestive hesitation. ". . . Magistra, please reassure the high masters that I have no doubts about the integrity of the Temple. But I prefer to leave the contract with Magister Tammorn in place. I look for a quick resolution and so will use all the resources I can command."

She did not rise. "A number of contracts arranged with your father will need to be renewed."

Essential contracts, like those of the mages vigilant, were inheritable, and he was glad at the moment they were, and not adding to his growing list. Of the others, he had a feeling the price had just gone up. ". . . Magistra," he said.

The man said, "If I were you, I would ask Magister Tammorn what he stole from your father's room yesterday."

Fejelis couldn't quite conceal his surprise. "What do you mean, stole?"

One of the mages vigilant stepped forward, at no prompt Fejelis could see. She was a slight, fair-haired woman with a high arched nose and prominent cheekbones, a face idiosyncratically interesting rather than beautiful. "I was one of those called to inspect your father's room. I noticed a small box of Darkborn design and workmanship. After Tammorn left, the box was no longer there."

While Tammorn's checkered career included petty larceny, this seemed an oddly trivial accusation. And why would the mages vigilant be paying attention to the ornaments in the prince's room? ". . . A talisman," Fejelis answered himself, ruminatively. "Did you find one?"

There was a silence of several beats. Fejelis said, ". . . I take that as a no."

Nobody contradicted him. ". . . Thank you," he said, mildly. "Be assured I will turn my attention to the renewal of contracts as soon as I can."

They stood with a disconcerting synchrony. "Your sister sends her best wishes," the woman said. He blinked at her, taken aback. She smiled, and the three turned and went out, the mages vigilant following them.

The secretary, experienced in court matters, conducted them out and closed the doors behind them, giving Fejelis a momentary respite. He used it to put his cauled head in his hands, rubbing his forehead to ease the ache.

Perrin—or whatever her name was now—would be twenty. She had been ten when the mages vigilant detected emergent magic in her. The compact dictated that no mage could hold secular rank, much less that of heir. By the time Fejelis had been able to leave his rooms after the poisoning, she was gone, her name barely mentioned. As if she herself had been part of the conspiracy. That was the greatest of cruelties.

For nearly ten years, he had schooled himself to forget he had another sister. And now, in violation of custom if not law, *Your sister sends her best wishes*.

Mother of All Things Born, what scheme was the *Temple* engaged in?

Tammorn

In his distraction, Tam sensed Lukfer's visitors only almost at Lukfer's door. By then there was no effacing himself. Lukfer said, <Come in, Tam, and meet my guests.>

He opened the door not on painful shadow but on sunlight. The curtains had been flung wide. The door to the seldom-used balcony stood open, and Lukfer was lounging against the balustrade, talking to two other mages. His magic eddied and rippled around the room, twitching the curtains and rattling the contents of cabinet drawers. It prodded and nudged Tam toward the balcony, playfully.

"Ah, Tam," Lukfer said, with a wave of a hand that was empty of any glass. "I believe you know Magister Pardel, and I believe you have met Magistra Viola, in her former life. Pardel, Viola, Magister Tammorn, who I believe needs no introduction."

Magistra Viola returned his stare with gray eyes as pale and unrevealing of her thoughts as mirrors. Her warm sandy hair was close-woven in an ornate southern style. She had the oval face, broad cheekbones, and brow of the young prince consort Helenja, but her nose and mouth were those of her father and the elder of her brothers. She had their height, too. Her ankle-length overjacket, her sleeveless shirt and full skirts, all were made of cloth enspelled to pass light in one direction only, and all were red as blood. On the notch at the base of her throat rested the twin of the pendant Fejelis wore, except that the stone was colorless, not blue.

"Magister Tam," Fejelis's elder sister murmured.

From his brief visits to the palace before Fejelis's poisoning, he remembered Perrin as a leggy hoyden of a child, the then favorite of Helenja's circle. By the time he returned from banishment, she was long gone into her own exile, as far away from court as the Temple could place her.

What else he knew of her was through Fejelis's very occasional mention.

Magister Pardel he also knew. A broad, black-haired, dark-skinned man, with something of the gait, still, of the young sailor he had been when his magic unexpectedly manifested. Shrewd and adaptable, he was the highest ranked of all sports within the Temple, both magically and materially successful. Almost the last person Tam would expect to find chatting on the balcony with Lukfer.

"So," Pardel said, with a glance at Viola, "a contract with the prince. That'll set them by their ears."

Viola caught and held Tam's eyes, drawing aside the collar of her jacket to show the chains of rank around her neck. "I am ranked and of age," she said, in a sweet, light voice. "I am no longer obliged to pretend that I had no life before the Temple."

Second-rank, only. Gossip had told him her magic had proved weak, cruelly so to have cost her her earthborn rank. He looked at her silver eyes and wondered what she felt about that.

"How is Jay?"

The name startled him into a twitch. A logical nickname amongst children, he told himself sternly. "He's holding up well," he said.

"Do you think he'd like to see me?" she said.

"I think he might," he said, though cautiously.

"Would you be prepared to arrange it?"

He made a sound intended to be neither agreement nor rejection. She did not press further, but engaged him in conversation around the doings and politics within the Temple that deftly trod away from matters of legitimacy and history. He would have enjoyed it but for wondering what Lukfer, and she, and Pardel, were all about.

"An interesting young woman," Lukfer noted after the two were well gone, "who has not forgotten that, but for a chance gift of fate, she might have been princess herself."

Tam gave him a sharp look—Lukfer's fluctuating magic could be intrusive in more than physical ways, though Pardel would have shielded the weaker mage. Lukfer merely raised a brow, inviting him to voice his thoughts.

"Why were they here? Did you invite them?"

"I did. I'm afraid, my young thief, that your reversion to your former habits did not go entirely unnoticed."

"The box—" And then he realized that he had no more sense of that noxious talisman.

Lukfer followed the turn of his head. "I decided," the older mage said, "partly for my edification, and partly as a precaution, to annul the ensorcellment."

"Dear Mother of All," Tam breathed at the thought of the intimacy that that implied. Little wonder Lukfer was out in the sunshine, and looked, now he paid more attention, a little sickly.

"It was not," Lukfer said, "a pleasant experience, but very educational. Now my guests have gone, I would quite like a glass of that fine Isles wine—the decanter is standing out. Pour a glass for yourself, if you would."

Given his precarious control, Lukfer rarely indulged. Nor did Tam: beer and spirits had played too large a part in the disasters of his youth. He poured—by hand, not magic—and carried the glasses back onto the balcony.

"So somebody noticed I had taken the box," he said. "How much difficulty is that likely to cause? Was that why you—?" He gestured toward the interior and the quenched box.

Lukfer held the wineglass lightly, contemplating the golden depths. "Aside from its general unpleasantness, I decided I would rather not have *my* lights go out at some unpredictable moment." His eyes lifted. "You think I did it to remove evidence?"

"I hope," Tam said slowly, "that wasn't the reason."

"I cannot say it was not," the other mage said.

Tam tamped down his temper. Getting himself tossed off the balcony by Lukfer's stirred-up magic would attract attention. "I had breakfast with Fejelis and his relatives— both sides. There was poison in one of the sauces—the heavily spiced ones that only the southerners would eat— and what was probably a staged episode on the part of Orlanjis. The attempt wasn't likely to have killed anyone, given the concentration of magic at the table, but I annulled it. I tried tasting it to see if I could learn more, but Fejelis stopped me out of a care for my palate."

Lukfer grunted. "Confused the one responsible no end, no doubt."

Tam rubbed his forehead, squinting in the late-afternoon sunlight. "Fejelis believes the solution is in identifying his father's assassin. I don't think he recognizes how much of the stability he was used to was because his father had ruled so well for so long. He won't get it back just by implicating the responsible faction. He is so young, Lukfer. Idealistic and fatalistic. Convinced he's invulnerable and equally convinced he will die young. And either way, bent on taking the most appalling risks."

He began to pace. "Last night I sensed more Shadowborn magic. I placed it in the archduke's palace on the Darkborn side. The worker was strong, but not particularly skillful. I wanted to examine the box again, to see if I could tell if it was the same mage."

"Ah," Lukfer said. "The talisman was enspelled by two mages, one powerful and skilled, and one powerful and less skilled. A master and student, perhaps; perhaps you sensed the student." Very soberly, "They understand our form of magic very well indeed, Tam. I could not have designed a more efficient annulment myself." Lukfer, after decades struggling to control his strength, had as much theoretical insight into magic as anyone in the tower.

But he would never be able to pass it on, neither the strength nor the insight. The masters of lineage had been unable to capture his strength for the lines; of his several children, born to carefully selected mothers, none were more than fourth-rank. His one strong granddaughter had vanished years ago. Tam was his only student in the last four decades, the only one who had the patience to receive understanding piecemeal, since even normal magespeech could be hazardous.

"Why did you have Pardel and the—Magistra Viola here?"

"You asked me—challenged me, even—to find a way to destroy this magic."

"You *told* them?" That came out offended, but he could not forget how he had had to drag an admission out of Lukfer. He shook his head, by way of apology

Lukfer's faint smile conveyed warmth and forgiveness. "Not yet. I have to be very sure that we can trust them, before we draw them into working outside the compact."

Outside the . . . "That's not possible."

"Is it not?" There was a surge of chill and foulness, and Lukfer's wine flared into a transparent blue flame. Tam gagged at the unexpected proximity of it. Lukfer raised the glass and, gently, quenched the flame with another pulse of the vile magic. "It is undetectable, at least by the lineage mages. And it is not nearly as unpleasant to use as to be around."

"Mother of All Things," Tam whispered. "You mean you're able to—"

He never finished the sentence, or the thought. His persistent sense of Fejelis's vitality suddenly flared bright with a sense of danger, and brighter still with agony. He choked out, "Jay—" Lukfer's broad, white hands caught and steadied him and chaotic power suddenly surged around him. Tam caught it as it crested, heedless of the danger, wrapped it in his will, and *lifted*.

Fejelis

Fejelis found his younger brother on his balcony, standing in the one corner that was still not in shadow at this hour, and looking out over the late-afternoon city. Orlanjis had, by all reports, kept to his rooms all day. He was not dressed for a public appearance. His auburn hair was worked into a simple braid, held with a red ribbon.

He started as Fejelis's name was announced, his shoulders stiffening.

". . . I'm glad to see you didn't suffer too many ill effects from breakfast," Fejelis said, to his back.

Orlanjis turned, posture and expression braced, lower lip protruding slightly. "I spoiled it, didn't I?"

". . . If that was your intention, yes."

"I didn't want to, but Sharel . . . and I wasn't feeling well anyway. . . ."

Sharel was their mother's sister, younger by twelve years, who had joined Helenja's entourage after the purge that had followed Fejelis's poisoning. Fejelis was not surprised that Sharel had suggested the masquerade, or that Orlanjis had taken the suggestion; when he was younger, he had adored her, and even now, plainly he was under her influence.

"I'm ashamed of myself," said Orlanjis, eyes downcast behind thick ginger lashes.

Which he might well be, as well as realizing that the potential consequences of offending Prince Fejelis were quite a bit more severe than the consequences of offending a mere elder brother. Fejelis rubbed thoughtfully at the callus on his right index finger, where his fencing glove had worn thin and the pommel rubbed, and looked around him. Of all the prince's children, Orlanjis had spent the longest in their mother's lands, in the desert, and was acutely homesick in the north. Along this narrow balcony, he had created a miniature desert, the sands sheltered and contained by glass.

Orlanjis said, dolefully, "I suppose if I want to go south for the winter, it's you I should ask."

Along the side of the building, blocking one of the windows, a portion of a canyon wall had been sculpted from porous clay and planted with cacti and epiphytes. Rather than answer his brother's implied request, Fejelis crouched to study the feathery sprigs of the plants that lived on moisture from the air. After a silence, Orlanjis said, "It shouldn't be that yellow on the tips. It needs more sun."

Hand on the glass to balance himself, Fejelis stood, trying not to make it apparent he did so to avoid having his brother at his back. Orlanjis seemed not to notice. His eyes, dark like their mother's, avoided Fejelis's. "Jay," he said more clearly, "I'd like to go south as soon as you'll let me. I don't want to be here while—"

While things worked themselves out around their father's deposition, Fejelis understood. ". . . I'd miss you."

Orlanjis took a step back. Fejelis shrugged, inviting him to believe it or not. ". . . I was thinking to ask if you would like the vacant rooms on the top floor. A far bigger balcony than this, and much more sun."

Orlanjis blinked. "Those were Perrin's rooms."

Your sister sends her regards.

". . . Even if she were ever to come back to the palace, it would be as a mage." And it was not likely, he knew, from Tam. The Temple disapproved of emotional ties with earthborn. Few mages were like Tam, prepared to flout that disapproval to love and befriend earthborn. "I don't think she would mind."

"It's on the same floor as Fath—you," Orlanjis said, suspiciously. "Do you *want* me there?"

". . . Yes," said Fejelis. ". . . I do. And yes. It's a bribe. I would far rather have you working with me than against me."

Orlanjis's lips parted.

"Father always said you had more imagination than the rest of us put together. . . . The lack spares my nerves, in these circumstances, but it does not help me solve the problems I face—the rift between north and south, the impoverishment of the earthborn lineages, the artisans' discontent, the effect on us of the Darkborn's progress. . . . To find solutions, I need people who can envision something new." He gestured to the model cliff. ". . . What I can do is make sure they and their ideas have opportunity to thrive."

"You sound—like Father," Orlanjis said, his brows drawing together.

"Thank you," Fejelis said.

"Mother won't like it if I move," Orlanjis said, toeing a twig on the balcony.

". . . I have to try and reach an accommodation with her, too," Fejelis said. An imp of mischief prompted him to say, ". . . Would you be willing to have breakfast with me tomorrow? Exonerate me of the suspicion of having tried to poison you this morning?"

Orlanjis's dark eyes widened at the blunt phrasing. "... Bring whomever you wish," Fejelis said, lightly.

"Jay, that mage—Tammorn—has associations with the radical artisans' movement."

". . . I'm aware of that," Fejelis said, wondering how Orlanjis had come by that information. "But thank you. Magister Tammorn came from the western provinces, so he has considerable sympathy with the artisans, though not, I think, with the radical factions." He knew not, in fact. The radicals recruited from the dispossessed incomers to the cities, of whom, decades ago, Tam had been one. Their advocacy of revolt put at risk the innovators Tam nurtured like tender plants. "I need that sympathy. Their brightnesses of both the court and the Temple are too far removed from the hardships of ordinary people. If we can address those, the radicals will lose their support."

Orlanjis's cynical expression was unpleasant on so roundly appealing a face.

"... You think I'm being naive," Fejelis said. "... So be it. Let the argument be simple compassion."

"How do you know so much?" Orlanjis said, a little sulkily. Perhaps measuring his potential as prince against Fejelis, and not liking the contrast.

Fejelis shrugged. ". . . I went out and about when I was younger—unobserved, I thought, though Father eventually disavowed me of that notion." Except where Tam was involved; the mage subtly used his magic to protect his meetings with Fejelis and the others from observation. "Father talked to me about what I learned, much as he talked to you about the southerners."

"You were close to him," Orlanjis said. "Closer than either he or you let us think."

Fejelis let silence be his answer. He felt an involuntary tightening in his throat at the reminder that that closeness was lost to him. Orlanjis's fingers worried at his sleeve. "I feel such a coward, Jay, not wearing red for him."

The corner of Fejelis's mouth quirked. ". . . 'Be your own man' is advice given cheaply by people who have no idea what it is to be the sons of a northern-southern marriage. But you're not a child anymore, 'Jis; you're a man, a prince's son, and could well be my successor. Like it or not, you have to make those decisions for yourself, and accept the risk. . . . And here endeth the lesson," he added, wryly, seeing the resentful flash in his brother's dark eyes.

There was a long silence. Orlanjis, he saw, was struggling with himself over a question. He feared he knew what it was.

"Jay, who do you think killed him?"

". . . I don't know," Fejelis said, leaning his elbow on the balustrade. "There is no doubt that magic was involved. The palace judiciary is reviewing all contracts, to try and identify any worded so as to permit an attack on the prince, that they missed. . . . The Temple is investigating magic outside contract." He hesitated, and then decided on a deeper candor than he had dared up until now, leaning close to say softly, ". . . Tammorn represents our best hope for learning anything the Temple does not want us to know."

"Oh," said Orlanjis, staring at his brother. "But we can't . . ."

That "we" echoed, made his heart lift, but Orlanjis did not finish the sentence. No matter, they had time. "I'm cold," Orlanjis muttered, and retreated back into the sunlit corner. Fejelis went with him. He should, he knew, get back to his receiving room and continue with his endless work, but this new rapport he was nurturing was precious. He did not know when he would have another opportunity to speak to Orlanjis like this, without interference.

He propped himself against the balcony, enjoying the warmth on his back. Mage light might sustain life, but it did not nourish it, not as the sun did. ". . . You were going to say . . ."

Orlanjis glanced toward him. Fejelis glimpsed the flash of white around his pupils as his eyes widened. He did not consciously register the sudden horror; he was not aware of recognizing the implications, nor did he formulate intent. He simply threw himself on Orlanjis, twisting to heave him bodily behind the shield of the glassed garden. He heard a coarse hiss behind him, and something thumped his back with a sound like a stone striking a hung carcass, and enough force to drive the breath from him. He crashed forward across his brother's legs, the impact jarring loose searing pain and a gush of salty warmth in his throat. He felt Orlanjis's thrashing efforts to free himself, but already his senses were being stripped from him, his hearing reduced to the fading rushing of his pulse, his sight entirely red shadows darkening to black. His last sensation was of peach fuzz against his palms.

Seven

Tammorn

$\mathcal{T}$ am dropped to his knees, gasping, as Lukfer's chaotic magic unraveled from his. Miraculously, he was alive and intact and not bisected by a plane of grass or planted knee-deep with the sands of this toy garden, or, worst of all, conjoined with one of the vigilants or servants clustered in the sunlight corner. His magic, wielded without thought, thrust them all aside, and he caught his first glimpse of Fejelis lying facedown and unmoving, impaled through the back by a wooden bolt. Just beyond his head, Orlanjis lay curled up against the balustrade, face twisted away in panicked, revolted denial. Even before he saw Fejelis, Tam had sensed the foul aura of the bolt itself, something crafted not for the annulment of light but for the annulment of life itself.

The mage vigilant who had been down on her knees beside Fejelis struggled against the pressure of Tam's greater strength, shouting something at him that he ignored, as he ignored the useless fluttering of her magic. They told him later he had *lifted* the length of the balcony. He knew only that he found himself crouching over Fejelis, tearing away the bloodied fabric around the bolt as simultaneously his magic tore at the killing ensorcellment. Then he felt his own heart suddenly falter within him, his hands go numb, the bolt darken in his sight, as his nemesis, shockingly, seized upon *his* vitality.

Until Lukfer reached across the distance between them

to hook the core out of the ensorcellment with a single practiced twist.

The bolt had driven all the way through Fejelis's lung, lodging in a rib. Its tip was bone, exempt, like the wood, from the talisman against metal bullets. It was barbed, designed to tear flesh when it was withdrawn. Tam growled, and felt the bolt vibrate with the sound, warping and withering like a stick in a flame, the barbs shriveling away. He drew it out, casting it aside; he did not know where, or toward whom. Fejelis choked, strangling on blood, an excruciatingly familiar sound. *<Lukfer!>* He reached out for the other mage, despite the danger, and felt a great surge of vitality flood him. Feverish with the excess of it, he bullied together blood vessels, spun together tissues, purged the blood from Fejelis's lungs and windpipe, and swept closed the skin around the wound so brusquely it shivered like the film on heated milk. Then he gathered Fejelis into his lap.

"Cloth," he croaked. Someone handed him a cloth, and turning Fejelis faceup, he began to wipe his bloodstained lips and cheek and scrub at the gore in his fair hair. He was hardly aware that the name he whispered was not Fejelis's, but that of his younger brother, now years dead. But this time it was a still-breathing body he cradled, not one still and beginning to stiffen in death.

Tammorn

"Here," said Captain Lapaxo. He stepped aside as he spoke, removing himself with alacrity from Tam's path, giving Tam and Fejelis a view of the balcony and the black tarpaulin heaped on it. Partly hidden beneath its folds was a southern-style crossbow, of wood and horn, with a powerful draw. A sideways glance confirmed that from here they could see the corner of Orlanjis's balcony, some seventy yards away. Shadows had claimed that balcony entirely now. Overhead, the clouds were tinged with sunset gold. But that he was feverish with borrowed vitality, he would have shivered.

Fejelis stooped, lifted the edge of the tarpaulin, studied the brown residue left by a man's quenching, and let the tarpaulin down again. The captain of vigilants looked at his pallid face, his blood-soaked, torn shirt, and the tidemarks of dried blood on his cheek, and winced, visibly.

". . . Can you tell anything?" Fejelis said to Tam. "Who was he?"

Vitality was fled, gone the instant the bowman pulled the tarpaulin over himself. Or had it pulled over him, Tam reminded himself; murder was entirely possible. Gone, too, was any trace of ensorcellment. The mages vigilant had sensed nothing. "No," he said. "I presume there's nothing to identify him or her."

"That's a southern bow," the captain said.

Fejelis's head turned, his eyes unreadable as mirrors. ". . . And how many from the north are experts with the weapon," he said, calmly, "including your own peers?"

The captain lowered his head. "Prince," he acknowledged.

". . . Do not let anything close your mind, Captain," the prince advised. "There were two men on that balcony; the bolt may not even have hit the right one."

Do you believe that? hovered unasked in the air. Orlanjis, hysterical, had claimed the bowman was aiming at himself, and that Fejelis had pushed him out of the way and thereby saved Orlanjis's life. "He moved so *fast*," Orlanjis had protested his perceptions of a brother known for his hesitations and spidery build.

But Orlanjis, by all reports, had drawn his brother into that exposed corner, just before the bowman fired the bolt.

A touch could answer that question, were Fejelis to ask Tam, but Fejelis had not asked.

"We're starting a census of everyone who's still in residence," Lapaxo said. "While it's possible *this* came from outside, it's more likely it was in the household all along. We'll find out who was in and out of these rooms, and check why the group they were supposed to house wasn't in them."

". . . Very good," Fejelis said. "I'll stop trying to tell you how to do your job now."

The captain accorded that a nerve twitch of a smile. "It's possible he tossed something identifying over the side, when he decided he could not escape, so we will need to search below."

Fejelis, looking down at the tarpaulin, said, ". . . He—or someone—was prepared. I would interpret that as meaning he was not meant to escape. . . . But I will leave you to your inquiries. I need to get cleaned up. I shall be opening the general receiving room in about an hour. Could you please arrange cover accordingly?" He raised a hand, preempting objections. Quite likely none of those watching would notice the tremor of those fingertips for seeing the blood that streaked them. ". . . We have a palace full of their brightnesses, and it is crucial that they see me."

"I do understand, my prince," said Lapaxo stoically.

". . . Actually," Fejelis said, in his rooms some time later, ". . . I believe Orlanjis." Bathed and scrubbed, his hair clean and drying, he sat gathering himself for his next public appearance. ". . . He thinks the bowman was aiming at him, and Orlanjis is very good with a bow—Sharel's teaching. . . . It was his reaction, when he saw the bowman—"

"Whom he claimed he didn't recognize," Tam could not help but say.

Fejelis continued his thought, "—that prompted mine. He was terrified."

Which did not, Tam thought, exempt the possibility that Orlanjis was merely playing out his assigned part. Fejelis was capable of steadily watching murder done in front of him; Orlanjis was not. "You saved his life, nearly at the cost of your own."

". . . I'm sure the mage vigilant would have dealt with any wounds."

Fejelis had not been conscious to hear the mage vigilant demand, "What did you *do*? I couldn't—" She had drawn back from publicly admitting that she had felt Fejelis dying under her hands. When Helenja had arrived with her entourage, Tam had watched the mage convince herself that she had simply not had time to muster effective healing magic before Tam had preempted her.

There was a short, suspended pause. ". . . But thank you," Fejelis said. "Again."

"I wish," Tam started, and stopped. The wish he was about to express was that either he or Lukfer had sensed the talisman before the bolt had been fired. It had certainly been potent enough to touch.

If Lukfer had not annulled the ensorcellment on the box, he might have been able to get a sense of distance. But if Lukfer had not annulled the ensorcellment on the box, he could not have annulled the ensorcellment on the bolt so deftly, and Fejelis might have died. "Are you warm enough yet?" he filled in the unfinished question.

He himself felt the room near stifling, but Fejelis had complained of cold even after a hot shower. He had hidden the worst of his reaction behind a locked bathroom door, and the accounts of his composure would be flying through the halls even now. Tam had seen his accomplishment in Lapaxo's response to him.

". . . It is a pity," Fejelis said, "we did not take the bowman alive, or find anything other than the bow. . . . If it was retaliation from the northern faction for my father's death . . ."

"Jay," Tam said, a little raggedly, "the Vigilance will take care of it. They have rather a lot to live down now."

Fejelis considered him, his expression oddly thoughtful and compassionate for so young a man. ". . . You called me by the name Artarian, back . . . then. Your son's name."

Mother of All, he had been distraught, to let that name slip. "Artarian was . . . my younger brother. He died at eighteen, defending me, after one of my messes. Stabbed . . . in the back. I reached him just in time to feel the life go out of him. I didn't know how to help him."

"Ah," Fejelis said, quietly. "Thank you. I'm honored that you would think of me in that way. I'm glad, too . . . that there is someone in the palace who will understand why I simply reacted."

Not exactly, thought Tam, for he was far less sure of Orlanjis than Fejelis seemed. He wanted to remonstrate, to warn Fejelis that even magic might not always be able to rescue him, and to tell him how nearly it had not, this time.

The prince got to his feet, testing his legs. ". . . I must show myself. I will keep the room open for an hour." With wintry amusement, "Anyone who does not appear by then is so far removed from either information or influence to be irrelevant, and can wait until morning."

Tam stood behind Fejelis's chair, listening as the prince exchanged brief words and assurances with the seemingly endless procession of people filing past him. Word seemed to have reached all the palace's guests, and they had all turned out to inspect their prince. "For cracks," as Fejelis had put it, with that dry detachment that was sustaining him. Vigilants flanked Fejelis, vigilants guarded all the entrances, and vigilants had been stationed on all the balconies. The full contingent of the mages vigilant contracted to the palace had been turned out as well. With the exception of one Captain Beaudry, who was missing, and Floria White Hand.

The corner of Fejelis's mouth had quirked at the sight of his massed guardians, but one look at Lapaxo's face and he had yielded without a word. On his left, within their own stockades of vigilants, sat the dowager consort with a shocky-looking Orlanjis, and other members of the southern faction. The dowager consort did not disguise her speculative attention on her elder son. On his right were Prasav and his cousins of the northern faction. Tam could not tell, from the surface, what they felt beyond their carefully expressed outrage.

All the time the pageant continued, Tam watched the steady blue-cauled head in front of him, and felt his rage grow. This extraordinary young man, this bright hope of the forgotten and dispossessed, had nearly died on the first day of his reign. Tam, for all his power, had failed to anticipate it and nearly failed to prevent it. Lukfer's wariness of their Temple superiors, justified as it may be, deprived them of potential allies and of latitude of action. But behind Tam's anger were fear and an appalling sense of powerlessness. He had not even sensed that bolt, except through Fejelis's agony as it struck.

The taking of a life, as he well knew, required no magic whatsoever. Even a first-rank mage could heal—or cause sickness—and execute elementary talismanic magic. A third-rank mage could have created that bolt—perhaps the apprentice who had had a part in creating the box.

Unlike most mages, Tam had no natural bent for healing, though with considerable effort he had grown skilled. He was a master of matter, not vitality. Had he not sensed the bolt, might he not sense other magic as inimical to life, because he lacked the sensitivity?

He thought of the mage he had sensed in the archduke's palace. The vitality was Darkborn, but the magic was Shadowborn. Could the archduke of the Darkborn know what he harbored? Sejanus Plantageter distrusted magic, but he was scrupulous in ensuring the law was observed even as it applied to mages and Lightborn. Or were the Shadowborn attacking the Darkborn, too? It was the Darkborn who had suffered most from the Shadowborn-set fires.

If that was the Shadowborn apprentice, or if that was a Darkborn mage allied with the Shadowborn, then there was only one way to be certain that he did no more harm. Tam's conscience would not allow killing on mere suspicion, but after twenty years around Lukfer, he knew how to bind another mage's magic. And perhaps, in so doing, he might learn enough of the other's purposes to know what additional action he must take.

He would not tell Lukfer; it would distress the older mage, and alarm him with the possibility Tam might rouse the interest of the Temple Vigilance. But he doubted that those worthies would much concern themselves with an assault on an unknown, low-ranked Darkborn mage. And it was worth the risk, to protect Fejelis. Let Tam get through this interminable hour, and let him get Fejelis back to his rooms and resting safely, and then he would deal with this mage, and his magic.

Telmaine

After a sleep broken by strange dreams and anxieties, Telmaine's evening toilette was interrupted by the arrival of her mother and, shortly thereafter, Merivan. Telmaine's brother the duke had received an invitation to breakfast at the archducal palace, and his duchess was still at their country estates for the summer, so he had appealed to his mother for support. The dowager duchess had brought two of the best early-evening dresses of Telmaine's wardrobe, and supervised Telmaine's maid with an anxious expression meant to reassure, though she said only, "We will discuss it later, dear," when Telmaine asked.

Telmaine had expected that they would be escorted to one of the more intimate receiving rooms on the upper floor, but they made their way to the main and public part of the palace and down to the level of the grand ballroom. A steady flow of people—couples and families with their retinues—were crossing the wide foyer from the doors and entering the ballroom. Telmaine swept out before her with her mage sense, and her next step stumbled over the density of vitality it met. The entire ballroom had been opened out and was filling up with people.

Behind her, Merivan said, sharply, "What is it?"

She regained her balance and her nerve, having confirmed that amongst the mass she sensed no taint of Shadowborn. "I was a little—startled, that was all," she said. "When you said breakfast—I expected—something—*small*."

"Lady Telmaine." A footman stepped up to her side. "Lord Vladimer requests a moment of your time." Even as he did so, another footman was leading her mother, brother, and sister into the ballroom, letting her detach herself. She trailed the footman between the rows of seated guests and the rows of poised servants, trying at once to hurry and to be unobtrusive. Surely Vladimer must have had word of Bal.

An exquisitely dressed young woman suddenly twisted in her chair with a rasp of lace. "Telmaine!"

"Sylvide!"

Her dearest friend, Sylvide di Reuther, caught her skirts; she had to stop. "What *happened* to you?" Sylvide cried. "Where did you go?"

Yes, the last Sylvide had known, she had set Telmaine down at Bolingbroke Circle, ostensibly to hire a carriage to take her back to the archducal palace and safety. Instead, Telmaine had taken a carriage to the docks and a walk through the fire. So the question absolutely could not be answered with the truth. Telmaine stooped low, easing Sylvide's grip, and bringing her mouth close to Sylvide's veiled ear. "I'll have to tell you later. Lord Vladimer wants to talk to me."

"Lord *Vladimer*? Why ever—"

Telmaine became aware of the silence around them, Sylvide's neighbors—her husband, her mother-in-law, her sister-in-law—all listening intently. She patted Sylvide's hand, whispered, "Tell you later"—though what, exactly, she had no idea—and bade them all good evening in the dulcet tones of a blameless woman. Sylvide's husband was the only one who replied. Oh, dear.

Vladimer was waiting for her in a small side room, standing propped on his cane. A cup and saucer sat within reach on a high table, but there was otherwise no sign of breakfast. Vladimer was finely groomed and as elegantly dressed as she had ever known him be. The lines of current fashion should have suited him, with his height and the angular lines of his face, but the skin seemed tight-drawn on the bones, and his vitality quivered in her awareness with pain and the hectic energy of fever and stimulants.

"Before you ask, there's been no further word from the Borders, bad or good," he began without a greeting. "There's been a report from the Stranhorne train station of abnormal weather, a very heavy snow, immediately around Stranhorne."

"Snow in summer?" Her voice rose. "Surely that's not natural."

"I am well aware of that," Vladimer said. "Console yourself, if you will, that it will hamper Ferdenzil Mycene's movements and communications as much as your husband's, Strumheller's, and mine." He hooked the cane on the edge of the table, lifted the cup, and drank thirstily. Teacup landed on saucer with the chime of fine china and the trill of an unsteady hand. "Now, as to this evening, this is a command performance. Rumor is rife. The evening broadsheets are full of speculations of such lush inventiveness that even I do not know whether to be impressed or appalled. Ishmael di Studier's name figures largely in them, as does your husband's. Even Strumheller's escape from the prison is being attributed to him in some quarters; he is quite the mastermind."

He was not so ill that his malicious humor was in abeyance. She supposed she should be grateful for the warning. "*What* am I supposed to *say* when people ask me where my husband *is*?" she demanded, but challenge quickly succumbed to panic. "I never expected this. Why has the archduke invited—"

"To quell rumor and alarm at the ducal orders. We are to conduct ourselves with apparent confidence that everything is on its way to resolution. Depending upon your audience, you may choose to pretend you have no knowledge of your husband's mission, though I doubt anyone who knows you well will credit that. Anyone too persistent, you may simply refer them to me."

"Lord Vladimer," she said plaintively, "can't I simply have the vapors and lie down?"

A brief taut smile, startled out of him. "If *I* may not, you certainly may not."

"And what are *you* going to say?" she challenged. "Or *will* my husband have a profession and reputation to return to?"

"I am not," he said flatly, "in the habit of discussing my activities, or my agents' activities, with the gossips of society. Be assured that the men who matter *will* know the services your husband has rendered."

And will they be grateful? Telmaine thought—but managed to stop herself from saying. *Oh, Bal, what a reward for your loyalty: social ruin.*

"Lord Vladimer," she murmured, and, hiding alarm and resentment behind a practiced, social smile, let herself be escorted from the room. She would *not* let Bal be sacrificed, not even for Sejanus Plantageter. She *would* not.

Sylvide di Reuther, at once the first and the very last person she wished to talk to, had inveigled the footmen to bring an extra chair and set an additional place next to her. The one consolation was that they were adjacent to the archducal table, close enough to sonn without her being obtrusive. She did not need magic to sense the thunderous atmosphere around her; Lady di Reuther was in fine high dudgeon, and Sylvide's breathing was quick and shallow and her heart-shaped face set. Telmaine ducked her head and nodded assent to the hovering footmen. Even if she could not eat, she could be spared having to speak while she picked at her plate. She lifted her fork in a trembling hand.

She had not thought she could eat—had expected even to be sickened by the smell of it—but when the first slice of breakfast pie was laid on her plate, she found herself having to restrain herself from an unladylike greed. The aroma of island spices poignantly evoked the memory of the imprisoned Ishmael confiding a wish or whimsy to retire to the Islands and grow spices.

"Telmaine," Sylvide said, from beside her, "how is little Florilinde?"

As safe, and unsafe, a question as any. "Back with us now," she said, laying down her fork. "And unharmed."

Sylvide breathed out. "That is so good. I hear Master di Maurier is still holding his own, and I'm sure that knowing she is safe will do him good."

"You are *not* communicating with that reprobate, Sylvide," decreed Lady di Reuther. "I was *appalled* to hear that you had visited him—and you, Telmaine. I thought better of you."

"Master di Maurier is a *hero*," Sylvide said, her voice pinched.

"Master di Maurier is a disgrace," Lady di Reuther declared.

Sylvide confined her argument to a tight little shake of the head. Softhearted Sylvide remembered Gil di Maurier from the nursery, her little boy cousin. To Telmaine's mind he was both hero and disgrace, but the experience of the underworld that he had gained pursuing his dissipations had let him find Florilinde. Her covert attempt to heal him had been no more than she owed him.

"Are you aware of the *reason* for your daughter's travail?" Lady di Reuther demanded.

"Yes," Telmaine said. "Confidential information that my husband refused to divulge."

"You do realize, Telmaine, even if your husband does not, that it is not appropriate for men and women of our

class to become the subject of such reporting as has sur-
rounded this affair."

"And little Amerdale," Sylvide said, desperately. "How
is she?"

Telmaine took firm control of herself, knowing that
she was merely a goad or two from some unwise outburst.
"Counting the days to her sixth birthday," she said, brittle
and airy. "We have promised her a kitten. She is quite in-
fatuated with them."

"My Dorian is the same, only with him it is birds. There
was an aviary in the Islands court; he would have stayed
there night and day if he could. Once," she said to the table,
"he persuaded me to take him to an all-day opening. The
visiting area was covered with a canvas, set up so that the
birds can go outside by a series of tunnels that don't pass
light. It was quite terrifying, and at the same time utterly
diverting, because the birds are so much busier and sing
so much more by day. The staff made up beds for us, but
neither of us slept at all."

"Dani," said Lady Calliope, "did you know about this?"

"Of course, Mother. If I had not had work, I would have
gone as well."

"Reckless," Lady Calliope deemed it. "Dorian is your
heir."

"It was quite safe," Sylvide said, breathing quickly.
"Dorian is my *son*."

"No, Dani, it was reckless. I trust there will be no
repetition."

Sylvide jabbed at a piece of bacon and sent it skittering across the plate and onto Telmaine's napkin. Telmaine
snatched it up and quickly laid it aside on the plate, trying
equally to avoid a stain and further comment from Lady
Calliope.

Sylvide said, "Your *hand*, Telmaine. It's all right."

"Quite all right," Telmaine said, remembering too late
she had planned to favor that hand when next she met Sylvide. "Oh, it stings still, but it must not have been as bad a
burn as we feared. It was fright as much as anything that
made me faint."

"I am so glad," Sylvide said. She caught Telmaine's wrist, pulling her close to whisper, "Telmaine, whatever they say, I don't believe any of it."

"About what?" Telmaine whispered back, wondering if there was more than Vladimer had hinted at, but Sylvide said nothing more. Telmaine cast a wary sonn around her dining companions. Across the table, Lady Calliope's aspect was haughty and disapproving, but she was ever thus. Beside his mother, Daniver di Reuther sat in sullen obedience. Telmaine thought guiltily of her lapsed resolve to speak to her brother the duke on Dani's behalf. Dani had been ousted from his post in the Scallon Islands by Mycene's intrigues, and the sooner he found another, the sooner he and poor Sylvide would escape his mother's reach. At Dani's side, his unmarried sister was teasing the food on an almost full plate, thin wrists protruding from her fashionably puffed sleeves. She was twenty-seven and still unwed, having outlived two fiancés and been jilted by the last. On Lady Calliope's right sat her older son, on whose account she had no right whatsoever to sneer at Gil di Maurier. By his drooping posture and sagging face Xavier di Reuther had planned to be abed by now, sleeping off a day's excess, rather than socializing to ducal order. At least the table should be spared his thumping wit, though not his heavy cologne. Merivan had stationed herself on his far side as sentinel to her erratic sister and was manifestly unhappy; her pregnancy made her extremely sensitive to odors.

Lady di Reuther was opining, disapprovingly, upon the behavior of her southern neighbors, and in particular the wayward daughters of the barony. Knowing that Ishmael was fugitive in Stranhorne lands made Telmaine listen, though she did find herself rather shocked; surely it was not true that the Baronettes Stranhorne had dressed in boys' garb to ride out to hunt Shadowborn.

Sylvide said, unexpectedly, "I thought it was very brave of them."

Xavier roused himself to a chortled "Like to sonn you in breeches, sister dear."

Dani started to stand, his expression ominous. His mother put a manacling hand on his arm.

"I don't think you would, sir," Telmaine said. With her early-maturing figure, her sweet nature, and a family who showed scant concern for the security and happiness of a girl, Sylvide had suffered far more presumption and trespass than she deserved. Xavier was more bluster than malice, but he still would not say such things to a woman he respected—Telmaine, for instance. She smiled sweetly into his bleary face and reached across the table with her magic. "I understand your sister-in-law is quite a fair shot." A delicate, internal nudge—it didn't take much—and he was pushing back from the table, stumbling away with a hand clapped over his mouth. She felt an indecent thrill as two footmen swiftly converged to steer him into a side room.

<You should not have done that.>

Her blood chilled. The voice had the crystal edges of a Lightborn, and the touch, brief as it was, exuded power.

"Telmaine?" said Sylvide.

She gripped the table, to hold herself in place. <*Who are you?*>

There was no answer. For a moment she struggled with the urge to flee—but where could she possibly flee to, if the Lightborn Temple Vigilance had discovered her? A whimper tried to escape; she swallowed it down.

"Telmaine!" Merivan hissed across the table. "Control yourself!"

"Daniver," Lady Calliope said, far more audibly. "Sit *down*. One of you making an exhibition of himself is quite enough."

Sylvide turned in her chair and took Telmaine's hands. "Telmaine, dear, are you ill?"

Quite possibly she was going mad. Quite possibly she had, under strain, imagined that voice in her mind. Had Sylvide not captured her hands, she would have chewed on her gloved fingertip. Instead, she bit her inner lip until she tasted salt and iron.

"You've had a bad few days," Sylvide commiserated. "I know."

The intrusive voice stayed silent. She breathed more steadily and managed to smile at Sylvide. "Tell me," she said, her voice almost under her control, "what absurd things *are* the broadsheets saying about my husband?"

Across the table, Lady Calliope drew breath at her audacity at approaching the subject so brazenly.

Sylvide's smile wavered. "They're saying that he—that he—oh, Telmaine, *must* you ask?"

"I'm sorry, dear Sylvide, but how else am I to know what nonsense I am to refute? A lady came to him in distress; he aided her. Should he be condemned for that?"

"I hardly think," Lady Calliope said, frostily, "this is a suitable topic for this breakfast table."

Telmaine set her hands beside her plate, and leaned forward. "Why *not*? Why should everyone be free to whisper slander at the breakfast table, and I not be allowed to speak truth? My husband is innocent."

"Then where is he?" Dani asked her.

She drew a deep breath. "Balthasar is undertaking an errand on request of Lord Vladimer. That is all I can say; you must take it up with Lord Vladimer himself."

"How convenient," said Lady Calliope, frigidly.

"Not at all," Telmaine said, with feeling. "I would much rather he were here than risking his life and health on this errand."

"With Ishmael di Studier," Lady Calliope said. "That is what the broadsheets say, that he is in collusion with that—practitioner."

"Baron Strumheller is no sorcerer. There"—she pointed in the direction of the ducal table—"sits your proof. Lord Vladimer, here, and willing to testify in Baron Strumheller's defense. And Baron Strumheller never laid a *hand* on Tercelle Amberley."

"Telmaine!" said Merivan.

Belatedly she recalled that one of the rumors accused Ishmael of fathering Tercelle's children. She was too angry to be embarrassed. "I will not listen in silence to this slander of two good men."

Over at the archduke's table, where Sejanus Plantageter sat with his brother, the Duke of Imbré, and his eldest daughter, a footman stooped to speak quietly in Lord Vladimer's ear. Telmaine's attention was caught as Vladimer's thin frame went rigid. The footman laid something in his hand. Lady Calliope was talking still; Telmaine hardly heard. Without warning, ignoring his brother's effort to speak to him, Vladimer stood up, spilling his cane on the floor. As he did so, the object he was holding tumbled free and swung from the chain tangled in his fingers. Telmaine recognized the shape of the large amulet she had last sonned hanging around Casamir Blondell's neck, the amulet of protection against magic. Sejanus Plantageter reached for it, steadied it. Telmaine could not resist extending her magic to gather in the words he murmured to his brother, "*Face*, Vladimer."

He lifted the amulet into Vladimer's hand and let Vladimer close his fingers on it, then patted Vladimer's hand, rising with an easy smile. The entire table, as etiquette demanded, stood with him. As Sejanus moved away, drawing attention with him, Vladimer thrust the amulet into his pocket, accepted back his cane, and limped toward the door. Her sonn caught his face, still an imperfect mask over shock. Only the fear of gossip inhibited her from rising to hurry after him. Something terrible had happened.

Surely if it were to do with Ishmael or Balthasar, Vladimer would have given her some signal.

And if she went after Vladimer, it would draw people's attention to his state, attention that the archduke was skillfully diverting. Sejanus was making his progress around the table next to Telmaine's, receiving bows and curtsies from intimidated heirs and heiresses, and exchanging easy pleasantries with their elders. Like his brother, Sejanus suited the lines of current fashion very well, though he was the bolder dresser.

He reached their table and they all rose as one, Sylvide with a soft gulp. Telmaine squeezed her hand, though her own racing heart betrayed her nervousness. She had ceased to be socially intimidated by the archduke years ago, but that was before she had brazened her way into his higher councils, attached herself inexplicably to his brother, and, worst of all, started to spy on him with magic. Feeling the vibrant presence of his vitality, so close to her, gave her a mortifying sense of having been revealed in turn. She tucked her magic as tightly within her skin as ever she had.

Lady Calliope, the terror of her family and inferiors, was utterly charming to the archduke, who charmed her right back. Dani was stiff and shamefaced when brought to admit to the loss of his diplomatic post, but the archduke assured him that there was always work for able men, and left Dani standing straighter. He was gentle with Dani's sister, managing to elicit her whispered agreement to his mention of the beauty of the city's botanic gardens in late summer. Merivan's courtesies were initially subdued, but the archduke's sly reference to a particularly controversial play to be staged that autumn drew the true Merivan out of cover, and he gave every indication of appreciating her tart opinions.

He moved on to speak to the couple between Merivan and Sylvide. Telmaine leaned over and murmured, "Courage, he doesn't bite," to Sylvide.

"That's all very well for you to say," Sylvide whispered, but she acquitted herself with poise, even warmth, as the archduke commented on the hunting in her home area of the near Borders. Sylvide was, as Telmaine had said, a good shot. Many women who lived in and around the Borders were.

And there was Vladimer, returning along the far side of the table, unnoticed by most, his aspect grim. Something must have befallen Casamir Blondell; that seemed the only plausible reason for his amulet to have come into Vladimer's hand in such a way. . . . Then Sejanus Plantageter turned to her. "Lady Telmaine," he said, taking her hand as she curtsied. "How is little Florilinde?"

"Quite well," she mustered in response. "Thank you."

"I gather from this evening's broadsheets that I ought to find something to divert your husband's talents."

She managed not to wince at his turn of humor, not so unlike his brother's. He patted her hand lightly and said, distinctly enough to carry, "I am well aware of the reasons he undertook this errand and am satisfied of his good intentions."

That might not be the most he could have said in Bal's defense, perhaps, but it was not the least, either. She sustained her grateful smile as the archduke moved on. Sylvide caught and squeezed her hand in return.

She had just drawn breath when she felt a sudden flush of heat across her skin, like a wind up a hot summer street, like the sheet of flame from her bumbling effort at Shadowborn magic. Frightened, she swept out with her magical senses, and felt, closing around her, a smothering net of Lightborn magic.

She gasped. The net burst with her frantic counterstroke; she felt the wielder's surprise at the force, and knew her assailant was the Lightborn mage who had spoken silently to her moments before, the one whose power she had measured. *<What are you doing?>* In response, he swept his power around her again, no hotter, no harder, and she deflected it again, clumsily. *<Who are you?>*

No answer came, no acknowledgment, no mockery. Momentarily, there was calm. Momentarily, she was able to realize that she was still in the ducal ballroom, in the presence of her betters and peers, before whom she had just done—what? What of the magical assault had manifested, besides her gasp? Sonn outlined Merivan just starting around the table, righteous purpose but no horror on her face. Sylvide, at her side, steadied her, saying in innocent dismay, "Telmaine, what is it? Are you feeling faint?" At her other side, the archduke's voice—oh, sweet Lady Imogene, no—the archduke himself was saying, "Lady Telmaine?"

"I have—," she managed, amazed that smoke did not stream from her mouth with her words. "I have—"

And the burning net fell on her again. "No! Leave me alone!" She was back in the warehouse, where flame roared and beams ruptured and Florilinde screamed, thin and high as a trapped kitten. Beside her, the archduke shouted unintelligible words that turned into a cry of agony. Shrieks and crashing followed. Cries of, *The archduke! Dani! Water! I'm burning!* The voice in her mind said, *<No, oh, no,>* and she staggered back with arms thrown over her head, thrusting him away. *<Stop it. I'm trying to—>*

"Sejanus!" A raw shout from Vladimer, and a scream from Sylvide, "Lord Vladimer, no!" Out of the surging echoes one threw itself against her, arms around her; as they reeled together she felt Sylvide's panic, her friend understanding nothing except some horrific, inexplicable threat to Telmaine. The explosion of a revolver, like that heard as she lay across the threshold of Vladimer's room. She knew what must happen now, but still screamed rejection of the blunt rupture of a bullet into a flesh, the violation, the unimaginable pain, the sudden, liquid surge of mortal blood up her throat.

Sylvide did not scream. She clutched briefly at Telmaine, her cheek pressed against Telmaine's collarbone, her ornately decorated hair scratching Telmaine's cheek, her hat tilted askew and about to tumble away. The impact of the bullet had driven her last breath out of her and she made no effort to draw another. Without a sound, her arms loosened, and she began to slip toward the floor. Telmaine tried to hold her, but her arms had lost their strength; they fell together. She felt the scour of the Lightborn's power across her mind, hot and harsh and lacerating as sand, and waited to be burned out, destroyed, killed. The gem-hard mind behind the magic brushed up against that seed of Shadowborn and suddenly she sensed realization, shock, and remorse. <*Why?*> she whispered, and in a rustle of dry grains, the other magic swept outward, effortlessly quenching flames. She was aware of a last receding, <*Forgive me. It wasn't you.*>

Vladimer's voice shouted, "Get your *hands off me*! Sejanus! *Janus*, answer me! Let me go—leave my arm—"

Someone said, bewildered, "He *shot* Sylvide. But why?"

Her attention was riveted by the touch of skin, the last sinking spark of vitality in the woman lying beneath her. She plunged after that spark into the lake of blood spilled by the bullet's passage through Sylvide's heart. The destruction was almost beyond her comprehension. Painfully, she began to draw together the burst and shredded valves and muscle, reaching deep into her own reserves of bodily health and vitality. But those were already nearly spent, drained by her struggle against the Lightborn, and Sylvide had already gone beyond consciousness and almost life itself. Ishmael's experience whispered within her that it was already too late. Then she felt hands on her, lifting her away from Sylvide, tearing skin from skin, severing the flow of magic. Her reach fell short, even at this small distance. She could no longer sense the spark within Sylvide. Someone breathed, *"Sweet Imogene—"*

"Sylvide," someone said, and she recognized the voice, that of Dani, Sylvide's husband. "Someone get a doctor," he said, his voice shrill with panic. "A doctor, quickly."

A hot, dusty wind blew out of the Shadowlands, out of Ishmael's memories; Telmaine shrieked, fought briefly— real Darkborn or dream-born Shadowborn, how could she know?—and fainted.

Eight

Floria

*T*he sound of the door opening on the other side of the paper wall woke Floria from a light sleep. Her right hand brushed her revolver, then her rapier; her eyes sought her lights, noting their true color. On the other side of the wall she could hear the creaks and rustling of heavy Darkborn clothing, the soft chink of metal kissing metal. Three, maybe four individuals, spreading out.

She scooped up the nearest light and slid noiselessly from the bed into the corner adjacent to the paper wall. Here, she was sheltered by stone from all but the most oblique shots, within reach of the *passe-muraille*. The paper was heavily reinforced, with a grille over it that limited any damage to it. If these were assassins, they would be counting on being able to survive the light spill from a few bullet holes, and on her not being able to slash open the mesh before she died—one man might choose a suicide attack, but numbers suggested they intended to survive, even if they needed their numbers for bravado or collusion. But they had neglected the *passe-muraille*. She had spent several awkward minutes earlier jimmying the catch so she could open both hatches from this side. A light, pushed inside, would be deadly.

"Mistress Floria White Hand," said a man's voice from the other side. He had come up close to the paper wall. Posturing for his audience, which might or might not include her. "Lightborn, I know you are in there. I am Sachever, Duke of Mycene."

Patriarch of the most prominent and ambitious of the dukedoms, whose lineage had held the archducal seat for hundreds of years before losing it to the Plantageters when Mycene policies led to Borders rebellion and civil war. Under the Mycene archdukes, Darkborn and Lightborn had held themselves strictly apart; Minhorne had come to be the city it was under the Plantageters.

"You sought sanctuary here because Prince Fejelis had ordered your arrest in connection with the murder of his father. Vladimer Plantageter did not have the authority to grant you sanctuary, and did so without his brother's knowledge."

This did not sound good, Floria thought.

"By my authority as a member of the regency council convened during the incapacity of Archduke Sejanus Plantageter, I am here to review your position."

That sounded even worse.

She left her light and her rapier ready beside the *passe-muraille* and moved noiselessly back to the head of the bed. "How has the archduke become incapacitated?" Even as she spoke, she was moving off-line.

"Magic," came back the one word.

Whose? And how incapacitated was he? "I wish him a quick recovery," she murmured, and moved again.

"His physicians do not hold out much hope for his survival."

She checked her glide, involuntarily. That was unwelcome knowledge—aside from the implications for her of candor from her jailers. The archduke and his consort had had three daughters and one son. Because the absurd Darkborn convention insisted on male inheritance, Plantageter's death would leave Darkborn power in the hands of a child and his regency council—as it had been left nearly forty years ago. And the Duke of Imbré, the moderating force on that earlier council, was old now.

Mycene would not be telling her this—a mere vigilant of the Lightborn court—without some purpose. Magic—did he mean to imply they suspected the Lightborn?

"Your Grace," she said, "have you had a report from Lord Vladimer?"

"Lord Vladimer has suffered a complete mental collapse and been confined for his own safety."

"Lord Vladimer believes that many recent events can be attributed to the actions of Shadowborn agents."

The unseen duke scoffed. "Infidelity, mendacity, venality, corruption, arson, and murder—we hardly need postulate a type of magic that no one has ever heard of, from a race that has bred nothing but beasts, to explain ordinary vice. No, my lady"—and the Darkborn courtesy was, from his mouth, definitely an insult—"our enemies are closer to home."

"I . . . do not like the sound of that, Your Grace," she said, quietly, circling the room in a slow arc. "Are you accusing the Lightborn?"

There was a silence. Mother of All, did Fejelis know yet that, instead of the stable and established regimen of Sejanus Plantageter, he had to contend with a regency council ruthless in its seizure of legitimacy—Vladimer Plantageter had shown no signs of imminent mental collapse when he questioned her—and that had condemned the Lightborn unquestioned and unseen?

If the prince did not know, he needed to.

How to persuade them to release her? She said, in tones of quiet resignation, "Then if you do not accept the existence of Shadowborn, I expect you will be surrendering me to the Prince's Vigilance."

"That need not be so. Why, after all, should you suffer for actions undertaken under ensorcellment?"

If her actions had led to Isidore's death, ensorcelled or not, she would live with that knowledge for the rest of her life. And if this duke did not understand that, then he had never served, truly served, anything other than his own base self-interest.

"Tell me about Isidore's son," the duke said, "this boy Fejelis."

Cheap, Your Grace, Floria thought. "Prince Fejelis is nineteen, which I believe is considered of age amongst Darkborn." She well knew it was; Balthasar had told her about the bitter debates around the raising of the age of legal marriage to sixteen, to protect young heirs and heiresses against coercion, and girls against too-early pregnancy.

"Just. And inexperienced."

"Inexperienced, perhaps, but he has years of his father's tutelage." Which could not be said for the archduke's own heir, who was being raised in the Plantageter country properties, sheltered by a father whose own responsibilities had fallen on him cruelly young.

"I'm told he has ties to a mage who is not well regarded by the Temple."

Tammorn? "I am not certain I know who you mean."

"One Magister Tammorn, peasant-born, and associated with the artisans' republican movements."

Having had Balthasar's perspective on the Darkborn republicans to match up against the Vigilance's impression of the Lightborn revolutionaries, she thought something had been lost in translation. But how had the Darkborn duke come to know about Tammorn? Was he accusing *Tammorn* of having injured the archduke? On Fejelis's behest . . . *Mother of All.*

"I know Magister Tammorn, as it happens," Floria said, carefully. "Any difficulties between himself and the Temple are long resolved."

Mycene questioned her for some minutes longer, regarding Fejelis: his relationship to the mages, his acceptance by their brightnesses of the court, his adherence to southern alliances and values. And regarding Tammorn: his power, his politics and affiliations. She stepped carefully through the answers, paying close attention to a man who was—or thought he was—Fejelis's peer. He had little regard for Fejelis's youth, though that should not have surprised her; his reputation on the other side of sunrise was of one who kept his own son down.

At last, he seemed satisfied. She had moved back toward the corner where the lamp sat, and now glanced down at it at her feet. She detested the thought of exposing her vulnerability, but it was as foolish to put her life at risk through paranoia as through recklessness—"Your Grace," she said. "Would you be able to arrange it so that the skylight in this room could be opened when morning comes? I have lights with me, but they need daylight to recharge."

She heard the soft creak of leather and chime of metal as he moved to square himself before the paper wall. "I will consider it." But there was neither concern nor promise in his voice. She slipped down to a sitting position, back against the stone, rapier held balanced between her hands, and, listening as they withdrew, stared at her light.

Was it more yellow? The color change that indicated impending extinction progressed over several hours. But if they did not open the skylight above her, the lights would fail by tomorrow's sunset.

She pushed herself out of her crouch and began to circle the refuge that had become a prison. Tested the grille over the paper wall, but that seemed entirely solid, and even if she could break through, it would simply move her deeper into the darkness. She returned to the door by which she had entered, like all Darkborn doors finished but not stained, its woods matched for texture but not color. Its closed blankness was a reproach to her lack of foresight. If she did not find a way out, she would die in the same manner as her prince.

Fejelis

For the second time that night, Fejelis jerked awake, sweating, at the shock of the blow beneath his shoulder blade. This time, he did not shout out, and the taste of peach and blood was faint and easily swallowed. He carefully lifted his head to favor his attendants with his best effort at a drowsy smile. Two palace vigilants, armed men in loose crimson tunics and trousers, stood on either side of the door. A mage vigilant occupied a chair several yards to his right, her eyes closed, her strained face indicating she was attending to her other senses.

Tam sat at the end of the bed, a letter in his hand, green gray eyes staring into an unseen distance.

Fejelis threw off sleep and sat up. When he had awakened before, Tam had been the first to reach him, the first to speak to him, the first to recognize his need for a basin as the taste of blood and peach sickened him. Now the mage slowly turned an ashen face toward him. Fejelis's heart jumped as he thought of Tammorn's small children, of Beatrice, of the artisans—all the people whom Tammorn passionately cared about. If any of their enemies wished to strike at him—"...Trouble?"

At the mage's incomprehension, Fejelis indicated the letter. Tam went to thrust it out of sight. Then his hunched shoulders sagged, and he pushed it toward Fejelis. "Read it."

Fejelis took it, noticing that the paper was stiff and smooth to the touch and blemished to the eye, of Darkborn rather than Lightborn manufacture. But the script was Lightborn, a spare cursive hand devoid of the flourishes fashionable in court circles. He flipped it over to read the signature: Floria.

"I have done," Tam said, in low voice, "a great deal of harm. I intended ill to one person, but what I have done ..." His voice shook and broke off as Fejelis lowered the letter. "Read it. It ... starts to explain."

In terse summary the letter told of attacks on the Darkborn, of fires and assassinations, of the attempted ensorcellment of Vladimer Plantageter ... and of the speculations of Vladimer Plantageter and this Darkborn lady, Telmaine, that the reason the Lightborn Temple had not reacted to these abuses was that they could not sense the magic used. He lifted his eyes. "... Do you believe this?"

"I have no reason to doubt," Tam said, heavily.

"...Explain," Fejelis said, after a long silence of disbelief.

Tam glanced toward the mage vigilant, met her eyes, gave a wan and apologetic smile, and traced a small loop in the air, trapping sound. "When ... I visited your father's rooms, I found a box of Darkborn design that was imbued with an unfamiliar form of magic—at least, I had only sensed its like recently. Its aura was extremely unpleasant, yet the Temple mages behaved as though they were unaware of it. I palmed the box and took it to Magister Lukfer."

So that explained the theft. Fejelis kept a studied neutral attentiveness in his expression, wanting no omissions.

"Lukfer identified the box as a talisman to annul magic. Specifically, of ensorcelled lights."

Fejelis strove to keep all emotion off his face, hard as it was.

"Another talisman of that same magic nearly killed you last night. The crossbow bolt was ensorcelled to annul *life*."

Fejelis flinched, the reaction unavoidable, and rebuked himself for doing so, for Tam fell silent. ". . . Whose magic is it?" he asked, what was to him the most salient question.

"Lukfer believes it is Shadowborn."

". . . Shadowborn?"

"Lukfer visited the Borders some years ago; he sensed it there. He corresponded with a Darkborn mage who identified it as Shadowborn."

". . . A *Darkborn* mage? . . . Then why does Lukfer believe it is Shadowborn magic, and not a variant of magic as practiced by Darkborn?"

"To a mage, the nature of the vitality behind a magic reveals itself." His eyes shifted away, as if recoiling from that thought.

Fejelis noted the reaction for a later question. ". . . I was under the impression," he said, slowly, "that the Shadowborn were entirely animal."

"I, too. But the fires in the city, the murder of your father, the ensorcellment of Lord Vladimer . . . all these suggest a mind or minds, though what purpose besides chaos, we do not know."

". . . And are Lightborn and Darkborn mages incapable of these things—annulling lights, sparking fires?"

"No, but . . . Shadowborn magic is distinct. We *can* use it—Lukfer annulled the magic on the box, learning its structure. He annulled the magic on the bolt, knowing that. He can kindle a fire, in the way they can."

". . . I think I must speak to your Magister Lukfer, as soon as possible. . . . What else?"

Tam's expression seemed to collapse in on itself. He gulped in a breath, like a novice swimmer in choppy water. "Lukfer said that the box had been enspelled by two mages, one skilled and one less so, master and student, he thought. The talisman of the crossbow bolt was a grotesque perversion of healing practice, but not one that requires great strength. I had not even been able to detect it until it struck you. If Lukfer hadn't . . ." He checked himself. "When I sensed Shadowborn magic being wielded within the archducal palace of the Darkborn, I thought it might be the student. So I made an attempt to bind the mage responsible. She was stronger than I thought; she fought me—"

"She?"

"A woman. Potentially sixth-rank, by her strength, but entirely untrained. She was in the same room as the archduke. She had been experimenting with the Shadowborn magic, and when she resisted me, it—expressed itself. Sejanus Plantageter tried to help her, and was badly—critically—burned."

Fejelis's eyes closed. Aside from any compassion due the man, the loss of an experienced and moderate leader on the other side of sunrise would add incalculably to the tensions. The archduke's heir was still a boy, and the regency council . . . the major dukes who would compose it included Duke Kalamay, whose hatred of Lightborn and mages had been controlled in its expression only by the archduke. If yesterday's crossbow bolt had been aimed to kill Fejelis and leave Orlanjis prince, with the southern faction behind him—

He had only Tam's word that Tam's intent was to bind the Darkborn mage and not kill the archduke. He watched Tam's eyes, steadily. ". . . They're trying to start a war between us."

The mage closed his eyes, in pain. "Oh, Mother of All."

There had been no surprise, or hostility, or dismay, or satisfaction—none of the reactions Fejelis would have expected in an enemy hearing his intent divined. He knew he should not be overconfident of his interpretation, but he could think of nothing else that fitted. And as for overconfidence in his perceptions—were it not for Tam, he would be twice dead. He had heard the mage vigilant protest her helplessness while he lay in Tam's arms. The wound itself might have been mortal. Tam had healed it, and wiped the blood from Fejelis's face, and called him by his dead brother's name.

If you've looked your hardest, trust what you see, his father had told him, on more than one occasion.

". . . Was it with the Temple's leave that you attempted to
bind this mage?" Fejelis said.

"No," Tam said. "It's not . . . Lukfer thinks it would be
dangerous for me, for the other sports, if the Temple mages
knew that we knew this magic existed. As best Lukfer can
tell, the ability to sense and use it was lost to the lineages
about five hundred years ago."

". . . Five *hundred* . . ." About the time the Lightborn
ceded the Borders entirely to the Darkborn. "But the
Darkborn can—you can. Lukfer . . ." He saw, then, the connection. "All sports."

"Yes."

". . . This may—change a great deal," Fejelis said, a weak
expression of possibilities beyond his prosaic imagination.
"It may be the basis of a true challenge to the mages' he-
gemony. It may also be the spark to tinder of all the resent-
ments." What he could imagine terrified him.

He drew a deep breath. ". . . We *cannot* let Sejanus Plantageter die," he said. "We need him, not a regency council
run by Kalamay and Mycene. . . . I am putting you under
contract—we will have to find language that would stand
up to challenge without being too specific—to find a way
to prevent his death that does not violate the compact. If
at all possible."

"The Darkborn mage—might," Tam said. "But I don't
know if she—"

". . . Be persuasive," Fejelis said, grimly.

Telmaine

She was aware of nothing outside herself, nothing but the
need to tamp her terrible magic down, bind it within her
skin. People spoke around and to her and she did not acknowledge them; they touched her and she winced away
from their consternation and worry. Intermittently, she felt
a hovering awareness, sensed a half-voiced mental whisper,
<Telmaine.> She drew her awareness deeper and deeper
within herself, sitting in the wide armchair with a dress-

ing gown wrapped around her, unprotected hands tucked under her arms.

"And she has been like this since—"

"Since we brought her back from the ballroom."

Sonn stroked her, a harsh intrusive touch. Her fingers sought a veil that was not there, found only tangled and uncombed hair.

"Mrs. Hearne"—Sachevar Mycene's voice—"do you know who was responsible for what happened in the ballroom?"

I was, tried to start out of her mouth. Her hand slid down her cheek and found her lips, sealing them.

"If you please, my lord duke"—that was Merivan—"my sister is Lady Telmaine Stott by birth."

"Madam, I am trying to get answers."

"My lord, my sister is in deep shock. Her closest friend was killed in front of her; we brought her back here with her clothes soaked in Lady Sylvide's blood."

The words evoked the sticky warmth of it, the iron stink. Telmaine retched into her hands, though there was little to bring up but bile. Mycene swiftly stood and stepped away, and the maid bent over her. Her touch was unsettling, the tumble of arcane symbols replaced by suspicion and fear of the men, protectiveness of Telmaine, worry for herself.

"Please," Merivan said, "leave my poor sister to rest."

The intruders retreated, their voices withdrawing into the next room. "My lady, Lord Vladimer accuses Lady Telmaine of being responsible for this catastrophe. He claims he was aiming at *her*, not Lady Sylvide."

"How utterly extraordinary," Merivan said, in fluting skepticism. "Why ever should Lord Vladimer do that?"

Another voice, Malachi Plantageter's. "Lady Erskane, someone or some*thing* caused materials in that room to ignite, causing injuries to over two dozen people, including the archduke."

I'm so sorry, Telmaine's lips shaped.

"I am *well* aware of that, gentlemen, as my own burns attest. If you have an actual accusation to make, do so, and let me deny it on my sister's behalf."

Malachi Plantageter said wearily, "Lady Merivan, several days ago, a part of the Rivermarch burned down in daylight, killing hundreds. Three days ago, four men died in a warehouse blaze that started so suddenly and burned so fiercely that they had no chance to escape. Lady Telmaine admits to having been on the scene at the time the fire began, rescuing her daughter. Lord Vladimer and Lady Telmaine arrived in Bolingbroke Station two evenings ago, and the train they had arrived in burst into flame. This evening the archduke and others were injured by fire. Immediately prior to that, Lady Telmaine showed signs of great distress. She was heard to cry out, 'No,' and 'Leave me alone.' When I examined the damage, it was apparent that the damage and the injury centered around herself and the unfortunate Lady Sylvide, who were the only people in that part of the room completely untouched."

"Your sister"—that was Kalamay—"was also keeping company with Ishmael di Studier."

"My lords," Merivan said, coolly, "you cannot persuade me that my poor sister has been guilty of anything other than ill-chosen company and being the victim of her husband's ill-considered decisions."

Telmaine made a low sound in her throat, too low to carry.

"But as soon as Lady Telmaine becomes capable of talking, I will ensure she speaks to you. In the meantime, I wish you well in finding those *truly* responsible."

"Lady Erskane," Mycene said, "what is your sister's relationship with—" The sound was abruptly pinched off. Telmaine's head came up; her sonn caught the maid with her hand on the door. The maid snatched her hand away from the door handle. She tiptoed back to Telmaine, bending to breathe, "M'lady?" Telmaine ignored her, listening with her skin.

Merivan was saying, ". . . no more of a relationship with the Lightborn than you or I."

"Mistress White Hand, a member of the Lightborn court, is in custody here in the archducal palace. She was granted sanctuary last night by Lord Vladimer, as she was being hunted by the Palace Vigilance under suspicion of having had a part in the death of the prince."

"And what," Merivan said, "has that to do with Telmaine?"

"Mistress White Hand is a known acquaintance of Balthasar Hearne. Lady Telmaine visited her twice last night, once in the company of Lord Vladimer, and once alone."

"My sister—," Merivan said, with feeling, stopped herself, and said, with a calculation Telmaine at least could hear, "My lords, certainly Telmaine has never confided in *me*—but a woman may be driven to confront a presumed rival for her husband's affections."

"A *Lightborn*?" Kalamay said.

"For a woman," Merivan said, sadly, "infidelity is a matter of the heart. My sister has been unwise, unwise in her marriage, and it seems unwise in her conduct. But I am certain that she would never be part of any conspiracy to harm the archduke."

Kalamay and Mycene took their leave, wishing Telmaine a quick recovery and saying that they must attend to other matters. Their voices were respectful and dissatisfied; Merivan had, for the moment, bested them. Telmaine did not realize that Malachi Plantageter had remained behind until he spoke. "Lady Erskane, how much has Lady Telmaine told you?"

With a brittle laugh, Merivan said, "Superintendent, my sister tells me as little as she possibly can. I do know that, on account of some embarrassment of Balthasar's, their daughter was abducted and held in captivity and Telmaine turned to other persons for help while Balthasar languished in bed. He does seem to have made quite a remarkable recovery," she said, maliciously.

There was a brief silence; then Malachi Plantageter said, "I would not burden a lady with this, but I do not know whether I would have the opportunity to tell your husband or your brother in a timely fashion. . . ." He hesitated. "In confidence I tell you that the archduke's condition is very grave. He is not expected to live." Merivan caught her breath, audibly. Telmaine whimpered and began to rock again. The maid twitched toward the door. "Even if he does live, he may never be able to resume his responsibilities.

The regency council has been convened for his son, under the leadership of Duke Mycene and Duke Kalamay. They have confined Lord Vladimer, considering his mental stability suspect."

"And yet they—and you—give weight to Vladimer's accusations," Merivan pointed out.

"Lady Erskane, I have the deepest respect for your family and that of Balthasar Hearne. But over the past several days, Lady Telmaine and her husband have been repeatedly connected with bizarre and fatal events. I cannot ignore that, and still fulfill the responsibilities entrusted to me."

There was a silence. "Thank you, Superintendent, for your candor," Merivan said, her voice breathy. "Be assured I *shall* advise my husband and my brother of this conversation."

"I ask that your sister remain here. She may keep her maid with her, and the household will attend to her needs. If she needs a physician—"

"I will arrange that our own physician attend her." With an exchange of brittle pleasantries, the superintendent departed. The door closed; the room outside was utterly still. "What has she *done*?" Merivan said, in a low voice.

"Merivan," said her mother's voice, unheard until now.

"I must sit down; I feel faint," Merivan said. Dresses and petticoats moved toward the armchair that Mycene had occupied; hems brushed Telmaine's ankles; fabric whispered upon upholstery as Merivan collapsed into the chair. The dowager said, in a low voice. "You did magnificently, my dear."

Merivan did not answer the praise. Her sonn rasped against Telmaine's skin. "Telmaine, *what have you done*?"

"Merivan!" the dowager hissed. "Do not undo all your good work."

Telmaine's lips moved, soundlessly. *Nobody's listening, Mama. I would know.*

"Vladimer has gone quite mad," Merivan said.

"Merivan," warningly.

"He tried to kill Telmaine, Mama, and he did kill Sylvide.
  ⸻e is accusing Telmaine of—of *sorcery*." Merivan's

teeth chattered on the last word. "I'm shaking," she said, in an affronted voice, Merivan, who prided herself on her composure and propriety. "Thank the Sole God that the dukes don't believe him, even if the superintendent—oh, I do feel unwell. . . ."

"Lord Vladimer," the dowager said, slowly, "has made a great many enemies over the years." And then she added, oddly, "Poor boy."

The hard knock on the door, quickly repeated, startled Merivan into a blurt of sonn. The dowager said to the maid, "Answer that, please," with admirable calm. Merivan cast around the room, and her mother said, "Don't be ridiculous, dear. We can't hide her, nor shall we be taking up pistols and pokers in her defense, given your condition and my age. *Yes?*" This sharply.

"Need t'talk to Lady Telmaine," Kingsley's voice said.

"Lady Telmaine is not fit to receive anyone," the dowager said, "and this is most importunate of you."

"I'll be worse than importunate, if need be," Kingsley returned, and cast his sonn over Telmaine. "M'lady, the dukes and the super are having their word in the halls right now. The super's minded to arrest you for collusion with sorcery, if nothing else, though the dukes favor the Lightborn having done the archduke. The one thing they're all agreed upon is that they want you caged up, the same way they've caged up Lord V. You're best away from here now."

"How dare—," Merivan said, but the dowager said, "Go on."

"Not much more to be said. It's no more healthy for me here, now, for my part in—well, since I've taken the lady's silver." Kingsley abruptly took a long stride and dropped on one knee beside her chair. "Come on, m'lady, show some of that fine spirit of yours. I'm in no position to smuggle you from the asylum they want you in, but I can do my best to get you out of here. The baron would strip the hide off me if I didn't."

The dowager said, "What is your name?"

"Kip—Kingsley, your ladyship."

"You have not been in service long," she observed, "and certainly not in the archducal household. What is your *real* name, and how do you claim to be in my daughter's service?"

Kingsley stood quickly up. Telmaine lifted her drooping head enough to sonn him, standing before her with closed fists, as though to champion her even against her family. "M'name's Kip, your ladyship; none other, you can guess why. A fistful of days ago I was apothecary to the main prison. That job's gone, the price of a good deed and hopes for vengeance. I lost a bonny child in the Rivermarch fire, your ladyship, and I want blood for my child's life. Now another fire's taken the archduke and maybe the lady's mind. I won't see her suffer more."

"Thank you, Kingsley, that is satisfactory. Wait outside. We will not be long. Girl, help me out of my dress."

"Mother," said Merivan, in a strangled voice. Farther away the door closed, Kip retreating in some haste.

"Do take a moment to compose yourself, Merivan; this will all rest on you." Fabric rustled and slithered, and buttons popped under hasty fingers, as the duchess divested herself of her outer dress. "Telmaine will wear my clothes, and the two of you will leave with that young man out there. I rely on you to decide where to go next, but I suggest it not be within the city. I will remain here. I am sure the good superintendent will be vexed, but I doubt he would turn the law upon the Dowager Duchess Stott. Though I do confess I have always wondered what it was to be on the inside of a cell. One should seek out new experiences at one's time of life."

"Mother," said Merivan, an oddly weak reflexive bluster.

"But perhaps you should advise Theophile and Eduard, just in case." The slithering and rustling ceased. "Now, Telmaine, you must put my dress on—"

"We'll have to pad her. Come on, Telmaine, stand up."

Hard fingers dug through the dressing gown into Telmaine's right elbow, sending lancinations along her arm. Through the touch, she felt Merivan's alarm, outrage—at Telmaine and the dukes, equally—nausea, and hurt. Over it all blazed the longing for the safety and order of her own household and the determination that the family reputation must be spared from the scandal of having a mad relative—or worse. Telmaine stood like a mannequin as they padded her torso, threw the petticoats and gown over her head, and buttoned the bodice. Padded into a semblance of her mother's shape, she could scarcely breathe.

Merivan threw a thick cloak around her and tugged the hood down over Telmaine's head until she felt its hem rest upon her nose. "There's no need to make me fit for the road. The more raddled I seem, the better. You'd best stay with the duchess. Else someone might wonder why you're going."

"Yes, m'lady," the maid said, in a small voice.

"Brave girl," the duchess approved. "We shall do well together. Go now, my dears. We shall be along presently."

Merivan spared no time for her own farewells, but forced Telmaine along the passageway, pulling her on when she balked on the stairs, remembering Ishmael sprawled chained and senseless over his captors' arms. In the vestibule Kingsley supported her while Merivan swept forward, raising her voice to demand why the coach she had ordered was not waiting.

"The—the regency council—has ordered that no one is to go outdoors, m'lady," the footman said. "There is a curfew—"

"I very much doubt," Merivan said, with fine imperiousness, "it applies to *me*, or to my mother, the Dowager Duchess Stott. I am feeling most unwell, and I wish to be attended by my own physicians. Bring me a carriage."

"My lady, the risk of further Lightborn—"

"My dear man, I am *well* acquainted with the harms of Lightborn magic, as you could observe if you chose to do so. I shall feel safer by far in my own home. Now, a cab, or we *walk*, and you may account of yourself to the master footman."

Merivan's bullying hauteur bore them past the footmen, down the steps. Kingsley and the coachman hefted Telmaine into the coach, leaving her to grope blindly up onto the seat. Merivan climbed in behind her, the sharp breath she drew as she seated herself suddenly reminiscent of Ishmael di Studier as they fled Balthasar's town house, he suffering from burns sustained escaping the blazing Rivermarch.

"Meri—," she croaked.

"For pity's sake," her sister rasped, "hold your tongue!"

Kingsley climbed up beside the coachman, ready to stiffen his resolve if need be. The gates that enclosed the entrance ground open; the carriage lurched forward and gained speed down the narrow driveway, throwing them against the side on the sharp turn. At the main gates, which were closed, Merivan renewed her argument with the guards—of course the archduke's curfew could not possibly refer to *her*, wife of Lord Theophile, sister to Duke Eduard Stott, daughter of, et cetera. . . . The gates were swung open, releasing them; the carriage turned sharply and the pulse of the cobbles evened.

Suddenly stifled, Telmaine pushed back the hood. Merivan was wearing an odd expression, exhilarated, queasy, and triumphant all at once. Her left sleeve had been cut away and a bandage covered her arm from wrist to shoulder. Her coiffeur was a tangled relic of its former self; the curls on the left side had been singed to frizz and bristles. Telmaine, anguished, whispered, "Merivan."

"Don't *bleat*, Telmaine," Merivan said tartly. "I've been brought to bed of six children; this hardly bears mention. Be thankful you're completely untouched. The archduke was only a few steps from you."

The dowager had been there when the archduke was carried out, arching his burned back away from the stretcher. When one of his bearers jarred a chair, he had screamed. Touch had given Telmaine that memory, too. Bile rose in her throat; she gagged against her sleeve.

"Pull yourself together!" Merivan said. "Be glad you're still alive."

Telmaine started to laugh at the bitter horror of it all. To laugh, and then to sob, crying through her sobs, "Be thankful! This is my fault!"

Merivan reached over and pinched her. "Not. One. Word," she said. Telmaine hiccuped into her hands. "When we get home—," she began.

<Telmaine,> said the voice, and she gave a short shriek of horror. <No!> said the Lightborn mage—she felt his magic grip and bear down on hers, hard, his will lock and

mute her voice. <I'm sorry to do this, but you mustn't scream. I'm *not* going to hurt you, I promise. What happened back there, I never meant. I didn't understand—but you truly cannot go on—>

<*Go away.*>

<My name's Tammorn. Floria White Hand wrote me a letter explaining what she thought—what you thought—was happening. I think you're right. I think we have to help each—>

And then the night split open with a sound like thunder, but a thunder low to the ground across the river. She had heard that very sound—or she had not heard it, but she had imagined it—or Sachever Mycene had imagined it, and she had swept the imagining from his mind. Out of the reverberations came the great shells howling overhead. Barely, she heard Kip's yell, and the carriage lurched into a gallop and a careening turn, crashing against a wall, rebounding onto four wheels with a rain of splinters. Merivan fell against her legs. She caught at her sister with one hand, striving to keep herself upright with the other, feeling her sister's fright for her unborn child. The guns across the river boomed again, deafening her to the sound of the impact of the first flight, which she felt only as a shudder through the floor of the coach, almost lost in the jolting. Another flight of shells raved overhead. The near side of the coach ground against stone, and it dragged to a stop. The far door opened; Kingsley seized the sprawled Merivan around the waist. "*Come*," he screamed, "or we're all dead." He dragged her out, threw her away from the coach. "In there!" Even as Telmaine started to follow, he seized her arm and hauled her out. Her skin was suddenly stinging, the stinging building up to a sear. She remembered, suddenly, the light that had burned her hand through the keyhole of Balthasar's house. She struggled against his grip, sonning wildly around her. "Get in*side*!" he shouted, and thrust her into a dank-smelling doorway, following at her heels to grab and slam the damp-swollen door behind them. Cheek almost against the scarred, splitting wood, he sobbed, "Bastards. Lunatic crazy *bastards*. Every cursed one of them ought to be in an asylum!"

Merivan and the coachman were both there, as stunned as she. Kip turned on them. "What are y'standing there for like sheep? This door's rotten and misfit." He pounded it, a sodden sound. "We've got to go down." All veneer of the genteel footman or educated apothecary abandoned, he grabbed Telmaine's cloak and dragged her toward worn stone steps. They breathed damp and old sewers. "We'll be—," he started to say.

Then she lost him, the steps beneath her feet, and everything else around her. Magic surged up around her, at first with the familiar lightness, but swiftly beyond mere lightness, a dissociating thrust as though the very earth repelled her. As it had done before, when the Lightborn mages conjured a storm to quench the fires of the Rivermarch, the magic—Lightborn magic—caught her as it blazed out of the ruin of the Mages' Tower. It burst apart the third salvo of incoming shells—and plunged down onto the gun emplacements on the slopes above the river. Fleetingly she sensed the vitality of the men there, before the magic plunged into the carefully stacked boxes of fuses and shells. A final, immense concussion pounded across the city as the gun emplacements exploded, annihilating the men servicing them, and half the hillside surrounding.

She came back to herself, slowly. Ishmael's memories whispered of this, of being so utterly spent in magic and body that even breathing seemed too much effort. Her mouth tasted of blood from her bitten tongue; she was lying on the uneven stone stairs, each step marking a bruise from her hips to the back of her head. She swallowed blood and turned her head to one side, struggling against the need to inhale, mortally terrified that she should breathe in smoke and seared flesh.

Her cheek brushed skirts, spread upon the stairs around their owner's ankles. She gasped in the stench of damp and old drains with profound gratitude. The skirts belonged to Merivan, who was sitting above her with one hand on her stomach and her face set in resentful nausea. On her far side, Kingsley crouched with his back braced against the rough wall. He sonned her, an odd, unsettled expression on his face. "Sorry, m'lady. I should'a warned you that it was slippery," he said. A threadbare excuse for her collapse; did he realize, then, what had happened to her?

"And *why*, exactly," Merivan said, and swallowed, "did you bring us down here?"

He shifted his attention from Telmaine to Merivan, very slowly. "The Lightborn tower's been breached."

But it was supposed to happen near sunset, not sunrise, floated out from behind Telmaine's eyes. Nobody reacted; she had not spoken aloud. She was still drifting, mind detached from body, thought from emotion. That, she thought lucidly, was why the curfew: Dukes Mycene and Kalamay clearing the streets before the attack began.

"How do *you* know?" demanded Merivan.

"Overheard Lord V. and Blondell arguing. Didn't make sense of what I'd heard, until now." His hands hung between his knees, fingers apart; his skin must be stinging even more than hers was, since he had been the longest exposed, pulling them all to safety. "Lord V. knew, I'm sure of it. That was what Blondell called treason."

"He was supposed to stop it," Telmaine heard her own, faint declaration.

Sonn snapped at her. *"What?"* Merivan said, and Kingsley, flatly, "He didn't."

Telmaine pushed herself up on the damp steps, elbow still on the hem of Merivan's dress. "He wouldn't—" But wouldn't he? He had defined the Mages' Temple as one threat, and Kalamay and Mycene as another. Set one at the other, and let them destroy each other, was that it? He said he understood the threat of magic, but *could* he, truly? Could *anyone* who had not felt what she had felt, in the storm that quenched the Rivermarch fire, and in the howling roar of magic that ruptured the gun emplacements, truly understand what Lightborn power meant?

But could anyone who had not heard the thunder of those guns appreciate the power of gunpowder and iron? Her own smarting skin attested to the ruin of the Mages' Tower.

<Tammorn?> The barest whisper, almost all she was capable of and all she dared. There was no answer.

"Telmaine," Merivan said, "from your bizarre behavior,

I suspect you know rather more than you have admitted. Let us find shelter, if such is to be had, and then, by the Sole God, you *will tell me*. Or I swear that I shall return you to the palace, and let the dukes do with you what they will."

Tammorn

Tam had twice in his life been caught in an earthquake in the mountain hamlet of his birth, and when the guns boomed, when the ground trembled with their consequence, it was the first thing he thought of. Then Lukfer's agony ripped across his mind, shearing away his connection with the resistant Darkborn mage.

Fejelis had rolled from a restless doze onto his feet, and had his hand on the window shutter before he remembered night and Darkborn and law, and hesitated. That gave Lapaxo time to seize upon him, and bellow, "Downstairs!" to his lieutenant. The vigilant caught Fejelis's other arm and between them they ran the prince out of the door while Fejelis was still trying to muster resistance. The mage vigilant who had been guarding Fejelis swung wildly around, her hair unraveling as Lukfer's turbulence manifested itself in physical form. With a cry of dread, she fled after the prince and vigilants, leaving Tam alone in the room.

Through the link with Lukfer he sensed foulness, cold, life's antithesis, life's annulment, *darkness*. He smelled stone dust, brimstone, blood. He felt pain, shocking pain, utter disbelief, outrage, *death*. From the direction of the tower he felt a massive gathering surge of magic, magic with such rage impelling it as he'd never felt; he felt the magic rise, surge, shape itself, and plunge toward the far side of the river. With his own ears he heard the last immense explosion.

He found himself down on hands and knees, in the brightly lit bedroom. On the bed, the bedsheets spun themselves into cords and danced like entranced serpents to a piper's flute. Books leaped from the shelves to swirl, birdlike, around the ceiling. He came to his knees, panting, and sweeping out his magic to sense first Fejelis, deep in the palace, and then Beatrice and the children, across the river, and the artisans at their various lodgings, all waking in fear at the sound.

Suddenly the dancing snakes collapsed back into mere bedsheets and the bird-books tumbled from the air. All that wild magic coiled and tightened around him. Lukfer's strength shattered his like an eggshell. *<Come.>*

There was no refusing magic and will united to such purpose. As he felt himself being wrenched out of place, he brought his arms across his chest and bent over, as though by physical effort he could resist even a magical dismemberment.

He landed whole, amidst billowing dust and the stench of brimstone, in Lukfer's fine, wide main room. Shutters and window had been blown in, showing darkness beyond. The curtains lay shredded across the rubble. Part of the ceiling had collapsed. There was barely enough light to live by. Gasping, holding the hem of his jacket to his nose to filter the worst of the dust, he lurched toward Lukfer's bedroom.

He did not at first see Lukfer, for the great slabs of ceiling and wall that had fallen across the bed, but he could sense him. His eye went at once to the red gray ooze creeping outward across the sheets. The magic pummeled him, sending him stumbling forward, enough to see that Lukfer's upper body and head were still intact. A fallen light, resting on the pillow, blazed upon the bloodless skin of Lukfer's face as his head turned, wolf yellow eyes glaring up at him, pupils constricted with bright light and pain. Tam reached for the slabs, but Lukfer's magic caught his. *<Leave it alone,>* Lukfer said. *<Help me.>*

Lukfer's hand lay flung out and palm up, dust coated, its fingers clenching and unclenching. Tam fumbled for it as tears blurred his ordinary sight. All his magic sensed was Lukfer's injury, legs and pelvis crushed, right arm and shoulder mangled, heart straining as blood saturated the mattress beneath him.

<Pay attention!> Magic drew him in like a hand on the scruff of his neck, shook him, forced his attention outward. He could sense ripples of magic spreading out from the dying mage, a profligate and senseless expenditure of vitality. All around him he could sense the fragments of

antithesis-of-life that had penetrated stone, wood, *flesh*, the same lethal magic that had been on the bolt that had brought down Fejelis, that had nearly killed himself. The ruins of the tower were riddled with it.

But there was none of it in these rooms, he realized, as Lukfer's magic cuffed him hard, so that, physically, he staggered. *<Follow me.>* . . . There was no residue in Lukfer or these rooms, and he realized then that the spreading ripples of Lukfer's magic were not random agonal spasms. He was purposefully rooting out the shell fragments, crushing and annulling them.

Shocked, he recognized that not only was the power not random, but it was controlled, and with every second growing more so. After a hundred and thirty years a prisoner to his wild magic, and even as he died, Lukfer was finally becoming the mage he should have been. Tam could sense his exhilaration, his hunger to *have this*, to know this, no matter how briefly. It was not a hunger he could refuse. Lukfer's power raced outward, and Tam scrambled after, sensing the faltering vitalities around them, feeling lineage mages struggling to weave integrity back into flesh, and failing and knowing their failure, and knowing despair. His magic caught and merged with Lukfer's, spinning wide to destroy the many—so many—deadly fragments of magic-imbued matter. He had never, in his own turbulence and ambivalence around his own power, known anything so purely glorious. But gradually the effort was less and less Lukfer's, more and more Tam's own, as the body pinned beneath the stone slabs steadily weakened. But Lukfer's will and magic were still strong enough, aware enough, to thrust aside one last effort at healing. *<Leave be,>* Lukfer said. *<I've no pain.>*

A lie; there was great pain, though it was starting to recede. The exhilaration was dwindling away to a sense of repletion, of resignation, a mortal weariness. Tam let the vast mesh of magic dispersed throughout the tower slip away from him, and crouched beside Lukfer. He did not care about others' needs, only Lukfer's. He felt no grief, only devastation and outrage at having to *accept* this. *<There's more Temple in you than you thought, lad,>* Lukfer whispered in his mind. <I am well content to have been able to do this ... once. ... Tell Jo I did think of her. ... I did love her. ...> He moved his head slightly, glazed yellow eyes seeking Tam. <But you are the one I would gift. ...>

Tam felt Lukfer's strained heart lose its rhythm, starved of blood and poisoned by the damaged body. His instinctive reaction was enacted before he thought; he reached in and caught Lukfer's heart with his magic.

Lukfer gasped. His stare returned from a great distance; he was frowning as though he had been interrupted in pleasant thought. The fingertips of Tam's hand blanched with pressure on Lukfer's chest. He would have to let go, Tam thought, he would have to let go, and for good. It had been wrong for him to take hold as he had. In another beat or two, he would let go. *I would gift*, Lukfer had said, before his heart tried to stop. Surely he meant the gift between mage and student of the master's lifetime knowledge, seldom given in full. But surely, though Lukfer deserved to give it, he did not deserve to receive it.

Lukfer's eyes suddenly crinkled in a smile. <Surely, you do.>

And he opened his mind and his magic to Tam, delivering up all the experience and knowledge of a lifetime trying to tame his untamable strength, accrued unrealized until the final moments of his life.

<Now *let me go*,> that wolf-bristle inner voice growled, and Lukfer's magic surged up for the last time, sweeping away Tam's hold on his heart, his hand on his chest, his touch on his mind—tossing Tam himself away to sprawl across rubble with bruising and winding force. Tam's own magic snapped him upright; magic reached for Lukfer; magic grasped the fibrillating heart and tried to restore it once more, but Lukfer's eyes were already fixed, their pupils slowly opening wide to death, and Tam had no more sense of Lukfer's magic or presence in the world.

With a stab of his hand Tam blasted apart the murdering slabs of stone and tile, flicking aside the splinters, punching away the billows of dust. He wound the blood-sodden sheets around Lukfer's body, lifted the body into his arms, gathered the lights around himself with a twist of the will, and launched himself and Lukfer and the lights through the shattered window and over the balustrade, plunging in the heart of whirling points of light toward the rubble-strewn and half-lit plaza below. Whether he would have caught himself, he would never know, but magic surged up around him, snared him, and set him down as light as a mote of dust settling in a still afternoon. A voice shouted, "Tam!" and beyond the spinning lights, he glimpsed a figure hurdling rubble with an agility its gangliness belied. Light flickered across Fejelis's dusty face as he halted, squinted, and tried to duck between the spinning lights. One hit his ribs; a second glanced off his head. Tam slapped the ensemble to the ground, where they shattered, the shards still brightly glowing.

Fejelis scrambled to his feet as the Vigilance reached them. "I'm all right—my fault . . . entirely my fault . . . stupid of me." He glanced around, seemed satisfied that violence was not going to be offered by his protectors, and then his eyes slid down to the burden in Tam's arms. ". . . Magister Lukfer?" He took a long, shivering breath, and returned his silvery gaze to Tam's face again, stepping close enough that his chest touched Tam's encircling arm. ". . . Don't crack on me, Tam," he said, in a low voice. "Don't you *dare* crack on me."

He caught Tam's arm as someone went to take Lukfer's body from him and he thrust them back with his magic. ". . . Let go," Fejelis ordered, but gently. "I know how hard it is for you, but it's time to let him go."

So Lukfer had commanded him. He yielded up the lifeless shell that had held great and frustrated magic and a great and frustrated heart, and left the others to discover for themselves that no act of healing would recapture lost life. Their magic lapped around him, leaving him untouched. Their voices lapped against him, going unheard. Fejelis abruptly kicked his knees out from underneath him to dump him sitting on a stone slab, and called for more light.

Tam blinked Fejelis's face into focus, wondering how long he had been in the tower, that Fejelis, whom he had last seen being bundled into the safer interior, could now be outside. He felt chilled and ill, too aware of the *wrong-*

ness of the night pressing down on him, as though the light of the world itself had been annulled.

Fejelis gripped his shoulder. ". . . Tam, I am so sorry."

An echo of his own words to Fejelis, after Isidore's death. How inadequate they were. He focused a small part of a mind roiling with grief and magic on his young charge. "You shouldn't be out here."

". . . I know." Fejelis was wearing a plain vigilant's uniform and helmet, though the disguise would not deceive anyone who observed the way the vigilants aligned themselves toward him. "My word was needed for them to bring lights out here." He gestured, indicating the night, province of Darkborn. ". . . I justified it to myself with the thought that anyone who had been caught outside had found shelter or would already be dead or dying. . . ."

"What . . . happened?"

". . . As far as I know, the tower was fired upon by cannon—Darkborn cannon—emplaced across the river. We had no prior warning, no prior information. The damage done is—" He gestured upward, up the great flank of the tower above them, dim above the lights except where light shone outward through gaps in the walls, limning broken stone or fractured windows.

A bristle and plush voice said in Tam's mind, *You're not done yet.* His head jerked up, his magic, groping toward the vitality that belonged to that voice, finding the points of chill antipathy that were the fragments of Shadowborn magic, strewn across the plaza. He shuddered.

Fejelis squeezed his shoulder again. ". . . I'm going to offer them shelter. . . . It's the least I can do." To someone else unseen, "Look after him, please." Tam's eyes followed the lanky figure as Fejelis picked his way across the rubble toward a group that Tam recognized as the few surviving high masters. Then Fejelis's foot brushed a fragment of shell and he stumbled, his vitality flickering. Tam surged to his feet, reaching to crush the ensorcellment and matter both. The captain of vigilants hefted and threw the prince aside from the bursting fragment. They argued briefly, the vigilant gesturing toward the palace, Fejelis toward the mages. Fejelis won.

Tam turned, spreading his awareness out, placing each lethal scrap. He wanted to stamp them to fragments beneath his sandals, and grind the fragments into dust. He wanted to pick each one up and feel its useless assault before he annihilated it. These were luxuries he could not permit himself, knowing that he must deal first and mindfully with those that threatened life.

A woman's voice said, "What are you doing?"

Perrin's silver eyes were inflamed with dust, and her right wept steady tears. Her pale hair hung in a tangled mat to the middle of her back, and her gauzy nightdress was caked with dust and clinging to her long, gangly body. Her bare toes curled, wincingly, on rock. ". . . I can feel them. I can feel them sucking the *life* out. . . ." Her voice trembled, and like Fejelis, she held back her next words, lest she show her loss of composure.

He said, hoarsely, "I'll explain later."

She nodded and wiped her eyes. "I saw you bring down Magister Lukfer. I'm so sorry. We just met the once. I liked him."

Her girlish ingenuousness moved him, absurd as it was to express trivial *liking* for that vanished giant of person and magic. He said, "While I'm doing this—will you guard Fejelis?"

"Fejelis?"

"He holds my contract; I'm seconding you while I deal with"—two more shards burst in the rubble—"this. Don't touch it. I don't want—" It was simpler for him to share his memory of Fejelis's life being annulled. She might have the strength to deal with these, but she might not, and he had neither strength nor time to expend in protecting her. She straightened in shock, her head turning toward her brother. "Mother's Milk," she breathed.

He watched her stumble on bruised feet toward Fejelis, and then returned to his grim task.

Telmaine

Kingsley—Kip—led them through the old underground streets of Minhorne, once the day and night byways of the Darkborn. As a giggling gaggle on a birthday outing, Telmaine and her small friends had once been herded round one of the most majestic examples of restoration, an underground square as large as Bolingbroke Station concourse. Here, in a much poorer area, the decay would have shocked her had she not heard Ishmael's account of his underground escape from the Rivermarch fire. In places they had to trudge ankle deep through reeking mud, which made Merivan gag and Telmaine unwillingly remember Balthasar's terse condemnation of the neglect of sewers in the Rivermarch. In other places, boards had been laid, or even boardwalk built, though the boards were unsteady and the boardwalk ramshackle. Along some stretches, the tunnels had been quartered length-ways with stone, to preserve a dry passage and let the rest go to ruin. And all the way along, they had to step, and in places climb over, the rubble of torn-down stone and brick entryways.

Merivan noted aloud that a number of the changes ap-peared to be recent, the rubble new and the boards still free of rot.

"Yes, m'lady," Kip said. "Since the—since the fire over to th'west of here, everyone's thinking to have an escape route."

They were now no longer alone, encountering people spilling in fours or eights or more from the underground doors into the passageway, to accost others as they tried to pass with demands or appeals for information, or specula-tions about noises heard outside. Kip deflected their que-ries in the dense cant of the Rivermarch. On they went, turn after turn, tunnel after tunnel, and when they stopped, it was in one of the half-closed tunnels against a crumbled underground entrance no different from any of the dozens they'd passed.

"This is the boardinghouse where I was t'live after the Rivermarch was burned out," she heard Kip say. "It's not—the place for ladies of your quality. It's not really the place for ladies at all, if you get my meaning—"

"I'm sure I don't," said Merivan, so briskly as to give the lie. "But the saying is 'any port in a storm,' is it not?"

"If half of what I hear's true," Kip said, "that's not t'be said of parts of the Scallon Isles."

Merivan huffed, not unappreciatively. "Kindly show us in and introduce us."

It was a lodging house where, Telmaine shortly understood, Ishmael di Studier had lately kept rooms, rooms that he had turned over to the displaced apothecary. The tall, effete old man who greeted them made haste to inform them that, in his prime, he had been the toast of the theaters and promised to show them his memorabilia. But for all his languishing manner and theatrical flourishes, he briskly reordered his household around their needs, opened a vacant suite to the sisters, and assigned the coachman a room. Only Kip's guarded, "Ruther, where's Seigfried?" perturbed his voluble poise. "Dear one, I do not know. He went out. We can but hope."

And so Telmaine found herself alone with her sister, in an upstairs, interior sitting room with the same cluttered shabby splendor of the rest. Through the walls she could hear the incessant tolling of the warning bell, but otherwise little else—no voices outside, no rattle of coaches on the uneven flagstones, no sound of horses. Merivan sluiced tea into a surprisingly dainty cup and set it down before Telmaine. The smell of the tea wrenched her heart: it was the same cheap, tarry brew that Bal preferred. She cradled the cup and the warmth to her. Merivan sipped, grimaced, and set her cup away. "*Now*, Telmaine," she said.

"Do you really want to hear?" Telmaine said. Her voice creaked as though it had gone unused for more than a night.

Merivan's expression turned disconcerted, as though she was recognizing that she had insisted out of habit. Bored, stifled, and imperious, she had long tried to rule her sisters as she did her children.

"Merivan," Telmaine said, slowly. "My clever sister. If only you'd been able to do what your talents fitted you for. You had to marry the man you wanted to be. To aspire for more means being the object of caricature and cruel jokes. So you fight boredom with society by staying pregnant, though you loathe the tedium of confinement more than you dread the lying-in."

"Telmaine," Merivan said, "whatever has got into you?"

"What do you think happened," she floated her question softly, so as not to rouse the terror, "there at breakfast?"

"The Lightborn—," Merivan said, and stopped. The haughty social mask was gone, and in its place was a fierce gratification at a puzzle coming together, and horror at the solution it showed. That gratification Telmaine remembered from the schoolroom, before Merivan's presentation year and the lessons taken from it. The horror was something new, something surely rare in Merivan's pugnaciously ordered life. Merivan breathed, *"Uncle Artos."*

"What?" Telmaine said, nerves too taut-strung for a moderated tone.

With a trace of her maddening elder-sister superiority, "Of course you wouldn't know."

"Uncle Artos died when we were small, I knew that," Telmaine said, piqued. "He was caught outside by accident."

"No," Merivan said. "Not accident."

And now it was Telmaine's turn to sense pieces falling into a pattern. Fragments of conversations overheard in the nursery and halls, feelings and thoughts sensed when she was still too young to shirk all touch. The grief and shame and guilt and worry were the first such adult emotions she knew. She hardly remembered now whether they were from her mother or her father. But they had centered around her mother's brother, Artos.

From the moment she knew she was pregnant with Florilinde, she had promised herself that magic could not be inherited. But Vladimer had said that the Lightborn bred their lineages to strengthen them.

"If—," she started. Stopped, gathered strength. "If you mean what I think you mean, yes, I am like Uncle Artos."

"Imposs—," Merivan began, a reflexive bark, but she didn't even complete the word. "No," Telmaine blurted. "I *am* a mage."

She heard her sister lurch forward; sonn caught Merivan's descending hand. The emotion conveyed through the touch was as much slap as the blow itself. "How *dare* you!"

"I was born this way!" Telmaine cried. Merivan did not

answer, still standing over her, her breathing quick and harsh. Telmaine splashed her with sonn, a slap in turn.

"Keep your voice down!" Merivan said, hands to her head, in a rare dramatic gesture. "Let me *think*. I feel so *sick*. This wretched indisposition—and now *this*. Mama—poor Mama, how *dare* you suggest—does she—no, *don't answer that*."

"I don't know if she knows. I never knew to—to touch—but after what happened—I don't *know*."

"Who else knows?" Merivan said, calming.

"Balthasar. Baron Strumheller," Telmaine said. "Lord Vladimer. And Kip suspects, I am sure of it."

Merivan gathered her skirts and sat down. "Strumheller is discredited. Vladimer is mad. Kip will stay silent, or go to jail; Theophile will make sure of that. And your husband had better hold his tongue."

"Merivan!" Telmaine cried out, "I *can't*—" But what it was—which of *can't go back*, *can't do this*, *can't bear it*, she meant—she did not know, maybe all together. She bent forward and put her face in her hands.

Merivan said, harshly, "If you are to have any hope of a decent life, you shall."

"A decent life!" said Telmaine, through her fingers. She wanted to laugh; she wanted to shriek. "All hope of a decent life died when I—" *When I first sensed another's thoughts? Why should a five-year-old child be condemned? When I chose to keep my secret, though I scarcely knew what being a mage meant, except that my one confession shocked my nanny to tears? When I used my touch-sense to find a man who could cherish me, rather than treat me as a step for his ambition and a vessel for his children? When I danced with the notorious Baron Strumheller, despite his gloved hands and his reputation? When I let Ishmael teach me how to save Balthasar from dying? When I walked into the heart of flame to retrieve my daughter? When I fought, magic to magic, against the Shadowborn? Agreed to guard Vladimer? Let Vladimer exploit my love, my loyalty, and my fear of being known for what I am? When I told him what Kalamay and Mycene planned, and failed to guess what he would do with it?*

What would Merivan have done, if she had been born a mage? Which of the two choices, Ishmael's or her own, would Merivan have made? Or—would she have taken the third, Uncle Artos's?

"You *are* my sister," Merivan said, her voice brittle. "I have known you since you were an infant in your cradle. Whatever you are, you are still my sister."

"Merivan," said Telmaine, into her hands, "I burned the archduke." If Sejanus Plantageter died, what would she do then? Sit outside and wait for the sunrise, as Artos had done. Balthasar would be furious at her, Ishmael equally so. Neither of them would do less than their all to set things right. And she had assumed they could do so, and that Vladimer would do so, and she could go on as she had always been. Go back to her parties, as Bal's sister had accused.

"There was a Lightborn mage, there in my mind. And I had been—I had been trying to understand, trying to do something with, with Shadowborn magic. So when the Lightborn mage—stabbed at me, I—the fires—burst out. It was an *accident*. Lord Vladimer tried to stop me, because—because the magic dies with the mage—and he *shot* Sylvide." A tremor went through her at the remembered bubbling of blood in her throat, of Sylvide's arms sliding away, of the spark of her *life* drowning. "I had found out—by magic—that Kalamay and Mycene planned to use artillery to attack the Lightborn Temple. I thought Vladimer would stop it, but he didn't. I don't know why."

That was sheer disingenuousness; he had declared himself plainly enough, had she but listened. He had chosen to let his enemies engage each other to their mutual destruction, calculating, maybe, that Sejanus would be able to prevent retaliation spreading, calculating, even, that Sejanus might disown him to do so. Poor Vladimer, she thought, in a perverse impulse of sympathy, her partner in choices and misuse of powers that led to ruin. Poor possessive, scheming Vladimer, to have so harmed the brother he loved, to have betrayed his archduke in trying to serve him.

"The guns were destroyed by the Lightborn mages—I *felt* it happen." She grew breathless again, remembering that flight of magic. It still seemed impossible that she had returned to earth whole. "I don't know how many of them—of the mages—survived, or what they will do now, or what the followers of Duke Mycene and Duke Kalamay will do. Or how many of them are still alive. Duke Mycene—meant to be beside the guns when the attack was launched." Again Merivan stirred as though to ask a question; again she swallowed it down. "That's all," Telmaine said, with a sob. "I've been—I've been doing my *best* to be Lady Telmaine, Mrs. Balthasar Hearne, good wife, good mother, good society lady. I've been—doing what I was told, doing what was expected of me—trying so *hard*. And it's all gone *wrong*. And I don't know what to do."

"There is no call on you to do anything," Merivan said, recovering some sense of balance in her own authoritarian role. "When it is safe, we will go on to my house, and Theophile—" Her voice stumbled; she recovered. "*No*, he should have been already home. But the children—"

Oh, sweet Imogene, the children. Reaching out felt like stretching a muscle scarred and contracted with injury, but she found Amerdale and Florilinde and the six—yes, six—vitalities of their cousins, and the equally familiar vitality of Merivan's husband, which she knew from being in his presence the day before. "No," she said. "No, they're all all right."

"Then we will return to my house," Merivan said.

But Telmaine, reaching farther, had found the archduke. Even at this remove, she sensed his grievous hurt. "No," she said, breathless.

"Telmaine, it is quite obvious to me—"

"Everyone," she gasped, "has been telling me what to do. Balthasar. Ishmael. *Vladimer.* You. I *wanted* them to. I thought they knew better and that I could trust them. But they didn't—and I couldn't—and I'm the one—" Suddenly she remembered the last hour of her labor with Florilinde, when, after screaming her refusal to go on, after sinking her teeth into Balthasar's hand to punish his false show of confidence in her, she had found strength she knew she did not have to do the impossible. Now she summoned up her strength for this assertion, for this—birth. "*I* am the one with the power. *I* will live or die with the consequences. So *don't* tell me what to do."

Merivan's mouth opened. Closed. Opened again. "Telmaine," she said. "You do surprise me." A silence followed, in which they both inspected that statement.

Telmaine said, in a voice that shook only a little, "I have to make it right, Merivan. I have to go back and make it right. But I'm going to need help." She cast around the room, a small room, its shabbiness enlivened by decorations—props, really—a fretwork fan, a spray of peacock feathers, surely artificial in their crispness, a large mass of tired silk flowers. But there was a fireplace, and the fire was set. She drew a deep breath, gripping her hands one in the other, and reached tentatively out toward the tinder. The effort felt like pressing on a bruise. With a soft *whumph* of bursting flame, the fire caught. Merivan shrieked, springing from her chair. Telmaine remembered then her sister's burned arm. "It's all right," she said, quickly. "It's just—" But Merivan, clinging to the chair, sonned her and the fire, her and the fire, her expression raw with fright. Whatever Telmaine had said up until now, this demonstration had made it real. "Meri—"

<*What are you doing?*>

<Getting your attention,> she managed, though her heart promptly started to thump with fright. "Meri— Merivan," she tried, as her sister bolted past her into the bedroom of the suite. She started to go after her; the Lightborn's will collapsed her legs beneath her. <Stop that!> she demanded, and pushed back hard. At least no one was near enough to be injured, should the fire erupt around her.

That thought stayed the Lightborn's assault. <You're a menace.>

<Would you please *listen* to me!> she said. And bringing to the forefront of her mind her mother's memory of the suffering archduke. <This would never have happened if you hadn't attacked me.>

<And what about *this*?> returned the Lightborn mage, and through her awareness tumbled his impressions of the destruction and carnage around the fallen tower. They came almost too quickly to leave individual impressions; all that remained was horror, death, suffering—and fury. She found herself pressed back in the chair, physically cowering.

<I'm sorry,> blurted out of her. <I'm sorry. I thought when I told him, I thought he'd stop it.>

She thought he had gone, with his final cruel sally, but he said, <*You knew? He*—sweet Mother, this is impossible with someone as untrained as you.>

As if his mental voice wasn't like being rubbed with ground glass, she thought. She sensed him making an effort to contain himself. Pride was at stake, the pride of the trained Temple mage. Another thought jumped, flealike, between them, her opinion of their training, and their principles, that they had neither sensed the Shadowborn nor moved against them. She sensed his sudden, acute attention, a focus sharp as a meat knife. <Explain,> he said. <But let me put that fire out first.>

<I can do that,> she said, and did so, smothering the flames as readily as she had done those kindled in her folded papers.

<This will go a lot more quickly if you just hold back and let me look for myself.>

<I don't know you well enough, *sir*. And I have no reason whatsoever to trust you.>

<Point—taken,> he said, suddenly sounding desperately tired. Like Ishmael, at times, she thought, and fought a softening. <Then just tell me—explain to me—how you came to be working with *that* magic.>

She began again, from her meeting with Ishmael di Studier and their arrival on her husband's doorstep to find Balthasar battered and dying. . . . He asked no questions; perhaps he did not need to, understanding far more of magic than she. The truth, unadorned, did not take very long. At the end she said, <I can heal the archduke, I know I can. But I can't get there as long as you are out with your lights.>

<We won't be taking our lights in until we're sure we have *everyone* accounted for.> Utter lack of compromise in his tone.

And after sunrise, she could not travel at all. Maybe there was a way through the tunnels that would bring them close to the archducal palace. Maybe since the archducal palace was well away from the prince's palace, maybe being a healer mage, she might last long enough outside . . . if she did not lose her reason first. Her courage shriveled at the memory of the sear of light on her skin.

<*Stop*,> he said, anguished again at some memory. She sensed him fighting for composure. <Floria's letter . . . Floria's letter said that you believed that she had been ensorcelled to take a talisman into the prince's room, and that the people responsible for the ensorcellment were Shadowborn. You did not tell her, did you, that you are mageborn?>

I am not—a twitch of old reflex. <You most certainly are,> he said, his tone a slap. <You met the Shadowborn— the one that ensorcelled your Vladimer—as mage to mage, yes? That is where you came by your knowledge.>

<He forced it on me,> she said, with all the outrage a woman could summon.

<But you've been—experimenting with it—since. Mother of All, woman, I took you for one of *them*!>

<Does that mean you *knew about the Shadowborn*?> she demanded—thinking of Ishmael returning burned, shocked, and reeking from beneath the burning Rivermarch, thinking of her daughter screaming as the warehouse blazed around her, thinking of Vladimer, laid out unconscious on his bed. Of Sylvide's fading presence, and the wet warmth of her blood. And them, the Lightborn mages, aloof in their superiority.

<Not all that!> he defended himself. <I didn't know all that. But I did sense the magic, and know it was something *wrong*.> A moment's wrestling with himself, quite palpable across the link between them. <I can get you back to the palace without your needing to go outside. But there's a condition.>

The overtones of his mental voice made her wary. <Yes?>

<By rights I should turn you over to the Temple Vigilance. But I wasn't born a Temple mage; I was born a sport, like you. So I propose to bind your powers myself, until I—we—can deal with them safely.> He was remembering a much-beloved, dangerous man, and the measures that the mages had taken to restrain that man's powers. <*No*,> she said, in horror.

<It won't be like that,> he said, and she sensed a surge of bitter grief—the man had died with the others in the tower. <Lukfer was more powerful and less controlled than either of us—except at the end. I'll be doing what the mages did to me, when I broke the law. I healed a child, outside contract.> There was, she thought, something calculated about that disclosure, for all she felt it to be true. And his feelings around his own binding were almost—content. As though being bound had let him set aside his responsibility for his powers and be other than he was for a while. She could understand. <As long as you do not fight me, it will be gentler than what I tried to do earlier, when I was trying to disable you outright.>

How very kind of you, she thought, not quite back at him. <How can I trust you?>

<I don't know. How can you?> His mental voice was slightly mocking, but she did not doubt, and let him know she did not doubt, a mage of his power and experience could hide any malign intent until it was too late. <I don't think you have any choice.>

<I would like a little while—to—to consider it.>

<Do. There's no need to light a beacon this time. Just project my name.>

And she was again alone, in a small suite decorated with the fading grandeur of burlesque memories. Merely another of the extraordinary places she had passed through since she had met Ishmael di Studier. She pushed herself out of her chair and went through to the bedroom. Merivan was lying limply on the bed, on her back, damp cloth on her forehead. By the fullness in her figure, she would have no choice but to retire from society very soon.

"Oh, Meri." She reached out a consoling hand, both for her sister's present misery and future unhappiness, remembering just in time that she wore no gloves. "I'm sorry," she said. "I didn't mean to alarm you. I've just had a—conversation—with a Lightborn mage. I lit the fire to attract his attention. If it's any consolation to you, I have been most roundly scolded."

"It's no consolation," Merivan said, faintly. She lifted the cloth and sat up, mustering her authority. "I had entertained some foolish hope that this was—some fantasy, some exaggeration, something that—we could *recover* from. But that—demonstration of yours . . ." She paused to dab her face and throat with the cloth. "It is one thing, Telmaine, to trespass with touch. Another to . . ." Do *that*, her wordless gesture said.

Telmaine had also cherished hopes that Merivan might bring herself to accept Telmaine-the-mage, or at least forgive her, as their mother seemed ready to do. Vain hopes, it seemed. She said, quietly, bare hands clasped together, "You thought something like Ish—Baron Strumheller's. Truly, so did I. I had no idea myself what I was capable of; I still don't."

"Baron Strumheller," Merivan said, with a wraith of her old ire. "This is all his doing. And that husband of yours."

"And what does it matter whose doing it is, mine, theirs, or the gods? If the archduke dies—particularly now, with what Mycene and Kalamay have done—it will all be on my conscience." She paused. "The Lightborn mage said he could help me get back to the palace safely. In return he wants to bind my magic so I will no longer be a danger."

"Is that possible?" Merivan said.

"He seems to think so."

"It would be better," Merivan said slowly, "if he could take it away entirely." The stroke of sonn that followed was as deliberate as a gallant's glove slap.

She remembered the crumbled-charcoal sense of Ishmael's magic. She remembered the dread with which he had warned her against the Temple Vigilance, who would burn out the magic and perhaps the mind of a renegade mage.

"I don't know what the effect would be on me," Telmaine said.

"But if it could be done without ill effect, you would have it done."

How typical of Merivan, Telmaine thought, to deliver such a question in a manner that was no question, was a decree. And if it *could* be done, if she could surrender it in a way that did her no harm, if she could be what she had always—until this last week—taken care to seem to be . . .

She realized she did not want to answer that question, here and now, much less give any kind of promise to Merivan, who would surely hold her to it.

"Telmaine? You surely cannot want to go through the rest of your life—and have your daughters go through theirs—known as a mage."

"I'll decide later," she said, bravely, knowing that quite insufficient even for a sickly Merivan. "Meri, I can—help your arm. And your indisposition."

Merivan had drawn breath to interrogate Telmaine's hesitation, but at the offer her expression suddenly rippled between nausea, uncertainty, and fascination. Suddenly, wincing, she thrust out her bandaged hand, fist clenched. "You know it all anyway."

Telmaine brought both hands around her sister's, warily, but could not repress a whimper as she received the full force of Merivan's thoughts, directed straight through their touch at Telmaine's heart: bitter accusation of the ruin Telmaine had made of her life and of her innocent daughters' lives, and the shame she had brought to her family. She whispered, *"You don't understand,"* but gathered her magic. It flooded up Merivan's burned arm, closing raw and weeping skin. She heard Merivan gasp, felt her appalled wonderment for several heartbeats before she snatched her hand away.

"I feel quite restored," she allowed, with suffused civility. "Thank you."

Telmaine smiled sadly. Whether her healing had in any way mitigated Merivan's anger and estrangement, her relationship to her sister would never be the same. Merivan was the determined upholder of society's norms and prejudices, and Telmaine had just shattered those norms. She said, "I'm going to go to the archduke now. I don't know how long it will be before it will be safe for you to go home. But your children and husband should be safe."

"Assuming," Merivan said, "the Lightborn do not retaliate against us for the toppling of their tower. Sweet Imogene, what were Mycene and Kalamay *thinking*?"

Telmaine could have answered that, had she chosen. Merivan said, "Yes, it is imperative that Sejanus live. We cannot have a regency council ruled by. the very same dukes who might already have had us at war with the Lightborn." At Telmaine's drawn breath, she tilted her head and cast a cool splash of sonn over her. "Little sister, your tender conscience is the least of this. Hasn't that husband of yours educated you at all? A twelve-year-old archduke and a nineteen-year-old prince cannot possibly manage this crisis."

And in that, Telmaine thought, was the reason for the mage's willingness to help her. He loved the prince, as a younger brother, a hope for the future, a son, even.

Merivan crossed to the little sink and hung the towel over the edge. Without turning, she said, "It is as well Mama encouraged a little independence in her daughters, or else I would be quite helpless without a maid. Do go, if you are going."

Mage sense led her up another flight of stairs, to Kip's room. The apothecary answered the door to her knock, his face relaxing as he sonned her. "Lady Telmaine."

"Do let me in," she said. Despite the gravity of her errand, she could not avoid sonning the room itself, curiously, since it had until recently been Ishmael's. She was disappointed: Ishmael did not accumulate possessions. He would be even more appalled than Balthasar, who at least had a weakness for books, at her accumulations of trinkets and jars and jewelry.

"Good t'have you up and about again," Kip said, his face wary.

"You know, don't you?" she said, simply.

A half shrug, spread hands. "Don't prevaricate," she said. "You know what I am."

"A mage," he said, cautiously. When she did not take prompt umbrage, he grinned cheekily. "So *that* was why Magister di Studier was so taken with you." His next voiced thought quenched the grin even more quickly than she would have quenched it with a cutting remark. "We've a cursed disaster on our hands, m'lady, if Kalamay and Mycene brought down the Mages' Tower, and the archduke's dying."

"I'm going back to the palace," she said.

"There's no way, from here," he said, flatly. "The underground streets near it were filled in during the Borders uprising."

"There's a Lightborn mage going to help me." She decided to omit the price of that help. "I need you to look after my sister. She knows—I've just told her—about me. I need you to help her get home. Then if you want to risk coming back to the palace . . ."

"They'll not let you at the archduke," he said. "Not to heal, not after—" He stopped suddenly.

She did not read magic to know his thoughts, the conclusion he had reached. She said in a low voice, "I never meant to hurt him, or anyone. The Lightborn mage thought I was a Shadowborn, or Shadowborn agent, because I had been experimenting with Shadowborn magic. He tried to disable me, and I lost control. We've reached a better understanding since."

"What a cursed mess," he said, with feeling. "No need to get further into it with me. I can guess some of th'rest, from what Magister di Studier said. A high-society lady, and a mage." His grin was wicked. "I *do* like it."

"I'd rather," she said stiffly, "you said nothing about this to anyone else."

A flicker of an ironic expression warned her that he appreciated how hollow the request was. "Lord V. know?"

"Yes."

"Th'Mother help you, Lady Telmaine. That's not a man you want for an enemy."

Her thought exactly. But she could not help asking, "Do you not *mind* magic?"

"Because society doesn't?" he returned. "What's society ever done for the likes of me but toss a few coin our way and deride us from its pulpits as drunks, whores, and bastards? We've had far more good of magic than we have had of virtue." He paused, and then remarked, with breathtaking gentleness and impertinence, "You'll be welcome among us, if they turn you out."

Tammorn

<Magister Tammorn,> said the Darkborn lady. <I'm ready.>

He had been aware of her, ready to restrain her magic, if need be, though he had hoped it would not be necessary. She had a natural gift for healing, he thought, and was displaying something of the profligate exuberance of a younger mage, newly come to her full strength. As well as a desperation to recoup as much virtue as she could from her fallen state.

Lightborn customs were cruel and self-serving, imposed by the Temple in their own self-interest; knowing that, living that, had turned him to rebellion. Yet Darkborn beliefs were as cruel, allowing the earthborn to condemn the mageborn merely for their very nature.

<I'll set the binding first,> he said. <I will be using my magic to annul yours. You will only be able to work through touch, not at a distance, while it is in effect. It won't affect your ability to heal by touch.>

He was aware of her ambivalent relief, though she tried to mask it from him, that she might be safer, but also that he might be sparing the greater part of her power. She had little sense of her own true potential. But were he to explain all that he was taking away from her, she might refuse to let him do it, and if she understood her own strength, she might resist his restraint—successfully, perhaps. Leaving him with the problems of her untrammeled power, and the dying archduke. This was for the best. It was only temporary.

<Will I still be able to sleep people?> she said, and while he was puzzling over the word, she explained, <They won't let me close to the archduke.>

<I'll see to that. Just—sit quietly a moment.>

She did. A Lightborn, man or woman, would be asking questions, not waiting with this semblance of docility—a semblance, he knew, because he could sense the conflict in her between the wish to question him and the wish to know no more than she did.

<When I bind your magic, you will not be able to reach

out to me anymore, though I will be able to reach you. I
will . . . sleep the people around your archduke, and then
set you down beside him. I will give you five minutes, which
should be more than enough time for you to do what you
need to. However, lifting you will leave me close to spent.
I've had a busy night.> He could not miss a sudden rill of
fear and rejection from her at a memory of another mage's
mental scream of agony. Piqued at the comparison between
himself and a Darkborn first-ranker, he said, <I *have* done
this before.>

She was not reassured, but said nothing.

<What I mean is, I may not be able to get you away
afterward.>

<I will find my own way,> she said, but he could not help
but feel her hope that once she healed the archduke, everything would start to come right. As gently as he could,
he said, <Don't you think you are being overoptimistic?>

She didn't answer.

<Then . . . one last question, do you sense your archduke,
and the people with him?>

<Yes,> she said, flinching, and he felt her flex her magic
and reach out. He took from her mind the sense of that
vitality, agonized and failing as it was, and expanded his
awareness around it. <There are three people in the room
with him.> Two old men, one younger, the younger one
with his own quota of physical and, especially, mental torment. He lingered over that vitality, realizing it must be
the Lord Vladimer who had permitted the slaughter of the
tower to proceed. It would be so simple to tear open the
vessels in his wounded shoulder in such a way that no one
could stanch the bleeding. Darien or Floria White Hand
would. But he, he was no assassin. The man was who he
was, had done what he had done for his own reasons. And,
as such unprincipled men often did, he would likely find his
own punishment.

Tam extinguished the three consciousnesses with the
lightest of touches and the reverence the task required, like
pinching off the wick of a ceremonial candle.

He slipped the sheath of his magic over her, just as he
had watched be done with Lukfer and experienced himself,

letting it shape itself around her form as around the form of a talisman. He left only her hands free. It was not a perfect binding, but he did not believe she had the conscious mastery to use that gap in the binding to free herself. Her understanding of her magic was still too much influenced by the first-rank mage who had made himself, inappropriately, her teacher.

He felt the binding quiver slightly; she must, he thought, have tried to speak to him. <It's done,> he said.

He centered himself, concentrating inwardly for a few heartbeats to ensure he had no physical weakness primed to bloom as the magic drained his vitality. The Temple trainers had a wide repertoire of cautionary tales, some grotesque. Then he coiled his magic around the woman and *lifted*.

Nine

Telmaine

*T*elmaine felt the Lightborn magic swirl and flex around her, and the sense of weightlessness that great magic evoked in her. She had a sudden, vagrant memory of herself as a small child delighting in jumping from chairs, from stairs, and even—when she could cozen a male relative into lifting her up—from high garden walls. Before jumping became yet another thing a duke's daughter did not do.

And she was simply *elsewhere*. She stifled a cry behind her hands. Yes, she had been witness and privy to the impossible since she and Ishmael had arrived on Balthasar's doorstep, but not direct witness to something as impossible as *this*.

Then she heard the rasping, rattling breathing from in front of her. Smelled mint and dried flower petals that could not mask the reek of disinfectant and medicinal alcohol, burned flesh, and dire illness. Her first fluttering sonn returned a vague outline of a raised, rectangular shape, not a man, but a coffin. She had no sense of his vitality. She all but fainted before reason overruled the horror with the certainty that if he were not still alive, she would not be hearing that *breathing*.

She cast again, more firmly. Tam had placed her at the foot of the bed. The form was a cage beneath the bedclothes, so that they not press against his burns. She could lift the bedclothes and reach beneath; that would be practical, but a trespass so indecent she could not consider it, absurd as that might seem.

Dukes Imbré and Rohan slumped in chairs on one side of the bed, Vladimer on the other. He had been leaning forward when Tam stripped awareness from him, and had slipped from the chair partially across the bed, and now lay awkwardly hunched with his wounded shoulder beneath him, his head turned away and resting on his brother's pillow. He wore a heavy dressing gown, and his feet were bare, exposing the deformity of the one leg. There was no cane within his reach.

Even so, she instinctively put space between herself and him. Steadying herself briefly on Rohan's chair, she moved between them, her skirts brushing Duke Imbré's sprawled legs, wincing for the indignity at so noble and faithful an old man. He had slumped sideways in his chair, his outstretched hand lightly clasping the archduke's, as a man might a sick boy's. He had been a father himself when the archduke was born; his daughter had been the archduke's wife.

She knelt, crushing her mother's skirts, and crept her fingers forward, nudging aside the upper slopes of the tent, touching bandages. Even through the bandages, she could feel the heat of the archduke's fever. His skin, raw with burns and pain, scorched her fingers and burned through to her heart.

Now that she had touched him, she dared sonn his sunken face, thinking it must offer no new horrors. But it was an accusation in itself, the ruin of all that graciousness, strength, and abundant vitality. She made a sound half sob, half plea for forgiveness. The man under her hand groaned and twitched his head toward the sound. A breath shaped itself around a name, a woman's name. Briefly, amidst pain, came the memory of a woman's laughter, a silk-sheathed waist supple between his hands, a woman's fingers walking, teasingly, down the skin of his abdomen. Telmaine's face heated in a most incongruous embarrassment. The name had sounded quite unlike the name of his wife, and no respectable woman wore clothes that left the body so reveal-

ing to touch. That the widowed archduke had a mistress
was common knowledge, amongst men, at least.

She pushed her left hand forward, beside her right, as
though he were a weight she expected to lift, spreading the
load. She took a deep breath, and let her magic, her healing,
surge into him. And instead of an immensely heavy load,
suddenly she had a lofting spirit, light as air, beneath her
hands.

<Careful!> said Tam.

But the archduke was smiling, dreaming of the lady with
the supple waist and lewd manners. Telmaine was the one
who was leaden-boned, scarcely able to brace her hands
against the bed and Rohan's chair and get her feet under her
without tearing out the hem of her mother's dress.

<You are all or nothing, aren't you?> Tam said. <Di
Studier's influence. He has to be; you don't. Time to leave,
Lady Telmaine.>

The archduke sat up. He jarred and caught the protective cage and sheets in both hands with a startled, "What?"
His forceful, resonant sonn impaled her like a butterfly,
and swept over the sleeping Imbré and Rohan. His hands
explored the cage, the sheets, the bandages on chest and
arms, the unmarked skin of his face—there they moved
with a flinching uncertainty that told her just how much
he remembered. In one motion, he threw the cage and
sheets aside, tucked his feet beneath himself, and rolled to
a crouch, confronting her, naked but for the bandages and
quite oblivious to it. *"Is this your doing?"* he demanded of
her, low, intense.

She recoiled, but the archduke lunged for her, seizing
her wrist, sliding off the bed onto his feet. "You are not
leaving," he said, "until I get answers." Tethered by his
hand, she could not escape the force of his feeling, the
memories of agony, of voices talking above him of death,
of a man weeping.

<Telmaine,> Tam said, <watch out. You're about to
be—>

His sentence went unfinished, cut off as suddenly as it
had been when the Mages' Tower came under attack. The
archduke's head came up and around at sounds from out-

side; then the bedroom's heavy double door was flung open before a wave of men, the Duke of Mycene in the lead. She had the vagrant thought, *He moves like Ishmael*—and then he had his revolver against her head.

"Release them, *sorceress*."

Behind him, Phineas Broome cried out, "I sense *Lightborn*."

"Release them *now*." Mycene dug the muzzle of the revolver hard into the tender skin beneath her ear. As his very last act of will he would blow her brains out—as he had been prepared by his very last act of will to bring down the Mages' Tower. The archduke's grip shackled her to his memories of torment and fire.

"I can't," she appealed. "I can't release them. They'll wake up soon, I promise."

Phineas Broome, at Mycene's shoulder, said, "The ensorcellment on them is Lightborn. There's one on her, too."

"It's not an ensorcellment," Telmaine gasped. "They will wake up, if you would only wait a moment or two."

"Don't trust her," Kalamay said. "She's a sorceress."

Blessedly, Imbré's legs twitched. Rohan stirred in his chair and sat up, "What . . . *Janus*?" Through Sejanus's touch, she felt his sear of alarm as Vladimer groaned. The archduke said to Mycene, "Hold her," and rolled across the bed to land beside Vladimer. He slid an arm beneath Vladimer, eased him off his wounded shoulder, then shifted his stance and lifted him easily onto the bed.

"*Sorcery*," Kalamay breathed, in horrified awe.

Telmaine, released, swayed. Claudius Rohan, not Sachevar Mycene, caught her and helped her into the chair he had just vacated, and waved Mycene's revolver away to a modest distance. She could have wept at the kindness, knowing that in a moment, he might loathe her for what she was and what she had done.

"Sejanus," Rohan said, conversationally, "might I suggest a dressing gown? There is a lady present."

The archduke gave an odd laugh. She thought she recognized that laugh, one at the absurdity of social conventions measured against matters of magic, life, and death. One of Mycene's followers brought the archduke a dressing gown and he wrapped it around himself, whipping the cord into a knot in a few brisk moves. He brushed Vladimer's forehead lightly with the back of his hand, then straightened. "Claudius," he said, "would you be so good as to stay here by Dimi while I sort this out?" He spoke with resonant authority and his actor's confidence, betraying no doubt that he could.

He swung back around the end of the bed. Old Duke Imbré struggled stiff-jointed out of his chair and caught him in a hard hug that abandoned all pretensions of dignity. "It's a miracle," the old man said, hoarsely.

"Both less and more than that, I fear," murmured the archduke, and more quietly, "If that is dying, Imbré, once is enough for me." He clapped the old man lightly on the back with a carelessness that his words belied, and steadied Imbré's arm as he sat. He directed the footmen—who were hovering with less than their usual unobtrusiveness—to bring chairs for himself and the dukes, and firmly dismissed the dozen or so men who had come with Kalamay. He would have dismissed Phineas Broome, with them, but Mycene said, "He is working for me. He is needed for your safety, Your Grace."

A brief, recollecting pause. "Strange service, for a republican."

Broome was disconcerted; Mycene, familiar with the archduke's ability to retain the details of men and events, was less so. "He did us all the great service of warning me that Vladimer was harboring a dangerous sorceress."

The archduke's expression became remarkably unrevealing. "You gentlemen have the advantage of me. How long was I—indisposed? Is that the sunrise bell I hear?"

"It's been about eight hours," Rohan said. His face and shoulders sagged briefly with the intensity of those hours. "And no, it's the warning bell, though sunrise itself is very close. About three hours ago, Lord Mycene's men launched an artillery barrage against the Mages' Tower, from emplacements on Kalamay's land on the other bank. The tower has been, at the very least, breached, if not toppled outright."

That, if nothing else, shook the archduke's composure.

"The *Mages' Tower*? The *Temple* itself? Sweet Lady Imogene, Mycene, *were you mad*?"

Mycene's falcon's head jerked slightly and his nostrils flared in offense. Kalamay said, "Only if it is madness to seek to please the Sole God."

The archduke ran a hand down his face, the gesture reminiscent of Ishmael. "And have we heard from the Lightborn since?" he said, in a strained voice. "Do we know how many of them were killed?"

"Not a word," said Rohan.

Did they know, Telmaine wondered, that the gun emplacements had been demolished by the Lightborn mages? If so, neither the dukes nor Phineas Broome said so.

"Sweet Imogene," said the archduke again. "During the night—how many of our *own* people died, do you suppose?"

"We imposed a curfew on the city. Those who obeyed it would have been quite safe."

"Which was the reason for your rather odd request last night," said Sejanus Plantageter, tight-jawed. "Congratulations, my lords, for having lowered us to the level of Odon the Breaker."

"They were mages, Sejanus. You said yourself—"

"I said *what*?" said the archduke, with ripening fury. "That I wished them *slaughtered*? That I counted their lives for nothing? I might not be prepared to let magic ruin us, morally and materially, but that did not mean that I am prepared to declare war unilaterally on its practitioners and murder them in their beds."

"You will not recognize it would come to that in the end," Mycene said.

"Will not, or *cannot*," Kalamay said, voice heavy with implication.

The archduke's drawn breath checked. "What do you mean by that?" he said, dangerously quiet.

"Your Grace, magic left you on the verge of death, and yet we find you restored to full health."

A muscle twitched at the corner of the archduke's mouth. "No expressions of pleasure at my recovery, my lords?"

"I cannot express such gladness, Your Grace, not given the agency."

A beat. "You are implying, my lord duke, that my will is not my own, is that it?"

There was a silence—none of them would be so ill-bred, or treasonous, as to say it aloud, but their silence did so. The archduke's expression grew fixed. "Lady Telmaine," said the archduke. "What do you have to say to these accusations?"

"I'm sorry, Your Grace," she said to her lap. "It is my fault you were hurt." She bared her face to his sonn. "I am not a sorceress, but I *am* a mage. I have not practiced magic until this last week, when I began to do so to keep my husband and children alive. Everything I told you was true, except I left out the part about my own magic. I was doing my best to help protect you—and Lord Vladimer—from the Shadowborn. But there was a Lightborn mage who thought I *was* Shadowborn, because I was—trying to learn how to use their magic. When he tried to bind my magic, the fires—burst out. He helped me come back here—to put right what he and I did. What that man calls ensorcellment is the binding he put around my magic to—to make it safe. I will swear any oath that you ask of me that I did not ensorcell you. And I did not ensorcell Lord Vladimer."

Before the archduke could respond, Vladimer suddenly pushed himself up on the pillow, casting a ragged sonn across them. *"Janus,"* he croaked. "Sweet Imogene, Janus." The archduke did not turn this time, but said levelly, "Yes, Vladimer. Come round here, if you would."

Nobody spoke as Rohan helped Vladimer to his feet and the two of them came around the end of the bed, Vladimer leaning on Rohan's shoulder. With his awareness focused entirely on his brother, he did not perceive Telmaine until he brushed her skirts, but when he did, Rohan needed to catch at him to steady him. The violence in his expression as he stood over her made her tremble. "Dimi," the archduke said quietly, rising to rest a light hand on his injured arm, "sit down. Help me unravel this."

Vladimer released Rohan to grip the breast of his brother's dressing gown with his sound hand. "Janus," he whispered, "by all the gods, I am sorry."

"You, too, Dimi? Perhaps I *am* dead," the archduke said, with harrowed levity, "to be hearing those words from you of all people."

"I failed you," Vladimer said, hoarsely, speaking as though the two of them were alone in the room. "Casamir had suspicions. I confess I did not give full hearing to those suspicions. I believe he was investigating them, when he was caught outside—or trapped outside—and died."

His mendacity was breathtaking: he had *known*. He had *known*, because she had told him, and he had done nothing to stop it.

This is for Sylvide, she thought. She said in a whisper, "Lord Vladimer, *you did know*."

"I failed you, too," Vladimer rasped, "when I trusted this woman. It was her magic that nearly killed you. Had my hand been steadier, she would already be dead."

The silence lasted several heartbeats. "Sit down, if you would, Vladimer," the archduke said. "My lords, it seems this is becoming more tangled, not less. Leave us, please. I need to speak first to my brother, who is obviously not well enough for a prolonged interview. Then I will speak with yourselves. Rohan, would you remain, please, since you have been privy to this strange affair from the beginning."

"And the sorceress?" said Kalamay.

To Telmaine's wavering sonn, his expression was unreadable. "Lady Telmaine," he said, with deliberate courtesy. "I must also ask you to wait as well."

By a sickening irony, of which the archduke was surely unaware, they were escorted into the same waiting room as the one that Mycene and Kalamay had been waiting in when Vladimer set her to discover their plot. As she preceded them into the room, Mycene said from behind her, "The penalty for sorcery is death. Rank is no protection, as Strumheller has cause to know."

"And the penalty for treason, Your Grace?" she managed, though her voice was little more than a whisper.

"Is irrelevant," Mycene said, gesturing her to an armchair with a mockery of courtesy. "The Lightborn are not our masters. Indeed, they are not even our peers. Plantageter will acknowledge that—if his will and wits are still his own."

"Mycene," said Kalamay from the door. "Are you prepared to wait in here, with this *sorceress*?"

The Duke of Mycene did not answer him directly but waved his men to flank the facing armchair, and Phineas Broome to their side, disregarding the mage's hesitation. "He reluctantly admits you are his superior in magic, but claims you could not overwhelm him before he could give warning. At my word or his, my men have orders to shoot, and not to stop shooting until I personally order them to do so." He sat down, even as she still stood, a studied insult. "Do sit down, Lady Telmaine."

"Mycene, have a care," said Kalamay.

"All my life," the Duke of Mycene said, carelessly, "timid people have urged me to have a care, and all my life, I have disregarded them, to my gain."

"This is for your good standing with the Sole God and His Church," Kalamay said. "The woman's power has too much fascination for you."

"All power has a fascination for me," Mycene allowed. "I admit it does fascinate me to know that a young woman has managed for decades to conceal her true nature."

She needed only her ears, not her magic, to hear the appetite in the words.

"And it is power, Lady Telmaine," he said, unknowingly echoing Ishmael. But, sweet Imogene, the difference between Ishmael and this man . . .

"A venal, corrupting power," Kalamay said.

"Oh, do stop cawing, Kalamay," Mycene advised, without turning his head.

"There are penalties for associating with mages."

"Vladimer Plantageter is much more guilty of that than I, and Sejanus cannot impugn me without impugning Vladimer, which he will not do. I sometimes wonder if there is not something unhealthy between those two. Their mother's behavior certainly was never constrained by decency."

"You have a foul mind," Kalamay said. He had sat down on a chair close to the door.

Telmaine, her head low, said, "He simply measures love as he knows it, Duke Kalamay."

She was rewarded by a sucked-in breath. "Don't speak to me, sorceress."

"I am no sorceress."

"In law," Mycene purred, unprovoked, "you are."

Broome shifted uneasily, his expression that of a deeply unhappy man. <Phineas Broome?> she said, but had the sense that she had spoken in a heavily curtained room that swallowed up all sound, all echoes.

"I wonder if there are others like you," Mycene mused.

"If there are, we must find them," Kalamay said.

"I have no doubt the church has its ways," Mycene said, silkily. To Telmaine, "You told Sejanus that Vladimer knew of our plans. Was it you who told Vladimer?"

She set her lips and refused to answer.

"No matter," Mycene said. "Sejanus will accept what is already done. The Lightborn will protest, of course—"

"They destroyed your guns," Telmaine said. "The *mages* destroyed your guns."

"In an impulse of anger that I understand," he said, with no apparent thought of the men who had died manning them. "Still, it is a pity. I doubt a lady can appreciate what an achievement of precision engineering those were. Though I suspect Ishmael di Studier might."

Telmaine choked back her anger at merely hearing him speak the name, never mind in such context.

"Was he your lover?" Mycene said, idly.

He would twist even her rightful denial upon itself. She turned her head away, signaling her refusal to entertain the conversation further. Presently, the footman arrived to advise Mycene that the archduke would speak to him now. Kalamay promptly demanded to wait elsewhere than in the company of two mages. He left, bound for the palace chapel, leaving Telmaine with Mycene's men, and Phineas Broome.

She had thought to ignore Broome, but in the absence of Mycene's baiting, her fear for herself returned, and it was as much to distract herself as to challenge him that she said, "Does your sister know you are here?"

"What's between me and my sister is none of your business."

"How long have you been working for Duke Mycene? Did you *help* him plan this attack? The Lightborn will know about you, Phineas Broome. And unlike the dukes, *you* are not immune from mages' justice."

"If she says another word, shoot her," Phineas Broome said, savagely.

She gripped the armrests, her heart racing, as she heard men's stances shift, holsters snapping open.

"I *didn't* help him plan this attack. I didn't even know about it. I went to him to tell him about *you*."

His tone, near panic, sounded genuine. If he had gone to betray her to Mycene—either sensing the Shadowborn magic about her or to compromise Vladimer—and then found himself allied with men who had slaughtered Lightborn mages—little wonder he sounded so panicked.

As before when frightened, he turned to righteous anger. "You think your birth entitles you to—" A footman interrupted what promised to be a familiar peroration against aristocratic privilege. The archduke, he said, was offering Lady Telmaine a more comfortable suite. With several of the palace guards at his back, he overrode Phineas's invocation of Duke Mycene's orders to escort her off to a small suite used, by the smell of dried flowers, by one or more of the dowagers of the connection. She declined food, drink, and the services of a maid, but she did ask for one of her own dresses, and gloves. Whatever fate awaited her, she would meet it as a lady, not a criminal. The bone heaviness had returned, the exhaustion of emotion and magic expended. She could hear the warning bells still ringing, marking the danger and chaos outside.

Fejelis

Fejelis stared down at the draft contract on the desk before him, marked by his dusty fingers.

He was aware of the mages watching him: three mages, high masters all, his lost and found sister, three members of the mages vigilant contracted to the palace. And of the earthborn: his mother, dowager consort and leader of the southern faction; his cousin Prasav, leader of the northern faction; several senior advisers of the palace judiciary, expert in reviewing contracts; Captain Lapaxo of the Palace Vigilance and his vigilants; and the prince's secretary. He was aware of the pressure of all their eyes on his lowered, cauled head.

". . . I cannot sign this," the prince said, quietly.

Having spoken, he looked up at the three high masters. The spokeswoman was the drab woman who had raised the Temple's concerns over the contract with Tam, now introduced as Magistra Valetta, mage judiciar and eighth-rank. In Isidore's ordered days, Fejelis doubted a single high master had set foot in the palace, much less three of them at once.

For people with such control over matter and vitality, they looked . . . much like the survivors of an explosion in an artisans' foundry he had once witnessed. Dazed and disoriented and very vulnerable.

". . . I think I understand your—need," he said, choosing the word with some care. Because he was not sure that he *could* understand. An ordinary earthborn would have trouble enough, but he, son of a prince, and of the north-south alliance, had been profoundly aware of his own mortality since the age of nine. The high masters in their tower had not been aware of theirs until now.

As with him, their enemies had cruelly taught it them.

If he had been able to be present at the trials and punishments of his poisoners, would he have wished to be?

If anyone had told him that these trials and punishments would not take place, that the guilty would be spared, what would he have thought?

"You will not deny us *justice*," the second of the high masters rasped.

"Shh!" said Magistra Valetta. "Let us find out what he *is* willing to do."

Fejelis looked down at the document before him. It was a contract, between himself and the Temple judiciary, enabling its retaliation, in his name, against the Darkborn responsible for the Temple's destruction. It was properly constituted according to the compact, save that it also sought to license, retroactively, the magical destruction of the artillery batteries.

That, he could almost give his name to. No earthly power could have ended that lethal barrage so swiftly. Never mind that retroactive permission violated the proper-notification statutes and that neither earthborn nor mageborn judiciary normally accepted insufficient time as an argument. This time, neither would dare object. Never mind that if he did give his name to the deed, it would make him responsible in law and before the Darkborn state. It would damage the Darkborn's trust, and damage—he did not know by how much—the artisans' projects, which relied upon Darkborn goodwill. But even so, he could still bring himself to give his name to it, if it stood alone.

But the rest of it . . .

Mother of All, he wished he had Tam here. He needed the mage's seasoning and advice, his insight into mortality and loss from the first twenty-five years of his life, his understanding of magic and the Temple from the second. In scattered moments, he worried about the man he had last seen sitting blank-eyed and bloodied on a slab of broken marble. *Don't break*, he had demanded, but it was not a demand that might be met. A wide heart could be as great a weakness as a pinched one.

He looked up at Tam's substitute, the sister he had lost as a child, so startlingly returned in the midst of ruin as a willowy young woman in a nightdress. In that chiaroscuro nightmare, her hissed, "Fejelis, I'm your *sister*. I'll thank you to look at my *face*," had lent a comic grace note.

But she, too, had almost died. The older mage who had been her lover had died.

He said, to her, "I . . . can't. It violates the compact. I am not sure I could even do it, had it been—" He realized then that Tam would be furious at him, for seeding the notion that such a danger could come from the *Lightborn* side. ". . . Had it been Lightborn. Because the perpetrators were earthborn. And the means, nonmagical." He saw Perrin draw in her breath, sharply. Her eyes flicked to the high masters, questioning. Fejelis followed her gaze, saw a quizzical expression cross Valetta's face, swiftly masked when she realized his attention. She frowned at Perrin.

"...Was there," he said, "a magical component?"

Valetta's hesitation was longer than his. "No," she said.

Perrin's face showed nothing now. He had not yet learned to read her.

"Then it *is* a matter for earthborn. If anything, this contract should be written so that we might act as *your* agents."

The angry mage snatched a sharp breath of profound offense at the suggestion. Fejelis kept his eyes level, his expression steady, thinking neutrality challenge enough. Change-and-about was perhaps a needed lesson here, but not one to be emphasized.

He was aware, though, from the sound of his mother's breathing, that the mage was not the only one offended. A sideways glance found Prasav's eye on him, calculating.

"But I do not think any such contract will be needed. Numerous Darkborn also died, caught outside in the city when the tower was breached. There is no obstacle to their answering to *Darkborn* law for those crimes. One death is all anyone can give."

Though where vengeful mages were involved, he was far from certain of that. He trusted that the Temple would not like to draw attention to that.

He said more softly, "I will see it done, Magistra Valetta. There is a principle of justice beyond contract or compact that made what my ancestor Odon did unacceptable, and that has made this unacceptable." He slipped his fingers beneath the stiff paper of the offered contract and held it out to her. "Please convey my respects, and my regrets, to your archmage and high masters."

"You had better," Prasav said as the door closed behind the mages, "be prepared for when they come back."

Fejelis turned to look at him, past Perrin. "...Why so?"

Prasav's attention shifted to Perrin, instead. "You're not contracted to him."

She bristled a little. "I was seconded when the mage who is contracted was otherwise occupied."

"Otherwise occupied?" said Helenja.

He knew better than to admit Tam might be incapacitated. "With casualties. Contracts do allow reassignment of certain duties."

If it were written into the contract, which Fejelis knew it was not; no one could substitute for Tam in his trust. He resisted the urge to rub his temples, where the caul seemed to press. "Perrin," he said, "could you please leave us for a moment. I need to talk to Prasav and Helenja—" Though he'd separate them, too, on the least provocation. He had no patience whatsoever with courtly warfare today.

"Magister Tam asked me to watch you."

". . . Outside. Now I have the mages vigilant." He made his glance a warning one. "I'll come back to you in a moment, if you would wait."

Straight-backed, she stalked from the room. She never had liked being excluded, from anything. He would have to talk to her alone, too, probe for what lay under Magistra Valetta's long hesitation in answer to his question.

But if the attack was other than purely material, why should the Temple deny it?

He glanced at the mages vigilant, but he had to trust in their discretion under contract, even in such circumstances, because he would be an utter fool to uncover himself further. ". . . Why should I expect them to come back?"

"Because word is that Sejanus Plantageter's not in charge anymore, and if the high masters don't know that already, they shortly will." Prasav inspected Fejelis for confirmation as to whether this was new to him. "My informants tell me that he was injured by an apparent magical attack—a crude one, with fire—last night, and is probably dying."

"Did you know this?" Helenja said, from behind him.

A poisoned question, for he had no doubt Helenja's and Isidore's informants had informed on each other for years, and she probably knew everything he did—through those channels. He suddenly felt the need to stand up, rather than have them picking over him like an unsatisfactory child. ". . . Yes." Those seconds he could spare from worrying about Tam, he spent hoping that Tam succeeded in finding a way to help Plantageter in a way that did not violate the compact.

Helenja's eyes narrowed in suspicion. "And when the mages do come back, your answer will be the same."

"... I am glad you are so sure of it ... since all I know is that the circumstances are likely to be different. ..."

"They are *Darkborn*," said the granddaughter of Odon.

"If the Darkborn will not bring them to justice," Prasav said, "we must."

"Did you *mean* to insult the high masters with that notion of *them* contracting *us*?" Helenja said.

"I thought it a potentially fruitful idea," Prasav said.

"... If we retaliate, either by contracting magic or without magic, it could put us at war with the Darkborn."

Fejelis remembered then his conversation with Tam, and the moment at which the pattern seemed to fall into place, of attacks intended to decapitate both leaderships and inflame their followers.

He gestured in the direction of the tower. "It's not ... a war we would necessarily win."

That made them think: good. "... I have sent a message to Sejanus Plantageter, asking for a meeting. If I must meet with a regency council, then I will meet with them. But in matters criminal, there is also Vladimer Plantageter, the brother."

Who by all accounts could match Fejelis's own relations for cunning, and who might, from the other side of sunset, have discerned the Temple's weakness. "... He has brought down more than one of their own aristocracy for less significant crimes than this."

Before either his mother or his cousin could resume, he said, "... I need a moment to speak to Per—Magistra Viola now."

Prasav and Helenja retreated, with their vigilants, and Perrin returned through the door of lesser privilege, her face heated. Her glance back at the door of greater privilege told him what had gone on out of his sight: the vigilants, or Helenja and Prasav, had blocked her entry through the door that had, once, been her right.

Now, he thought, what could he risk saying to her, a member of the Temple, with mages vigilant present? If he only had Tam's letter to hand to her—which was possibly back in his bedchambers, or equally possibly with Tam, and if so—did mages burn ruined clothing?

". . . Do you know," he asked, "how is Magister Tam?"

"I don't," she said, obviously startled that that was his first question.

They looked at each other across the desk, nearly eye to eye. Her face was both familiar and strange; he wondered if she found his likewise. He wished he had the opportunity to learn more about her, for simple—kinship—as well as the need to decide whether to trust her.

He sat down instead, by far the easier decision. ". . . Magistra Valetta seemed to hesitate when I asked her if there was magic behind the attack on the tower."

Her expression became wary, and stayed so. "She said there was none."

"Was that your sense as well?"

". . . I sensed . . . something. But I am not very strong."

Fejelis laid his hands fingertip to fingertip in front of him. ". . . How many of you died, Perrin?"

She flinched. "Do the numbers *matter*?"

To the mages, it seemed so.

". . . Tam—Magister Tammorn—brought down the body of Magister Lukfer. I am finding it a little . . . difficult to understand how Darkborn shells could kill a mage so highly ranked, and although no one will tell me numbers, I am certain he is not the only one."

"Magister Lukfer wasn't highly ranked, but he was— very strong." She blinked rapidly, her inflamed eyes bright with tears. "Fejelis, I'm not *contracted* to you. I did this because Magister Tammorn asked me to, because he—had something else to do. I didn't expect to still be doing it now. It's allowed, but it's limited."

Her flickering glances toward the mages vigilant made him dearly wish for a private place, a corridor, a balcony . . . though look how that last had turned out.

". . . And I'm very grateful to you," he said. "Would you like to stand down, then? I won't need you, I don't think, unless I need to go back outside."

Her wordless gratitude confirmed her dread of incurring the Temple's displeasure. He felt a moment's regret—the sister he remembered would not have yielded to *anyone's* displeasure. Very conscious of being heir, she was, even arrogant. How bitter it have must been to her to lose such a place for second-rank magic.

He could not, he realized, thank her for her service in the conventional terms, which would seem to her as condescending. "When everything is close to normal again"—assuming that they both survived—"will you join me for a beer?"

"A *beer*?" she said, widening her eyes. "My princely little brother likes *beer*."

"Or wine, if you prefer." Consorting with the artisans had given him low tastes, indeed, but he much preferred artisans' bitter to anything sweet or fruity. He might explain that to her, over that beer.

At the door, there seemed to be a quiet stirring, his secretary gesturing to one of the Vigilance, the vigilant gesturing to Lapaxo. What new crisis was upon him?

"Fejelis," she said, suddenly leaning forward, *"ask Tammorn your questions."*

Then she was gone, and Lapaxo was coming forward to tell him that protests had begun in Darkborn areas of the city, and that mobs were gathering outside the archducal palace and Bolingbroke Station.

Telmaine

Sejanus Plantageter arrived alone, in midmorning. He was dressed as elaborately as she had ever seen him, with all the elegance and artistry of his class and talents. There were no marks about him of his injuries, but his face was weary and strained.

"Lady Telmaine," the archduke said. And then, quietly, "I am so sorry."

Her sonn caught him as he drew back a chair and sat down. There was a guardedness about his movements, a constraint that set distance between them and that attested to his fear of her. But there was also a somber resolution.

"I have spoken to Vladimer and my dukes. Now I would like to hear what you have to say."

I am so sorry, he had said, as if a physician announcing a death, or a father a punishment. "Will it make any difference?" she whispered.

She held back her sonn; she did not want to know the expression on his face.

"No," he said, at last. "If I did not believe you at some level blameless, I would not have entered this room." Her lips parted, but to what purpose? "By your confession, you did not intend to injure me or the others; nor, I believe, did your Lightborn companion. Is he with you now?"

"No," she said. "I think—I think something has happened to him. Maybe in the attack on the tower . . ."

There was a silence.

"Will I be tried for sorcery?" she asked quietly.

"No," the archduke said, quietly. "You already have been."

Her panicked stroke of sonn made him flinch; the flinch angered him, but at himself, not her, she realized as, deliberately, pointedly, he leaned forward in his chair, toward her.

"I have had no trial. No defense. My husband—" And then she pressed her hand to her lips in shame. Law might hold Balthasar as her husband responsible for her deeds, as under it he and she were one. Should she try to shelter behind him, she might drag him to her fate. "You *can't*," she blurted, through her fingers. "Balthasar didn't even know. You cannot condemn him. This is all my fault."

"I don't," said the archduke. "I don't condemn your husband. I don't even condemn you." He smiled, strangely. "Arthritis of the joints is a family weakness. Even at my age, I no longer knew what it was to leap out of bed. Now my knees feel as though they belong to a man of twenty. And as for this being all your fault—dear lady, this one took a committee."

"But I am the one condemned," she murmured.

"I will deal with the rest in good time," the archduke said. "Even, the Sole God help me, with my brother, who told me the truth at last. But if I am to do that, there must be no question whatsoever that my will is my own." A pause. "Do you understand me, Lady Telmaine?"

Oh, God. Sorcery, the very charge that pursued Ishmael, carried a penalty of death—for magic died with the mage and only thus could sorcery assuredly be lifted. "I did not ensorcell you!" she whispered.

"Can you prove it? Can I prove it? Can I even *know* it?" In that last question, in that raw undertone, she heard her fate. It was his own fear of magic that condemned her, as it had condemned Ishmael.

He said, steady again, "What Mycene and Kalamay have done, what Vladimer permitted them to do, could start a civil war with the Lightborn. I do not know whether the mages are satisfied with their retribution, or whether there will be more. But if I am to deal with the Lightborn, and Mycene and Kalamay, I must have the unequivocal support of all my remaining dukes and barons, and of most of the lesser nobility. And I will not have that if there is any question of a magical influence."

She was utterly numb, insensitive to either feeling or heat, the dreadful power of her fires as remote as the never-felt sun.

"A trial for sorcery," the archduke said, "would allow unacceptable publicity. Because you are Anaxamander Stott's daughter, the law allows for an in-camera judgment of your peers in a case prejudicial to the interests of the archdukedom. Which this surely is. Of his own volition, and bravely so, Claudius spoke in your defense."

He did not state what the judgment had been. He did not need to. "Balthasar?" she whispered.

"You have my personal guarantee that any charges against him arising from this will be stricken. He will, however, remain responsible for his own actions; I cannot spare him that."

"Amerdale? Florilinde?" She would not pray to the Sole God, who had renounced all bonds of family. And she could not pray to the Mother, patroness of Lightborn and mages. So who would watch over her children?

"I will do everything I can for them," he said. Perhaps he might be thinking of his own children, younger than her daughters when their mother died.

"Mama . . . ? Merivan . . . ?"

"I doubt," the archduke said slowly, "they will be blamed." Ensorcellment, she understood. She would be blamed for ensorcelling them to help her escape. Once she was dead, so, too, was their guilt.

Her brothers? Her sisters—Anarysinde . . . ? Surely An-arys would have no appeal as a bride to Ferdenzil Mycene now. Except that his father . . . but she could not think of that. Sylvide—but Sylvide was dead. The people she had known, well and less well, liked and disliked, in society . . . to whom else did she owe a plea for the archduke's mercy?

Ishmael? She whispered, "You're wrong about him."

"About whom?"

"Baron Strumheller."

The archduke said nothing. He did not agree; he would offer neither hope nor forgiveness there. Perhaps he even blamed Ishmael for her disaster.

Could she go well to her death, and hope he would think better of her, and spare Ishmael and Balthasar on her be-half? She was not sure she knew how. Death, as she knew it in life, had been sudden and savage, the wrenching loss of a friend from a sickness in the blood when she was a child, the death of one of her young suitors in a hunting accident, the shocking death in childbirth of a girl from her presen-tation year, not a year after her wedding. Her father's sud-den death, unexpected to her, not to him. She had touched death in others, chance-brushed soft old skin and felt the pain of tumors, the failing of heart or lungs or kidneys. She had sensed, over and over again, the fear of death in her female friends, for themselves and their children, and the grief of death in her grandparents' peers. During her long labor with Florilinde she had been convinced she would die. A moment before Ishmael had shot the Shadowborn, she had felt her life being uprooted, with her magic, from her flesh; when he had shot it, she had felt *its* death.

But none of the deaths she had felt or observed, none of the deaths she had enacted as a child making believe in the nursery, none of the deaths she had ever feared, included being shackled to a post before sunrise, or placed in a box with slits in it—the traditional death by blades of light.

"How will it be done?" she heard herself say, in the cool tones of a lady forced to discuss a most disagreeable subject.

He made a sound in his throat, as though he had choked back an involuntary protest.

She had no sense of whether it was light or dark outside, whether she must linger one hour or twelve in this condemned but not yet dead state. "Is it light outside yet?"

"It is," he said, in a half-strangled voice. "But—there is an execution room within the palace." She remembered Vladimer's grisly tour of the palace's halls and history and that room that could be opened to sunlight, for the discreet disposal of the condemned. That was what Vladimer had meant, about protections not available to the common-born: in the interests of the state, she would be denied a trial.

The archduke came to his feet. She did not need magic to feel the effort it took for him to do so without rushing. "I can give you—I *will* give you time to say good-bye to your mother, write your letters, set your affairs in order. If you need a physician, one will be called. If you need a priest, there is one in the palace. I give you my word that inasmuch as it is in my power, your family will not suffer for your being condemned as a sorceress."

But it is not in your power, she thought. *You already said so. Nor is it in your power to grant me what I most wish, the chance to say farewell to my husband and daughters. I wonder if you tried to persuade each other it is a kindness that I not speak to them, or they to me. Or a kindness that you have treated me to a swift execution, and not slow death by blades of light.*

I do not like your notions of kindness, my lords.

"Your Grace," she said, more firmly, lowering her hands from her face. "Would you please tell me one thing? What was your vote?"

"I . . . abstained," he said, his voice very quiet.

Ten

Telmaine

*S*he wrote no letters of farewell, but entrusted messages to Balthasar and the children to her mother. Had they been alone, she would have left a message for Ishmael, too, but Mycene's guards would not leave them.

They did not touch until the last, until the archduke's guards came to take her to the execution room. Then Telmaine kissed her mother, and her mother laid her hand along Telmaine's face, although the turmoil in her mother's heart and thoughts, and her memories of her brother—all of which perhaps she meant to conceal with her thoughts of love—were nearly unbearable. "Take good care of my children, Mama," she said huskily. "And Balthasar."

Her mother's brave smile trembled. "Of course, my dear girl. Though I cannot help but *wish* that he had not opened his door to that woman."

"Oh, I, too," Telmaine said. "But had he not, he would not have been my Balthasar. Do take care of him, please. Don't let anyone blame him. He has made me very happy, all my married life."

Her mother pulled her into her arms, embracing her with a ferocity Telmaine had not expected to find in that small, placid body. "This is so *unjust*," she said, not troubling to lower her voice.

"Pray for me, Mama," Telmaine said, just loud enough to carry, and then, as though her voice had failed her, breathed, "I mean to escape if I can."

In the long walk through the corridors to her place of execution, she discovered for herself what Ishmael already knew, that while the determination to resist required courage, it also lent courage.

The room to which they led her was the one Vladimer had pointed out. The air inside it was warm, warm with the sun on the outer walls. It had a bare wooden floor and a single wooden chair with no padding or covering—the easier to sweep away the remains, Telmaine realized. She gasped shallowly for air, and nearly shied as the guards told her to sit down. But her faintness decided for her, and probably sensibly so, though her skin crept away from contact with the wood. The guards might have forced and shackled her otherwise. She had hardly noticed them until now; now, listening to them, she wondered what made them so willing to conduct a woman, even a mage, to such a death. Phineas Broome had been noticeably absent during these last hours. Had *he* objected that she, an outrage to his pride but a mage nonetheless, had been sentenced outright to death? Or was it delicacy of feeling on his part? Or cowardice, pure and simple?

She could but hope he was nowhere near, or that he had rethought his service, because she could not think of a way out of this trap other than by magic.

As soon as the door closed behind the guards, she was out of the chair, sonning around the room. All the walls were solid, but the ceiling—the ceiling had a large recessed area, like the sealed windows in a house once Lightborn. It would open to flood the room with sunlight, and it was far beyond her reach. She set her ear against the door, listening with all her being for sound outside. Nothing. She pressed bare hands against the metal of the lock, concentrating on the structures within. If she could sense the working of a body through her hands, and heal tissues with her will, why shouldn't she realign the mechanism of a lock? Though the anatomy of locks was another thing Balthasar had not thought to learn, or Ishmael to teach her—surely his eclectic knowledge included *that*—and she would be sure to tax them each with that when they met again.

She prodded frantically at surfaces. Oh, sweet Imogene, let this work; let her live, to tax them.

She felt something shift within the lock, and pressed deeper, and felt the soft vibrations as cylinders fell and the pronounced click as the shaft dropped back. She groped for the handle, turned it. A thin sheet of cool air, redolent of darkness and safety, washed over her fingers as the door cracked open. No shouts of alarm came, no heavy shoulder jammed the door closed. She eased the door just wide enough, and slid through, and closed it very quietly behind her.

No one sonned or seized her. For several breaths she simply stood with her back against the wall, coming to believe both that she had been put in the room to die and that she had escaped it.

Escaped *it*, but not the archducal palace itself. They would be back to confirm her execution. She must find somewhere to hide until sunset, when she might escape in truth.

Then she heard a door close, very softly, at the far end of the corridor. Someone had come into the corridor, someone moving as stealthily as she. More so, because the murmur of skirts would be audible. A man, therefore, and alone.

She heard a click against the baseboard, as though a shoe had tapped it. The brush of a foot on carpet, close. A breath, almost at her ear. She swung her bare hand up, clouted a head with her forearm. Sonn rang off the bones of her skull, but she had him, her hand gripping the side of his face, her magic pouring into him. Recognition came with the touch of the feverish heat of his skin, the feverish workings of thought. She caught him as he slumped against her, unable to do more than slow both of them in their fall, and shield as best she could his right arm. They sprawled together on the bare floor, his cane toppling heavily across her skirts.

She struggled up on her elbow, her fingers reaching for his face. *Vladimer.* He was dressed for travel in a long coat and stout boots that would give his ankle support, his right arm held in a sling. Her sonn resolved a revolver in a waist holster, and a bulky bag of something soft in his left pocket. His blood was sour with drugs, the strong sedatives that had surely been used to subdue him and the stimulants he must have taken to counteract them. Within the wound, the torn muscles were beginning to heal, but the bullet had cracked bone, and the inflammation around that was still fiery. She had to struggle not to extend healing. She did not want him fit and able to thwart her. And for Sylvide, he deserved to suffer.

What could she do with him? The moment she released him, he would start to wake. Once he woke, he would raise the alarm, if he did not hunt her down himself.

But if anyone knew how to hide in the palace, and to leave unobtrusively, *he* did. She slipped her left hand into his coat and eased out the revolver. She remembered the gunman at the station, dying with a bolt from Vladimer's cane in him, and nudged its weight off her skirts. Oh, sweet Imogene, she was not Vladimer's equal, in speed or cunning.

Should she simply compel him? If anyone deserved it, he did. And she still had her touch; she had just proved so.

But if she did so, it would make her the sorceress she was accused of being.

His sonn caught her as she backed away, his revolver in her right hand, trained on him, his cane in her left. Her sonn caught him as he pushed himself to a sitting position. His hand went to his empty holster, clenched, and twitched away. "Lady Telmaine." His expression was angrily ironic. "Congratulations."

"*I'm leaving.* Don't try and stop me."

Vladimer levered himself to his knees, and climbed slowly to his feet, bracing his elbow as he leaned against the wall. The posture was painfully reminiscent of Ishmael. "May I have my cane, please?"

"Not unless you help me."

He reached into his pocket and pulled out the bulky roll of soft material. "That's exactly what I came to do. Take off your jewelry, open the door, and spread this"—he held out the roll—"on the chair. *Hurry!*"

She propped the cane against the wall, well out of his reach, and inched forward to take the bag. It was surprisingly heavy and filled with a soft fine powder that smelled of ash. Vladimer's expression shaded from sardonic into savage at her recoil. "It's a cursed poor reward for Blondell to be used this way, but do it, woman! Spread him out, drop your baubles on top of him, and let's go."

"But why—"

"Because Sejanus ordered me to."

The ferocity in Vladimer's tone told her how intensely he resented those orders, and how much they bound him. *That* made her believe him. Nevertheless, she used the cane to jam the door, knowing that mere threat of death would not deter him from her destruction. One-handed, she spilled the residue of a man on the chair and on the floor, and then fumbled Bal's love knot from her neck, her wedding rings from her hands, and dropped the necklace on the chair, the rings on the floor. As she did so, she heard from overhead a heavy mechanical thud and the grinding of gears. Vladimer lunged for her, caught her sleeved wrist, and heaved her out of the room. The door slammed.

The sear on her skin faded. When he lunged, she had been convinced she was dead, there and then. She scarcely believed that he had chosen to pull her from the room rather than trap her there. She scarcely believed, again, that she was alive.

"Pick up the cane," Vladimer said hoarsely, leaning against the door.

She crouched, and did so, handing it warily to him, lethal tip leading. He had shot Sylvide, betrayed herself, deceived his brother, and just risked and saved her life. Was he now playing out a cruel, subtle game of revenge that would still end in her death in an unknown place?

"The Borders are under attack," Vladimer said. "Janus just had a telegram from Stranhorne."

"Bal?" she said breathlessly. "Ishmael?"

"Would you move, woman? We can't stay here to debate it."

She leveled the revolver. "Mistress White Hand. We're going to let her out."

From his poised stillness and his intent expression, he was considering his options. Anger steadied her hand, lent her expression a hardness he must believe.

"If that woman were Darkborn, she would be your husband's mistress."

He knew how to cut deep, Vladimer did. She was not going to explain to him that this was the obligation of one prisoner to another. "That is my business," she said with a lady's cool disdain, "and none of yours."

Grimly, he yielded. "We need to get out of the corridor, anyway; they'll be down any minute."

There was no sound from the other side of the paper wall when they entered Floria's room. Suddenly dreading the implications, she whispered, "Mistress White Hand?"

"Telmaine?" The Lightborn woman's voice was husky, with fear or shouting. "Telmaine, my lights are orange. I could have less than an hour before they go out completely. If your being here means anything, please, get them to open the skylight!"

She had thought as much. "That's what—" A signal from Vladimer changed a *we* to an *I*. "I'm here to let you out." She waved to Vladimer, resolved that if he did not understand, or refused to understand, she would repeat her request aloud. He was at the desk, feeling under it; she tensed, but he came up holding a key. She said, "I'm going to put the key to the outer door into the *passe-muraille*. The rest is up to you."

"Thank the Mother, Telmaine," Floria breathed. "I thought I was going to die like . . ."

You need not tell me. She took the key from Vladimer, laid the key inside the *passe-muraille*, and closed the hatch. "Done," she said.

She heard Floria's hand scrabble in the hatch. "Thank you," she breathed.

Telmaine set her back against the paper wall, something she would never have imagined doing before last week, preferring the Lightborn to the Darkborn behind her. Vladimer had withdrawn to the door, his head angled to listen to the sounds outside. And there were sounds outside—men's voices, speaking low as they passed by. Floria started to say something, and Telmaine hushed her sharply. She did not need to expand on it, not to the vigilant. She heard footsteps whisper away on the other side of the paper wall, and was trapped in the dilemma of either risking speech or risking having Floria leave before Telmaine asked her what she *must*. She strained uselessly to sense what lay behind the wall, appalled at how, in a bare few days, she should have become so dependent on her magic.

Vladimer sonned her, drawing her attention; when she sonned him in return, he beckoned her, commandingly. "Mistress White Hand," she hissed, and then, *"Floria?"*

From farther away. *"Telmaine?"*

"Please get a message to Balthasar. Tell him we spoke. It's *very* important."

"Telmaine—what's been happening? I heard a terrible sound a while ago—a booming, and voices screaming from the street—"

"I have no time," she breathed. "I have to go." She followed Vladimer into the small antechamber, and waited while he listened at the door until he was satisfied. Then she followed him out, revolver in her hand. The spreading of the ashes, the leaving behind of her jewelry, those signaled the depth of his planning, the gravity of his masquerade. He meant to leave, and he meant to take her with him; that, for the moment, was sufficient.

Just before the heavy double doors, he turned right, and unlocked the small side door, opening it on a spiral stairwell that breathed coldly and moistly of underground. He started down it, moving carefully on steps that were dipped with centuries of wear. She went after, silently until the question became pressing, "Vladimer, *where are we going?*"

"I told you: the Borders."

He had *not* told her—but she let that pass. "Kip said there was no underground connection between the city and the palace."

"Did he?" Vladimer said, sounding almost amused.

"And even if there were, it's miles to the station." He could never walk it, even healthy.

He did not answer. They emerged in catacombs, storerooms of the old, underground palace, now occupied only by moldering crates and barrels of supplies long forgotten. Between vast stone pillars and beneath immense buttresses, she followed him. If he had brought her here to murder her, she would never be found. If she shot him now, she might never find her way out. One or the other, or both of them, would slowly rot. Immolation seemed the less obscene fate now.

He reached a gnarled wall, felt in his pocket. She hitched the revolver, but he only produced a piece of metal, with a hook on the end, dug it into a hole in the stone, and pulled. Stones ground on one another and drew apart. He slid through into the space beyond. She balked. His sonn caught her; before she could react, his cane was leveled, and if the tip wavered, at this distance he would not miss.

"I cannot leave you alive," he rasped. "Sejanus wants you out of the city, where you'd be unable to twist any ensorcellment over him."

"There is no ensorcellment!"

"*He doesn't know that.* Nor do I. The dukes will be satisfied with a heap of ash, but Sejanus wants you gone."

"And you gone as well?" she returned.

"And me, too." His voice so dull with pain she nearly pitied him.

"We're under the garden now," he said, once more in control of himself. "It's just a few hundred yards more. You might as well give me back that revolver if you're not going to use it."

Lips compressed, she shook her head. He shrugged, one-shouldered, and stepped back to let her through.

The few hundred yards felt like several miles. Her shoes had never been made for slippery flagstone, or for walking any distance, and she had neither coat nor shawl over her light indoor dress. Even when she pulled her gloves back on, her hands felt icy. She missed, acutely, the tiny weight of Balthasar's love knot nestled against her throat. Back in the palace, was the evidence now being put before the archduke? When would they tell Balthasar—*the children*? She shivered and bit her gloved finger, tasting salt.

When Vladimer halted, she nearly collided with him from behind. The underground passageway continued, but he was stooping beside a low grille, and struggling one-handed with its mechanism. She let him struggle until it was plain that he was making no progress, and then silently offered her right hand to partner his left. Between them they got the grille open. On the far side, there was a long step down. He offered his sound hand to steady her as she slith-ered through, and accepted her bracing arms on his own de-scent. She sonned around herself in amazement. They were but a few steps from the edge of an underground canal. To their right, in a bay, a dozen flat-bottomed riverboats, like the ones she had played in in her youth, nuzzled the stone pier. Vladimer said, "Give me the cursed gun. You'll need both hands, and I don't want it going overboard."

She hesitated, and finally yielded the revolver. He checked it by touch, and returned it to its holster. Nothing in his face suggested that he thought of using it here and now, on her. He directed her to cast off the lead boat—"You've two sound hands"—while he climbed carefully in and settled himself by the tiller. The moment the line slipped free, the boat began to move on the current. To his barked, "Jump!" she tossed the line before her, hitched up her skirts, and leaped, landing low and light, gripping the gunnels. The boat rocked, and settled. He said, "Good. Take up the pole, and help keep us straight."

Useless to protest she had not punted a riverboat for years, and then only on her boy cousins' rare sufferance. She knelt in the bow and tilted at the walls, nearly losing her seat on occasion, but he had a practiced hand on the tiller, and as the current caught and began to carry them, their course steadied, and she drew the pole back in.

"Come back here," he said, sliding off the seat to sit on the floor, without relinquishing his grip on the tiller. "The canal runs parallel to the creek for a mile or so, and there are open grilles to level the water. At this time of day there's enough light coming through to burn us."

Bent low, she clambered over the seats. "Tarpaulins, under that last seat; get two out and cover us." She dragged out the heavy, waxy sheets, and struggled to unfold them. He released the tiller only as long as he needed to shift his hand to grip through the tarpaulin, then had her draw it over his head. Her heart beating quickly, she shrouded herself as well. She heard the crackle of waxed fabric as he shifted, his breathing harsh with the discomfort of moving. "Don't talk; we might be heard. And don't move until I say."

Huddled under the heavy fabric, breathing her own exhalations, she fought panic. Perhaps he felt the same, for it was he who broke the silence, in a rasp. "First day I ever spent in the open under tarp, it was with Ishmael di Studier, trussed like a roast for the pot because he didn't know if I was friend or enemy." It was a sketch that begged a story, but if Vladimer had hoped she would ask him, she determined to disappoint him. But speculation was distraction from panic, and the notion of Vladimer bound and helpless, quite consoling. In the stuffy warmth of her own body heat and exhaled air, she grew calmer and then drowsy with broken sleep and strain.

She jumped awake to a foot prodding her through the stiff tarp and the sound of spattering water. "Are you dead, woman? If you're not, take the pole. There's a confluence just ahead that we need to negotiate."

"Is it—?"

"*Yes, it's safe*, but in half a minute it won't be. *Move.*"

She struggled from under the tarpaulin and crawled to the front of the boat, taking up the pole. From ahead, she could hear bubbling water. Sonn resolved a ceiling lower than her standing height and close parallel walls that ended in a void a dozen boat lengths away. Vladimer raised his voice. "The current will take us to the right. Brace us so we don't collide with the walls. If we swing too wide, fend us off the far side of the canal. And sonn ahead for obstructions."

She gasped, and readied her pole, feeling the boat quiver with the first turbulence. Current snatched at the bow. Vladimer snapped, "Brace!" and she jammed the pole into the looming wall, scrabbling to find purchase with her feet. "Don't stall us!" Vladimer said. "Push us forward!" Feet jammed against the side of the boat, gloved hands slipping, she strained, trying to convert her brace to a forward push. The boat lurched, wobbled, turned slowly out of the side channel into the main. *"Sonn front!"* The channel was wide, much wider than the creek tributary, and its ceiling was higher than she might reach, standing—should she be foolish enough to stand. They were moving briskly enough that if an obstacle snagged them unawares, they might capsize. She could swim, but not well, and Vladimer had one arm unusable.

But the way seemed clear. She risked sonning behind her. Vladimer was hunched painfully in the stern, still gripping the tiller. "Lord Vladimer—"

"Attend—front. In two miles—we pull off. So don't—go to sleep on me." She realized, after a disbelieving moment, that he meant it in jest, delivered through gritted teeth though it was.

She crouched in the bow, sonning ahead until her neck and head began to ache from the strain. At irregular intervals a spatter of droplets doused her from above. Vladimer, she noticed, was using the tarpaulin to spare *himself*. At last he said, "We are coming up on the station docks now. There's a bay on the right. Tell me 'one' as soon as you sonn it, and 'two' as it's within a pole's reach. Do it smartly. I didn't intend these boats to be handled by two people alone."

She acknowledged him, voice husky. "One . . . two."

"Fend off ahead!" and he forced the tiller over, sending them straight for the wall that split the main stream from the bay. The force of the rod striking the wall nearly tore it from her hands. *"Bring us right!"* Vladimer shouted, as the stern began to swing round in the current. He abandoned the tiller and scrambled forward to grip the wall one-handed, lending his strength to hers. Slowly, grindingly, the boat scraped past and into the gentler current of the bay. Vladimer half sat, half fell against one of the middle benches.

She sonned around them. They were drifting in calm water. On the far side, only five or six boat widths away, a series of steps led down to the water's edge, each wide enough to receive a single boat, separated by a wall with iron rings at various levels.

If Vladimer had not fainted, he was close enough to it to be of little use. She poled them toward the steps, and retrieved the wet bow rope from where she had thrown it. But for one impossible knot, she managed to untangle it, and leaned from the bow to capture the iron ring and thread the rope through it.

Behind her, Vladimer noted in a tone of remote interest, "We're taking on water."

Their last collision had split boards, and they were indeed taking on water. Their exit was graceless and urgent, accomplished by crawling onto the stone steps. She left Vladimer propped against the stone block while she retrieved his cane from the half-sunk boat.

"I think," she said, "your evacuation plan still needs work."

He made a sound at the back of his throat that indicated agreement, possibly even amusement. She pulled him to his feet, and up the steps, finding a grille not unlike the one they had negotiated on the way out. He let her ply the key and pull away the grille, alone. She scrambled up the waist-high step, and helped him haul himself up, which he did in teeth-clenched misery.

"How far do we have to go to the station?" she said.

"We can't . . . not until sunset," he said. "The day trains are not running. There are rooms. . . ."

The rooms, off a side tunnel and up a short flight of stairs, were appallingly primitive and an utter delight. A small central sitting room with four bedrooms, each containing several narrow beds with chests and cabinets with clothes, carefully folded and preserved with sachets of flowers. Telmaine, with her wet skirts dragging around her ankles, nearly sobbed with relief at the scent of them.

"How long has this *been* here?" she said, rummaging for something that might fit.

"The underground aqueduct . . . is as old as the city itself," Vladimer said, leaning painfully in the doorway. "When this leg of mine made me realize I hadn't allowed in my plan for anyone who couldn't walk the distance—I had it reopened."

"And what did you do to the workmen?" she said, tone biting. Plainly, Vladimer's intent was to have an escape route for the archduke and his family, and for that, secrecy was essential.

"Selectivity, good pay, and intimidation," Vladimer said, taking no apparent offense at her implication. "Change," he ordered, "and join me."

What she wanted to do most of all was *sleep*. No, what she wanted was *him* to sleep, so that she could relax her guard, think what to do next, where to go. He seemed set on taking her with him, to the Borders. One man and one woman against an invasion: what new madness was he planning? She pulled on a sensible traveling dress made for a woman slightly taller and fuller-bodied than she, but still a passable fit.

She found Vladimer at the table central to the sitting room, a dry jacket thrown over his shoulders and a corked bottle and glasses in front of him. He sonned her and drew his breath in sharply, his expression going taut with shock and then anger and finally a strange, wounded ambivalence. She had not thought to wonder whose dress this might be, but if he had first arranged this egress years ago, then— gossip had had Vladimer in love with his brother's wife. Before she had spent time in his company, before she had brushed his mind, she would not have believed it of a man with his reputation, but the Vladimer who had revealed himself to her was capable of intense loves and hatreds.

She sat down opposite him, affecting to have noticed nothing. Vladimer pushed the bottle toward her and handed her the cork twist. Removing corks from bottles was not something a lady did, but she succeeded in extracting a mangled cork and carefully poured out two glasses. She had been afraid it might be beer, but it smelled, quite pleasantly and not at all headily, of early-summer cider. Vladimer produced a small medicine bottle and added a carefully measured quantity of its contents to his glass. She caught the familiar musty scent of a strong pain reliever.

"You said there was a report of an invasion in the Borders, and that you intend to go there, and take me there. What do you intend us to do?"

Vladimer leaned back, bracing his arm. "First, confirm the report. It may be wrong, or exaggerated."

"And if not? What can you and I do alone?"

"Sejanus was not prepared to send reinforcements of the usual sort, at least not without more information. Which I fear might come too late. So I sent a message to Magistra Broome by daylight runner." He paused, but the name had evoked her habitual blank response to any mention of mages and magic, born of long years of concealment. "I asked her to join me with as many of her people as would come."

She discovered then that the thought of meeting Darkborn mages openly no longer dismayed her. The worst, after all, had already happened. "What did you do to Phineas Broome?"

Vladimer smiled, thinly. "What makes you think I did anything?"

That smile, for one. "I tripped the lock by magic. Put you out by magic." His lips tightened at the reminder. "He raised no alarm. Is he dead?"

"No," Vladimer said. "He listened to reason—or at least to my reasoning as to his motives for putting himself at Mycene's service." He paused, inviting the question, but she was cursed if she would oblige. "I believe, for all his claims of concern about threats from Shadowborn against the dukedom, he also intended to divert arms to his revolutionary colleagues. I was able to tell him enough to convince him I could make such an accusation stick, whether or not it was true. I bought his silence with my own."

He sipped the cider, frowning at the taste, or maybe only his thoughts. "He insists that he went to Mycene *after* my interview with himself and his sister, because he was disturbed by your presence. . . ."

She would rather not think about that interview, Phineas Broome, or the Shadowborn taint on her. "So you and I and Magistra Broome's mages are supposed to do what?"

"The Borders has a full standing force and as large a trained reserve as creative accounting allows." *Whose?* Creative accounting was not likely to be one of Ishmael's skills; the man was direct to a fault. "If they have proven unequal to the forces moving against them, then atypical reinforcements may better serve. In any case, it is quite certain we will be facing mages, and mages capable of ensorcelling people against their loyalties." He flinched, as at a sudden assault of pain. Not physical, she thought; no, for if it had been physical, he would have turned to his drugged cider.

"If Magistra Olivede Hearne comes," Telmaine said, "you could send her to the palace. She is only third-rank, but she is Balthasar's sister, and she has a great deal in common with him."

He reacted rather as she had reacted to the mention of mages. She saw the old mask of suspicion drop over his face. Already regretting her compassionate impulse—to this man of all people—she snapped, "For pity's sake, Vladimer, my magic's—what was your phrase?—trussed like a roast for the pot. I don't need it to know how much you hate these orders, *hate* leaving your brother, even though he gave you no choice."

"No," he said. "He did not."

If Sejanus Plantageter had dealt harshly with him, it *was* no more than he deserved. There were things she supposed he and she needed to say to each other, but she did not have the strength. "If there's anything else, I expect it can wait for nightfall. We're both tired. I'm going to get some rest."

She picked up her glass and left him sitting there, alone.

Floria

In the doorway, Floria halted at her first sight of the Mages' Tower under the bright midday sun. Its flanks gaped. Its domed top was an irregular spire, the dome itself reduced to broken ribs. The carved upper balconies gaped like an old brawler's teeth, and the tiling and reliefs were staved in or cracked. In the stillness of noon, a trembling haze of dust shimmered over the ruin.

Her first thought was *None of them told me*—not Mycene, not Telmaine, not Vladimer.

A shout pulled her attention back to the street, to the small mob of men and women at the archducal palace's main gates. Their yells had, until now, merely formed part of the overall city racket, but the shout that had drawn her attention had been, ". . . Hold that door!" Several were looking at her; one was pointing; two, then four, then several, began running in her direction. Instinctively responding as a vigilant, she stepped clear of the doorway, pulling the heavy door shut behind her, slid open the small *passe-muraille* beside the door, and, thrusting her left arm deep into shadow, let the key drop to the tiles on the far side.

The first man to reach her pushed her aside, and groped briefly and futilely into the shadows, until the pain of the dark made him rear back, dragging out a blanched and nerveless arm. "Why'd you do that?" he screamed at her. He was a handsome youth, for all his glossy white gold curls were gray with dust, his kohl-rimmed eyes reddened, and his skin piebald with bruises. His tunic, gaudy beneath its dust and bloodstains, suggested he was an entertainer. She recognized him then as the male ingenue in an acting troupe whose theater home was close to the tower. The performers often rehearsed late, and slept in the theater. "She threw away the key," the actor cried to his audience, voice trembling with emotion. "She *threw away the key*."

Floria eased away, not allowing them to encircle her, while two of the heavier men, one of whom was as dusty and tattered as the actor, took turns kicking and shoulder-tackling the door. "Don't you have any idea what they've done?" The actor swung his arm toward the ruined tower.

Floria followed the gesture, let her eyes widen and glaze with shock, as though she were seeing it for the first time. "Mother of All Things," she breathed. "The tower? *What happened to the tower?*"

Pinning her against the wall, they pelted her with the account of explosions in the night, of slabs of the tower crashing through roofs and crushing out lives and light, of survivors waiting huddled in dusty shelter until dawn, emerging to dig with bloodied fingers for the crushed bodies or quenched residue of loved ones and friends. She assumed the role of an innocent courier, forced by sunset to remain at her destination overnight, only to emerge to meet horror. She gasped; she wept; she cast oblique glances across the group to check whether any one of them might question why a courier went armed like a palace vigilant. Her vest, blessedly, covered the tattoo. Finding nothing more blameworthy about her than ignorance, the most aggressive of the group returned to shouting and pounding on the doors. The others were too absorbed in their own anguish to question hers.

Begging their leave to go and check on her sister who lived close, so close, to the tower, she escaped them. At

the first corner that put a wall between her and them, she
started to run.

The street was Darkborn, a most select neighborhood,
given its proximity to the archducal palace, tall row houses
describing graceful arcs around manicured gardens. There
was horror here, too, muted and subtle horror. Metal
glinted dully from an upper step, marking a thin film of
ash that trailed down the stairs: residue of a Darkborn im-
molated on the very threshold of safety. A smudge of ash
lingered before an open gate to a servants' entrance, while
the gate itself rocked gently in the breeze. Her foot flashed
by a lady's reticule, fallen in the middle of the pavement.
Burned ghosts swirled at her heels, and she could imagine
the Darkborn huddled within their windowless walls, uncomprehending. What *madness* had overtaken whoever
had conceived of this?

Away from the archducal palace, even the Lightborn
streets were lightly traveled. There were none of the open
Lightborn cabs. A Darkborn carriage had overturned
against a railing; the spiked uprights had staved in its sides.
The horse lay dead in its traces, shot through the back of
its head—a runaway, brought down too late? She did not
look inside the carriage, or too closely at the driver's seat.
She shied at the flash of chain armor and polished helmets
from an approaching party of city guards or vigilants, the
very people who would be holding her warrant. She could
not let herself be taken short of the palace vestibule, where
she might have a chance of being brought promptly before ... before Fejelis. The sight of the tower, the urgency of
her flight, had driven Isidore's loss from her mind. She had
been homing on the man who had had her service all her
adult life, when that man was already gone.

Because of her.

Leaving an inexperienced son suspected of his father's
unrighteous deposition, of which, if Telmaine's account was
true—if Tam could verify it—he was far more blameless
than Floria herself. She owed Fejelis his exoneration, if
nothing more.

She opened the nearest gate and ducked into the garden, listening for the sound of chain armor marching by.

Bound for the archducal palace, perhaps. She gave them time to reach the end of the street, and then slid her head around the gate.

At least the momentary pause had renewed her wind. She ran another mile, passing the occasional huddle of pedestrians exchanging shocked news, as well as people proceeding on their daily round with an expression of grim purposefulness. Twice, she came on groups conferring over mounds of ash. As she passed the second, one of them, a student artisan by his dress, smeared the ash with his foot. Two of his companions jerked him away. He remonstrated, his voice rising in self-justification.

She heard the mob around Bolingbroke Station and concourse before she saw it, deep, repeated booms, such as she had heard only from Darkborn factories with heavy machinery, and the dull roar of many voices. Once she reached the approach street itself, she could see the mob itself at the doors, yelling in synchrony with the booming.

She checked her stride, coming to a halt. Fejelis needed the information she brought, would be at risk without it, but Fejelis had the palace vigilants and his own skills, and the Darkborn inside the station had no defenders, and no means of defense that also kept them safe from the deadly sunlight. If those doors gave, the sun would massacre them to a one, railway workers and shopkeepers, businessmen and students, men, women, and children, none of them dukes and few of them soldiers—Balthasar's people.

She knew what Isidore's orders would have been, and she thought she knew what Fejelis would say. But it was the baying of the mob that evoked an atavistic fury in her. On a day when madness abounded, let this be hers.

The crowd already almost filled the apron in front of the old station building. Onlookers draped the statues set at two and ten o'clock of the arc, and only the depth of the surrounding water had deterred most from mounting the central fountain. Floria set her foot on the rim of the fountain, jumped to catch the outstretched arm of the centerpiece, and swung herself up. Two of the youths occupying the statue took one look at her revolver and face, and abandoned their places. A shove dislodged the third. The centerpiece, with its wide metal vanes, was an outrage to conservative Darkborn sensibilities and none too beautiful to Lightborn eyes, but good cover and vantage. Stretched along one of those vanes, Floria could see the improvised ram, a metal-capped pole lashed to a carriage chassis. Its six drivers were lining it up for another run at the varnished station doors.

She thought to be surprised that the city guard were not here already, but feared she knew why. From Balthasar she knew that the old station building descended several levels underground, so even if the doors were breached, the Darkborn might find refuge until the crowd amassed sufficient lights and daring to follow them in. Unlike other places in the city, which might likewise be under siege.

Perhaps, she thought, she should let them expend their rage on the doors—but even as she had the thought, the ram struck with a yielding note, and the crowd raised a roar of triumph that made her flinch. She steadied her revolver and placed two bullets between the lead two bearers. One recoiled, and the ram missed its next stroke. A new man shouldered in to take his place. Floria shot again, and he leaped back, gripping the shoulder that had been set to the ram: either her bullet, or a sliver, had grazed it. Silence spread raggedly outward, people looking around, first randomly, then purposefully. She eased herself up on her elbows, revolver held ready, alert for any movement beneath her that might indicate that someone in the crowd was armed with other than the usual weapons of urban troublemakers.

"Let them be," she shouted. "They are not your enemies."

"Not our enemies! *Not our enemies!*" shrieked a woman from the crowd. By the layer of dust and wild look of her, she, too, had been all too close to the falling tower. "My brother's son was crushed in his bed, and his mother's likely to lose the babe she's carrying now, from grief."

"I am grieved for your grief." Floria shouted back, "But this would not *be* justice. This would be murder hot and foul, and I will not see it done."

"Who are you to judge?"

"Floria White Hand of Prince Isidore's and Prince Fejelis's Vigilance." Praying that the warrant had been kept within the Vigilance.

"Darkborn-lover!" A rock struck the edge of the vane. She did not know who had thrown it, had not seen him or her readying the throw. No, this was not tenable.

The people around the ram scrambled together another charge. She grimaced, sighted, and shot along the length of the ram as they rushed forward once more, but they barely stalled in their stroke. The crowd roared.

"Didn't you look down as you came through these streets?" she screamed. *"Darkborn died by the dozens. They did not know, any more than we did."*

"Someone knew," and more rocks rattled off the fan, hurled from either side, with shouts of "Darkborn-lover," and "Sons of Odon," and "...murdered mages."

Down the central corridor the six rolling the ram were joined by several more, jostling for position. She screamed, *"Next, I shoot to wound!"* She heard splashing below her, and someone seized her foot, using his body weight to drag her down. She passed her revolver to her left hand, caught the edge with the stronger right, hung on. Another solid boom with grace note of cracking hinge. Her assailant, scrambling for a higher grip on her leg, or her other ankle, brought his head within kicking distance, and she kicked, bloodying his mouth. With a wordless shout lost in the roar of the crowd she hauled herself higher, switched the revolver to her right hand, and shot twice on either side of the line defined by the ram. The ram faltered in its drive and struck off center. A flung rock split her scalp beneath the hairline; another numbed her right arm. The fountain was all white froth and thrashing limbs, the statue around her vibrating with blows. Something struck the fan beside her arm, harder than any rock: a bullet or a pistol ball. Hands clawed at her drawn-up legs, tearing clothing and skin. Over the edge of the fan she glimpsed flying rocks, flailing arms, and, behind them, the glitter of sunlight on armor, the gleam of polished helmets. For a heartbeat longer, her grip held; then she was torn free and falling into heaving bodies and white, pitching water.

She regained consciousness slung over the edge of the

fountain, turbid, reddish water inches from her face. Someone was supporting her head while she heaved up froth
and bile. Something rocked in her peripheral vision; rolling
her eyes, she saw a corpse floating facedown, its outspread
arms the fish-belly white of exsanguination.

"Done yet?" a woman's voice said. She croaked assent. Two people hefted her upright, turned her around,
and dumped her on the ground with her back against the
fountain. A question and an assurance were exchanged,
and others moved off. Her ribs ached, her limbs ached, her
stomach ached. She tried to swallow and retched dryly with
the scouring of her raw throat. Rubbed her mouth with a
sodden red sleeve, then her eyes, squinting around her.

Slowly, the scene cohered. The mob broke like surf
against armored and shield-holding guards. The cart holding the ram was overturned, the ram itself foundered and
a hazard more to the mob than the doors. The doors themselves stood at the guards' backs, unbreached, their polished surfaces—kept that way by the small cadre of Lightborn railway workers—gleaming with reflected sunlight.

"What exactly," said Tempe's voice, "did you think you
were doing?"

Floria rolled her head on the supporting tile of the fountain, blinking away trickling water. The vague throbbing
above her eye suggested she had already had a mage's attention. "The hinges were giving."

"We were *coming*," Tempe said.

"How could I know that?" Floria wheezed.

"If you had surrendered as you were supposed to,"
Tempe said, "you would have. Fejelis rescinded the warrant
last night. Now everyone is asking each other why you ran
if you were innocent."

Judiciar to the end, interrogating when Floria was half
drowned, bruised, and feeling vilely ill, in no condition to
do herself anything but a disservice. "Ask Beaudry why he
shot at me," she croaked.

"You were running."

"I *saw* him draw. *Then* I ran. . . . If you can't hear me
speak the truth, and you didn't see for yourself, ask *him*."

"Can't do that," Tempe said, leaning close to say, "Someone put a wood and bone crossbow bolt in Fejelis's back yesterday. Went right by his talisman, which is enspelled for metal. Residue and a southern crossbow were found on an adjacent balcony. Beaudry's unaccounted for on search, and he was skilled with the crossbow."

"What?" Floria scrambled to her feet, or tried to, finding herself in a dizzied half crouch with one hand on the fountain rim, Tempe's arm around her waist, gripping bruises. Her reflexes, it seemed to Floria, had already settled on Fejelis, for all her mind was undecided.

Tempe wrestled her onto the fountain's edge. "That sport mage Fejelis contracted *lifted* in from who knows where, threw everyone off him, and got the bolt out. I don't know how long Fejelis'll survive, but he's fine at the moment. He's put the entire Prince's Vigilance out on the street, to protect Darkborn."

"What . . . ?"

"It was quite a scene, they say. Fejelis said he'd be cursed if he'd be remembered in the same breath as Odon the Breaker and threatened to take it to a duel if Captain Lapaxo didn't obey his orders; Lapaxo vowed to take Fejelis over his knee and spank him if he didn't keep enough for his own protection. Each of them," she added with the insight of her asset, "meant every word he said."

"Mother of All," Floria breathed.

"I expect they'll be the best of friends hereafter," Tempe predicted, her tone adding an unspoken, *Men*.

"Who's back at the palace?"

"Six, under Rupertis. Orlanjis's vigilants are out here as well, though Helenja refused to let hers go. The mage seems to have vanished; word's out he's answering questions from the high masters."

"I have to get back there."

"I'll take you. I'll not be needed until later, when they're ready to sort and fillet their haul here." While the armed vigilants held their circle, the guards, expert in this work, were systematically shackling those who had not fled. Behind them, several mages vigilant moved amongst the fallen, ensuring their survival to trial. City taxes at work, Floria thought sourly. She felt at her waist. Revolver, gone.

At the bottom of the fountain, she hoped, though there'd be no finding it until the fountain was drained. Two corpses floated in the water, beyond saving. The nearest, she vaguely remembered. Following her gaze, Tempe silently handed her her ankle dagger.

"Did I—?" She remembered frantically trying to keep one arm, one knife, free of the hands that thrust her deep, and slashing at the black shapes eclipsing the surface.

"That one, yes." Tempe handed her her rapier in its soaked sheath. "Given that multiple witnesses truthfully attest he was trying to drown you, I doubt there will be more than a fine to pay. The blood money to the family will come out of city funds. The other seems to have been pushed under in the struggle. We didn't realize he was down there in time."

It was one of the youths she had frightened into retreat. Nineteen, at most, face bruised and blood-filled brown eyes turned blindly up to the sky. His last sight the white underside of foaming water and the shadows of people trampling him under? She looked away from the uncomprehending young face. "There was more than one trying to drown me," she said.

"We'll get descriptions," Tempe said. "And we'll need your testimony, too. You've me to thank that you're not joining the haul in the tank. And if you run again, Floria, it will be a vigilant's warrant on you, understand?"

She made a sound that she trusted could be interpreted as assent.

"I don't suppose you'll tell me about this box that the rumors keep mentioning."

"You'll have to wait until I speak to Fejelis." She twisted her neck to look at the other woman. "I'd appreciate having you there; maybe he'll believe I'm speaking the truth."

She pushed herself all the way to her feet, and this time her legs seemed to resign themselves to their task. Tempe beckoned to three trainee vigilants who had, Floria realized, been standing off close enough if they were needed, not close enough to hear what they shouldn't. They closed in around her; they, it seemed, would be their escort.

She cleared her throat. "What else has been happening at the palace?"

Fejelis

In the vast vestibule of the palace, Fejelis silently handed the crimson ribbons to Captain Rupertis, who did not protest the menial task, but patiently tied them in place around Fejelis's dusty red sleeves. They would stand out, clean and shiny as they were, distinct from the mourning garb of earlier grief.

To his hovering secretary, he said, ". . . Has there been any response from the Darkborn?"

"None, my prince."

He disliked that. He disliked that a great deal. In a city in chaos, a palace courier bound for the archducal palace could easily have fallen to a random attack. Even without the possibility of deliberate interception. He said, ". . . I have to know who is in charge over there, and what they plan to do with those responsible for this slaughter."

He bit off the end of the word, preventing others from escaping; he, of all people, could not afford intemperance of speech in a city reeling between paralysis and violence. But he had just come from the servants' quarters beneath the outer wall, adjacent to the tower. Blocks of dazzling carved alabaster fallen from the tower lay amongst shattered brick and adobe of the servants' homes. A glittering ice field of broken glass covered the roadway in front, and the servants' gardens. Glass frost rimed flowers and hedges. Servants, palace staff, and mages together searched for the residues of high masters and servants' children, mingling in death as they never would in life.

Having seen that, how could he not call it by name?

Perrin, recalled to guard him, had stood trembling by his side, tears streaking a face still dusty from their efforts on the far side of the wall, until he had insisted that she go indoors. As she walked away, he heard his sister beginning to sob aloud.

". . . I need an answer, Captain, even if I have to go over

to the palace, and demand it in person." Which he would, their murderous brightnesses, argumentative vigilants, and riots notwithstanding. To his secretary, ". . . Prepare another copy of the initial message." To the captain, ". . . Recall four vigilants—or as many as you think needed to get a message over to the archducal palace. I don't want to send another courier into that chaos. Ask them to wait half an hour for an answer, and if there is no answer, to come back and report to me."

"Yes, my—" Rupertis broke off and turned as five figures appeared in the outer doorway, thrusting Fejelis into the shelter of his body. Fejelis did not resist; he and Lapaxo had settled that, hours ago. But as the figures stepped out of the light, he recognized three cadet members of the Vigilance, Mistress Tempe, and Floria White Hand. Floria's red clothing was shredded and saturated, the skin it exposed mottled with purple and painted bruising, her hair hung in a wrung-out coil over her shoulder, and her eyes had the expression of glazed ferocity he had become all too used to seeing around him in the past hours. For all he knew, he would see in his own mirror, had he time to look. ". . . Mistress White Hand. Good—to see you."

Her smile had a crazed quality. "Prince Fejelis. Good to see you, too."

Tempe reported, to the prince and the captain equally, "We found her trying to stand off a mob in front of Bolingbroke Station, solo. Got there just as they dragged her off the fountain statuary and set out to drown her in it."

"The hinges of the station door were starting to give," Floria rasped, and coughed. "Prince, I've been at the archducal residence. Last person I spoke to, before the one who let me out, was Duke Sachevar Mycene. He claimed to be in charge of the regency council for the archducal heir, and that Sejanus Plantageter was dying of a magically induced injury. He said Vladimer Plantageter had had a mental collapse—though I spoke to the man only hours earlier and he was sharp as a stiletto. But Mycene seemed very sure of himself." Her gaze probed his face, looking for what, he did not know. "I've more information, but . . . I'd better give it you in a more private place."

". . . If it's what you put in a letter to Magister Tammorn, I've seen that."

Her shoulders slumped slightly, with what, he could not tell. He had not studied her nearly closely enough, trusting in his father's assessment of her as an unshakable loyalist. Could he have noticed any inconsistencies in her behavior, signifying her ensorcellment, if he had? *Most useless word in the language, "if,"* his father's phantom voice pointed out. He did need to know whether the ensorcellment persisted. He needed Tam or Perrin—and he was glad the doors stood wide at their backs, flooding the vestibule with sunlight.

". . . Go and get cleaned up, Mistress Floria." By the red seam of a fresh-healed wound above her brow, he inferred she had had a mage's attention already, and the Vigilance prided themselves on their stoicism. ". . . I'll speak to you presently."

It took an effort for her to move off with her old, deadly lightness of step, but he doubted that anyone other than he and her fellow vigilants would know it. Rupertis waved off one of the novices and one of the vigilants to escort her: wise, given that rumors of her wrongdoing would have sunk deeper into the cracks in the walls than word of his rescinding the warrant.

Tempe said, "She wouldn't answer questions on the way back. Without a warrant . . ."

Which frustrated the judiciar, that was plain. Fejelis had the vagrant thought that that asset of veracity must make for a difficult time in love.

When he proved resistant to the hint, she said to her captain, "If I'm not needed here, then I'll go over to the jail, help them sort out their catch." Rupertis, though he twitched a little, gave up the two novices to accompany her.

"Might I suggest . . . ?" Rupertis began to him, and then both he and Fejelis swung toward the sound of running footsteps.

". . . a stiff drink?" Fejelis said under his breath, drawing a startled look and a grim smile from the vigilant.

The runner was Perrin, still dusty and almost as distraught as he'd last seen her. She skidded up to him.

"They're going to burn him out," she blurted. "They've bound him and they're going to burn him out."

"Who?" said Fejelis, though he already knew. And she confirmed it, "The high masters. They're going to burn out Magister Tammorn."

"Come," said Fejelis, but three strides on, he caught Perrin's arm. "... I'm going to want backup for this. Find Orlanjis, Mother, Prasav, Ember. Bring them and their retinue, and anyone else of their brightnesses you think might carry weight. Floria White Hand as well." She gulped. Fejelis said, "... I know it'll cost me, but I owe Tam and I need him." Her eyes widened a little, but he didn't have time to settle gossip. He spun her toward the stairs, released her, and ran for his chambers, to exchange his vigilant's helmet for the caul. Prayed he was not too late.

The mages had eventually taken over the entire south wing of the palace, including the southwest-facing rooms that had once been Perrin's and he had offered to Orlanjis. He trusted that Orlanjis and the palace staff—whose labors since the coming-of-age ceremonial had been nothing short of heroic—would eventually forgive him. The archmage himself had appropriated Perrin's former suite.

It might be mannerly and politic for Fejelis to knock, but it was not tactical, since he was sure his entrance would be barred. He twisted the handle, shouldered open the door, and had crossed the threshold into the streaming sunlight from skylight and windows before he met an invisible wall.

Five people turned to look at him from where they stood encircling Tam, who lay facedown on the southern tent mat that served as carpet. Only his outflung hands moved, groping for purchase on the rough weave. His dusty auburn head lay between the bare feet of a small man in a clean white loincloth and a single chain of rank, and nothing else. The man's head would have come no higher than Fejelis's shoulder, and by eye, he was somewhat past middle age, his copper skin lacking the luster of youth, and his black hair thinning. They had never met, but he had heard Tam's descriptions often enough. The prince who had ruled when this little man was born, in a hidden mage's redoubt deep in the south, was three hundred years dead. It was not merely the pressure of the barrier that made Fejelis's breath shallow, his voice thin. ". . . Magister Archmage."

The archmage waved someone forward with a flick of his fingers, his gaze not leaving the intruder. His black eyes had the fierce, dislocated outrage of a newly trapped hawk.

". . . I am Fejelis, Isidore's son, and prince of the earth-born. Your host for the duration . . . I . . . . have an interest in this mage."

Magistra Valetta stepped into his line of sight, breaking his eye contact with the archmage. "Prince Fejelis," she said, "the contract was not finalized and has now been canceled."

". . . Actions taken even under provisional contract are covered by the compact, and are therefore the responsibility of the earthborn primary." He could feel the inexorable pressure of their magic, forcing him backward. He kept his voice level. ". . . Under whose contract do you use magic against me?"

The pressure stopped so suddenly, he nearly pitched on his knees, and by the thud behind him, someone else was less agile. He did not look behind him, merely found his balance, keeping his posture easy. It was entirely possible his relaxed stance meant no more to the high masters than a cat's lax sprawl. He did not know how mages so powerful would construe threat. As humans did, or otherwise?

The archmage said something in an archaic dialect. Valetta said, "Prince Fejelis, this mage is not under discipline for anything done under contract; it is a Temple matter entirely."

"I'm glad it is nothing that I asked Magister Tammorn to do. But I am not certain that this is *not* earthborn business, given how my father died."

He heard movement behind him, and despite himself, the skin of his back tightened against a blow. Helenja's voice said, "Fejelis, what is this?"

Orlanjis sidled up beside him on his left, his wide eyes taking in the bound Tam, and the archmage. By his indrawn breath, he recognized the latter immediately. The barest flicker of his attention betrayed his urge to look sideways at Fejelis, and then he stared front, unblinking, as he would a deadly sand viper. Fejelis heard their mother hiss Orlan-jis's name.

"Fejelis," Prasav said, "show some common sense. You cannot interfere in Temple matters."

Floria White Hand moved silently up on his other side. She had changed her clothes, but her hair was a toweled tangle and she was sashless and barefoot. And quite deadly, poised on the balls of her bare feet, her bruised face a cool, attentive fighter's mask. Remembering her ensorcellment, he felt his skin prickle.

Too few allies, and the man he most trusted lying bound on that tent rug. He had no choice but to risk—he did not know what. ". . . I think I must, since I believe it concerns the magic that killed my father, specifically, the magic of Shadowborn."

"Shadowborn are a myth," Prasav said, curtly. "You're just making a fool of yourself."

A flicker of movement to the right of him, Perrin, in her dusty clothes, reaching a hand toward him. "Jay," she said, voice urgent and low, "don't. I—mistook what was happening here. It's—it's Temple discipline. Yes, I know it looks bad—but—it's really not as bad as it looks. Just go now."

Did he know her well enough to believe her before the testimony of his eyes? *No.* And why, having summoned him here, was she so bent upon having him leave now? ". . . *Are* the Shadowborn a myth?" Fejelis asked the high masters quietly. "Or are they something you have known to fear for five hundred years, because lineage mages cannot sense their magic, and so cannot counter it?"

Valetta's eyes flicked past him to whoever stood behind him. He heard his mother breathe, "Oh, you young fool."

Valetta said, "Prince Fejelis, we forgive your confusion. This mage, Tammorn, was influenced by a deranged and uncontrolled master." From the mat, Tam gave a gargling shout of rage. "It is probably as well that Lukfer died in the Temple's ruin. We may still be able to salvage Tammorn."

She lied well, Fejelis thought, but watching her, watching her with all the experience gained in surviving court, he knew she lied.

He walked slowly forward, alert to any motion toward

him. The archmage watched his approach with those black eyes whose depths went down three hundred years. From the vantage of his mere nineteen, Fejelis tried to fathom those eyes, those centuries. How long since the ancient mage had spoken directly to an earthborn, even to a prince? Did he even know modern language? Was this by his preference, or that of the high masters around him? Had he been sealed away beneath layers of veneration, growing ever more isolated amongst his own? Princes had met that fate, too, though only over decades, not centuries.

Still holding the archmage's eyes, he knelt and gently squeezed Tam's outstretched hand, trusting that while the mages might have bound magic, mage sense, and speech, they had discounted touch and its consolations. He heard an indrawn breath from their brightnesses, likely offended by the symbolic submission in his kneeling, or maybe by the touch. He didn't care if their brightnesses were offended, if the mages respected compassion for one of their own.

He said quietly, ". . . I may be too willing to believe an explanation that implicates a third party and exonerates my family. But *no one else* has been able to tell me why the lights in my father's room failed."

The woman started to speak; the archmage held up his hand. Fejelis's heart beat faster, as the copper-skinned little man studied him. ". . . Magister Lukfer, Magister Tam, and at least two Darkborn mages sensed magic behind multiple fires that killed Darkborn, and the annulment of the lights that caused my father's death. Magister Lukfer said that he had come to associate such magic with the Shadowborn.

". . . Yet I have had no mention, no report whatsoever, from the Temple of this magic, or of justice meted out for its abuse. I was also informed that the Darkborn are beginning to wonder at the Temple's apparent inactivity. . . ." He paused, gathered himself. "Magister Tammorn told me that the crossbow bolt that nearly took my life, despite the initial efforts of a mage of the lineage, was ensorcelled to annul life. I—believe—that that same magic *might* have accounted for the many deaths among you, even more than the Darkborn's shells." He heard Perrin's indrawn breath, but the high masters were very still, frighteningly still. "To defeat this enemy, we need to come together—princes, brightnesses, earthborn, Lightborn *and* Darkborn. In the name of a compact that has served us for seven hundred years, please, help us, as Magisters Tam and Lukfer tried to do, in their own, perhaps flawed, way. And let us help you."

He had to wait for an answer now, thought it took all his courage to resist flinging more words after these, the best he could find.

"I find it hard to believe you care about the compact, Fejelis," said Prasav, from behind him.

Fejelis did not wish to turn away from the archmage, but even less did he wish Prasav at his back. He knee-stepped to one side and pivoted, to find Floria there, silent as ever, blocking Prasav's approach. Perrin had a hand on Orlanjis's arm, trying, against Orlanjis's resistance, to draw him back.

Prasav tossed something down onto the mat. "That mage," he said, "and this prince, who is hardly worthy of the name, have conspired together to undermine the compact, using Darkborn technologies to *replace* magic." He let the fragile electric bulb bobble around on the carpet until they had all recognized it and then, deliberately, stepped on it, crushing it to glass shards and wire. "Contrary to the impression they have so carefully conveyed, they've known each other for four years, during which the mage has drawn Fejelis into a circle of treasonous radicals he has cultivated."

". . . Innovation is not treason," Fejelis said, to the archmage. "The artisans are idealistic young people trying to find ways to ease the burden on the tower. And my father was well aware that I knew Tam."

Prasav smiled down at him, the expression a travesty of Isidore's. "Magistra Valetta, if you were to tell us the truth, might you not say that the murderer of Isidore, the captain of vigilants, and two others is that mage there, who ensorcelled the woman Floria White Hand to place a talisman capable of annulling the lights in Isidore's room, and then removed that talisman once it had done his work? He did so at the behest of the prince, his lover. He has violated the laws of the compact before, on behalf of this prince. It may be awkward to admit that any mage should be so corrupt, but there are always bad apples. You deal with your bad apple; leave us to deal with ours, and no word will ever leave this room."

". . . None of that is true," Fejelis said, surging to his feet. ". . . A touch will tell you." He offered his hand, striving neither to appeal nor importune by the gesture.

Valetta said nothing. Nor did she move to take his hand, and accept the truth. Fejelis felt suddenly chilled, tasting peach. Tasting betrayal. Floria, at his side, took the one measured side step needed to free them both for action, her hand slipping to her rapier pommel.

Rupertis said, "Floria, these men ensorcelled you. Move aside, if you can."

"If I am ensorcelled," the vigilant rasped, "then let the mages vigilant release me, if they can."

From outside the door, three vigilants stepped into the room, one moving up behind him and two to each side, crossbows coming to bear. It did not take Orlanjis's skill to triangulate their target. Floria stepped into the line of the woman on the right, though at this range, it might not matter.

Perrin cried out, "*Don't*. I won't take the caul stained with his blood. You promised!"

"You!" said Orlanjis and Helenja together. "You have no standing here," Helenja said. "You gave it up, ten years ago."

"It was *taken away* from me, ten years ago," Perrin spit. "And you let them do it to me, and you'll let them do it to *him*, all for your precious Orlanjis."

"Not for me!" Orlanjis cried out. In his horrified eyes, Fejelis could see his memory of the day before, his anticipation of what was about to happen.

"I'm *sorry*, Fejelis," Perrin said. "I *tried* to warn you. You just wouldn't understand what this outrage *meant* to the tower."

". . . The compact does not allow a mage to be . . . ," Fejelis said.

"Even the compact can be amended," said Prasav, and gestured. Orlanjis shouted, and lunged forward too late, too short. Fejelis twisted frantically sideways, knowing the futility. He had a blurred impression of Floria moving, her rapier's edge slicing light as she drew, and then Orlanjis tackled him and brought them both crashing down onto the mat.

Winded, gasping, he waited for the sear of pain in his chest, the gurgle of blood in his throat. Lying on his back and staring at the ceiling . . . where the painted sun had gained three extra rays.

He lifted his head. Floria half crouched over him, rapier drawn. The vigilants, Prasav, and Helenja stared up at the embedded crossbow bolts. Ember and the mages stared at Tam.

Who reared up straight-armed from the carpet, face flushed and wild and smeared with tears and mucus, saying to no one and everyone, *"You shall not have him."*

"Them!" gasped out Fejelis, having just enough time to sling an arm around Orlanjis and pull him close.

Eleven

Floria

*T*he crossbow bolt flashed as it spun in the air between the bow and her breast, and vanished. From overhead came a staccato triplet, almost unheard for the heavier thumps of Fejelis and Orlanjis tumbling to the carpet. She kept facing the bowmen, who were all staring upward. Rupertis swore vilely, staring past her to where Fejelis and Orlanjis must be lying. Then she turned, stomach clenching with trepidation at what she must see—one or both of them pierced and dying. But the brothers were gone. Tammorn, too. With that heightened awareness that comes with preparing to kill or die, she saw Valetta's head snap toward the archmage, who lifted his eyes from the empty carpet. In their exchanged glances, Floria saw avarice.

Prasav stepped forward. "Bring them back!"

The archmage regarded him in silence, across centuries and power. A distance far wider, Floria sensed, than the one between the archmage and the very young Fejelis.

Prasav, unlike Fejelis, could not sustain that eye contact. He turned to Valetta. "I'll contract with you to find and return the princes. I'll offer a good price."

The archmage said something. "The princes," Valetta said, "are irrelevant. The mage is ours to deal with." And that, Floria realized, explained the avarice. Tam had broken a binding imposed by the archmage and *four* high masters. *Now*, with their numbers decimated, they would want that power in their lineages.

Not least, if Tam could sense and manipulate magic lost to the lineages.

"All we need is to know where they are," Prasav said.

Perrin said, shrilly, "You promised me Fejelis would be deposed without killing him."

"Don't be naive, girl," Prasav tossed at her. "Nobody leaves a deposed prince alive."

"If the compact can be amended," Perrin snapped, "then this so-called tradition can be amended. It wasn't always this way, that princes killed each other. I don't want Fejelis dead." To Valetta, "You can have the mage."

Prasav turned back to Valetta. "You don't know, do you, where they are? You have no idea where he took them."

The archmage turned in dismissal and walked away into the inner room, sandals softly slapping his feet. The three high masters trailed at his heels. Valetta looked on as Prasav and Perrin argued, the girl's face pale, frightened even, the man allowing his anger to show, now it had found a safe target.

"If you think, after this display, that Fejelis is not dangerous to us, you're more than naive; you're a fool. You heard him speak. You heard me say he has radical contacts in the city. He's known at court—you aren't. That mage of his broke a binding imposed by the archmage and four high masters. Fejelis isn't the fool nine-year-old you remember and that mage is no fifth-rank mediocrity."

Perrin's head jerked back. Color rose in her cheeks as though he had slapped her—with the reminder of her own small powers. Mother's Milk, but she was easy to make dance. The question was, whose would be the tune: Prasav's, or the Temple's?

Neither was righteous. Floria supposed she should take some thought to her own survival, but she was still caught up in that vaulting disregard of life or death characteristic of the fighter's mind. Each breath gave her a small shock of delight, and was equally a matter of indifference.

At a sound behind her, she whirled, startling the vigilants who stood nearest, who had not yet registered it. Rupertis was the first to look over his shoulder to find the prince's secretary standing pale but determined on the threshold, four vigilants flanking him. "There is a message for Prince Fejelis," he said. "From the Darkborn. It is urgent."

Perrin sucked in a breath, "I'll take it."

The secretary looked at her, trying to parse the chains of rank around her neck, her uncauled head, and Fejelis's absence. "Give it to me," she ordered. "I am princess now."

The vigilants looked uncertainly to Rupertis, their captain; he nodded, and the secretary slowly proffered the letter. Prasav made a move for it; Perrin put her shoulder between him and it, turning away as she tore it open. The sheet of paper she extracted was unevenly colored and blank of any ink, but bore the characteristic stippling of Darkborn script. Perrin's brows drew beneath her crafted cap of hair. Unlike Fejelis, she had not learned to read Darkborn script.

Ember stepped forward, holding out her hand. "If I may, Princess."

Perrin looked sharply at the woman, surely her rival now, and reluctantly extended the letter. Ember studied it, reading with her eyes what Darkborn read with their fingers. "It is from Sejanus Plantageter, his hand, his signature," she said.

Yet Mycene had said the archduke was critically injured. Was this truly his hand? Was the Darkborn script not the subtlety of a man limiting a letter's readership, but an insult from one indifferent to the letter's audience? For that matter, was Ember's interpretation what the letter itself said?

Perhaps so, for having read it, she returned it without hesitation to Perrin. "He agrees to meet with Prince Fejelis. He offers the chambers of the Intercalatory Council: though it is humble, it is equipped for such discussions. He suggests an hour after sunset, to give both ourselves and him the chance to bring together our retinues, and offers to clear the streets so that we may travel with lights in the open.

"The other thing he says is that the Darkborn are having trouble in the Borders. He says that they have had a message from one of their manors indicating that it has been overrun, and names the enemy"—to the mage—"Shadowborn."

"So he will not wish to engage two enemies," Prasav noted. "This works to our advantage."

"And if . . . these enemies are ours as well," Perrin ventured. Ah, Perrin was herself a sport; she, too, should be able to sense Shadowborn magic.

And suffer the same consequences as her brother for saying so. Valetta, Prasav, and Ember regarded her with similar expressions—not, Floria thought, unlike expert swordsmen waiting for the novice to make an inevitable error. Helenja shook her head, very slightly, more in resignation than in warning. Perrin's lashes veiled her eyes, and she did not press for an answer. But she looked frightened.

"Princess," said Prasav, with a dangerous kindness. "We must discuss the terms of Darkborn surrender and reparations, so we can speak with a united voice. This gives us a fine opportunity to reestablish the relationship across the sunset on a basis satisfactory to ourselves. Magistra Valetta, we would be most grateful if you could attend, since you are the most gravely injured."

Valetta inclined her head, an expression of dark irony in her eyes.

"Please write the Darkborn archduke that we accept his invitation," Perrin said, thinly.

"Do so," Prasav added, "in Fejelis's name."

Helenja was watching the exchange with a curled lip. "Mistress White Hand," she murmured, just loudly enough for Floria to hear, "come with me."

Floria weighed the consequences, briefly, of refusal. But she had no wish to stay here until Prasav's or Ember's or Valetta's attention returned to her. If what Tam and Fejelis had said was true, Helenja and the southerners were innocent of Isidore's unrighteous deposition. And if Floria knew Helenja, she would want her younger son back, safe, whatever she intended for her elder. That desire, Floria thought, might be parlayed into help for Fejelis. Quietly, she sheathed her rapier and followed Helenja's Vigilance from the room.

One of Helenja's many minor offenses against custom was in preferring her ground-floor chambers to the consort's official chambers. Those could be approached only through the well-watched halls of the palace, while the ground-floor chambers opened out into gated gardens with at least six gates. Easy enough for messengers to go and come, or visitors to come and go. Floria, directed to the door of lesser privilege, found herself in a receiving room whose floor and skirting were sandy-hued stone, and whose walls were sandy-hued, fine-textured wood. The reflected light was warmer than the desert.

The dowager consort circled her. "Whose creature are you? I find that utterly impossible to decide."

Floria turned with her, alert for the smallest glance or gesture that might be a signal to dispatch Floria. Or try to. She had not yet returned to the world of multiple dimensions; her perceptions remained narrowed to single choices, single actions. Within that narrowed space, her focus was exquisite, her potential deadly.

"Were you ensorcelled, or did you willingly carry that talisman to my husband, and in whose service? Are you ensorcelled now, or did you willingly shield Fejelis with your body? Do you know?"

I know this, Floria thought. *I am not yours.*

"I would have said until yesterday that you were my husband's creature. Had you not been, he would have been dead at any one of a dozen times. You would have let him cut out your heart. But then, he never would have let a warrant be released against you. I was quite surprised that Fejelis did." She tapped her upper lip with a finger, and took it away to ask, "Was it the mage's influence? Was he jealous?"

Floria snorted, more in annoyance than amusement. Helenja's voice plucked and worried at the perfectly tucked-in corners of her awareness, threatening to expand it once more into multiple dimensions, blurring that perfect fighter's mind. She measured the distance of her hand to the pommel, the distance of the tip to Helenja's heart. Except that, in the presence of a mage, the assassination would be no more than a gesture.

"Or did he *know*, as Fejelis said?" To the mage, Helenja said, "*Is* this woman ensorcelled?"

Before the mage had taken a step toward her, Floria had the rapier drawn. "She can answer from there, or not at all."

"Madam consort," protested the mage, turning, and, meeting Helenja's gaze, wilted. "I sense no ensorcellment."

"But you were born of the lineages," Helenja said. "I wonder what the answer would be were I to put that question to my daughter."

She abandoned her circling, opening the space between them to set her hips on a high table, propping herself against it. Despite her bulk, she still moved like a young woman, the haughty desert rider Isidore had contracted with. "You hate me, understandably. I was just a girl when I came to this court, foolish, crude, and proud. I brought with me ambitious men and women, and I believed with them at my back I could rule this court. Instead, they nearly ruled me, and they did things that cost me—the regard of my son, for one. I am watching my daughter make the same mistake.

"Do you understand what you saw in there, Mistress White Hand? Through Perrin, the mages have taken control of the princedom. How long they have been planning this I do not know, though I suspect it was initially the work of a faction within the Temple, and would have come to nothing without this Darkborn madness. But Prasav wants the caul for himself, and if not himself, Ember. I doubt he will get it; whether he realizes it or not, if he makes a move, he will be lucky to live. Ember is more subtle; I have no doubt that she is already cultivating alliances."

Floria made her voice work, "I do not serve Prasav. I do not serve the mages. I am a member of the Prince's Vigilance; I serve the lawful prince."

Helenja heard the "lawful," and smiled. "Then it appears we have a common cause, and uncommon enemies. I am prepared to allow that you were ensorcelled, whether by one of our mages or a Shadowborn, and that any part you had in Isidore's death was an unwilling one. I will offer you my own protection, and the protection of my mages—of whatever worth that may prove. In exchange, you will help me find my sons. *Then* we will settle which one is to be prince. Do you agree?"

Fejelis

One moment he sprawled on the mat, looking up at the bolt-pierced ceiling, the next on hard ground and matted heather, looking up at—whiteness. Orlanjis struggled free of his grip and sat up, wild-eyed; Fejelis pushed himself up, feeling no less so.

"Where . . . ," said Orlanjis.

The light was filtered white, and directionless. His clothes and hair turned instantly clammy. Was this dusk? What should have been the agony of imminent dissolution was no more than a dull cramp in his limbs, no worse than when he dashed through the deep shade of full summer foliage. Not dusk, then, but cold mist.

". . . are we?"

Seacoast, island, or mountains. Much more pertinent was *when*? How near was sunset?

A few yards away, Tam lay on his face, one hand still braced flat, elbow jutting up, though he had collapsed over it. His breathing was imperceptible and his face—when Fejelis eased him over onto his back—mist gray. Even the freckles were grubby smudges under the smears and dirt. Fejelis's ear on his chest found a slow heartbeat; a cheek against his nose felt a wisp of stirring air. Fejelis pinched him, hard, eliciting no reaction.

"Is he . . . dead?" Orlanjis said, scrambling up beside him. "Did *he* do this?"

"No, he isn't, and yes, I think he did." He settled back on his heels, sweeping a damp sleeve across a damp forehead, and started to enumerate his wants. They had no food or water, no means of keeping themselves and especially Tam warm . . . and no lights.

"He *has* to take us back!" Orlanjis said, grabbing at the mage's shoulder. Fejelis caught his wrist, using his adult strength. The white of panic showed around Orlanjis's irises as they jerked to focus, dilated, on Fejelis. "When the sun sets, we're *dead*."

". . . Given that three crossbowmen just fired on us, having until sunset is an improvement. . . ." Orlanjis's rolling eyes reminded him that not everyone appreciated princely humor. He said more gently, "For the moment, we're safe."

"Safe . . . ? *He's* the only way back, and he's out cold."

"He'll have had a reason for bringing us here. Let's try and get our bearings." He laid a hand briefly on Tam's chest, trying to communicate reassurance, before standing up. "You and I are going to walk off until we can just still see Tam. I'm going to walk out from you until I can just see you, and then we're going to circle Tam, not losing sight of each other."

"Don't leave me," Orlanjis said to their feet.

". . . I won't." He smiled, and squeezed Orlanjis's shoulder, lightly. "Not knowing how you stood by me, back there. . . . Don't lose sight of Tam and if I'm moving out too far, beckon me back in, all right?" As from a skittish horse, he backed away until Orlanjis grew indistinct. He knew his reds would stand out, easing Orlanjis's panic. He turned shoulder on to his brother, and slowly began to pace out a circle. After two dozen slow paces, he spotted a distinct gray line almost at the limits of vision. He squinted; yes, it was real. "I see something—no, don't come!" He pulled off his jacket, bundled it, and laid it on the ground, crossed halfway to Orlanjis, and tipped the caul from his head and set it on the ground, before going the rest of the way.

". . . We'll pick it up on the way back," he promised his gaping brother. ". . . Stay there while I get Tam."

He returned to Tam, crouched, propped the limp mage up, and muscled him into an awkward shoulder carry. They followed the line of the caul and the mourning jacket to where Fejelis had seen the track, Orlanjis obeying without objection Fejelis's, "Pick these up, would you?" though he handled the caul like a ball of spines. The mist had closed in once more, but Orlanjis said, "I'll go," and walked forward. "It's a railway track. But where—"

Fejelis grunted, "Not so fast," as Orlanjis blurred in the mist, and followed with all the haste he could muster. He came upon Orlanjis standing on a narrow, paved road, staring down at the adjacent railway track.

"We're in the Borders," Orlanjis said, whitely.

Hilly terrain, no smell of the sea. ". . . You sound very certain."

"This kind of track was only laid between Stranhorne and the end of the southern railway. We're—in the Borders."

". . . That makes a certain sense," Fejelis said. It also suggested Tam had not been thinking as clearly as he might, to drop them in this barren land that the Lightborn had abandoned. He hid his despair as he looked along the empty track as it emerged on one side of him and disappeared into mist on the other, as uninformatively as it had come. In the sky, the position of the sun was not even marked with a brighter smudge. Orlanjis, picking his way along the track with apparent purpose, suddenly said, "Fejelis, we need to go this way."

"What is it?"

"Nearest railwayman's hut. There are dozens of them along the tracks, for the use of the people who maintain the tracks and switch points for the day trains. I know they *say* there are no Lightborn in the Borders, but there are. Because of our eyes, we're much more efficient at checking track."

". . . I never knew you were interested in railways."

Orlanjis's scowl deepened; he shrugged self-consciously. "I thought if I couldn't stand court anymore, I'd run away and work for the railways."

Fejelis managed to keep his lip from twitching. Orlanjis's knowledge could be lifesaving. ". . . So how far?"

Orlanjis looked at him, at the inert mage on his shoulder. "I don't know."

". . . Could you go ahead along the track, then? Get help, if possible. I will follow as I can." Then if sunset caught them, Orlanjis would have had the better chance of finding shelter.

Orlanjis swallowed. Fejelis waited, keeping his regard steady, confident, hiding his own fear. Orlanjis gave a single jerky nod, and then turned and plunged into the mist. Not daring to go more slowly. "Follow the track," Fejelis shouted after him. No answer came back, only a muffled suggestion of running feet. The mist closed around him, his sole companion now. Fejelis took a more solid grip of the awkward burden of his protector and friend—shoulder-carrying an adult was far more difficult than the vigilants made it look—and concentrated on placing one foot in front of the other for as long as he could.

When he saw the lights, some indeterminate time later, he took them at first for merely another illusion, one with the tunneled vision, the gray fogs, the sudden sprays of sparks that had invaded his field of view. With his heart-beat thumping in his ears, he did not hear voices. But the lights bobbed closer, and he caught sight of the moving vertical shapes of men. He raised his voice, and Orlanjis charged out of the mist, nearly colliding with him. "Jay!" he said loudly, and whispered urgently, "We're *his* servants, right? Play stupid." Fingers fumbled around Fejelis's neck, releasing the star sapphire and the talisman of immunity and shuffling both away into an inner pocket.

Behind him the other shapes expanded and took on den-sity and then color and detail—two men and a woman in leather and coarse open-weave fabric, clothed more heav-ily and completely than any city dweller. Orlanjis had on a similar vest, too large for him. All three of the railway work-ers were young, two fair-skinned and ginger-haired, with the west-mountains slur in their speech, and the second man copper-skinned and dark-haired, with a southwest accent. The westerners were Sorrel and Midha, and the southerner was Jade. They helped Fejelis off-shoulder the unconscious mage and laid him out on a mesh hammock. Exhaustion and relief at the arrival of not only men but blessed *light* made Fejelis every bit as stupid as Orlanjis's masquerade de-manded. When Jade said, "Mother's Milk, I know this man," he simply gawked.

Orlanjis recovered himself enough to say—chirp, rather, "You know him?"

"Aye, I know him," said the man, seemingly unaware of the panicked look Orlanjis sent Fejelis. Fejelis observed to his relief that he handled Tam carefully, and not as a man would an enemy. Fejelis tried to prompt him to elaborate, carefully using the accents of a city artisan, ". . . He's done a lot of good in the city."

"Thought you two were brothers," the woman put in, more suspiciously. "That one doesn't sound much like you."

"He's the one with ambitions to rise," Fejelis said. "Me, I dun' care." He wondered where Orlanjis had hidden the caul and equally distinctive jacket, but he decided he was glad, for the moment, that Orlanjis had found some story to tell. He doubted his own powers of invention, in his exhaustion.

With a worried sideways glance at his face, Orlanjis took the fourth corner of the hammock, unasked.

The light beyond the mist was definitely dulling, and he had had to take his turn with the carrying, before they reached shelter. Orlanjis must have run much of the way. It had been a largely silent walk, exchanges limited to those necessary to share the load. Though he had established that they were within the Darkborn barony of Strumheller, thirty miles west of Strumheller Crosstracks itself. The rail-waymen's hut was a pleasant surprise: not a hut, but a small house, raised well above head height for visibility and for protection against the occasional Shadowborn. Jade took malicious delight in pointing out the deep scores of claw marks on the supports for the edification of the city boys. Orlanjis swallowed, his eyes flashing white. Fejelis thought that the strop marks looked years, if not decades, old. He was too cursed tired to get exercised.

On the platform, a second young woman was waiting, standing guard, a bow slung on one shoulder, a Darkborn-made rifle on the other. She greeted them at the top of the stairs, and looked down at Tam's unconscious form in dismay. "Tam!"

Tam's choice of destination was appearing less and less random. The woman's eyes flickered up to Fejelis, wary and slightly dismayed as she became aware of his attention. She was short, stocky rather than slight; though she stood only as high as his midchest, she had shoulders as muscular as a vigilant's, full breasts and hips, and big, competent hands. Her skin was the deep olive of the southwest, with honey yellow eyes, and black hair so close-cropped it resembled fur. The hair was silvered with fine beads of mist dew. He wondered how it would feel to stroke it.

She broke their locked gazes, turning away. He shook
his head, disconcerted. Years of cultivating his resistance to
the stratagems of poisonous court beauties, not to mention
flirtatious artisans, and here he was, distracted by a name-
less railway woman off the edge of the civilized world.

"Jay?" Orlanjis said.

He gave his brother a wry half smile, and, stooping, followed their rescuers into their refuge. Inside, they were lifting the unconscious Tam into what looked to be the best
bed in the house. There was hardly enough space in the tiny
room for the four hammock bearers, much less Fejelis, so
he stood back. Orlanjis and two of the others came out; the
other man, who had also recognized Tam, stayed. The second
woman started to close the door, and met Fejelis's steady
gaze and his steady hand on the door. ". . . He's th'master,"
he said, trying to phrase a promise of silence in a dull-wit's
idiom. ". . . We dun say anything that he doesn't want said."

"Come in, then," she said, and, as the other man drew
breath, shook her head at him, firmly. They might be
brother and sister, Fejelis thought, with something of the
same broad build and cast of face, though the man's skin
was coppery, and his eyes dark, rather than that oddly familiar gold.

Fejelis closed the door carefully behind him. The woman
squared herself, facing him. "Before we go any further," she
said, softly, "who are you, really? Your . . . brother spun a
tale of rivalry between mages that *might* have been cred-
ible to someone who did not know Magister Tammorn, but
failed dismally to do other than entertain me."

He had feared Orlanjis had been overly creative.
". . . Mistress . . ." She volunteered no name. "I have . . . good
reason not to tell you my real name, since the trouble Magister Tammorn pulled us away from was mine more than
his. But he is my friend, and has been for several years."

Her eyes narrowed, seeming to measure the distance
between them. He in turn measured the strength in those
well-formed arms, and kept his hand on the door handle.

"What is his son's name?" she said.

"Artarian. After the brother he lost in the mountains,
years ago."

"And who is his master?"

"The only name he has ever mentioned is Lukfer."

"Can you describe Magister Lukfer?"

Not alive, he thought, remembering the body wrapped in its torn, dusty, blood-sodden sheets. If she had known the dead mage, it seemed too cruel to deceive her with a description from a death mask. And then he remembered where he had seen eyes as golden as hers before: staring in death. ". . . No. We never met."

"Ah." Aware that he was being less than candid. "If you are playing us false, I will deal with you. And if you don't appreciate that now, you will." She bent over Tam and set her fingers against his temples, uttering a suppressed "Oof," as though assuming an unexpectedly heavy load. Beneath her touch, Tam groaned, and then suddenly thrashed upright. Wide gray green eyes, as panicked as Orlanjis's had been, fixed on Fejelis. "Fejelis, look out!"

". . . I'm fine," Fejelis said, distinctly. "As is my brother. You got us both away."

"Him, too," said Tam, quite coherently. "No wonder it cursed near killed me. Where are we?"

". . . In the Borders. Where you brought us."

Tam swept his gaze round, saw the woman, and lost the little color he had regained. Tears came to his eyes. "Jo, I'd no idea where you'd gone. He didn't tell me until—Jo, he's *dead*. I couldn't—he wouldn't let me—but you'd have been so proud of him—" As suddenly as they had opened, his eyes rolled up, and he toppled sideways. As one, the man and woman snatched at him, heads colliding; Fejelis avoided becoming a third party only by being that step farther away. Jade and the woman disentangled themselves and laid Tam back on the pillows.

"I know of only one Fejelis," the woman said, without looking away from Tam's face.

Useless to deny it, now that Tam had spoken it aloud. ". . . I expect I am that one." He drew the sapphire pendant from his pocket, offered it to their inspection, and returned it to hiding.

"The prince's sons?" said the man.

". . . My father was assassinated two days ago."

"Mother's Milk. Then *you*—"

"Fejelis Grey Rapids was the style I had chosen for myself." When he thought about it, it was about the only routine decision he had managed to make amidst the cascading disasters of his brief reign. Not quite the briefest reign—history told of the nine-minute prince—but certainly one of the briefest. Shock had numbed him to catastrophe and failure. He hoped it would keep doing so, a little longer.

"Mother's Milk," the woman echoed, shakily, and added, "Your brightness." She glanced at Tam, who was muttering in his sleep. "We shouldn't disturb him. He's badly overspent. Even with my help it could be a few days before he's back to strength."

But he would recover; Fejelis drew reassurance from her simple confidence in her own abilities and Tam's strength. "... And you are?"

"Jovance. Yes, I'm a mage, and no, I'm not a member of the Temple—which is how I come to be here, working the railroads with the other misfits, rebels, and dropouts. Your brightness, may we please go into the main room, and you then can tell us the real story?"

Orlanjis was slumped in one of the worn sling chairs set close to the fire, his childishly supple neck awkwardly crooked. Thoughtless reflex made Fejelis's heart thump alarm, but Orlanjis's breathing was easy, his face almost its normal color, his trailing hands relaxed. The sleep was one of simple exhaustion. Fejelis lifted a cushion from one of the other chairs and used it to prop his brother's head in an easier position. Orlanjis did not even twitch.

Jovance, who had observed this, pointed him to the other chair close to the fire. She brought a high stool to his side, and the others took their places on chairs, stools, and the floor. "Looks like cursed politics has caught up with us," she remarked to her fellows. "Magister Tammorn—Tam—is my grandfather's student." To Fejelis, "That's Magister Lukfer." Then she continued, "And Tam's had almost as much trouble with the Temple as I have. But *this* is no servant, but his brightness himself, Prince Fejelis Grey Rapids. I've never seen him, but I have seen his father and I knew his sister, and there's enough of a likeness to be convincing, even without what I got from Tam—though that was pretty cursed confused. The youngster with the stories is the prince's brother, Orlanjis."

To Fejelis she said, "I would wait on asking you to confirm the truth of what you say"—by touch, she meant—"until Tam is well enough to stand by you; I know he would prefer that. He clearly cares about you." She straightened and drew in a breath. "But knowing that I will, would you tell me how you came to be here?"

He did so, starting from his being awakened by word of his father's death—filling in his relationship with Tam, Floria's suspected ensorcellment, and the Darkborn's crises. Jovance was the only one who asked questions, the others seemingly too intimidated to do so, though the copper-skinned man—half brother, perhaps—prompted her with glances she seemed to have little trouble interpreting. Half brother, some impossibly rash part of him *hoped*, for the longer they spoke, the more remarkable she seemed to him. When he came to describe Lukfer's death, he did so haltingly, groping for words that would not evoke in her mind the pictures that came so readily to his. Even his chosen words were cruel to speak, and to hear. She and Jade wept quietly, her arm around the young man's shoulder, but she wordlessly gestured Fejelis to go on. He finished with the Temple's betrayal, his fall, and Tam's desperate exertion in saving them all. Done, he sat spent of words and emotion.

There was a long, long silence. "Broke a binding by five high masters, did he?" she murmured, a growl beneath the murmur. "Did they *ever* underestimate him." A pause. "And the Temple finally made a move on the princedom. Doesn't surprise me, having met your sister. Shouldn't wonder if it weren't her idea in the first place."

She wiped her tear-streaked face, studied the moisture on her fingers with a bitter expression. "My turn, then. I'm the strongest of Lukfer's grandchildren—or children, for that matter. Jade"—she glanced at the other man—"didn't even get the magic. . . . But I fell in love with an earth-born, and the only children I wished to bear were *his*. *That* was what the Temple could not abide, that I not agree to be bred like a mare for their lineages. My lover—my *con-*

sort," she claimed him, "was a trader. Like one of those wild cranes, endlessly roaming, up and down the length of the lands, in and out, even. He was tall and gangly and fair, no beauty by any conventional measure, but with a bold spirit unlike any other." Her smile passed through and beyond tall, gangly, fair Fejelis. "We planned to make our lives outside the lands, beyond the reach of the Temple. Others had, not many, but a few. Then one day he went over the boundary and never came back." A silence opened up, filled only with the crackle and snap of sticks in the fire.

"I believed—still believe—the Temple arranged that," Jovance said, defying him to disbelieve her. "I didn't care then whether I lived or died, only that I thwart them. Lukfer brought me here, before I did something fatal. The one place they would not look." Her eyes slowly refocused on him; she returned to their close little shelter, and their situation. "I think you're probably safe here, at least for a little. If not—well, it's just trouble deferred, isn't it? *Theirs.*"

That sense of humor would not be misplaced amongst princes, he thought. "You said you weren't surprised that the Temple would break the compact."

She leaned forward, bracing herself with her elbows. "I knew the temptation was always there, though I doubted it would come to it. But now—do you know how many of them died?" An odd expression crossed her face, as though for the first time she was thinking of other people she, personally, knew.

He shook his head, now basely glad he did not know, and have to tell her.

"Course not. They must be beyond terrified that earthborn could do that to them. They've never had much respect for earthborn technology. And now you and Tam have brought into the open another failing." She tilted back to study him. "Your brightness," she said pointedly, "the way you told it suggests that you thought it a well-laid plot. To *my* ear, it sounds like desperate improvisation. I've no doubt that various people had schemes, but their coming together seems entirely fortuitous. Prasav ad-libbed an invitation, and Valetta seized upon it. The archmage didn't declare himself, either way; people may get a shock when he does. If it happened that way, it won't last. I could count three ways the Temple will split over Viola as princess, no fingers needed. Their brightnesses won't countenance a mage princess. Prasav won't countenance magic used against the Darkborn, any more than you would have. He'll see the precedent. *She* knows she's climbed on a tiger, politically as well as magically, if she can sense that magic—I *can't*, by the way, too much lineage in me. The Temple's bleeding in a shark pond, with the tower brought down and your revelations about the Shadowborn, though it's still a cursed big fish for the eating. Your court's going to get indigestion, trying. So for you it's just a matter of finding the right time to return with bandages and bellyache medicine."

Her incisive, derisive dissection of his usurpers' prospects had stirred an uncharitable sense of hope, where before there had been just a numb need to survive. At the mention of bandages and stomach medicine, he almost smiled. She was right, he thought; his reign, with all he wished to achieve, was not yet over. Alive, he remained undeposed.

She got abruptly to her feet, discomfited by his grateful look. "It's gone sunset, and we've no idea when the next train's going to come through. At least one of us has to be awake to man the telegraphs, but the rest of us should get some sleep. So we can deal with tomorrow, tomorrow."

His neck had never had Orlanjis's enviable bonelessness, precluding slithering down into the chair and sleeping until midwinter. He contemplated the enticing plane of the floor. Except that someone would probably tread on him.

"We've pallets for visitors. Not what you're used to, I'm sure, but"—she glanced down at the sleeping Orlanjis, with a wry smile—"I think you'll manage."

To say that he preferred a pallet on the floor amongst friends to luxury amongst enemies would be premature, as well as presumptuous, but he thought it, nonetheless. "Thank you."

Telmaine

When Telmaine and Vladimer emerged onto the station concourse, an emergence timed to meet the evening rush, they found it unnervingly empty. Vladimer halted and blocked her next step with his outstretched arm, cane in hand. "There's been trouble," he muttered.

She thought for a moment he would draw back, but instead, he handed her the cane and unholstered the revolver. "Take it." She did, setting down the carpetbag that held their few necessities. "Don't use it unless you're certain," he said, a warning with bitter meaning to her ears. She nodded curtly, handed him back the cane, and retrieved the bag.

She followed closely on his heels, closely enough to be aware of his stiffening. The concealing hat and veils he had insisted she wear hampered both her perceptions and her movement, and the muffling of her magical senses unnerved her. She could not help thinking what had happened the last time they passed through this station. Her sleep had been interspersed with wakeful spells of futilely plucking at the binding and dreams of being trapped in a spider's web, in a cocoon, in yards and yards of winding silk, smothering dreams—the very dreams she had suffered as a sought-after heiress, before she had met Balthasar.

Vladimer had suffered his share of nightmares, too; she had heard him grinding his teeth and muttering. She did not allude to it; nor did he mention whether he had heard her crying. They confined their conversation to practicalities, to gathering a change of clothing and a few necessities into a bag—which was left to her to lug.

Vladimer waylaid a passing engineer to question him about whether the trains would keep their schedule, given the crisis. Telmaine had not thought to wonder how they would find out what had happened outside without betraying that they had not come from outside, but Vladimer did it artfully.

"Sweet Imogene," Telmaine breathed after the engineer had gone his way, having delivered his pungent observations of the state of the doors after the Lightborn assault.

"Indeed," said Vladimer, grim. None of the trains were running to schedule; most would not leave until a preliminary inspection of track had been completed, and then they would go only slowly for fear of sabotage. The reports coming out of Stranhorne were few and contradictory, and the coastal Borders Express had been canceled for the day. The inland train itself was in question.

Until this moment, she had thought of this Borders trip with ambivalence; now she was desperate to get down there and find out what had happened to her husband, and to Ishmael. "Can't you commission a special?"

"Yes. But it will not leave for at least another hour, at the earliest. Maybe we should get a coach."

Shuddersome notion, since no coach even came close to a train's comforts, or speed. They would be a day on the road, another day in unwelcome proximity. For Vladimer, with his wound, it would be excruciating. "We should get breakfast," she said firmly. "It would be the *normal* thing for two delayed travelers. I'm sure you have a lounge you use, where you won't be pestered."

He did, a secluded, off-the-concourse bar, where, no doubt, assignations and illicit transactions could pass unobserved. It was not yet open for business, but the waiter recognized Vladimer, and allowed them in. Vladimer waited, standing, while she settled herself into the alcove. Then abruptly he said, "Stay here. I need to make arrangements." She got halfway to her feet before sense and temper both got the better of the impulse—whether to protect or to cling, she could not have said. He could cursed well mind his own safety, if he insisted. While she waited, she ordered tea for Vladimer, and hot chocolate for herself, and whatever leftovers remained from the night before, since no deliveries had reached the station yet. She hadn't eaten since the boardinghouse, and before that, at the archducal breakfast. And Vladimer couldn't keep going on the contents of his little bottles, whatever he fancied.

Vladimer returned before the food, easing himself down onto the bench seat, and laid his cane on the table between them with casual purpose, tip toward the door. "The railway officials have agreed to provide a special train, with a crew and guards," he said, in a low voice. "It will also carry a crew for the inspection of the tracks and the telegraph. We will be going first to Strumheller, then across to Stranhorne. It won't be the safest journey." Her expression conveyed her option of that useless and decidedly hypocritical concern. The corner of his mouth twitched in amusement, the rat bastard. "They'll tell us when it is ready. We may have company by then. If not, it is again you and I."

The steward arrived with their tea and hot chocolate, preventing any unwise comment on her part. The hot chocolate was a painful reminder of her and Balthasar's flight to the coast, where they had fortified themselves with hot chocolate for the final confrontation. Her throat tightened so that she could hardly swallow; she choked it, and a roll, down. Vladimer was doing the same, with equal resolution and lack of appetite.

There was one thing to be said for this. Life could not contain many social encounters more fraught and awkward than breakfast with a disgraced and possibly erstwhile spy-master who had saved one from death and killed one's best friend. She said, with a certain morbid curiosity, "I presume they're going to announce my passing at some point. And from what?"

"If it is left up to Kalamay and Mycene, it will be sooner rather than later. It will probably be put out as a sudden illness. There will be no mention of magic."

"Merivan—won't let it rest until she's satisfied she has had the truth."

"She would regret that," Vladimer noted. "I expect your mother to exert a restraining influence."

"You know my mother?" Telmaine said, startled out of her cynical pose, but remembering the dowager duchess speaking of Vladimer as a *poor boy*.

"She was always very gracious to me."

"Mama—is a kind person," Telmaine said, translating. "I hope she—" She could not finish. Her mother could not possibly know she had fulfilled her whispered promise to escape if she could, given such convincing evidence of Telmaine's destruction as she and Vladimer had left behind. She swallowed down a threatened sob.

"I must admit," Vladimer said, almost conversationally, "I was surprised by that deception your mother was party to, the first time you escaped the palace."

Was he asking who was responsible, or what had motivated her mother? There was nothing to be lost in concealing that now; the consequences to the family of that decades-old scandal were entirely outweighed by Telmaine's own. "Did you know about my uncle Artos?"

"The one who exposed himself, with no gambling debts, no unwise speculations, and—despite the gossip—no thwarted or shameful entanglements. I had presumed it was inborn melancholia...." And then he sonned her. "Ah."

She lowered her head, in acquiescence. "You, my lady," he said, his voice not quite as harsh, "are made of sterner stuff."

"Why, Lord Vladimer, a compliment."

Another twitch of the lips, at her acerbic tone. "If you will. It is not, I assure you from personal experience, consolation."

She knew she did not want to interpret that remark. She heard with relief the sudden commotion at the entrance to the bar, Phoebe Broome's clear voice saying, "Yes, I know he's there; he told me to meet him here, and he is very reliable. A tall, lean gentleman, with a limp and a cane, and a bad right arm."

Vladimer was not pleased with the mention of the last, but he mustered his manners and confirmed to the waiter that he was indeed expecting another lady and possible company. Phoebe Broome in person was taller than most men, dressed for practicality rather than fashion in a long, plain coat worn open over a divided skirt, and jacket, the attire of a modern city woman. On her small, dainty head, she wore a cloche hat, not unbecomingly. And on her hands, gloves. Her companion this time was an equally tall old man in a similar coat over a suit that was at least four decades out of fashion. He had the shriveled, puckish face of some forest sprite depicted in the legends as ancient, crazed, and full of mischief. He poked his head over Phoebe's shoulder, sonned Telmaine, and *tsk*ed like a tutor over a miscreant pupil. "My dear, you must have been quite wicked, though maybe not entirely so; either that or someone was careless, leaving that big hole."

"*Father—,*" said Phoebe Broome, though Telmaine was aware of her fascinated and perhaps appalled attention to herself and presumably the binding.

Vladimer recalled their attention to himself. "Magistra Broome. This, I deduce, is Magister Farquhar Broome himself."

"I'm sorry to intrude upon you this way, Lord Vladimer," Phoebe said, a little diffidently, "but you did indicate it was urgent, and—it was easiest to follow my sense of your vitality than start asking. It's—becoming quite busy out there. A lot of people trying to get out of the city, before things get worse."

Worse than—Telmaine wished she could ask. Farquhar Broome had slipped into place beside her, and like an idiot child entranced by a soft fur jacket was moving his hand up and down her arm, lingering over her wrist.

"*Father—*"

At that moment Broome made a small motion with his hand and Telmaine felt the binding unravel. Her mage sense bloomed with shocking, revelatory suddenness. She sensed the serene, quixotic personality of the odd old man beside her, a personality that overlaid a power like a vast lake. She sensed the narrower river of power, swift and disciplined, running through the woman, and Vladimer's familiar vitality, shot through with pain and stimulants. A little farther away she jolted up against a cluster of mages, twenty-five or thirty of them, including a vitality with an oddly familiar sense to it: Balthasar's sister—her sister in marriage—Olivede.

Telmaine snatched back her awareness with dizzying force, and sat trembling slightly, waiting for repercussions. But Olivede was not a woman given to flying into rooms and ready confrontations. And Tammorn was silent. Dead?

"Now that's much better," Farquhar Broome approved. "Now, about that nasty thing—"

"Father, what have you done?" Phoebe said. Vladimer brought his cane up and over, not violently, but decisively, setting the deadly tip on Farquhar Broome's wrist. "This woman's magic is uncontrolled and dangerous," he said, in a harsh voice.

Farquhar Broome reached over and gently set aside the cane. "My dear lady, my noble lord, I do apologize. It is so rare that I have a chance to examine novel magic, and it was a fascinating binding. I would—"

"No, Father, whatever it is," Phoebe said.

"But there is no need to worry. She is untrained, of course, and she has a nasty and rather powerful magical impression in her, but I am well able to manage that." He sounded now like one of Balthasar's older colleagues, briskly reassuring an anxious and difficult family member. "And you, young man, ought not to be stressing your system the way you are; you shall be ill if you go on like this—" He waved his hand. "Yes, yes, I know, the young; they are all immortal and invulnerable. . . . But we shall be traveling together, won't we, so we will have leisure to get to know each other." He smiled benignly over them all. "Let me go and reassure the rest of our party—hot chocolate seems an excellent idea—and let you have a chance to talk."

He sallied blithely forth, moving lightly for a man of his apparent age. Phoebe Broome's mouth opened, closed. "Please have . . . a seat, Magistra Broome," said Vladimer, at his most bland.

Self-consciously, she took the seat beside Telmaine her father had just vacated, facing Vladimer. Let out her breath, waiting for his reaction. "Well," she said at last. "You've now met my father. At his worst."

"Being myself widely considered my family's difficult member, I would not presume to comment."

"That is . . . gentlemanly of you," Magistra Broome murmured, and straightened, seeming at last to believe him. "You did ask me to bring the strongest mages amongst us, and he is the very strongest."

Telmaine, remembering her impression of vastness, nodded involuntarily, the motion catching both Vladimer's and Phoebe Broome's attention. Phoebe left anything she would have said unsaid for the moment. Bracing herself, she said, "Lord Vladimer, my brother . . ."

"Is, as far as I know, still at the palace. He took care to reassure me that you knew nothing of his activities."

She shook her head, denying the importance of that, but said, "I didn't. Until he left me a decidedly peculiar note. What . . . has he done?"

"I believe," Vladimer said, "he chose to warn Duke Mycene that I was consorting with a dangerous mage."

Phoebe's head twitched toward Telmaine, though she did not sonn. "Is he under arrest?"

"Not yet, at least not by my agents. I exchanged my silence for his silence on a matter essential to the state. Unfortunately, he has placed himself in the position where he may be implicated, amongst Darkborn at least, in last night's murder of the Lightborn mages. There was, apparently, a mage involved in the planning of it."

"If he enabled that slaughter in any way, he deserves to die," Phoebe said harshly. Vladimer's silence was reassessing.

"Lord Vladimer, you could only imagine what happened the night before last; we *lived through it*. We sensed the deaths, and we sensed the magic that slaughtered them."

She turned her head to Telmaine, her neat features hardening. "Please tell me," she said, "why *you* have the taint of Shadowborn on you."

A billowing surge of magic rippled from her to the group outside, not a simple communion, but a mustering of force.

"The binding that my father released was imposed by one of the Lightborn, was it not? For what reason?"

"Answer her, Lady Telmaine," Vladimer said, dispassionately. "It seems I have somewhat mistaken their purpose in coming here."

Her sonn showed his intense, poised expression, his hand on the hilt of his cane. She realized then what he meant—that Phoebe Broome, like her brother, like Tam, thought she was one with the Shadowborn. That Magistra Broome had come, with her fellows, to protect Vladimer, and to sit in judgment on her.

"If you knew," Telmaine burst out, "what I and my family have suffered at the—*hands*—of these creatures." She caught herself then, terrified that she would smell smoke, or sense the sudden heat of flame.

Vladimer, by his very stillness, by the rapid pulse in his throat, feared the same. Phoebe Broome seemed very calm.

"Ishmael told you," Telmaine said, struggling for composure, "about Tercelle Amberley's children, and what happened to my husband."

"Your ... husband is Balthasar Hearne? But Olivede—"

"Didn't know," Telmaine said. "Balthasar didn't know. *Nobody knew.* Ishmael was the first, ever . . ." Except, maybe, her mother. "I helped him save Balthasar's life. I walked through fire to rescue my daughter from her kidnappers, and Ishmael—Ishmael saved me from the flames when my magic failed."

"Oh, sweet Imogene, that was what happened. No wonder he . . ."

She did not want to think about Ishmael's sacrifice for her sake, any more than Phoebe wanted to name his loss. But the woman's obvious regret, for Ishmael at least, steadied her further. "When we reached Lord Vladimer's bedside, we fought the Shadowborn, only I was losing, and he— put his magic into my mind—before Ishmael killed him." She told how the taint had drawn Magister Tammorn's attention, and how, distraught by the attempt on the life of his prince, he had tried to bind her. How in throwing off the binding, she had critically injured the archduke. She did not notice, until Phoebe Broome laid her hand on its tip, how Vladimer's cane lay. He did not resist when she eased it off-line. Telmaine told of her return to save the archduke, its means, and its mortal consequences—Phoebe Broome made an inarticulate sound of protest at the sentence of execution, and breathed again only when she sketched her escape, without details as to how she and Vladimer had reached the station.

The mage was quiet for several breaths after she had done. "I am relieved that this is the way it is. You at least . . ." She stopped, certainly thinking of her brother.

Vladimer, unexpectedly, said, "It is more than likely that the mage involved in the planning of the destruction was one of our Shadowborn, rather than your brother. It is far more of a piece with their behavior than his." But as Phoebe turned a grateful expression on him, he continued. "It is, unfortunately, also more than likely that amongst the Darkborn, there is no one to appreciate the distinction. I did warn your brother; it is for him to save himself now."

She swallowed, and rubbed her trembling lips with a gloved hand. "I'm sorry—in many ways—that your magic has caused you, and others, such difficulty, Lady Telmaine. Father—will be able to help. When it comes to high-level magic, he really is quite sensible. Ishmael wasn't really—" Fortunately, she did not repeat Tammorn's opinion that Ishmael was no adequate tutor for Telmaine, if that was what she was thinking.

Phoebe turned to Vladimer. "I have a confession to make, Lord Vladimer. We have Tercelle Amberley's children. After Ishmael told me about them, I made it my business to find them."

Vladimer shook his head slightly. "It might have made a difference two days ago. Not now."

"For you, maybe," Phoebe Broome reminded him. "It still matters to them." Her shoulders shifted. "Aside from the fact that they do seem to be sighted, there is nothing about them that indicates they were not born to a Darkborn mother and father. But then Lightborn and Darkborn are of common stock. Why not Shadowborn, or at least some among them?"

The waiter arrived then, with a cup of coffee for the mage, and she smiled and thanked him, and sipped carefully at the pungent beverage. Vladimer shifted on the bench, drawing his hand away from his cane to brace his right arm unobtrusively against his body.

Phoebe Broome said, "Your message said that you wanted mages to accompany you to the Borders to investigate Shadowborn activities."

"Yes," Vladimer said. "Three nights ago Ishmael di Studier and Balthasar Hearne took the coastal train into the Borders. I have not heard from either of them since. The last information I had suggested that both were bound for Stranhorne, and that the weather around Stranhorne had

been extremely abnormal—a snowstorm, to be precise."
The mage straightened: it took a very strong mage to influence the weather. "The last message out of Stranhorne conveyed the impression it had been overrun by an unknown force. Have you had any sense of something amiss?"

"Father . . . may have, but none of the rest of us could have any sense of anything amiss. We decided to get out of the city tonight. It did not seem a safe place for mages anymore." She hesitated, as though waiting for a question, but none came. "The adults who did not want to join us have taken the children and dependents to a place we hope will be safe, in the northwest."

"In many respects, it is a wise decision. In others, a problematic one. If, as I have come to suspect, the Lightborn either cannot or will not contend with Shadowborn magic, it leaves the city uncovered."

And the archduke . . . Did Phoebe Broome hear the effort to achieve that indifferent tone?

She paused, seemed about to say one thing, said instead, "What did you think twenty-five mages—less if some of us stay—and yourselves could accomplish in the Borders?"

"I admit," Vladimer said, "I am not certain." His voice was bleak. "My concern was with invasion, and if it is that, and the Borders defenses have been overrun, then conventional forces are unlikely to fare better. You represent as unconventional a force as I could conceive of."

"You mean us to fight," Phoebe Broome said, somberly.

"I am aware, from what Ishmael has said of you, and from what you have said of yourself, that the idea is distasteful to you." She shook her head a little, as though at an oversimplification, but did not argue with him. "But magic is at the core of this, and magic is your province, Magistra Broome. Your province, and your calling, I believe."

"Yes."

"I do not know that you will receive any tangible reward for your service."

She sighed. "It does not matter. From what Ishmael said, from what you have said, and what we *know*, we have to help. Some of us will come. Some of us will stay. Will you trust us to divide our party as we think fit?"

"Yes," Vladimer said quietly. "We shall have to wait for our train, but I might as well begin by telling you what I know."

He did not sonn after Phoebe Broome's departing figure, but sat for a moment bracing his aching right arm with his left, before lifting his head. "So, another journey, Lady Telmaine?"

One to redemption or death, she thought, for both of them. She matched her tone to his. "I am ready, Lord Vladimer."

About the Author

ALISON SINCLAIR is the author of *Legacies, Blueheart,* and *Cavalcade* (which was nominated for the Arthur C. Clarke Award), as well as *Darkborn* and *Lightborn.* She lives in Montreal.

R0074